ALSO BY CHLOE WALSH

Boys of Tommen

Taming 7

CHLOE WALSH

Bloom books

Copyright © 2024 by Chloe Walsh
Cover and internal design © 2024 by Sourcebooks
Cover design by Brittany Vibbert/Sourcebooks
Cover images © Yamada Taro/Getty Images, Ekaterina Goncharova/Getty
Images, fotograzia/Getty Images, Biwa Studio/Getty Images

Published by Bloom Books, an imprint of Sourcebooks
P.O. Box 4410, Naperville, Illinois 60567-4410
(630) 961-3900
sourcebooks.com

Cataloging-in-Publication Data is on file with the Library of Congress

Printed and bound in the United States of America.
WOZ 10 9 8 7 6 5 4 3 2 1

For Caitlin.

Author's Note

Taming 7 is the fifth installment in the Boys of Tommen series, and the first book for Gerard Gibson and Claire Biggs.

Some scenes in this book may be extremely upsetting, therefore reader discretion is advised. Because of its explicit sexual content, graphic violence, mature themes, triggers, and bad language, the book is suitable for mature readers.

It is based in the south of Ireland, set during 2005, and contains Irish dialogue and slang. Terms, references, lingo, and characters' internal dialogue is in conjunction with that period in history and in no way reflects the author's personal opinions or values.

A detailed glossary can be found at the beginning of the book.

Thank you so much for joining me on this adventure.

Lots of love,
Chlo xxx

Name Pronunciations

Aoif: Eeef
Aoife: E-fa
Caoimhe: Kee-va
Gardaí: Gar-Dee
Sadhbh: Sigh-ve
Sean: Shawn
Sinead: Shin-aid
Neasa: Nasa
Eoghan: Owen
Tadhg: Tie-g (like *tiger* but without the *r* at the end)

Glossary

the Angelus: Every evening at six in Ireland, there is a minute of silence for prayer on the television.

bluey: porno movie

bonnet: hood of the car

boot: trunk of the car

Burdizzo: castration device

camogie: the female version of hurling

Child of Prague: a religious statue farmers place out in a field to encourage good weather (an old Irish superstition)

chipper: a restaurant that sells fast food

cooker: oven/stove/hob

corker: beautiful woman

cracking on: hooking up

craic: fun

Culchie: a person from the countryside or a county outside of Dublin. Usually used as a friendly insult.

daft: silly

daft as a brush: very silly

Dub: a person from Dublin

eejit: fool/idiot

Fair City: popular Irish television soap

fanny: vagina

feis: traditional Gaelic arts and culture festival/event

fortnight: two weeks

frigit: someone who has never been kissed

GAA: Gaelic Athletic Association

Garda: policeman (plural: Gardaí)

Gardaí Síochána: Irish police force

gas: funny

get your hole: have sex

gobshite: fool/idiot

grinds: tutoring

hatchet craic: great fun

hole: often said instead of ass/bottom

hurling: a hugely popular, amateur Irish sport played with wooden hurleys and sliotars (wooden sticks and small, hard balls)

Jackeen: a person from Dublin. A term sometimes used by people from other counties in Ireland to refer to a person from Dublin

jammy: lucky

jammiest: luckiest

jumper: sweater

junior cert: the compulsory state exam taken in third year, midway through the six-year cycle of secondary school

langer: idiot

langers: group of idiots and/or to be extremely drunk

leaving cert: the compulsory state exam taken in the final year of secondary school

messages: groceries

mickey/willy: penis

mope: idiot

on the hop: skipping school

on the lash: going out drinking

on the piss: going out drinking

poitín: Irish version of moonshine/illegal, home-brewed alcohol

pound shop: dollar store

primary school: elementary school, junior infants to sixth class

  playschool: preschool/nursery

  junior infants: equivalent to kindergarten

  senior infants: equivalent to second year of kindergarten

  first class: equivalent to first grade

  second class: equivalent to second grade

  third class: equivalent to third grade

  fourth class: equivalent to fourth grade

  fifth class: equivalent to fifth grade

  sixth class: equivalent to sixth grade

Rebel County: nickname for County Cork

ridey: a good-looking person

Rolos: popular brand of chocolate candy

rosary, removal, burial: the three days of a Catholic funeral in Ireland

runners: trainers/sneakers

Sacred Heart: the name of Shannon, Joey, Darren, Claire, Caoimhe, Lizzie, Tadhg, Ollie, Podge, and Alec's mixed primary school

sap: sad/pathetic

Scoil Eoin: the name of Johnny, Gibsie, Feely, Hughie, and Kevin's all-boys primary school

scoring: kissing

secondary school: high school—first year to sixth year

    first year: equivalent to seventh grade

    second year: equivalent to eighth grade

    third year: equivalent to ninth grade

    fourth year: transition year, equivalent to tenth grade

    fifth year: equivalent to eleventh grade

    sixth year: equivalent to twelfth grade

shades: police

shifting: kissing

shifting jackets: lucky piece of clothing, usually a jacket, when trying to pick up a girl

slab of beer: box of 24 bottles of beer

solicitor: lawyer

spanner: idiot

spanner: a wrench

spuds: potatoes

St. Bernadette's: the name of Aoife, Casey, and Katie's all-girls primary school

strop: mood-swing/pouting/sulking

St. Stephen's Day: Boxing Day/December 26th

swot: nerd/academically gifted

tog off: change into or out of training clothes

wellies: rubber boots worn in the rain

wheelie bin: trash can

yolk: nickname for an illegal drug

PREFACE

Moments before the pain in my lungs exploded and everything went dark, I saw it. A halo of light. An orb of pure sunshine.

Her.

I saw her.

And that's when I knew.

That's when I knew...

PROLOGUE
Don't Take the Girl

CLAIRE

MAY 1995

THE STENCH OF SMOKE WAS IN MY NOSE, AND I DIDN'T LIKE IT. MAMMY SAID IT WAS incense; the same stuff Father Murphy burned at mass on Sundays.

I didn't like going to mass. The church felt stuffy, and old, and sad.

Worst of all, you didn't get to talk for a whole hour.

An hour felt forever when you were five.

Somehow, the church was even worse today and it was Tuesday.

It was sadder.

Looking around at all the crying faces, I plucked at a loose thread on my cardigan and swung my legs back and forth, smiling to myself every time I kicked the back of the pew in front of me.

"Sit still, Claire," Daddy instructed, placing a hand on my knee. "It's almost over, pet."

"It's stinky," I whispered back, pinching my nose. "I don't like it, Daddy."

"I know, pet," he agreed, smoothing a hand over my curls. "Be a big girl for Daddy and stay nice and quiet for five more minutes."

"Then can I play with Gerard?"

He didn't answer me.

"Can I play with Gerard today, Daddy?" I repeated, pulling on the leg of his trouser suit. "Please? I miss him."

"Maybe not today, pet," he replied, and then he did what the other men were doing. He leaned forward and pushed his thumbs into his eyes to hide his tears.

"But how come?" I argued. "He's right up there." I pointed to the front of the church. "I can see him, Daddy."

"No, Claire."

"But—"

"Shh."

I didn't understand any of this.

Twisting sideways, I looked at my brother. He was crying, too. Mammy tucked him into her side as he cried against her shoulder.

"Hey, Hugh?" I whisper-hissed, covering my mouth with my hands. "Do you want to play with Gerard after mass?"

"Shh, Claire," Mammy sniffled, using the tissue tucked inside her sleeve to wipe her face. "Not here."

Not here?

What did that mean?

I couldn't figure out what was happening, but I didn't like it. I had a strange feeling in my tummy that got stronger every time I looked at the coffins. That's what Hugh called the boxes near the altar.

There was a big brown one and a small white one. Hugh said that Gerard's daddy, Joe, was in the big brown one and his sister, Bethany, was in the little white one.

Because they drowned last Saturday.

Drowned was a new word for me, and it was hard to understand, but it still made me super sad. Because when you drowned you went in a box.

"Drowned." Brows furrowed in concentration, I tried to spell out the word. "D-R..."

"Shh, Claire."

Nope, it was too big for me.

Folding and unfolding my hands, I looked around and waved when I spotted Hugh and Gerard's teacher across the row.

"Stop it, Claire," Mammy warned, snatching my hand out of the air and placing it on my lap. "Be good."

I thought I *was* being good.

Trying my best to be good for Mammy, I sat on my hands and didn't swing my legs anymore.

Not until the music started and everybody stood up.

"Oasis, Daddy," I squealed, barely able to contain my excitement. I knew this song. It was my daddy and Joe's favorite band. The song playing was called "Stop Crying Your Heart Out."

Daddy didn't smile. He was too sad. Joe was his bestest friend in the whole world, and he was in the brown coffin, but Gerard was my bestest friend in the whole wide world, and I was happy because he didn't get drowned with Joe and Bethany.

My daddy got Gerard out of the water. He jumped in and rescued him. With his suit and shoes on. And his socks. My daddy was a hero. That's what the neighbors said.

When Father Murphy walked down the aisle sprinkling that stinky smoke, I pegged my nose and squirmed in discomfort, but I quickly forgot about the smell when my gaze landed on the coffins. They were being carried down the aisle.

The big brown one first.

Then the little white one.

The crying got louder and louder then, making me super sad. When the white coffin passed by our pew, my brother burst into tears, crying loud and hard into my mother's chest.

"Shh, Hugh," I scolded. "Be good."

"Shh, Claire," both Mammy and Daddy said at the same time.

I didn't get it.

People started to follow the coffin.

Gerard's nana and granddad, his aunties and uncles, and cousins. His mammy, Sadhbh, who was being held up by her boyfriend, Keith, and his stinky son, Mark.

I didn't like Mark. I didn't like his mean eyes, or his big hands, or how he was always scowling at us.

Shuffling along behind him, with his aunty Jacqui, was my bestest friend in the whole world.

Gerard.

Excitement bubbled inside of me at the sight of him, and I could hardly stop myself from bouncing on the spot. Wide-eyed, I watched as the blond-haired boy, with the curls that matched mine, used the sleeve of his white shirt to wipe his nose before locking his gaze on me.

"Hi," I mouthed, waving at him.

His eyes looked so sad, and his cheeks were streaked with tears, but he raised his hand and waved back at me. "Hi."

My heart started to beat superfast, like I had been running a race, and my belly flip-flopped like a pancake in a frying pan.

"Don't move," Mammy began to say, but I couldn't help it. I was already slipping out of the pew and racing down the aisle. "Peter, stop her!"

"Claire," Dad whisper-hissed, but it was too late.

I had made it back to him. Not stopping until I was right beside my best friend, I slipped my hand into his and squeezed. "I missed you."

Sniffling, Gerard tightened his hold on my hand and wiped his cheek with the sleeve of his black suit jacket as we trailed out of the church after the coffins. "I missed you, too."

"I'm glad it's not you in the box," I whispered in his ear, leaning close enough so that only Gerard could hear me. "You're my favorite person in the whole wide world, and I would swap everyone for you. Even Hugh."

"You're not supposed to say things like that," he replied, but he didn't sound mad. Instead, he tightened his hold on my hand as we followed the crowd toward the graveyard.

"I prayed for it to be you," I said quickly, needing to tell him all the things I had saved up in my head since the boat. Since the drowning. "When they said someone had been saved from the water. I prayed for it to be you."

He choked out a sob and turned to look at me. "You d-did?"

I nodded. "I promised God I would do all the good things in the world if he brought you back." I beamed at him. "And he listened."

"That wasn't God, Claire," he whispered, wiping his nose with his sleeve. "That was your dad."

"I don't care who it was," I replied. "Just as long as you're here."

"I don't think my family thinks like that," he said, turning back to look at the ground as we walked. "I think they wanted your dad to save Bethany."

"I didn't," I admitted honestly. "I wanted to keep you most of all."

"Claire, come back to us please," Daddy interrupted, catching up with us and placing a hand on my shoulder. "You can't be with Gerard right now."

I opened my mouth to complain, but Gerard answered for me. "Please don't take her away from me."

"Leave them be, Pete," Aunty Jacqui told Daddy. "God knows the poor lad needs a familiar face at this time."

Daddy didn't look so sure, but he let me walk to the graveside with Gerard.

"I don't know what I'm going to do now," he said when we reached the grave. "I don't want to go home with them."

"With your mam and Keith?" Scrunching my nose up in disgust, I muttered, "And stinky Mark."

Gerard nodded stiffly. "I want my dad."

"Your dad's an angel now, though, right?"

He shrugged. "That's what Father Murphy said."

"Don't you believe him?"

"I don't know what I believe anymore," he replied, and then he went quiet for a long moment before blowing out a frustrated breath. "I looked stupid."

"When?"

"At mass."

"Why?"

"Because I couldn't read it," he said quietly.

"The prayer?" I asked, thinking back to the prayer Gerard read at the altar during mass. "I thought you were great."

"I couldn't fucking read the words, Claire," he choked out, tearful gray eyes locked on mine. "I made it up."

"That's okay, Gerard." I smiled extra hard to make him feel better. "I thought you were the bestest."

"Mark said it's because I'm stupid," he added, tightening his hold on my hand. "He whispered it in my ear when I came back from the altar."

"Mark's the stupid one," I growled, feeling cross. "You're the smartest person I know. Like supersmart."

"It's when the words are on a page," he said, releasing a frustrated breath. "I swear I can remember them just fine in my head. I could have said it no problem if I didn't look down at the stupid page."

"Gerard."

"It makes no sense to me," he hurried to add. "It doesn't matter if I write it down or Mam writes it. Not one word on the page makes sense to me."

"I can help you," I offered. "I'm getting really good at reading my *Tara and Ben* reader at school."

"Just stay." He squeezed my hand. "That helps."

"It does?"

Nodding stiffly, he took a step closer to the open grave and peeked in. "It's deep."

"Yeah, super deep," I agreed, peering into the big hole in the ground alongside him.

"It's dark."

"Uh-huh." I nodded eagerly. "Too dark."

"She's scared of the dark."

"Bethany?"

"Yeah."

"It's okay, though, because your daddy is with her, so he'll keep her safe."

"What about me?" he whispered as a lone tear trickled down his cheek. "Who'll keep me safe?"

"I will, silly," I replied, releasing his hand so that I could give him a hug. "I'll keep you safe, Gerard."

His breath hitched and I knew that he was about to cry again. But he didn't. Instead, he broke free from my hug, turned away from the big hole, and ran down the footpath away from the big crowd, ignoring his mammy and aunties who were calling his name.

He was faster than me.

He had longer legs.

But Gerard never ran away from me before.

It made me sad.

6

"Hey, Gerard!" I called out, huffing and puffing out big breaths as I raced after him. "Wait for me."

"I'll get him," Hugh and Patrick both said, bolting past me like the fastest runners in Ireland.

My brother and his friends were seven. I was only five. It wasn't fair that I couldn't keep up with them.

A small hand slipped into mine and I turned around to see a pair of bright-blue eyes. "Hey."

"Lizzie!" Smiling at the sight of my other best friend, I threw my arms around her and squeezed. "You came."

"We all came."

"Even Caoimhe?"

"Yep. Are you going back to your parents?"

"I need to find Gerard."

"Want me to come with you?"

I nodded happily.

Grinning back at me, Lizzie slipped her arm through mine and skipped along beside me in the direction of where the boys had gone. "I don't like the smell in the church."

"Me either," she agreed. "It stinks."

"And it's too hot," I added. "Mammy made me wear tights and this big cardigan." Feeling hot, I tugged at the buttons on my cardigan and sighed loudly when they wouldn't open. "I'm still not good with the buttons, Liz."

"That's okay," she replied, reaching for my cardigan. "I'm excellent."

She *was* excellent. Lizzie was so excellent she could even spell the word *excellent*. She always got the super-work stars from Teacher in class. I didn't mind, though. Apart from Gerard and Shannon, Lizzie was my third favorite friend in the world.

"Do you think he's going to be okay?" I asked a little while later when we turned a corner in the empty part of the graveyard and the boys came into sight.

Up ahead, I could see my brother, Hugh. He was holding Gerard in his arms. Keeping him close while their other friend, Patrick, sat on the footpath with his arm around the both of them. I couldn't hear what my brother was saying to Gerard, but I knew it was something smart. Hugh was good that way. He always knew what to say.

"Who?"

"Gerard."

"I don't know, Claire." Lizzie shrugged as she helped to retie my cardigan around my waist when it slipped off. "Caoimhe says that Gibsie's going to be sad for a long time."

"A really long time," I agreed, feeling sad thinking about it.

"She said we need to leave him alone and give him time."

"Time?"

"Yep."

"Time for what?"

"Don't know," she replied with a shrug. "But Caoimhe says it's important."

"I want to hug him."

"You should," she told me. "You give the best hugs."

"Your hugs are pretty good, too," I replied. "Super squishy."

"But your hugs feel like sunshine."

"Like sunshine?" I frowned in confusion. "How?"

"Because you are sunshine, silly," she laughed before skipping off in the direction of the boys. "Or maybe it's your shampoo."

"My shampoo?" Reaching around, I grabbed a curl and took a whiff. "That's not sunshine, Liz. That's strawberries."

"I'm really sorry about your dad, Gibsie," Lizzie said when she reached their huddle. Not stopping until she was kneeling on the footpath in front of him, she wrapped her arms around our friend and squeezed him tight. "And your sister, too."

"Thanks, Liz," Gerard sniffled, hugging her back.

"Oh, I brought this for you," she added, reaching into the pocket of her skirt. "Sorry, it got bent in my pocket." She placed a broken daisy on his lap before settling down on the footpath next to my brother. "It's for the grave."

"Thanks, Liz." He shoved the daisy into his pocket before turning to look at my brother and then Patrick. "Thanks for staying, lads."

"We'll always stay, Gibs," Hugh replied, keeping one arm wrapped around Gerard, while using the other to tuck Lizzie close to his side.

"Exactly," Patrick agreed, hooking his arm around Gerard from the other side. "What are friends for?"

A hot, angry feeling stabbed my belly.

It always happened when Liz and Hugh were together. She was supposed to be my friend, but she always played with my brother when she came over, and I didn't like it.

Sitting cross-legged on the footpath in front of them, I picked at a scab on my elbow and tried to think nicer thoughts. Kinder thoughts. I'd made a promise to God, after all. I got to keep Gerard.

"Liz!" Caoimhe's familiar voice drilled through the air. "What were you thinking running off like that? Mam's looking all over the place for you."

"Aw, crap," Lizzie grumbled, quickly climbing to her feet. "I better go back."

"I'll walk you back to your sister," Hugh said, springing up to join her. "I'll be right back, Gibs."

"He definitely has the hots for her," Patrick announced, staring after Hugh and Liz as they walked up the path.

"Oh yeah," Gerard agreed quietly. "He's so obvious."

Frowning, Patrick added, "I think she has the hots for him, too."

"Yep," Gerard replied. "She's obvious, too."

"What's the hots?" I asked them.

"It's when two people want to hold hands with each other and spend all of lunch-time playing together. Just the two of them," Patrick explained.

"But Hugh doesn't go to the same school as Liz, so how can they have the hots for each other if they don't play together at lunchtime?"

"They do it at home instead," Gerard offered.

"Playing?"

"Yep."

"But you play with Lizzie, too, Patrick," I added. "So, does that mean you have the hots for her, too?"

"I don't know. Maybe sometimes," he replied, looking distracted before quickly climbing to his feet. "I'll be right back."

"Sorry for running away earlier," Gerard said when Patrick was gone. "I wasn't running away from you."

"It was the big hole in the ground, wasn't it?" I asked, crawling over to sit beside him. "It scared me, too."

With teary gray eyes, he nodded slowly. "I didn't want to see them put my sister in the hole."

"Hey, Gerard?"

"Yeah, Claire?"

"Do you need time?"

"Time for what?"

"I don't know." I shrugged and readjusted the knot holding my cardigan to my waist. "Caoimhe said that you lots of need time and that we're to leave you alone."

"No, no, don't go," he blurted out, snatching up my hand in his. "Okay?"

"I wasn't going anywhere, silly." I chuckled, staring down at how his hand made my hand look super tiny. "I would never leave you, Gerard."

"That's what my dad said." He sucked in a shaky breath and clenched his eyes shut before whispering, "So just…please don't go, okay?"

"I'll never go, Gerard," I replied, shifting closer so that our shoulders were touching.

That was what happened when I was with Gerard. I wanted my hand to touch his hand all the time. Or my shoulder. Or my toes. I never wanted him to step back or leave. I just wanted him to stay right beside me. Even when he was super sad. "I'll never leave you."

"I mean it," he urged, turning to look at me now. "I can't lose another person I love."

"You love me?"

He nodded sadly as another tear trickled down his check. "I love you most of all."

I beamed up at him. "Even more than Hugh?"

He scrunched his nose up in disgust. "I don't love Hugh."

"Even more than Patrick?"

"I don't love Feely, either."

"You don't?"

"Just you."

"You know, Gerard, if you ever get super sad, I can be your sister, too. Hugh won't mind sharing."

"You can't be my sister, Claire."

"Why not?"

"Because you can't have the hots for your sister."

"You've got the hots for me?" My tummy flipped like a pancake again. "Not Lizzie? Because I heard Hugh say that she's super pretty once."

"Lizzie? Ugh. No way," he grumbled, lip curling up in disapproval. "I don't see Lizzie."

"You don't?"

"I don't see anyone." His lips tipped up in the smallest of smiles before he added, "Except for you."

"Gerard, sweetheart, it's time to go home," a familiar voice called out, and I felt him stiffen beside me when both of our families walked toward us. "We have mourners coming to the house."

"Five more minutes," he bit out, breathing hard and fast now. "Please."

"We have to go now, pet," his mammy pushed.

"Please," he repeated, glaring at the footpath. "Five minutes."

"Gerard…"

"He can come home with us, Sadhbh," I offered, wrapping my arm around his shoulders as best as I could. It wasn't easy when he was a lot bigger than me, but I tried. "We have room in the car."

"Not today, Claire pet," she replied, sniffling. "Gerard has to be with his family right now."

"They are not my family," he choked out, chest heaving. "They're my family," he added, pointing in the opposite direction, to where his daddy and sister were buried. "So just leave me alone, okay?"

"Gerard!" Sadhbh gasped, and then burst into another fit of crying. "I need you with me right now."

"Let him go with his friends, sweetheart," Keith tried to persuade. "He'll feel better around people his own age."

"Yeah, let him go," Mark grunted. "I'm sick of the crying."

"Mark, you're not helping!"

"I can't breathe," Gerard strangled out, turning to look at me, gray eyes wild with panic as he began to suck in deep, sharp gulps of air. "I can't breathe, Claire."

My eyes widened in horror. "You can't?"

He shook his head, looking terrified. "I'm drowning."

"You're drowning?" Yelping out a startled cry, I sprang to my feet and pulled him with me. "It's okay, Gerard. You just have to open your mouth and let the air go in."

"I c-can't!"

"You can't?"

"N-no…"

All hell broke loose after that.

"What's happening to him?"

"He's having a panic attack."

"Gibs?"

"Gerard, sweetheart, it's me, Sinead. Can you hear me?"

"I can't breathe!"

"Help him!"

"No, don't l-let g-go of my h-hand!"

"I won't, Gerard."

Lying in the darkness, I stared up at the ceiling and tried my best to be a brave girl. I didn't like sleeping in the dark, but I was staying in my brother's room tonight, so I didn't get to choose. It wasn't too scary, though. The moon was big and bright and shining through the window like a night-light.

"Are you still awake?"

That was Hugh.

"Yeah." I whispered back. "Are you?"

"Obviously. I asked you a question, didn't I?"

"Oh yeah."

"Is he still holding your hand?"

I looked down at where mine and Gerard's hands were still joined and nodded. "Yep."

Pulling himself up on his elbows, my brother leaned over Gerard's sleeping frame and whispered, "Do you need to use the bathroom before you go to sleep?"

"Super bad." I chewed on my lip, feeling worried. "What if I wet the bed?"

"Don't you dare wet my bed."

"But what if I fall asleep and it happens?"

"Go to the bathroom before you fall asleep."

"I can't. He won't let go and I've been holding his hand in all day."

"Well, he's out cold now," Hugh whispered back. "They gave him that medicine to make him sleep."

"Yeah," I replied, brows furrowing at the memory. "He was so sad."

"I know." Hugh sighed heavily. "Just slip your hand out of his and go."

"I've already tried." My palm was sweaty and hot, but Gerard was still holding onto it with both of his hands. He hadn't let go of it since the funeral. "I'm stuck, Hugh."

"Shit."

"Don't curse."

"Just give him the night with the kids, Sadhbh," I heard my mother say from the other side of the bedroom door. "He's already asleep, the poor crater. I'll bring him over first thing in the morning."

"Oh shit," Hugh mouthed, flopping back down into sleep position.

"Don't curse," I whisper-hissed, mirroring his actions.

"I don't know what to do here, Sinead," Gerard's mother sobbed. "He's so broken."

"He's a strong boy with a wonderful mother who loves him. He can get through anything."

"But it's just so awful because he was already struggling with the separation, but now with Joe gone and Keith having moved in last month—" Another pained sob. "I'm afraid he'll feel like I'm replacing his father."

More mumbling continued before the sound of footsteps retreating filled the silence.

"She did replace Joe," Hugh muttered under his breath.

"Hugh!"

"What? It's true."

"Yeah, but you still can't say it out loud."

"Whether I say it out loud or say it in my head, it's still true, Claire. Sadhbh dumped Joe for Keith, and everyone knows it."

"Even Gerard?"

"Especially Gibs."

"He never told me."

"Because he treats you like you're made of glass."

"He does?"

"Yup."

"Oh." Frowning, I twisted sideways to look at my brother. "Hey Hugh? What does 'dumped' mean?"

"It's when someone you love gets rid of you because they love someone else more," he replied, rolling onto his side to face me.

"Oh." I chewed my lip and thought about it for a moment. "Is Mammy going to dump Daddy like Sadhbh dumped Joe?"

"No way," Hugh replied in a reassuring tone. "Mam loves Dad the right way."

"Didn't Sadhbh love Joe the right way?"

"At one time she did," he replied with a shrug. "But I guess she stopped."

"That's super sad."

"Quit saying the word 'super' all the time, Claire."

"I like the word 'super,'" I protested. "I can even spell it."

"Yeah, yeah," he said, yawning. "Okay, I think I have a plan."

"You do?"

"Yep." Nodding, my brother leaned over Gerard's sleeping frame and reached for his hand. "I'll hold his hand while you go to the toilet."

"But what if he wakes up and gets another panic attack?"

"Then you better pee quickly," my brother grumbled as he pried Gerard's hands away from mine. "Now, Claire. Run fast."

The sound of crying woke me up later that night. "Hugh?" Blinking awake, I looked around my brother's room, feeling confused. "Is that you?"

"N-no, he's s-still asleep."

"Gerard?" My belly did the pancake flipping when I heard his voice, and I quickly flipped onto my side to look at him. "Hi."

He was already lying on his side facing me, with my right hand clasped between both of his. "Hi."

"Are you okay?"

Sniffling, he wiped his cheek against the pillow and slowly shook his head.

"Did you have a bad dream?"

He nodded once.

"About the boat?" I asked, resting my free hand on top of his. "About falling in the water?"

Another small nod.

"You're safe now," I tried to make him happy by saying. "Nice and warm and dry—and you're back with me."

He didn't smile. Instead, he continued to stare at me, while big, fat teardrops trickled down his cheeks. "What am I going to do, Claire?"

"What do you mean?" I asked, shifting closer so that our feet were touching. I had cold toes. Gerard's were always warm. Except for last Saturday. His and Hugh's First Holy Communion Day. The day our daddies took our families out on that big boat to celebrate. That day, Gerard was blue and cold all over.

"Without my dad," he whispered, covering my feet with his. He clenched his eyes shut before choking out, "And m-my s-sister." Sniffling back another sob, he blew out a shaky breath. "I'm all alone now."

"No, you're not," I whispered back, using my free hand to wipe a super big tear off my cheek. "You've got Sadhbh, and Keith, and Mark—"

"I hate him," he interrupted with a sharp hiss.

"Who? Keith?"

He nodded stiffly. "And n-not just him."

"Mark, too?"

Sniffling, he swallowed deeply before saying, "I don't like the way he looks at me."

My eyes widened. "He looks bad at you?"

"He looks evil at me," he explained. "Like he wants to hurt me."

Anger grew in my belly. "Hurt you?"

He nodded again. "Maybe even kill me."

"Well, I will kick him in his willy if he hurts you," I growled. "I know how to do it. Just ask Hugh. I kicked him in his willy last week for breaking my Barbie and he cried."

"Oh yeah." Gerard smiled. "I remember."

His first big smile since that day.

"I like your face when you do that," I told him, reaching up to touch the hole that appeared in his cheek when he smiled.

"Do what?"

"Smile," I explained. "It makes my tummy wobble."

"Wobble?"

"Uh-huh." Nodding eagerly, I snickered when it happened again. "Like jiggly jelly."

14

"Huh." Gerard's brows furrowed together, and he looked like he was concentrating superhard. "It's the same for me."

"Hey, Gerard?"

"Yeah, Claire?"

"You're still holding my hand."

"I know." A shiver rolled through him, and he tightened his hold on my hand. "Sorry. It's just…holding your hand makes me feel better."

"It does?"

"Yeah." He watched me cautiously. "Is that okay?"

"Yep." I beamed at him. "You can hold my hand forever."

"You promise?"

"Uh-huh." I yawned, feeling sleepy. "I promise."

1

Back with a Vengeance

GIBSIE

10 YEARS LATER

Scream, you pathetic piece of shit, the voice in my head commanded.

Was it my voice?

Was it someone else's?

I couldn't be sure anymore.

All I knew in this moment was that I wanted nothing more than to move, to run, to scream, but I *couldn't*.

Call for help, dammit!

I can't!

Nothing was working.

I couldn't move a muscle.

Not so much as a fingertip.

I was paralyzed with fear.

Again.

Rendered helpless, I drenched the part of my mattress that my face was pressed into with my tears.

Pressure.

It was climbing up my throat.

Pushing me deeper into the mattress.

Silent tears followed by silent screams that couldn't activate my vocal cords.

Drip. Drip. Drip.

The heavy weight above me kept me locked in my personal eternal pit of terror.

Drowning.

Pressing my face into the mattress until I couldn't breathe. Letting the water fill my lungs to the point of explosion.

Nostrils flaring.

It's not real.

Arms flailing.

You're not here.

Darkness seeping in.

It doesn't hurt anymore.

The image of crushing waves shifted to the familiar view of my upstairs landing.

I'm drowning, Mam.

I could see the hue of light from her bedroom lamp shining from underneath the doorframe.

I'm going under again.

That horrific, familiar scorching pain seared through me, causing my body to thrash helplessly.

Why can't you see me?

Death would be better than this.

It hurts.

I was already dying on the inside.

Make it stop.

My insides were already ruined.

Make him stop.

My heart slowly disintegrated in my chest.

No, don't take me away from them.

My heartbeat grew sluggish in my chest, but I could still hear my pulse thundering in my ears.

No. Please. Stop him from saving me.

Because I would never be healed.

It's your fault she's dead.

I could feel his hands on my body.

Keep your eyes on the door.

Pressure.

Please let me go.

It was building up in my chest.

I want my dad.

Clawing at my throat.

Don't make me let go of his hand.

Drowning me.

I can't see my sister.

Smothering me.

She's disappearing deeper and deeper into the darkness.

Pushing against my lungs to the point where I couldn't breathe.

He's coming closer.

"No!"

Go with her.

"Stop!"

I promise it'll be better down there.

"Dad!"

Hold your breath.

And then he was pulling me out of the water.

"Breathe, kid, breathe!"

You deserve to be punished.

"Keep trying, dammit!"

You deserve to be hurt.

"One, two, three, four, five!"

You deserve to be ruined.

"Stand clear."

From the inside out.

"We've got a pulse…"

"No!" Gasping for air, I scrambled out of bed, not stopping until I had collapsed in a heap on the bedroom floor. "Christ." Panic-stricken, I ran my hands through my sweat-soaked hair and then scrubbed my face. Anxiety was thrashing around inside of me, causing my heart to buck around like a demonic ping-pong ball in my chest.

I could still taste the water in my mouth, feel the panic as my lungs filled and burned to the point of bursting.

Chest heaving and breathing ragged, I stared up at the ceiling in the darkness, still desperately clawing for air.

Thud.

Thud.

Thud.

My heart was beating so hard, climbing so high in my chest, that I could almost taste it in my throat.

Metallic.

Sinful.

Wrong!

"You're okay," I tried to tell myself, but felt no comfort. "You're okay."

Thud.

Thud.

Thud.

I couldn't breathe.

Yes, you can.

You're breathing just fine, asshole.

It was a nightmare.

It wasn't real.

But it *was*.

It is real.

Wrong.

Wrong.

Wrong!

"Fucking stop it," I ordered my own wandering mind as I rolled onto my hands and knees, moving through the darkness blindly. "Just shut the fuck up for one goddamn minute!"

Thud.

Thud.

Thud.

Was I still awake?

Thud.

Thud.

Thud.

Or had I fallen back to sleep?

Thud.

Thud.

Thud.

I was definitely on the move now, stumbling around in the darkness, guided solely by memory.

Thud.

Thud.

Thud.

A severe wave of brain fog attacked my senses and I felt myself slipping.

Drifting away again.

Into another nightmare.

Jesus no!

"No, no, no…" Whimpering, I mentally fought against what I knew came next, but it was no use.

Even in my dreams, I couldn't change a thing.

"Gerard?"

Far out in the distance, I could hear her.

"Oh my god, Gerard."

My heart was thundering in my chest.

"You're okay. Shh, shh, it's okay."

My feet were moving.

"It's me. You're safe."

My hands were reaching for her.

"I've got you."

But I couldn't see a thing.

"Shh, baby, I've got you."

My pulse was roaring in my ears.

"I'm right here with you."

The waves were lapping over my body.

"Open your eyes, Gerard."

Her touch was crushing my soul.

"Come back to me…"

"Fuck!" I choked out, physically coughing and spluttering violently as the phantom sensation of drowning continued to cause havoc on my psyche. "Claire?" Frantic, my eyes sprang open. "Claire?" The fog lifted from my mind, and I felt like I could suddenly see again. "*Claire?*"

"It's me." A pair of familiar hands wrapped around my waist from behind, causing my entire body to simultaneously stiffen and jolt. "I'm right here, Gerard."

And then I could smell her shampoo, the washing powder her mother always used on her clothes, the feel of her chest pressed to my back as she cradled my body against her.

Relief.

It flooded my body with such force that it eradicated every ounce of adrenaline that had been thrashing around inside of me, leaving me a broken mess in her arms. "*Claire.*"

"I've got you."

When she put her hands on my body, I didn't flinch. I didn't feel the familiar swell of panic that consumed me when I was grabbed from behind.

I didn't have to open my eyes to know that I had somehow managed to sleepwalk into her bedroom. *Again.* It was the only place my legs ever took me. It was the only place I could *breathe.*

I also didn't have to look behind me to know that she was wearing her favorite pink unicorn onesie. I was so familiar with the fabric that I recognized the feel of it against my back as she continued to hold me.

Her senses became *my* senses, and I found a way to anchor myself in the moment. I found the strength to drag the present version of me out of my nightmares. *Out of my past.*

"You're safe now." Claire's voice was filled with a quiet, assured confidence that I desperately clung to in the moment. She had a right to feel confident. She had been the unfortunate candidate thrust into bringing me back from the edge every day since the drowning. "I've got your back."

Claire Biggs had a lot of things.

My back.

My attention.

My heart.

My soul.

Yeah, she had all of me and that wasn't an exaggeration.

I knew that gate-crashing her room wasn't fair to either of us—I wasn't stupid—but it was a habit I'd formed after my father died, and I just wasn't ready to kick it. She was the nicotine I couldn't walk away from. The crutch I hadn't learned to walk without.

Get out of her bedroom, asshole.

Get your shit together.

You have no right to lean on her like this.

"They're getting worse, Gerard."

It wasn't a question, but I forced myself to answer her anyway. "Yeah."

"More violent."

Again, it wasn't a question, but I responded with a shaky "yeah."

My nightmares had always been horrendous. Usually, I was good at hiding them from her, which was impressive considering I'd slept in her bed almost every night since I was seven.

When the night terrors were bad, like they had been this past summer, I tried to make myself scarce and made the conscious effort to sleep at my own house. It never seemed to make a difference, though, because even in sleep I found my way back to her.

"Why?" Concern filled her voice. "What's been happening to you?"

Nothing.

Nothing was happening to me, which was why I felt so goddamn frustrated. I'd been plagued by night terrors since the accident. Sure, they got progressively worse a few years back when I was dealing with shit, but I was *fine* now.

Being happy was a decision I made for myself and, miraculously, it helped. It wasn't real, I didn't truly feel that way, but I was a firm believer in faking it until you made it. After all, I would be dead without the sentiment.

21

It was like anything I had ever manifested for my life. Even if it didn't necessarily come true right away, I acted like it had until it did. For example, I wanted to be normal, therefore I was. I wanted to be talented like Johnny, to be smart like Hugh, to be creative like Patrick, therefore I did and *was* all those things.

Sure, I might not be any of those things naturally, but if I pretended like I was long enough, then there was a good chance it might happen.

Maybe Lizzie was right, and I was a thick fucker. I certainly wasn't getting into any universities after Tommen. But I always had my sense of humor to fall back on.

Bluffing my way through life had worked like a charm so far. Bonus points because I wasn't hurting anyone. Unlike Lizzie, I had found a way to cope, and grieve, and protect myself without tearing strips out of others.

Why be fucked-up Gerard when I could be Gibsie the fuckup? It couldn't hurt when I was Gibsie, because Gibsie was my armor, and humor was my sword.

I didn't think too much about the words that came out of my mouth. I usually said whatever was on my mind at the time, and that formed the person I had become in the minds of my friends. I was naturally self-deprecating, never purposefully cruel, and my attitude made people laugh. My mouth spurted shit at the expense of my own character, like a cloak of self-sabotaging protection.

Nothing I said was for venomous or boasting purposes. It was for sheer protection. It was my safety net. Because I had an acute need to protect myself and I didn't know how else to do that in a world where everyone aside from me seemed to have their shit together.

There was only one person in my life that still saw me as, well, *me.*

Only one person who refused to let go of the version of me from the past.

The girl with her arms around me.

My girl.

"Then it has to be what happened to you on the camping trip," she declared in a passionate tone of voice. "When Lizzie pushed you into the river, she must have triggered something inside of you—a memory of that day."

"Maybe," I replied, my breathing still uneven and ragged. "Whatever." Sitting forward, I pressed my face into my hands and tried to get a handle on myself. "Doesn't matter."

"It's *does* matter, Gerard. You've been a wreck almost every night since." Reaching up, she peeled my hands away from my face and entwined them with hers. "I'm worried about you."

I didn't have to force myself to look at the girl holding my hands; my eyes automatically sought her out, honing in on those blond curls and brown eyes like I had been programmed to seek them out since babyhood.

"Hey, hey, just talk to me," she instructed softly, reaching up to cup my face. "Come on, Gerard. Tell me what's happening in that head of yours."

I *couldn't* talk to her.

I couldn't talk to anyone.

The ugly side of life I had been exposed to was something I would take to the grave with me.

Stop.

Don't think about it.

Block it out.

The present was the safest place for my mind to reside because the past was horrific and the future terrified me.

"It's okay." I tried to appease her worrying, covering her hands with mine as I repressed the urge to shudder. "Don't worry about me."

"That's what friends do, Gerard." Never taking her big brown eyes off mine, she leaned in close to rest her forehead against mine. "They worry about each other."

If I could sew this girl to my skin without causing her an ounce of harm, then I would do it in a heartbeat. That's how vital she was to my life. How essential she was to my existence.

If drugs were to Joey Lynch what Claire Biggs was to me, then there was no amount of rehab that could sway me to kick the habit. Because she was the habit of *my* lifetime.

In a weird way, that's why I helped Aoife Molloy all those months ago. I would have helped her anyway, but the utter helplessness I saw in her eyes that night as she stared down the gun of love and pain, I knew there was something in her that I could relate to. I knew what it felt like to be that helpless, and I *never* wanted anyone to experience it. I saw the look in her eyes. I knew that look. I only wished that someone could have stepped in and saved me from that pain. But money couldn't soothe the pain of my past. From feeling that level of devastation and weakness. If giving the girl a few quid spared her from that ordeal, then I would gladly do it.

"You can talk to me," Claire continued to knock down my walls by saying. "I'm always here for you."

"Claire." Closing my eyes, I dragged in a steadying breath and forced myself to remember why I needed to *not* do what my heart was *strongly* urging me to do.

Christ, I wanted to kiss her. I wanted to do all the things lads did with their girls. I wanted to make her *mine*, but what if I was wrong? Not us as a couple, but me as a *man*? What if it didn't work? What if *I* didn't work? Because I didn't feel things with girls. I never felt anything. I was numb to the point of being dead, and if I didn't feel things with *Claire*, then it would confirm that my past had truly broken me beyond repair.

I could still remember how it felt the first time she put her lips on mine. Years had passed and several lips had replaced hers since, but I never forgot the spark. The ping. The ignited buzz that throttled my chest and caused my skin to grow hot and cold and warm and tingly all at once. It had only happened one time with one girl. She did something to me that day, gave me a sort of comfort only a person in my position could understand. I felt something. I felt for her. I enjoyed it. Her touch was welcome and wanted and wonderful. After that, I tried to forget about it for the sake of my friendship with Hugh, but I never could. Forgetting Claire wasn't something I was capable of doing and he knew it.

Any form of intimacy I could conjure up, I wanted to both give and have with her. *Just her.*

Because I cared about the girl. I cared to the point where she distracted my day. I cared when her cat was sick. I cared when she cried. I cared when her mam ran out of her favorite brand of cereal, and she had to eat porridge. I cared so fucking much it was hard to find where she started and I ended.

I knew her favorite song every year since August 7, 1989. I knew her secrets, her little habits, and traits that nobody else noticed. I wanted to waste my time on her. All of my time. All of the time.

She'd always been the curly-haired whirlwind across the street that made my heart go crackers, but after the accident, I projected a lot of my emotions onto her. Hell, maybe even into her.

Both sets of our parents had grown up together, and when they settled down and married, they decided to put down roots on the same street and raise their children together.

A little younger than Hugh and a little older than Claire, I had somehow slotted into the middle, destined to grow up alongside the Biggs siblings. I loved them both like they were my own flesh and blood, but it became very clear to me, at a young age, that the feelings I held for the youngest member of the Biggs family were *not* brotherly.

From as far back as I could remember, my mind had always been very clear about three things.

One: Hugh was my brother.

Two: Bethany was my sister.

Three: Claire was *mine*.

After the accident, once I learned how fickle life could be, how quickly a person you loved could be snatched away, it caused the feelings I had for Claire to deepen rapidly, growing wilder and stronger with every day that passed, spreading in intricate, permanent patterns around my heart like ivy.

The girl was everything to me, and that wasn't me being dramatic. It was a fact. The thought of letting her down made me feel physically sick. The thought of any form of harm coming to her, be it emotional or physical, made me feel homicidal.

So, I did the friend thing, played the role I had been assigned since birth, and tried my best not to fuck it up, while soaking in every spare second of time with her. I didn't call over at the Biggs house for Hugh. It was always for her. I would always look after her, even if looking at her from afar was all I could do. It would be enough for me. It would have to be. Because breaking her or corrupting her wasn't an option. Letting her down was even less of one.

Hugh didn't want me near his sister for all the reasons he didn't need to worry about. Because, as sure as there was a cat in County Cork, I would never cause harm to Claire Biggs.

She was too important to me.

She was *everything* to me.

Knowing that our mothers not only thought we would make a good couple, but strongly encouraged it on the daily warmed something inside of me, but it couldn't warm or quieten the niggling fear I had of fucking everything up and potentially driving away the only person I couldn't live without.

Because I never wanted her to run from me. To be afraid of me, or for me to make her feel the way I felt. I never wanted her to experience that form of helplessness.

I *wanted* the future I joked about with her. I wanted *everything* with her. Problem was, I didn't trust the person I was. I was too fucking scared of becoming what had ruined me. Of abusing her love and breaking her heart.

Because once we crossed that line, things would never be the same again. We couldn't come back from it. And I needed the guarantee that I wouldn't wreck it. That I wouldn't be reckless with her heart. That I could love her the right way. Because I loved this girl. With every fiber of my being. With every beat of my poor defective heart. I loved her fiercely, solely, wholeheartedly. I had so many physical urges directed solely toward her, but there were no guarantees in life, and I *couldn't* risk it.

Clenching my eyes shut, I took a moment to compose myself, to slide my comedic, carefree mask into place. It covered me like a blanket of deceit and protection.

This was how I had managed to reinvent myself when my world crashed down around me. Not just reinvent myself. No, it was more than that. It was my personal resurrection.

When I opened my eyes again, I was the version of me I could tolerate. The version that couldn't be hurt.

Never again.

"You know me, Claire-Bear," I offered with a reassuring smile. Because even though looking at her was effortless, seeing concern in her eyes was *not*. "I'm always okay."

She didn't look impressed. Or fooled. "So, it's like that again, huh?"

Guilt swam inside of me, but I doubled down and smiled harder. "Like what?"

She didn't respond. Instead, she stared at me for the longest time before shaking her head in resignation.

"Okay, Gerard." Releasing me, she climbed to her feet. "Build your walls back up all you want," she declared as she gathered up her pillows and duvet that were strewn everywhere, along with her nightstand and lamp. "I'm too tired to break them down tonight."

It was only then that I was registered the fact that not only did I wake her up with my bullshit, but I'd messed her room up in my pathetic attempt to find her in the dark.

"Shit, babe," I muttered, hurrying to fix my mistakes. "I didn't mean to do any of this." Standing the nightstand back up, I switched on the thankfully unbroken lamp and placed it back in its usual spot. "Fuck." Immediately, my gaze channeled in on the sleeping cat in the corner of her bedroom, with her litter of babies, and I sagged in relief, grateful that I hadn't disturbed them. "I'm so sorry."

"Yeah." Yawning, she clambered onto her bed, burrowed under the duvet, and then patted the empty patch of mattress beside her. "It was like you were trying to fight me and run to me all in one breath."

A shudder racked through me. "I'm sorry."

"Don't be. I'm glad you're here." She patted the mattress once more, causing a combination of guilt and relief to course through my veins. "Now, come here and snuggle me. You know I hate sleeping without you."

Yeah, I knew that, and it was a troubling piece of information because it meant that my fucked-up issues had managed to seep their way into her innocence.

It meant that I had infected her with my bullshit. It felt an awful lot like an unhealthy codependency technique, and that troubled me because I didn't want this girl to depend on me for anything. Because I wasn't worthy and I sure as hell wasn't good enough.

Still, like every night since the age of seven, I found myself climbing into bed beside her, with only one goal in mind: to get as close as humanly possible to the only form of physical comfort I had found in my seventeen years on earth.

When I was under the covers, I automatically moved into the middle of the bed and then rolled onto my right side, feeling the familiar dip in the mattress that had been put there from my body imprint.

Like clockwork, Claire rolled onto her side and raised her arm, waiting for mine to come around her. "Mmm," she purred like a little kitten. "You're always toasty warm."

"Yeah." I shifted closer until our bodies aligned, her back to my chest, my hand on her hip, her hand gripping my forearm. Perfectly in sync in every human way possible. "Claire?"

"Hmm?"

"I'm sorry." *Again.* "About tonight." *Again.*

"S'okay..." she mumbled drowsily, as she shimmied until her back was flush to my chest. "Night, Gerard... Love you."

"I love you, too," I whispered, feeling the familiar jolt of adrenaline rocket through my veins when those words spilled from her lips.

Claire meant it when she told me that she loved me. That was the first of two things in life I *was* sure of, and I meant it right back. That was the second thing I was sure of. If I knew nothing else in this world, then I knew that I loved Claire Biggs.

More than she could ever know.

More than one lousy four-letter word could ever depict.

And from my own limited experience, I was under no illusion as to how messy loving a person could be. Because love *hurt.* It burned like hell. I got that. I accepted the pain. The self-inflicted flesh wounds it took to love another human. I wasn't afraid of that. Of being hurt. Of anything for myself. My fear rested in my inability to love her the right way. In the potential I had to hurt her beyond repair or recourse.

The same way *he* hurt me.

2

Sleepwalking Sweethearts and Bonehead Brothers

CLAIRE

"I'M TELLING YOU, CLAIRE-BEAR, WE'VE GOT THIS," GERARD DECLARED, ARMED WITH Brian's cat cage. "It's in the bag." Marching us through the fair, he didn't stop until we reached the area of the field that was sporting the dog show. "Trust me."

"I don't know, Gerard," I replied, chewing on my bottom lip as I hurried along beside him. "What if they don't let us enter?"

"Bullshit," he shot back, and then jerked comically when Brian swiped a paw through the bars of the cage. "They can't do that."

"Brian's a cat."

"So?"

"So, this is a dog show."

"Nowhere in the rule books does it state that we have to enter a dog."

"I think because it's alluded to in the title 'dog show,' Gerard."

"Do you see a cat show being offered anywhere?"

"Nope."

"Me either, so this will work, Claire."

"What if they laugh at us?"

"So what if they do?" he scoffed, completely unaffected. "Let them. We need that prize money, babe—and we have more than earned that first-place trophy for washing that deranged bastard." Reaching up, he touched the part of his shoulder that had been mangled the worst. "I have the scratches to prove it."

"But you know Brian's not very friendly."

"No, he's not," Gerard agreed. "But I promised I would stand by you and provide for our babies so that's exactly what I'm going to do." Shrugging, he added, "Besides, he's the one tapping Cherub. He can do this for us."

"We should have brought Cherub."

"Yeah, well, she's a preoccupied right now," he shot back, "what with being in the family way and having a belly on her bigger than Fat Paddy." Slapping on a smile, he added, "Let's just work with what we've been given here. Brian might be a bastard, but he's a beautiful one."

That was true. Brian was a looker alright. A long-haired pedigreed Persian with a snow-white coat of perfectly combed fur. Too bad he was a demon on the inside. "What if he attacks the judges?"

"Don't worry, I've got that covered."

"Oh?" My eyes narrowed and I eyed him warily. "Gerard. What did you do?"

"Offered him a mild sedative before we left the house."

"You did what?"

"How else was I supposed to get him in the box?" he demanded, looking affronted. "You know how ratty he gets when I touch him."

"Oh god, this is a bad idea."

"It's a great idea," he corrected, wrapping his arm around my shoulders. "And we've got this."

"Oh, Gerard, look at the dog," I cooed, eyes locked on a pampered Pomeranian.

"He doesn't have shit on us…"

"Claire."

"Claire."

"*Claire!*" The sound of my brother's voice thundered through my ears, disrupting the most epically perfect memory dream I'd had in weeks and startling me into a sudden state of confused consciousness. "Come on, will you? It's gone seven. I'm leaving in ten minutes."

"Gone seven?" I called back sleepily. "In the morning?"

"Yeah, let's go," his deep voice boomed from the other side of my bedroom door. "Hurry up."

"But it's still summer, Hugh," I wailed, momentarily panicking that I'd somehow slept through the last few days of our summer holidays and was about to be thrust back into corridors of Tommen. "And it's Saturday!"

"Yeah, genius, I know it's Saturday," he drawled, tone laced with a healthy dollop of brotherly sarcasm. "Listen, Mam's been tormenting me since your birthday to get you a job at the hotel. Kim told me to bring you along this morning, there's an opening for a part-time lifeguard at the pool, and she wants to give you a trial run while I'm on duty, so get your ass in gear because my shift starts at eight, and I won't be late for you."

"A trial?" Scrunching my nose up in distaste, I stretched my legs out and yawned. "For what?"

"A job," came his sarcastic response.

"But I have a job."

"You volunteer at the public swimming pool, Claire," he replied, sounding more impatient by the second. "Lifeguarding at the hotel is a paying job."

"Smart-ass." Yawning sleepily, I snuggled deeper into the mattress, feeling beyond exhausted. "Give me five more minutes, will you? I'm just resting my eyes."

"Rest your eyes all you want," my brother replied. "But I'm leaving in ten minutes. Dad's holed up in the attic on a deadline, so he won't take you, and—"

"Then I'll ask Mam," I called back before he could finish.

Hah.

Take that, sucker.

"Mam's not back from the night shift at the hospital yet," he swiftly continued, not missing a beat. "She won't be back in time."

"Hugh, please," I complained, kicking my legs under my duvet in frustration. "Just give me five more minutes!"

"*No,* because I know that your version of five minutes really means forty minutes and I need to leave in ten," he replied, sounding more impatient by the second.

"Keep talking and you'll bore me back to sleep."

"Fine. Suit yourself," he called back. "But when Mam bitches about you not getting a job, don't even think about dropping the blame baton onto me, princess." There was a long pause before his voice boomed again. "Oh, and you can tell that asshole that he was supposed to meet Cap at the gym two hours ago."

That did the trick.

My eyes sprang open and I bolted out of my bed, only to ping back like a boomerang when my hand wouldn't comply with the rest of my body.

Of course it wouldn't.

Not when it was welded to a much larger hand.

"Five more minutes, babe." Gerard echoed my earlier words from under a mountain of pillows and teddy bears. "I'm resting my eyes."

"Come on, get up," I groaned, battling it out for dominion over my hand and losing when he pulled me back down on the mattress without breaking a sweat—or cracking open an eyelid. "Hugh's right outside my door. Apparently, you're supposed to be at the gym."

"The gym can suck my balls," he mumbled, rolling onto his side and pulling me flush against his chest to spoon. "Fucking Kav."

"Gerard!"

"Snuggling my Claire-Bear equals a happy Gibsie. Running laps on the treadmill until I puke equals a very unhappy Gibsie." The feel of his big body pressed to mine set loose what felt like a cage of wild butterflies in my chest. "It's all about priorities, babe."

"And I'm yours?" I teased.

"Always," he confirmed sleepily, tightening his hold on my waist.

Jesus.

Breath hitching, I forced myself to exhale slowly, all the while desperately trying to channel down the somersaulting sensation in my belly. The one that felt like I had just driven over a massive hump in the road, that caused my organs to shift around in my body.

Everything between us was starting to feel a whole lot different lately. More intense. More grown-up. Even though he was the same boy I'd spent most of my life adoring, he certainly didn't look like that boy anymore.

Sure, his silvery-gray eyes still sparkled with boyish mischief, but the puppy fat that had once lingered on his belly was long gone. High cheekbones and a defined jawline that was speckled with day-old stubble had replaced the chubby cheeks he once bore.

It was fair to say that Gerard Gibson was all man now, and that piece of knowledge caused something to stir inside of me.

I liked it, I realized—maybe even more than liked it.

My body seemed to react to the sight of him, causing my skin to flood with heat and my heart rate to skyrocket.

"Just relax," he mumbled sleepily. Not bothering to crack an eyelid open, he draped his big bicep around my body and pulled me back down. "Hmm." A deep rumble of approval escaped his lips when our bodies melded together once more. "Better."

Unable to repress the full-body shudder of pleasure that rippled through my core, I grew lax against him, knowing that it was a terrible idea with Hugh just outside and especially when I could feel Gerard's, uh, morning *ladder* steadily *erecting*, but I couldn't resist the temptation.

Completely aligned, with my back to his chest, Gerard buried his face in my neck and inhaled deeply before whispering the words, "Stay with me," in my ear.

Oh god.

"You're going to get in trouble with Johnny," I announced, repressing the urge to shiver in delight when his lips brushed the curve of my neck. The move was featherlight and clearly accidental on his behalf, but it caused my toes to curl. "And you're all sweaty."

"Kav will be grand." His breath fanned the back of my neck when he spoke. "And it always happens after, ah, you know."

After one of his night terrors, and, yeah, I knew all too well.

Last night was a bad one and I could still remember it vividly.

Heat emanated from his skin.

Sweat trickled from his neck to his shoulder.

I watched the glistening bead as it moved.

Sliding over his bare flesh, expunging itself from a body I could never get close enough to.

It wouldn't be long now.

The screaming would come.

Followed swiftly by the panic attack that always reduced him to a gasping, breathless, broken seven-year-old boy.

I remembered the first one just as vividly as the day it happened.

After all, I had been there to witness it firsthand.

The trauma.

The devastation.

The thought barely had time to register in my mind when the first cry ripped from his throat. It was a torn, shrill, agonizing sound that cultivated from a memory I couldn't erase for him.

"No!" Thrashing helplessly, he bolted out of bed, knocking over my nightstand in his bid to break free from the demons in his dreams. "Please don't..."

"Gerard!"

I had enough experience dealing with his night terrors to know that giving him space was the worst thing I could do. Therefore, I scrambled off my bed in my haste to get to him.

"Shh." Even in sleep, he knew my touch enough to let me cradle him in my arms. "It's me." His entire body was soaked with sweat but that didn't stop me. "I'm here." I leaned in close, nuzzling his cheek with mine. "Shh, Gerard, it's okay."

"No, no, no..." Pained groans turned to weak mewling as even in sleep, he frantically sought out my touch. "I can't make it stop."

"It's over," I tried to coax, cupping his cheeks with my hands. "It's just a nightmare now."

His sharp intakes of breath took on a desperate note, quickly shifting into panicked gasps.

Like he couldn't draw air into his lungs.

Like he was drowning.

With them.

"I've got you," I continued to whisper, melding my body to his, knowing this was exactly what he needed to come back down from the edge. From the pain. "I'm right here with you."

Slowly, his body relaxed to the feel of mine, taking me in, hearing my words, smelling my scent, breathing me in until he was mine and I was his. Until we were us again and he was safe.

"Claire?" His body stiffened then, and I knew he was awake. "Claire. Claire?"

"It's me." Releasing a shaky breath, I tightened my hold on him and buried my face in his neck. "I'm right here, Gerard. It's okay..."

"Yeah, I know," I whispered, blinking away the memories of last night when he wandered into my room in a frantic state of blind panic. "But they're getting a lot worse."

I felt him nod against me.

Lately, Gerard's nightmares had frequented to the point of being almost a nightly event. It was as unsettling as it was heartbreaking. Because I knew he was battling his demons—or should I say his ghosts. The ones from his childhood that he refused to talk about.

"What happened in last night's one?" I asked, feeling just as helpless this morning as I did every morning that I woke up with him in my bed.

Finding Gerard in my bed wasn't a new thing for us. In fact, in the past decade there was only a handful of nights he hadn't slept over.

"Same as always," he replied in a vulnerable tone, sounding nothing like the comedic joker the rest of the world was privy to. "Listen, I'll get you to wherever you need to be on time, I promise." He shifted closer, tightening his big arm around my waist. "Just snuggle me for a bit first."

The words were no sooner out of his mouth when my bedroom door swung inward with such force that it smacked off the plaster on my wall.

"Did I just hear that asshole ask you to *snuggle*?"

"What the hell, Hugh?" I shouted, wrestling free from the giant teenage boy in my bed to stop the giant teenage boy charging toward him from throwing down. "We have rules in this house, remember?" Scrambling off the bed, I rushed to intercept Hugh before either one could choose violence. Gerard and Hugh's relationship was more like brothers than friends and rarely came to any serious blows, but there had been a couple of occasions down through the years that I didn't want to see repeated. "Ever heard of knocking?"

"Gibs, you better not be naked in there," my brother warned, ignoring me entirely, while he focused on his friend who was sprawled out in my bed.

"Morning, stud," Gerard poked the bear by taunting, as he wiggled his fingers in salutation. "Any chance of some breakfast in bed for your favorite brother-in-law?"

And there it was.

His mask.

The divide that separated the sensitive boy I adored from the humorous one all our other friends enjoyed.

It slipped effortlessly into place.

Gibsie belonged to the rest of the world.

Gerard belonged just to me.

"I'll give you breakfast in bed, you little whore." My brother's face turned a freakish shade of purple. "I swear to Christ, lad, if you put so much as a finger on her, I will legit kill you dead this time."

"*On* her or *in* her?"

"Gibs!"

"Oh, get a grip, you big eejit." I rolled my eyes and stalked toward my brother. "He's only messing with you. We're clearly just friends."

"*Clearly*," came Hugh's sarcastic response. "You two are just friends and Bella's the Virgin Mary."

"Bella's a… What's the word those girls in pink use in the film, babe?" Gerard asked, twirling a finger around aimlessly. "An ugly clit?"

"A fugly slut, Gerard," I corrected with a smile. "But full marks for attempting a *Mean Girls* reference."

"Fugly slut," he chuckled, repeating the word to himself. "I love it."

"You won't be around to love anything if you don't get your hole out of my sister's bed," Hugh growled.

"Hey now, you listen up here, buddy," I huffed, catching ahold of his shoulders and pushing him toward my door. "I don't go in your room when your precious *Katie* is here, so you don't get to come into mine."

"There's a big goddamn difference in that equation, Claire," Hugh shot back. "Katie's a saint and he's a whore." Clearly furious, my older brother took in my appearance and seemed temporary appeased at the sight of my pink, fluffy onesie. "Oh, thank Jesus. You're fully clothed."

"Same as always," I drawled, folding my arms across my chest. "Talk about jumping to conclusions, Hugh. Jeez."

"Yeah, well, this sleepwalking bullshit has to stop," my brother commanded, turning his attention back to the boy in my bed. "It's getting beyond a joke."

"He can't help it," I protested, finding myself coming to the defense of the boy I'd adored since childhood. "You know it's not something he can control, Hugh. It just happens."

"Of course he can," Hugh shot back, giving me a look that said *don't be so gullible.* "He knows *exactly* what he's doing."

"No, he doesn't."

"Yes, he does," my brother clapped back. "You don't see him sleepwalking into my bed, do you?"

"If you're feeling left out, I can make it my mission to stop by your bed tonight, brother," Gerard said.

"Try it and I'll chop your nuts off."

"No need to get testy."

"Stay out of my sister's bed and we won't have a problem."

"Force of habit," Gerard mused as he stretched out on my bed like a big, lazy lion before pulling himself into a sitting position, Gibsie mode fully activated.

"Yeah," Hugh sneered in disgust. "A ten-year habit that stops today."

"What can I say." Chuckling softly to himself, Gerard stretched his arms above his head and yawned loudly. "I'm a creature of habit."

The move caused my duvet to slip downward, giving me a wonderful view of his naked chest.

"You're a creature alright," my brother growled, stalking toward him. "A fucking pest corrupting my sister."

"Oh, pack it in, Hugh!" I interrupted, tearing my eyes off Gerard's pierced nipples. "He's not corrupting me."

"See?" Grinning wickedly, Gerard waggled his brows at the same time as flexing his pecs. "I'm not corrupting her."

"Don't you shake your tits at me," Hugh warned, waving an accusing finger around. "And don't even think about cooking up anything fishy in here with my sister."

"I don't cook fish, Hugh, I bake buns," Gerard shot back with a wink. "In ovens."

"You cheeky—"

"Hey—no, no, no, don't come barge into my room banging your fists on your chest just because your pea brain can't process the fact that two people can sleep in the same bed and just sleep," I warned, quickly intercepting my brother when he made a beeline for Gerard. "Nuh-uh, don't even think about throwing down in here, buddy."

"Just sleep," Hugh sneered and then turned his attention back to Gerard. "You know what? The sooner you get back to school, the better, because you've been stuck on my sister like a fly to shit—"

"Are you calling your sister shit?"

"Yeah." I narrowed my eyes. "Did you just call me poo?"

"You know what I mean," Hugh grumbled. "He hasn't left this house—or your side, for that matter—all damn summer."

"So?" I laughed. "He's been here every day since forever. We've always hung out, Hugh. What's the big deal now?"

"The big deal now is that you're not a child anymore, Claire. You're a sixteen-year-old teenage girl and he's a fuckboy, with a lot of experience and a lot of hidden agendas."

"I beg your fucking pardon," Gerard spluttered, clearly taking offense to the statement. "I am *no* fuckboy."

"Gibs, you're the definition of a fuckboy," Hugh argued back. "People look up the word in the dictionary and find your face!"

"Actually, that word isn't in the dictionary." I decided to offer some common sense into the equation.

"Aha!" Gerard taunted, springing out of my bed. "Shows what you know, asshole."

"Well, at least you have jocks on," Hugh huffed, mildly appeased by the sight of Gerard's white Calvin Kleins.

"Yeah." Gerard snorted. "This time."

Hugh's eyes widened to the point where I thought they might pop. "Asshole, you are getting on my last nerve."

"Come on, Gerard," I groaned, shaking my head. "Don't rise him."

"That's what I tried to tell your sister last night."

A vein bulged in my brother's forehead. "What did you just *say*?" Hugh whisper-hissed, as his eyes widened in comical horror. "What the fuck did you just say about my sister?"

"Gerard," I half scolded, half laughed as I slapped a hand over my mouth.

Grinning wolfishly, he winked in response.

"Right. That's it. I can't take it anymore. Out," Hugh ordered, pointing to my bedroom door. "Take your filthy mouth and your even filthier cock back to your own side of the street."

"You've got me all wrong, lad," Gerard continued to taunt, as he threw on my dressing gown and then somersaulted over the bed to where I was standing. "I'm as pure as the driven snow."

"Yeah," Hugh grumbled sarcastically. "The snow outside a whorehouse."

"Good luck with your interview, Claire-Bear." Gerard pressed a featherlight kiss to my cheek before toeing on my at-least-five-sizes-too-small slippers. "Mind if I take a shower here? Keith always leaves a deposit worthy of an exorcism in the toilet before work that, I shit you not, takes a good three hours to fully flush down the—"

"Yes, we do. Now, get out!" Hugh instructed, pointing to the basket in the corner of my room that contained a sleeping Cherub and her brood of adorable offspring. "And take your share of those kittens back to your side of the street with you."

"And separate them from their mother?" Gerard gaped. "What kind of a monster are you?"

"Cherub will be grand," Hugh grumbled.

"I was *referring* to your sister."

"You're a head case, Gibs. Seriously fucking deranged."

"Ignore your cranky uncle, babies," Gerard called over his shoulder as he sauntered out of my room. "Daddy will be back tonight."

"Go the fuck home, Gibs!"

"Fine. I need to go check on your nephew anyway."

"He's not my nephew, you freak. He's a hedgehog in hibernation in your mam's hot press because you and my sister have issues with taking in strays."

"Whatever you say, lad. See you later for the beach trip, baby mama."

Snickering, I held up a hand and waved at his retreating frame. "See you later, baby daddy."

"Why do that?" Hugh demanded, tone resigned. "Why encourage the crazy?"

"Because I love his crazy." I laughed, still grinning from ear to ear. "And so do you."

"Yeah, and I'd love his crazy an awful lot more if it didn't involve spending time in my baby sister's bedroom," Hugh grumbled. "Come on, Claire, I know you have it bad for him, but make smart choices here, will you?"

"Make smart choices?" I asked and then laughed in his face. I couldn't help it. "What are you talking about?"

"I'm talking about you and Gibs and your warped little sleepover club."

"Oh my god, I *loved* those books," I chimed in with a smile. "I had the entire collection when we were kids, remember?"

"Yeah, I remember, now back to the real-life sleepovers," he grumbled, running a hand through his hair. "Listen, there's a reason Mam and Sadhbh put a stop to them when we left primary school."

"*Tried* to put a stop to them," I corrected with a snort. "And failed."

"Come on, Claire," he growled impatiently. "You know what can happen in the heat of the moment."

"The heat of the moment?" I laughed. "What moment?"

"I don't know," he snapped, flustered. "Whatever moments you and him have when you're alone."

I arched a brow. "Meaning?"

"Sex."

"Oh my god," I laughed. "You're so funny."

"Funny?" His eyes widened to saucers. "Sex isn't funny."

"No, sex isn't funny," I agreed with a snicker. "But you are."

"Two words, Claire," he shot back. "Joey and Aoife."

"That's three words."

"Fine," he countered, not missing a beat. "Here's two words for you: teen pregnancy. Have you seen the girl lately? She looks like she's ready to pop." His eyes bulged for emphasis. "If it can happen to Joey Lynch, it can happen to anyone of us."

"Not me." I smiled sweetly up at him. "Because I don't possess a penis."

"Yeah, well, your pillow pal certainly does."

"Hugh," I said as calmly as I could, while I tried to wipe the smile from my face in order to comfort my big dope of a brother. "I promise Gerard and I are just friends. Same as always."

"Yeah," he agreed, not sounding one bit comforted. "Friends that been getting awfully close since Cap left for tour back in June."

"We've always been close."

"True, but it's been different this summer, and you know it," he pushed, and I couldn't deny the hint of concern in his voice—or his eyes. "Come on, Claire. I'm not thick. I can see it, same as everyone else, and contrary to popular belief, I'm *not* trying to control your life. I'm just... I know Gibs better than anyone, and he...and you..." He shook his head and blew out a breath before adding, "Look, I just don't want to see you get hurt."

Hugh was right about one thing.

It *was* different us this summer.

We *were* closer.

It *was* more.

"Why would I get hurt?" I asked, folding my arms across my chest.

"Because he's fucked in the head."

"Hugh!"

"Stop it. Don't look at me like that. You know I love him like a brother," he hurried to explain, looking flustered. "I would take a bullet for him, lay down my life for him in a heartbeat, but he's damaged, Claire. I'm talking seriously damaged here. What happened to him when we were kids seriously screwed up his brain. He hasn't been the same since he was seven and we both know it."

Yeah, I knew it, but it wasn't nice to hear it out loud.

"Oh my god, Hugh, stop, will you?" I shook my head in disgust. "Half of our friendship circle is damaged. That hasn't stopped us being friends with any of them, has it?"

"Yeah, but you're not just friends with Gibs," he argued. "You're in love with him."

"So?" I'd given up denying it a long time ago. Besides, I was a terrible liar. "What's your point?"

"My point is that you're not damaged," he urged, tone laced with sincerity. "And I don't want that to change."

"And you think it will?" I pushed, folding my arms across my chest. "If I get too close to Gerard?"

"I'm afraid of what could happen if he gives in and it gets too deep and goes too far," he admitted, brown eyes locked on mine. "I'm afraid of the aftermath, Claire."

His words rattled me in a way they never had before.

Because I could hear the concern in his tone.

It was genuine.

It was valid.

But his warning would fall on deaf ears because I had a Gerard Gibson–sized blind spot on my heart.

"Would it make you feel better if I told you that I have never seen or touched Gerard's penis for sexual reasons?" I decided to throw my brother an olive branch by saying.

"What? No, Claire," Hugh groaned, looking thoroughly disturbed. "That wouldn't make me feel better at all…" He shook his head before quickly backpedaling, "Hold up, so that means you have?"

"Uh…maybe?" I chuckled sheepishly, unable to stop my mind from wandering back to a particularly strange *interaction* I shared with Gerard's ladder last Easter.

"Are you alone?" Gerard asked when he hobbled into my bedroom, kitted out in our town's rugby team kit—muddy boots and all. "There's no one else in here?" He looked around nervously, all while covering his crotch with his hands. "No evil Viper lurking behind a door with a knife in hand, waiting for the opportunity to take me out?"

"No, Gerard, I'm all alone." I laughed, still flipping through the pages of my favorite weekly magazine subscription. "Why are you back from the game early?" I narrowed my eyes, instantly suspicious. "Did you get sent off again?"

"Yes, but I sent myself off this time," he explained, as he hobbled comically toward me. "Care to explain why?"

"Because your brother couldn't protect a paper bag in a goddamn maul, that's why," he huffed. "Listen, what I'm about to show you is really bad, and I apologize in advance for the nightmares I'm about to unleash on you, but I'm in real danger of dying here, Claire-Bear." He sank down on my bed beside me, only to grunt in pain and spring back up. "As in fully dead with no comeback."

"Why?" I laughed, pulling myself into a sitting position. "What did you do?"

"It's my dick," he admitted in a pained tone. "Actually, it's my ladder."

"Your ladder?" My eyes widened. "Your dick is a ladder?"

"No, no, no," he groaned, gingerly lowering himself down on the mattress this time. "It's the ladder on my dick."

"Okay." I shook my head. "I am so confused right."

"Listen to me; I pierced my dick, it's called a Jacob's ladder, and some prick from the other team kicked me square in the nuts during the game," he said in a big whoosh. "I'm hurt, and I mean seriously hurt, Claire-Bear. We're talking 'Tom's down and Dick and Harry are missing in action' kind of hurt."

"Oh my god." My eyes widened in horror as I tried to make sense of the crazy spilling from his lips. "You did what?"

"Can you check it for me?" he asked, grimacing in discomfort. "And not in a 'I'm trying to get you to put it in your mouth' kind of way," he hurried to add. "More of a 'I really fucking love my dick and I don't want to get sepsis like Kav' kind of way?"

"Gerard!"

"Please, Claire," he begged, clutching his stomach. "You know I can't cope with blood, and if there's blood down there, then I'm going to pass out."

"You *can't* cope with blood? What about me?" I squealed, scrambling onto my knees in anticipation, as some sick wave of morbid curiosity washed over me. "What if it scares me? Oh god, what if I vomit? You know I hate vomiting."

"I'm not going to lie to you, Claire. It might scare you, and we could both vomit," he confirmed grimly. "But you're my best friend and I would do it for you in a heartbeat."

Dammit, that was true.

All jokes aside, if the shoe was on the other foot and I was stupid enough to pierce my genitals, he would help me. "Okay, okay, fine!"

"Thank you," he sighed in relief. "Okay, if it's bad, don't tell me. Just go outside and call an ambulance."

"And you're sure you don't want to ask one of the boys to check it for you?" I asked in a much calmer tone than I was feeling. "You wouldn't feel more comfortable with Hugh or Johnny, or Keith—"

"No," he choked out. "Jesus no. It can only be you."

"Okay."

He looked at me uncertainly. "Okay?"

"Okay," I confirmed with a determined nod. Climbing off the bed, I dropped to my knees in front him and reached for the waist of his shorts. "I'm ready."

"Wait, wait, wait," he choked out, batting my hands away as he squirmed in discomfort. "I've changed my mind."

"Gerard, come on, don't be a baby. You're in pain and need to get this ladder inspected," I urged, reaching for his shorts again. "Just be brave and take off your underpants."

"It's not a ladder right now, babe," he groaned, hands settling on the elastic waistband of his shorts. "The minute I saw you in those shorts, it turned into a full-blown fire-escape stairwell."

I grinned up at him. "It did?"

His eyes widened in horror. "Focus, Claire!"

"Okay, okay, let's not panic here." Rolling my shoulders, I sucked in a steadying breath and reached for his waistband again. This time, he let me. "Don't worry, Gerard. My mam's *a nurse," I added, as I carefully lowered his shorts and underpants. "Medicine is in my genes. I can absolutely help you with... Oh my god!"*

"What, what?" Gerard demanded, keeping a hand clamped over his eyes. "There's blood, isn't there? I broke it, didn't I?" He wailed loudly. "Oh Jesus, is it bad? Tell me it isn't bad? Is the piercing still there?"

"Uh..." My eyes widened to saucers when his fully erect ladder sprang free. "There's no blood." I crouched lower to get a good look at the underside of his genitals. "Oh, yeah, there it is."

"What?" he demanded, tone frantic, eyes still covered. "What's there?"

"The silver bar," I explained, leaning in closer to get a better look at it. "Wow. It's, ah—" Blowing out a shaky breath, I looked up at him and grinned. "It looks a lot different to what I pictured in my head."

"Bad different?"

"No, not bad different," I mused, pleasantly surprised. "It's like a trunk."

"Jesus!"

"Aren't willies weird, Gerard?"

"You've touched his *dick*?" Hugh bellowed, dragging me back to the present. "What the fuck?"

My cheeks flamed and I scurried over to my dressing table, busying myself with readjusting the photos of friends that I had tacked to the mirror. When my eyes locked on the blue rosette tacked onto the corner of my mirror with the words *Brian, Best in Show 2005, First Place*, I couldn't stop my smile from spreading.

"In my defense, I only used my pinkie finger," I said, turning my attention back to my agitated-looking brother. "And it was purely for medical purposes."

"*Medical* purposes?" Hugh's face turned a scary shade of purple. "Claire!"

"What?" I defended, squirming in sheepish discomfort. "Do you know how serious it can be when someone's ladder gets injured?"

"What in the name of Jesus does that even... You know what, forget it. I don't want to know," he groaned, clutching his stomach as he stomped toward my bedroom door. "Hurry up and get dressed. I'll be in the toilet with my head in the bowl when you're ready."

3
Calls from Cap

GIBSIE

THE ERRATIC HEARTBEAT THAT ACCOMPANIED LAST NIGHT'S NIGHTMARE HAD FOL-
lowed me into consciousness this morning, causing the drumming beat of my pulse to
keep me company on the walk home.

Duh, duh, duh.

Duh, duh, duh.

Duh, duh, duh, duh...du-duh...

It grew wilder, more frantic, and more deafening with every step I took away from
the Biggses' house. From *her*.

Go back.

Go back now.

Run.

Don't...

"Shut the fuck up!" Reaching a hand up, I slammed the palm of my hand against
my forehead, needing my stupid brain to just stop. "Calm down," I continued to coax,
using my other hand to rub my chest. "You're grand. Everything's grand."

It was no use.

I had never been able to self-soothe, not with my words or my touch. Not when
my brain didn't like my voice and my body didn't like my touch.

Refusing to give in to temptation by turning on my heels and bolting back to the
girl who had the innate ability to do for me what I could never do for myself, I crossed
the road toward my house.

Get a handle on yourself, you big eejit.

The sound of my mother's voice was the first thing that greeted me when I stepped
inside the front door, followed swiftly by the sound of my stepfather's grating one when
he called out, "Gibs, is that you, son?"

I'm not your son, asshole, I mouthed, sticking both fingers up at the kitchen door
animatedly before getting a handle on my emotions and composing myself.

"The one and only," I said, forcing myself to sound carefree, while I purposefully
ignored the way they were holding hands at the table.

Holding hands?

At their age.

Puke.

"You're supposed to be grounded," my stepfather informed me. "Or have you forgotten about the very expensive landscaping job you cost me last month at Mrs. Kingston's?"

"Nope." I grinned at the memory. "I remember."

"Jesus, Gibs." Keith narrowed his eyes. "You could pretend that you feel bad about it."

"I could," I agreed, still grinning. "But I'm no liar."

"You need to do something with him," he told my mother, tone laced with disgust. "Mark never gave us this trouble."

"I have," Mam urged. "I grounded him. He hasn't seen his friends in three weeks."

"Except that he has," Keith argued. "Considering he's rambling home at seven o'clock in the morning after spending the night at the neighbors like a whoring tomcat."

"You'd know all about that, wouldn't you, Keith?" I shot back, unable to stop myself. "Whoring around other people's houses?"

"Stop it, the pair of you," Mam snapped, turning her attention to me. "Your father's right—"

"He's *not* my father."

"This behavior has to stop," she pressed on. "What you did to Keith's machinery was completely out of order. You're supposed to be grounded and you've been sneaking out at night."

"I don't sneak anywhere," I countered. "I sleepwalk."

"And I've indulged your late-night walkabouts because, well, we both understand about the nightmares," she continued, not missing a beat. "But school is starting back next week. It's a serious time in your life. Sixth year is important, and we both feel that it's high time you knuckled…" Her voice trailed off when her eyes trailed over me. "What in the name of Jesus are you wearing, Gerard Gibson?"

Confused, I glanced down at myself and then smirked when I noted the silky pink dressing gown with the pom-pom tassels. "Do you like it?" Grinning, I twirled the tassel around aimlessly. "It's my new look, Mam."

"*Why*, Gerard?"

"Why not?"

"Oh, Jesus, Keith." Mam dropped her head in her hands and groaned. "Take this one for me, will you?"

"Don't feed into it," Keith the killjoy interjected, giving my mother's hand a squeeze. "He'll keep it going forever."

"Oh do, Keith," I shot back, unable to keep my tone light when I was addressing him. "Feed into it. I beg you."

Shaking his head, my stepfather stood up and moved for the kettle. "Your mother's right, Gibs. You need to start taking life more seriously."

And you need to take a long walk off a short cliff, asshole. "Is that so?"

"And take that jewelry out of your nipples," Mam wailed. "It's dangerous to play rugby with body piercings."

"Then you better not check my cock," I muttered under my breath, making a beeline for the fridge.

"What was that, Bubba?"

"I said I never wear jewelry when I'm on Coach's clock," I clarified—and by clarifying I meant I bullshitted my way out of losing my car privileges. "I follow the rules, Mam. No need to worry about me."

"Have you come off your medication?" Concern filled her eyes. "Because I've noticed you've been sleepwalking a lot more this summer."

"Nope," I replied with a shit-eating grin. "Still taking my pill a day to keep the voices away."

"Oh, Gerard, you know that's not what you have to take it for."

"Which Gerard are you talking to?"

"Stop it!" Keith snapped, looking flustered. "You know that kind of talk worries your mother."

"My bad," I replied, and then proceeded to spray the contents of a whipped cream can into my mouth. "I'll...be...the...good...Gerard."

"Aren't you supposed to be at the bakery?" Keith pressed. "You work Saturdays, too, don't you? Or have you decided to add skiving off work to the CV? Because I have to tell you, boy, that makes one hell of a read to potential college admission offices. Unreliable work ethic, unintelligible academic portfolio, not to mention your complete disregard to rules."

"Jesus, I'm a real catch, aren't I?" I taunted; tone laced with sarcasm. "They'll be lining up for me."

"It's his day off," Mam explained for me, which pissed me off on a whole new level because I didn't need to explain shit to this man. "His grounding is up today, remember?"

"He's not finished paying off the machinery he damaged."

"I've already paid for that, Keith."

"I don't remember agreeing to him being ungrounded, Sadhbh."

"I don't remember your name being on my birth certificate."

"Gerard!"

"Since when does he have Saturdays off?"

"Since it's my last weekend before school starts back up and I have plans with my friends," I snapped. *Asshole.*

"What's with the tone?"

"There's no tone."

"You definitely have a tone."

"How would you both feel if I booked you a family session with Anne?" Mam interjected before a full-blown argument could ensue. Wise woman. She knew us well.

"I don't need another session with Anne," I replied in between mouthfuls of cream. *Not with him, or on my own.* "I saw her the other week."

Good old Anne. I'd been seeing her on the third Friday of every month since I was seven years old. Mam thought she was a miracle worker and the reason I had come out of the other side of my father and sister's deaths without having a mental breakdown.

She wasn't.

I was just that fucking awesome at reinventing myself. Aside from the label of hyperactive dyslexic hanging over my head, I was doing pretty damn well for myself.

Snatching up the bottle of pills on top of the fridge, I unscrewed the cap and popped a Ritalin into my mouth. "Happy now?"

"You just seem so restless lately, pet."

"Don't know what to tell you, Mam. I'm always restless." Shrugging, I added, "I'll see Anne next month, like arranged, and not a minute before it."

"We don't want to see you spiral."

We.

I rolled my eyes at that. "When have I ever spiraled?"

"You do a lot of things you don't tell us about."

Us. "I don't spiral."

"Sometimes I wonder if it would be better if you did."

"Come again?"

"Anger, Gerard," she pushed. "It's okay to feel angry, pet."

"Why would I be angry?"

"Maybe because sixth year is almost upon you and your father's not here to see you off."

Every ounce of joy in my heart evaporated. "Don't do this."

"It's okay to be angry with the world."

"I'm *not* angry with the world." I was quick to shoot the idea down. *I'm angry with him.*

"Speaking of sixth year. You failed three of your subjects last year, son," Keith chimed in. Good-for-nothing bastard. "We need to put a plan together for this coming school year if we want you to get into university."

Maybe I'll follow in my good old stepdaddy's shoes and hook up with a wealthy man's wife? Because that sure as shit seems to have turned out well for you. "I'll figure it out."

"Do you need grinds?" Mam asked. "Because if you do, Keith can phone Mr. Twomey and have that arranged for you. He's goods friends with him—"

"I don't need *Keith* to do anything for me," I bit out, feeling the mask slip as a surge of rage rocketed up my body. "I've got it all under control," I forced myself to add. "I'm grand, Mam."

"Well, hopefully Mark will be able to make it home from India for Christmas this year," she hurried to add, causing stepdaddy dearest to puff his chest out with pride. Ah yes, the perfect one. The un-fucked-up son. "I'm sure he could help you with your schoolwork over the Christmas break. We could set up some sort of schedule for him to tutor you…"

"I said I'm fine!" I snapped, slamming the fridge door closed and stalking for the door. "Everything's grand. I'm grand. I don't need any favors from your husband, and I sure as shit don't need any fucking grinds from his son!"

"Gerard!" Mam gasped. "Excuse me. Don't just storm off."

Too late.

I was already bolting for the stairs.

"Come on, son," Keith called after me. "After all these years, we can have a civil conversation, can't we?"

"No," I roared over my shoulder. "And I'm *not* your son."

"Gibsie?"

Thud. Thud. Thud.

"This house is home to all of us."

Thud. Thud. Thud.

"Can't we just try to get along."

Thud. Thud. Thud.

"For my sake, Bubba, please!"

"I'm done, Mam!" I called over my shoulder as I narrowly avoided Brian in the landing in my haste to reach my room. "Conversation over."

Feeling my mood grow darker with every step I took, I blew out a breath and shook my hands.

"Calm the fuck down," I instructed myself when my heartbeat rocketed to new heights. "Just breathe, asshole."

Using every ounce of willpower that I had inside of me, I forced myself not to take my bedroom door off its hinges when I reached it.

This house didn't belong to Keith.

It didn't even belong to Mam.

Nor did the bakery.

The name *Gibson* was on the deeds of every financial asset in my mother's possession, not *Allen*. This was my father's house. That bed Keith slept in every night belonged to my father, just like the woman who slept beside him every night for that past ten years.

So much for true love.

Mam and Dad had been together since they were twelve and this was their end result: Mam shagging the prick laying down the new patio in our garden, while Dad worked his bollocks off to pay for said patio and give her everything else she wanted.

Fucking typical.

Now, I loved my mother with all my heart, I truly did, but the fact that she shacked up with that man in a house my father had paid for made me sick to my goddamn stomach.

Remembering that Dad used to have to pick us up on the weekends and wait for us at the front door that he paid for, while Keith was warming his bed, made the bitterness inside of me fester and stew.

I tolerated their relationship because what other choice had I? I was polite and civil when I could be, but that's where I drew the line. I didn't want a relationship with the man. In fact, I wanted as little as humanly possible to do with him and everyone related to him.

The bitter taste in my mouth was only intensified by the fact that she allowed her *husband's* son to use *my* dead sister's bedroom for his own. In my eyes, the man who married my mother represented the beginning of the end for my family.

For my father.

For my sister.

For me.

Goddammit, I didn't like to dwell in the past. It was behind us for a reason. I was okay now. I had a good life, with good friends. Everything was *good*, dammit, and I refused to think otherwise. I refused to let my mind fuck that up for me.

I could handle Keith and the grief and the anger. I could handle the bad days. Really, I could. But the sleeping—or lack of it—was a real problem for me.

It was hard to function on little to no sleep, and the nightmares... Jesus Christ, the nightmares were beyond disturbing. It made me so fucking angry that my subconscious refused to move on from something I'd put to bed years ago. I didn't need the reminders of all the horrors of my childhood. Of the image of my sister disappearing beneath the surface, or the feel of my father's hand, or the look of fear in his eyes, or the feel of *his*…

"Fuck!" I snapped, springing up from my perch to pace the room. "Not cool. Not fucking cool, dick!"

Wisps of echoed voices and memories bombarded my mind, setting me into sensory overload. On mornings like this one, everything was a trigger, spurring me into an agitated state of needing to move. Unease thrummed inside of my veins like a drum, pushing me to move and laugh and run and do anything I could to get the feeling out of me. To push *him* away.

Because it was too hard to remember.

I was, as my mother once referred to me, "wearing." Meaning I was exhausting to handle, and that drove people away.

Not Claire-Bear.

She never left. She always seemed to have a level of energy that balanced mine. Our personalities complemented the other, and when I was little, I used to believe that Holy God had put her on earth just for me. Because she was the only person I didn't seem to scare off. Hell, even Hugh and Feely got tired of me. But never her.

I guess that's why she had always been so perfect for me. I was boisterous and she was full of beans. We went together like bacon and cabbage. It just worked. She never seemed to grow tired of me, which was something I couldn't say about everyone else in my life.

Our bedroom windows faced each other's, and it gave me a strange sort of comfort, knowing that she was close by. After all, she was the best part of a broken childhood, because the pictures hanging on the walls at home sure as shit represented anything but. Those pictures were a cold reminder of a childhood that ended too soon. I couldn't smile when I looked at any of the family portraits adorning the walls of my house. I couldn't muster up good memories because since that day, all I had in my head were bad.

My life changed in the blink of an eye, changing me irrevocably, and the only way I could move past it was to forget it.

So, I didn't remember any of it. I blocked it out. The good, the bad, and the depressing. I froze it all out of my mind, choosing to allow myself to remember only one face in a lifetime of haze. Her. She was the safest memory my mind contained, the only face I could trust not to hurt me.

Beyond flustered, I snatched my phone off my nightstand and scrolled through my contacts, not stopping until I settled on a familiar name.

Pressing Call, I held the phone to my ear and paced the room. My body was bristling with energy, and the urge to escape was so intense that I momentarily thought about throwing myself out the window.

The fall wouldn't kill me. Hell, I wouldn't even break a bone, but it might distract me from the fucked-up thoughts rushing around in my head.

Because this room.

That ceiling.

Their ghosts.

My memories.

I couldn't fucking take it.

Relief flooded my body at a rapid rate when his familiar Dublin accent came down the line. "About bleeding time." For whatever reason, Johnny's voice was like an immediate shot of relief to my senses. "Ever heard of answering your phone, Gibs? I've called you five times already, lad. I thought your ma was unleashing you from the doghouse today. What's the story? I haven't seen you in weeks."

For a brief moment, I contemplated spilling my guts out to the lad on the other side of the line. I certainly trusted him enough to tell him. Johnny tolerated me in a way that most of the lads couldn't. He seemed to get me, even without me telling him one word of my past.

Spending most of the summer without him had been torture, and that wasn't an exaggeration. It fucking sucked balls, because his absence gave me far too much time to think.

I had trouble being alone with myself. It didn't feel good to be on my own. In company was when I worked best. Being alone fucked with my head worse than anything else. Because being alone meant that I had to think. And I fucking hated thinking. I had a chaotic thought process that had been given a formal diagnosis from doctors but no reprieve.

Aside from Claire, Johnny was my closest friend in the world, and quite possibly the best person I knew. He would know what to do. He was good at fixing things.

Do it.

Tell him.

Let him help you.

Don't you dare.

Remember what happened the last time you tried to tell.

"Sorry about missing your calls, Kav. I was over in Claire's place last night—left my phone in my room," I heard myself explain instead. "And I'm officially ungrounded. I just overslept."

Johnny didn't know about the ins and outs of my family drama, and that was exactly how I liked it. He had enough problems of his own to deal with, not to mention two epic parents that provided him with a home that made it hard for him to relate.

Johnny had the kind of structured will about him that appealed to me. He was safe. He was steady and stable and dependable, and I would die on my hill of loyalty to him. Because aside from Claire, I'd never had a friend I could find peace with like him.

He was the protector. Fuck knows how he came to be what he was, but Mammy K and John Sr. did a fantastic fucking job. Without realizing it, they had created a personal savior in their son.

We had our own little world and I refused to fuck that up with any bullshit memories. I would rather stew in silence than expose myself to that potential pain. So, I smacked on a smile whenever Johnny came over and said all the right things to the man that had broken up my family, all the while silently simmering on the inside.

"Yeah, I heard all about it," he replied with a weary sigh. "I've had Hugh on the phone, ranting and raving about how he was going to borrow a Burdizzo off Feely's da to castrate you."

"Nice," I snickered, reveling in Hugh's discomfort. "Sorry about missing the gym, lad."

"Story of your life, Gibs," he replied, but the humor in his tone assured me that he wasn't about to hold a grudge over it. "Are we still on for the beach later?"

"We better be," I shot back. "I booked the day off work for it."

"And overnight camping? Is that still the plan."

"Yep. I have my tent ready to go and the boot of the car filled with beer and bog roll."

"Nice." He chuckled. "Listen, I might be late. The Academy called. I've a meeting with the heads before lunch. They want my da with me to sign extension contracts, so he'll drop me off at the beach afterward."

"Contracts?" My brows shot up. "I don't like the sound of that."

"It's just protocol," my best friend replied breezily. "Nothing to worry about, Gibs. I'll be back with you at Tommen next Thursday. No worries."

I felt my body physically sag in relief. The thought of my best friend being snatched away by the pros was a much bigger fear these days since they were quite literally banging on his back door with contracts and offers galore. Johnny would be leaving Ballylaggin, but we got to keep him for one more school year.

"You promise?"

"Yeah, Gibs, I promise, lad."

"Good," I said, momentarily appeased that he wasn't leaving again. "So, how's life at the manor?"

"Bleeding manic." He chuckled, and then he paused before asking, "You okay, Gibs?"

Fucked in the head and getting progressively worse by the day. "You know me, Johnny lad, I'm always grand," I replied, leaning against the windowsill as I spoke. "Why'd you ask?"

"Don't know," he replied, and I didn't have to be with him to know that he was scratching his jaw. It was a trait of his that I had grown accustomed to. "Just felt like I should."

"So, how's little Shannon?" Balancing the phone between my ear and shoulder, I rummaged in the top drawer of my nightstand for a packet of chewing gum I knew I put there last week. "Are you feeling suffocated yet?"

"Suffocated?"

"Having so many people in your house."

"Gibs, I'd let my ma adopt the whole bleeding school if it meant that I got to keep that girl."

"Little Shannon, huh?" I grinned. "What a number she did on your heart, lad."

"Tell me about it."

"She really came into her own this summer."

"I know, lad," he agreed, tone far more enthusiastic now that we were talking about his favorite topic of conversation. "You know the way Claire's been giving her lessons at the public pool all summer? Well, Ma took her and the boys to the pool yesterday." I could hear the smile in his voice when he said, "And she did three full lengths of the pool."

"She did?"

"Without stopping," he added. "I'm so bleeding proud of her, Gibs."

"Yeah," I agreed, feeling equally proud. "According to Claire, she's a natural."

"Shan's a natural at everything."

"Did she tell you that McGarry was sniffing around the pool during their sessions when you were away on tour?" I asked, delighted when I found the packet of chewing gum. Score. "Circling the girls like a fucking great white."

"No," Johnny bit out. "And you didn't tell me, either."

"Because I didn't want to be responsible for distracting you and ruining your future prospects."

"Well, I'm home now and my prospects are bright," Johnny replied, tone hard. "I'll deal with him at school next week."

"No need." Unwrapping half a dozen sticks of gum, I popped them all into my mouth. "I handled it ages ago."

"You did? At the pool?" Surprise filled his tone. "You went in the water?"

"Get real, Cap." I rolled my eyes. "I found him in the changing rooms after one of his stalking sessions." Grinning, I added, "Suffice to say he hasn't been doing much swimming with a cast on his arm."

"Tell me you didn't break his bleeding arm, Gibs."

"Give me some credit, will you?" I snorted. "He tripped."

"Over what?"

"The contents of his shampoo bottle." I sprayed another dollop of cream into my mouth. "And my foot."

"Nice," he replied, sounding distant. There was another long pause before his voice returned on the line, this time all professional. "Listen, Gibs, I have to get ready for that meeting. I'll see you this afternoon, okay?"

A pang of sadness hit me hard in the chest, making it momentarily hard to breathe, before I quickly got a handle on myself. "Give them hell, Cap." Pinching the bridge of my nose, I forced another smile, even though I was alone in my room. "See you later."

"Bye, Gibs."

"Bye, Kav."

When the line went dead, I stood there for a long time with the receiver in my hand, just staring out my bedroom window.

The sky was blue outside.

The birds were out.

The sun was shining.

It was another blissful morning.

And I wanted to *scream*.

4

Jagged Little Scars

CLAIRE

"Well?" Hugh asked, when I joined him at the edge of the pool after my interview. "How did it go?"

"Okay, I guess?" I shrugged, feeling slightly disheartened by my earlier meeting with his boss. "She said she would get back to me." I looked to my brother for some much-needed emotional support. "Is that a bad thing?"

"Nah, if Kim didn't like you, trust me, you'd know it." Setting his mop down, he patted my shoulder and walked back to his deck chair. "I bet you a tenner you'll get the job."

"She was sort of terrifying, Hugh."

"Yeah, Kim can be a fair bit of a ballbuster," he agreed, eyes focusing on the bodies splashing around in the water as he spoke. "She has this hard, take-no-shit approach, but she's fair."

I wasn't sure about that. My brother's boss, from our brief encounter, had given me some serious Mr. Twomey vibes. I was half hoping that she *didn't* call me back. Sure, a paying job would be super, but I enjoyed volunteering at the community pool, and I was a firm believer in life being about more than just a paycheck.

"Oh my god," I choked out when a familiar blond shimmied into my peripheral vision. "What the hell happened to you?"

"I fell," Lizzie explained, joining us at Hugh's deck chair.

The fact that she was here wasn't surprising. Her family had been members for years, same as ours, but it was the scar she bore that took my breath away.

I'd seen similar cuts on Lizzie's body in the past, but not for a very long time. The faint scars that adorned her inner wrists had appeared in the months that followed her sister's passing. After her parents put her in counseling, it seemed to stop. I thought she had it under control. Apparently not.

"On what?" I demanded, gaping at the huge, jagged, freshly scabbed cut going the entire length of her thigh. "A chain saw?"

"No, on a barbed-wire fence I was climbing over, actually." Clad in a white bikini, Lizzie pulled her hair up into a makeshift ponytail and offered me a half-hearted smile. Scars or not, Lizzie was ridiculously beautiful. Like for real. She looked like some sort of angel, with a halo of messy blond hair. "It's all good, Claire. It happened ages ago. It doesn't even hurt anymore."

"Are you sure?" I squirmed in discomfort, eyeing the horrendous-looking cut. "Because it looks recent and it's hurting me just to look at it."

"Yeah," Hugh agreed, tone hard as his eyes locked on her thigh.

"Didn't know you were working today," she replied, folding her arms across her chest.

"Wasn't supposed to be," Hugh replied, not taking his eyes off her thigh. "What happened?"

Ignoring my brother, Lizzie moved for the edge of the pool, not stopping until she had eased herself into the water. "I'll see you later, Claire."

"Yeah, okay," I called after her, worrying my lip. "Are you coming to the beach campout?"

"Is Thor going?"

"You already know the answer."

"Then you already know my answer."

"Are you sure you don't want to come?" I asked, forcefully cheerful. "It's going to be super fun."

"I'm sure I'd rather drown than voluntarily spend time with him," she called back and then she disappeared beneath the water.

"Oh crap." I turned back to my brother, feeling a surge of anxiety fill my chest. "That's weird, right?" I gestured to where Lizzie had disappeared beneath the water. "She's not okay, is she?"

"How am I supposed to know?" my brother bit out, tone thick with emotion. "I'm hardly her confidante these days, am I?"

"Yeah, but you used to be," I blurted out, uttering the words I'd vowed many years ago to never repeat. Seriously, speaking about it was as taboo at Tommen as saying the name Voldemort at Hogwarts. A big no-no.

Hugh and Lizzie's fractured relationship was one that was stored in the memory vault labeled *Never bring up again for the good of our friendship circle.*

My brother's eyes flashed with pain, and I felt like the biggest jerk in the world.

"Yikes." Squirming in discomfort, I reached out and patted his shoulder. "Sorry."

"I don't know," he repeated in a low tone—I presumed to hide the tremor in his voice. Because Lizzie affected Hugh badly, and she always had. For some reason, my brother had been infatuated with my prickly bestie since the beginning of time. And for some even stranger reason, the feeling had been mutual for Lizzie.

Throughout the course of our entire childhood, they'd stuck together like peas in a pod. By the time we'd made it to fifth class of primary school, their friendship title had been upgraded to that of boyfriend and girlfriend. Not that any of us had a clue of what that meant. In our young minds, it simply meant that they were each other's favorite.

Either way, they were together for a *really* long time, even after everything seemed to fall apart for Liz after her sister died. Hugh was the one she leaned on back then. Come to think about it, he was the only one she was willing to speak to for *months*. It was a pretty dark time in our lives that had followed us long into secondary school.

Over time, Lizzie's grief had taken ahold of her in ways none of us were equipped or mature enough to handle, and by the start of second year, Lizzie and Hugh's relationship, along with a lot of her relationships with other friends, had completely unraveled.

I stuck in there with her, taking on her mood swings and erratic behavior because I loved her like a sister, but it wasn't easy. Especially when she focused all of her pain on Gerard because of a rumor that involved his stepbrother.

It sucked because Liz and Gerard used to be really good friends before that. We all were. We had this tight little circle that had been shattered after Caoimhe died.

After the breakup, the rest of our close-knit circle mentally vowed to never discuss it or bring it up again. To this day, we were completely oblivious as to the inside details of their breakup because Hugh and Liz could hardly bear to spend more than a few minutes in each other's company, let alone talk about it.

Even though they'd been together since primary school, the breakup didn't seem to affect Lizzie too deeply because she started seeing someone else within days of them calling it off. Hugh, on the other hand, spent several months moping around the house like a dark cloud until he collided with Katie in the hallways of Tommen and the sun started shining for him again.

Deep down inside, I knew the reason Hugh tried to keep me away from Gerard was because he was projecting his own experience on me. When my brother said that he was afraid of me getting hurt, what he really meant was that he didn't want me to get hurt like *he* had.

"Hugh, it's happening again, isn't it?"

He flicked his gaze to me, and I could tell from one glimpse of his brown eyes that I wasn't alone in my worrying. "I don't know."

"She's still so angry."

"Yeah, Claire, I *know*."

"Should we…" Shrugging, I chewed anxiously on my lip and flicked my attention back to our friend who was now swimming laps. "I don't know, do something?"

"Like what?"

"I don't know. *Anything*?"

"I'm not the one, Claire," Hugh choked out and I watched as a full-body shudder rippled through him. "Not this time. Not anymore. I can't keep saving…" Dropping his head in his hands, he sucked in a sharp breath, shoulders slumped. "I have Katie now… I *can't* do this with her again."

I got that, but I was scared, and he was my big brother who always seemed to know what to do. After all, Hugh was the one who knew more about Lizzie than any of the rest of us. He'd been there, right there in the middle of her personal breakdown the last time. Before the shutters came down around her heart blocking all of us out, he was the last person to be pushed away. He knew her better than anyone. The old her, at least.

"I could talk to her parents," I offered, feeling lost and way out of my depth. "Or Pierce."

"Pierce?" Hugh gaped at me like I had lost my mind. "Like he's worth a fucking conversation." His eyes narrowed in fury as he spoke. "He's not blind, Claire. He just doesn't care."

"He has to care," I urged. "He *has* to see. He's her boyfriend, Hugh."

"He only sees the parts of her he wants to see," Hugh spat out. "He won't do a damn thing, Claire, which suits Liz perfectly, considering that's the only reason she's with him."

"Then we need to talk to Mam," I blurted out. "She'll talk to Lizzie's mam and sort it out again."

"Sort it out again," Hugh repeated under his breath. "She's not a computer that needs resetting, Claire. It's not that simple." Muttering something unintelligible under his breath, he abruptly stood and rolled his shoulders. "Fine."

"Fine?" Hope filled my heart. "You'll do something."

"Yeah, Claire." Another shudder racked through my brother, and he nodded solemnly. "I'll do something."

5

Evil Cats and Helicopter Mothers

GIBSIE

Gripping the porcelain sink in our upstairs bathroom, I stared at my reflection in the mirror and honed in on the droplets of water dripping from my hair to my face, courtesy of the water I'd just splashed on my face.

A shiver racked through me at the sight, and I sucked back a groan. Shuddering in a combination of disgust and self-loathing, I licked my lips and forced myself to get a grip. "Get a handle on yourself."

Because this was pathetic.

You *are pathetic.*

While the rest of my friends had spent their summer holidays neck deep in the Atlantic Ocean, I sat it out on the sand like the coward I was. Sure, I had an epic tan to show for myself, sun-bleached streaks in my hair that lads paid good money for, and had constructed some seriously impressive sand forts and castles, but it was such a damn waste of a summer.

Pathetic as it was, I struggled to cope with anything more than dipping my toes in the water. Seriously, submerging my body in water was an abhorrent thought. I could never get out of my head, or my past, long enough to attempt it.

Showers I could manage because I was upright and in no danger of going under. But I couldn't remember the last time I'd taken a bath. It must have been before that day. I'd definitely been joined by Batman and my Teenage Turtles figurines.

Come to think about it, where did Raphael ever go?

"Gibs?" Mam called from the bottom of the staircase. "The girls are here."

Cowa-fucking-bunga. I smiled to myself, bad mood forgotten, and grabbed a towel off the rack to quickly dry my face. The knowledge that Keith had left the house an hour ago was another huge mood booster. "On the way, ladies."

Freewheeling out of the bathroom, I grabbed a floral shirt from my wardrobe, pocketed a bottle of baby oil, and snatched up my sunglasses, determined to make the most of the late August sunshine.

It was Saturday afternoon, our last one before school started back on Thursday, and I was determined to put a tan on my skin that would last until Mr. Sun made a reappearance next summer.

Batting down all worries of hazardous currents and riptides, I made a bolt for the staircase. Narrowly avoiding a side swipe from the demon my mother had christened Brian on the turn of the staircase, I trip-tumbled off the last four steps.

"Did you just see that?" I demanded in outrage, pointing an accusing finger in the direction of my mother's one-balled Persian. "He tried to push me down the stairs."

"Don't be so dramatic, Gibs," Mam scolded, scooping up the snow-white ball of fluff. "Brian has a heart of gold."

Brian purred in response to my mother's welcomed affection but narrowed his beady green eyes at me in warning. As if to say, *I'll get you next time.*

Not if I get you first, fucker.

"Yeah, well, if I'm found mangled in my bed some morning, with cat scratches all over my body, don't say I didn't warn you," I huffed as I shrugged on my shirt, not bothering to button it. "Because you've had plenty warnings, woman."

"That will never happen."

"It could."

"You'd have to sleep in your bed for that to happen."

"Hi, Gibs," the smallest of the three acknowledged with a shy smile.

"Little Shannon." I smiled warmly at my best friend's girl as she stood in my front hall, armed with what I knew was a mountain of picnic food—courtesy of Mammy K—all ready for a day at the beach.

"Thanks for offering to drive us," she said when I took the basket from her and set it down on the sideboard. "Johnny has that meeting with the Academy heads." Blowing out a breath, she flicked her ponytail over her shoulder and smiled up at me. "His dad is going to drop him off afterward."

The girl standing beside Shan cleared her throat, and that was all it took for my body to ignite. And holy shit, If I thought my heart had beat hard at the fear of water earlier, it paled in comparison to the tornado of internal tremors that ricocheted through every chamber of my heart at the sight of *her.*

While I worked hard to keep my head on my shoulders and my heart in my chest, my eyes gave her face their undivided attention. Something that had never been a challenge. Not when she'd been successfully garnering every ounce of my attention since the beginning of time. "Claire-Bear."

Big brown doe eyes smiled back at me. Yeah, she had eyes that *smiled.* Her usual mountain of wild blond curls was piled on top of her head and barely contained by what I could only describe as a hair claw. I didn't know the correct terminology for such feminine creations, but having messed around in her room enough times, I knew it to be a tricky bastard, with a surprisingly forceful sting if it clamped your skin.

Not as bad as a scratch to the gooch from Brian when getting out of the shower, but still.

"Gerard," Claire replied in that upbeat, lyrical tone of voice I adored. "It's twenty-six degrees outside and you're clearly caked in baby oil." Shaking her head, she tutted in disapproval. "You're going to burn your nipples again."

"Ah Jesus, Gerard," Mam scolded with a heavy sigh. "What did I tell you about protecting yourself in the sun?"

"I already told you, Mam; the sun loves me," I shot back before turning to Claire. "And if I do burn my tits, you can nurse me back to full health again."

Shannon laughed. "Again?"

"It's a long story," Claire explained, stepping forward to fix the buttons on my shirt. "One full of peeling skin and bleeding nipples that I don't care to repeat anytime soon."

"Don't listen to her, little Shannon," I offered with a chuckle. "She loves minding me."

"So, who else is going to be at this beach campout?" Mam inquired, smiling lovingly at Shan who was rubbing the demon in her arms.

"The usual gang," Claire offered, keeping a wide berth of Brian.

"The usual gang?" Mam's frown deepened, and I felt myself stiffen.

This was it.

She was about to start.

"Who does that include exactly?"

"It's okay," I started to say. "I'll be okay, Mam—"

"Stay away from the water," she ordered, cutting me off and delivering her own water balloon of misery on what I hoped would be a good day—and I *needed* it to be a good day, dammit. I hadn't slept more than three hours last night, what with my subconscious trying to lure me to a dark corner of my mind.

Good day.

Good day.

Good day.

I was manifesting the hell out of it.

"And stay away from that—"

"Mam," I warned, cutting her off before she went there. Because I couldn't go there. Not today. "It'll be grand."

"I mean it, young man," Mam argued. "Play in the sand to your heart's content but steer clear of the water. Don't even paddle. Not after what happened last time."

Last time being Johnny's birthday back in May. The disastrous camping trip where I'd nearly met my watery grave. *Again.* Damn Johnny for telling my mam about the whole being thrown in the river incident. She hadn't slept through the night since, and I would know since I hadn't slept through the night since I was seven.

"Play in the sand? Paddle?" I gaped at her, feigning outrage, while desperately trying to steer the conversation to safer waters—pun intended. "Jesus Christ, Mam, I'm seventeen, not seven." Bending down, I snatched up the picnic basket and headed for the door, needing to get out of this house. "Do you want to slap SPF 50 on me and hide me under an umbrella to build sandcastles for the day?"

"Wouldn't be the first time," Shannon snickered from behind the hand she was using to bury her smile.

"Hey now, that wasn't a castle, it was a man-sized fort," I accused, pointing a finger at her. "And *you* two were the architects!"

"Yes, we were, Gerard, and you were a wonderful minion." Claire laughed, catching ahold of my hand and pulling me toward the door, with a snickering Shannon in tow. "Don't worry about him, Sadhbh. Gerard's perfectly safe with us."

"Yeah," Shannon agreed, playfully slipping her arm through mine. "We've got his back."

"I'll hold you to that, girls," Mam called after us. "Look after each other."

"Always," all three of us chorused in unison.

"Sadhbh is such a helicopter mam," Claire cackled when she climbed into the passenger seat of my Ford Focus. "It's cute."

Not when I needed her to be. "It's annoying is what it is," I offered, climbing into the driver's seat beside her.

"Well, I think she's a sweetheart," Shannon chimed in from the back seat.

"Yeah, a sweetheart with invisible rotor blades attached to her back," I grumbled, cranking the engine, and tearing away from the house. "The woman is relentless. Guaranteed I'll have at least three texts on my phone when I park up warning me to stay out of the water."

"I suppose you can't blame her for worrying," Shannon offered quietly. "You know, all things considered."

"Hmm," was all I replied, because in all truth, I had no intention of going there today. *Good day, good day, good day.*

"Sorry, Gibs."

"For what?" I asked, casting a glance in the rearview mirror.

"For bringing it up," she replied with a small shrug. "I mean, I of all people should know better."

"No worries, little Shannon." I forced a huge smile. "It's all good."

A warm hand settled on my lap then and I felt immense comfort. Fuck it, I had no clue how the girl did it, but she could ground me with her fingertip.

One touch and I was okay again.

I could breathe again.

For a little while, at least.

"So, what's the gossip, girls?" I asked, sick to death of being in my own head. I needed an out. A distraction. Anything but my memories for company. "How was the interview, Claire-Bear?"

"Terrible," Claire groaned, folding her arms across her chest. "Hugh's boss is a mean old biddy."

"So, you didn't get the job?"

"Oh god, I hope not, guys." Flicking through songs on my car stereo, she settled on one of our favorites; Matt Nathanson's "Laid." "I'm perfectly content as I am."

"Yes, you *are* perfect as you are," I agreed.

She rolled her eyes in response. "Oh, and fair warning, Hugh is like a demon since he got home from work."

"Why?"

"It's my fault," she muttered, drumming her fingers on the car door. "Liz was at the pool this morning, and I asked him to talk to her about something." She shrugged in defeat. "Obviously, it didn't go well because he's been banging around the house like a bear with a sore head since he got home. I mean, God only knows why. It's not like his life is terrible. Pretty girlfriend. Pretty sister. Pretty fantastic life if you ask me."

"You *are* fantastic."

"You're a dope."

"I'd gladly be dope if you put me in your mouth."

"Gibs, you're getting worse." Shannon laughed from the back seat. "That was weak."

"It's because I'm rusty," I defended with a huff. "I haven't seen anyone in weeks to practice on. I've been on house arrest, remember?"

"Well, it serves you right for doing what you did," Claire cackled. "In all fairness, Gerard, what did you expect them to do?"

"Not ruin my summer."

"You stole your stepfather's *tractor*."

"A digger," I corrected with a huff. "It was a digger, not a tractor, and I borrowed it."

"And then you rolled all over Mrs. Kingston's flower bed with the wheels."

"Only because I couldn't get a handle on the pedals." I narrowed my eyes. "And if I recall correctly, I wasn't alone in my mission, either."

"I plead the Fifth," Claire snickered.

"You would."

"Why would you guys steal a digger?" Shannon laughed.

"No idea." I laughed.

"Seemed like a good idea at the time," Claire added.

"And now?"

"Now?" Scratching my chin, I grinned sheepishly. "Maybe not so much."

"You ruined her petunias," Claire reminded me with a mischievous grin.

My mouth fell open in outrage. "That was *you*!"

"Nuh-uh." She patted my thigh. "Not according to our parents."

6
Boys, Beaches, and Besties

CLAIRE

Our trip to the beach turned out to be a glorious one. Surrounded by friendly faces, and on a day filled with sunshine, sandcastles, and seaside paddling, we celebrated our last days of freedom before school returned and the summer gave way to autumn.

In between spending copious amounts of time trying to drown each other in the ocean, Shan and I had lazed idly on the toasty sand for most of the evening, carefree and untroubled by the world that was waiting for us just around the corner.

"Remember when I told you that beautiful boys with big muscles complicate every-thing?" I declared several hours later, sprawled out on my belly, enjoying the last of the evening sun rays, while the boys tossed a ball around further up the beach. The sun was setting, the tents had been pitched, and I was reveling in the last wisps of heat. "Well, I was right."

"Understatement of the century," Shan agreed from her perch beside me. "But they're so pretty to look at."

"True." Pulling up on my elbows, I twisted around just in time to see Gerard leap into the air to catch the ball. "Oh, sweet baby Jesus." He looked so damn good today. Clad in nothing but a pair of white shorts, he filled every inch of his skin like a dream. No, like a demigod. Yeah, a demigod was so much more fitting.

"I get it." Shannon smiled knowingly. "I feel the same about Johnny."

"It's hard to concentrate, huh?"

"Definitely," she agreed. "And then it gets deeper because you start to crave their words as much as their kisses."

"Whoa," I breathed. "Sounds intense."

"You should tell Gibs how you feel, Claire."

"He already knows how I feel," I replied, settling back down on my stomach. "He's just…Gerard."

"And you're Claire," she added. "And together you make a perfect team."

"Yeah, maybe."

"Definitely," she assured me. "It'll happen. I can feel it in my bones."

I hope so. "I'm going to miss this," I changed the subject by saying. "I wish we lived in a world where summer never ended."

"But then we wouldn't have autumn," Shan offered, happy to follow my lead. "And you know how much we love Octobers."

"True," I agreed dreamily. "Woolly jumpers and falling leaves."

"Hot chocolate and Halloween," she added with a wistful sigh.

"Bonfires."

"Dark evenings."

"Trick-or-treating."

"Snuggling under blankets."

"Okay, new plan. Let's build a world full of Octobers."

"Now that's a world I want to live in," Shan agreed.

"We can be queens."

"Or presidents."

"Rulers."

"Yes, joint rulers of all things autumn."

"Genius."

"Hey, Shan?"

"Hmm?"

Rolling onto my side, I pushed my curls back and gave my bestie my full attention. "Do you hold it against me?"

"I would never hold anything against you, Claire," she replied, mirroring my actions.

I smiled sadly. "You don't even know what I'm referring to."

"Because it doesn't matter." She reached out with her foot and poked my leg with her toe. "It would never happen."

"But I knew, Shan. I *knew* something was wrong in your house," I confessed, repeating a conversation we'd had a couple of times this summer. "I didn't do anything about it, and the guilt is still eating me."

"Claire, you have nothing to feel guilty about. You didn't know. Not really. I never told you anything. You had a feeling. And you did everything you could have done for me. Trust me, I know." Pushing up onto her knees, Shannon grabbed a hair tie off her wrist and pulled her hair into a makeshift bun. "I'm still here. I made it. He didn't beat me." Smiling softly, she gestured to herself and then our surroundings. "And look at my life now."

"I know and I'm so thankful you're here," I strangled out, feeling overwhelmed with emotion.

Johnny's family had taken Shannon and her brothers in when their parents died in a house fire earlier this year. A fire that had been purposefully set by their abusive, alcoholic father.

The six Lynch siblings had been through hell and back this year and had finally found a soft landing in the Kavanagh home.

Their oldest brother, Darren, was grown and lived up north. Meanwhile, Joey was in therapy for his addiction issues. Shannon and the three younger boys—Tadhg, Ollie, and Sean—resided in the manor with the Kavanaghs. And boy were those kids *thriving*.

Springing forward, I threw my arms around her and squeezed tightly. "I don't know what I'd do without you."

"Okay, what's really wrong?" she asked with a small chuckle as she hugged me back.

"What do you mean?"

"Something's on your mind."

"How can you tell?"

"Because you're an open book," Shannon explained. "I'm not going to force you into telling me anything, but know that you can, and I'll never judge. No matter what."

"It's Liz," I admitted, pulling back to look at her. "I think she might be hurting herself again."

"Again?" Shannon's face paled. "What do you mean 'again'?"

"Aw crap, I keep forgetting you weren't around much back then. Even though we've been friends forever, there are huge patches of time you weren't there when we were growing up."

"Focus, Claire," Shannon urged, sounding panicked. "When did this happen before?"

"After Caoimhe passed away." Swallowing deeply, I pressed a hand to my brow and fought the internal panic clawing at me. "She was cutting for a while back then."

"Cutting?" Her blue eyes widened in horror. "Are you talking about self-harm?"

I nodded grimly. "Um, it was a really dark time in her life, and I told my mam who then told her mam."

"Good," Shannon urged, offering me a supportive nod. "That's good, Claire."

"And I thought it helped, you know? Her parents got her into counseling and the cutting stopped, but then I saw her at the pool this morning and she has this huge scar on her thigh, and it looked so much like the ones I used to see on her..." My words broke off and I blew out a shaky breath. "She said she fell on barbed wire, but that's not true, Shan. I know it in my gut."

"Oh god," Shannon whispered, covering her mouth with her hand. "Poor Lizzie."

"So, I guess I'm asking you to tell me what to do," I added, feeling nervous and uncertain. "I don't want to upset her or make things harder for her than they already are, but I can't sit back and do nothing." *Like I did with you.*

"No," Shannon agreed quietly.

"So, what do I do?"

"What about talking to her about it?"

"She's been pulling away from me for months," I explained, using my toe to dig a hole in the sand as I spoke. "Because of Gerard."

"Because she blames Gibs for what happened between Mark and Caoimhe."

"Yep. Pretty much." Releasing a pained sigh, I scooped up a handful of sand and then watched as it slowly trickled from my fingertips. "I understand where she is coming from. Really, I do. But I won't ever walk away from him." *Not even for Lizzie.* "And she sees my friendship with him as one giant betrayal to her." I shrugged, feeling helpless. "The closer I get to Gerard, the further Lizzie pulls away."

"That's a horrible situation to be put in," Shannon offered, reaching over to cover my hand with hers. "One I think you've been doing a wonderful job of navigating."

"I used to think so, too," I admitted. "That I was good at navigating my friendships with them both. But not lately." *Not since the last camping trip.* "Not anymore."

"I'm going to help," Shannon declared, squeezing my hand. "You're not alone in this. She's our best friend and I'm right here with you, Claire. We'll do something about this."

"What though?"

"We'll talk to Liz," she replied. "And we'll talk to her mother, too."

"She might freak," I offered warily.

"She might," Shannon agreed with a nod. "But it's a risk worth taking."

"Sorry we're so late, guys. I didn't get off work until eight," Katie announced, causing our conversation to be cut short when she hurried up the beach in our direction. "Room for one more?"

Clearing her throat, Shannon smiled brightly and patted her towel. "Always."

"Thanks," Katie replied, sinking down on the edge of Shannon's towel. Her cheeks were flushed, and she was still wearing her work uniform. "I have no idea what's getting into that brother of yours, Claire, but he's like a monk that's taken a vow of silence."

"Really?" I glanced over my shoulder and spotted my brother who had just arrived. Clad in board shorts and an oversized hoodie, he pitched their tent with effortless ease before turning his attention to the makeshift fire that was dying out.

Oh god.

This was my fault.

It clearly went very badly with Lizzie earlier.

"I'll be right back," I announced, climbing to my feet. "Two secs, guys."

"Can you grab a hoodie for me?" Shan called after me. "The sun's going down and it's getting chilly."

"On it," I called back, not stopping until I reached my brother. "Are you okay?"

"Never better," he replied, attention glued to the flames he was teasing back to life. "You?"

"Come on, Hugh." I stepped closer. "What happened?"

"What do you mean?"

"With Lizzie," I pushed. "Was she mean to you?"

"When isn't she mean, Claire?" he replied flatly.

Oh god, she *was* mean.

"You know she doesn't mean it, right?" I tried to sway. "It's her coping mechanism."

"I don't need anyone to explain Lizzie Young's coping mechanisms to me," came his hard response. "I'm well versed in them."

"So, you asked her about it?" I chewed on my lip, anxious. "About the cutting?"

"Yes, Claire, I asked her about it."

"And?"

"And it was a huge fucking mistake," Hugh spat out, tossing the stick in the fire. "There's a reason we steer clear of each other, and I was reminded of that today."

"Hugh," I began to say, but he shook his head.

"I'm done, Claire." Rolling his shoulders, he pushed the sleeves of his hoodie up to his elbows and stalked off in the direction of the boys, kicking at the sand as he went. "Ask Feely to talk to her because I'm so fucking done."

"See?" Katie exclaimed when I returned to her and Shan. "He's clearly in a mood about something, right?"

"Maybe," I mumbled, feeling terrible for pushing my brother into doing something that I knew full well would affect him.

"Liz!" Shannon squealed, scrambling to her feet and making a beeline for the sand dune our willowy friend was standing on. Standing beside her with his arms full of camping equipment was Pierce. "You came!"

"I came." She laughed, reciprocating Shannon's hug with a rare show of affection.

Shifting in discomfort, Pierce stepped around the girls and headed straight for the boys who were on their way to investigate our new guests.

"I thought you said you weren't coming?" Patrick called out good-naturedly, shielding his eyes from the late evening sun, as he looked up at her.

"Yeah, well, I figured you'd be bored without me," Lizzie called back, covering her mouth with her hands to send her voice further.

"Peace," Katie mumbled under her breath. "We would have had *peace* without her."

Choosing not to call her out on her mutterings, because in all honesty the girl wasn't wrong, I stood up to make room for my brother, who had joined his girlfriend.

Dusting the sand off my thighs, I offered Lizzie a big wave. She began to reciprocate with a wave of her own but quickly stopped and veered her attention back to Shannon when I was joined by the boys.

"No fighting," Johnny was instructing Gerard. He had his hands on Gerard's shoulders like he was priming him for a boxing match. "No matter what she says, no matter how low she hits you below the belt, no bleeding fighting, Gibs."

"I've got it," Gerard grumbled, shaking out of Johnny's hold. "I won't even look in her direction."

"Good man yourself," Johnny encouraged. "Because we want a peaceful night."

"Yes, we do," Katie agreed, hooking arms with Hugh. "*Peaceful.*"

"You'll have no drama from me, boss," Gerard offered in a teasing tone, attention locked on me as he prowled toward me with mischief dancing in his eyes. "I only have eyes for one blond."

He had a twinkle of mischief in his eyes that was addictive. Seriously, being with Gerard felt like when you were five and waiting for Santa to come on Christmas Eve. He drew every element of emotion from my heart, and he did it without breaking a sweat.

"Don't you dare," I squealed, as I scampered to the side and narrowly avoided his playful onslaught. "Gerard Gibson, I'm warning you—ahhh!"

"What's that, lover? You fancy a moonlight stroll on the beach?" Throwing me over his shoulder, Gerard proceeded to run down the beach. "Anything for you, my sweetheart."

"Oh my god," I half laughed, half screamed, as my face bounced helplessly against his back. "Let me down or I'll pinch your ass."

"Is that a promise?"

"I'll do it," I warned through fits of laughter. "I will, Gerard." Sliding my hand into the waistband of his short, I pushed my hand inside. "Ooh, what's this? A round, hairy ass cheek!"

"Okay, okay." He laughed, surprising me as he quickly forfeited and set me down on my feet. "You win."

"I do?" I replied, breathless. "Since when?"

"Since I can't take it." He chuckled, still smiling down at me.

"Can't take what?"

"Being touched there."

It was only then that I realized that I still had my hand in his shorts. "Oh crap." Cheeks flaming, I quickly yanked my hand free and grinned up at him. "Oops."

"Oops," he mimicked affectionately, hands resting on my shoulders.

"Why can't you take being touched there?"

"Because I have the worst tickles known to mankind on my hole."

"Tickles." I arched a brow. "On your ass?"

"Yep. So bad." He nodded eagerly. "I lose total control of my limbs. Seriously. Try it and I'm like a ninja with a black belt."

"And how do you know you have a tickly ass?"

"Do you really want to know the answer to that question."

"Uh, no," I confirmed with a grimace. "On second thoughts, don't tell me."

"Come on." He chuckled, draping his arm over my shoulders. "Let's take that moonlight stroll."

"This is entirely inappropriate behavior."

"Duly noted. Should we continue?"

"Of course."

"Okay then."

"Hey, remember that song about the summertime?" Entwining my hand with his, I twirled out of his hold before returning to his side. "The one our dads used to play all the time when we were little."

Shifting our bodies so that he was behind me, he wrapped his arms around my waist and leaned in close. "'In the Summertime' by Mungo Jerry." Mimicking the singer's voice, he broke into the chorus, giving me a hilarious rendition of one of my favorite childhood songs. "Is that the one?"

"Yes!" Biting down on my lip with sheer delight, I gripped his forearms for dear life when he began to swing me around in circles. "Oh my god," I squealed, feeling safer in this boy's arms than anywhere else on earth. "Please don't let go."

"Never," he vowed. "Not in a million years."

7

Lord of the Dance Beach

GIBSIE

Several hours later, the tunes were cranking on Feely's boom box, and the drink was flowing. My valiant efforts of manifesting a good day seemed to have worked because not only had the Viper steered clear of me all night, but she taken to her tent with Lover Boy over an hour ago and hadn't resurfaced since.

Taking it as a nod from my old man in the sky looking out for me, I had decided to celebrate by necking half my weight in cider. To be honest, I pitied Feely, the poor misfortunate bastard, for having to share a tent with me later, but I was having too much fun to care—or stop.

"And here we have it, folks," Feely declared, turning up the volume on his boom box to the maximum. The familiar beat of Gaelic Storm's "Irish Party in Third Class" boomed loudly, causing every limb in my body to react on instinct to the sound of the bodhran as it played a tune in rhythm to the beat of my eternally Irish heart. "Baby Biggs and Lord of the Dance himself."

My eyes were bleary and unfocused, but I would have to be blind not to see her. Ringlets of golden sunshine bounced in the air as she moved around the campfire like she had been put on this earth to dance with me.

Keeping my hands rigid by my sides, I concentrated really hard on keeping my back straight and my body upright, not an easy feat after a slab of cider, but the girl dancing in circles around me was worth the effort.

Grinning devilishly when it was time to join her, Claire offered me a knowing tilt of her chin and off I went, flying through the air like a demented fucking lunatic with perfectly pointed toes.

"They're going to fall into the fire," Hugh slurred, pointing with his beer canto where I was standing precariously close to the flames. "Gibs, you better not burn my baby sister!"

"Shush you, they clearly know what they're doing." Katie laughed, slapping at his hand. "Keep going, guys. You're amazing. Like the couple in Riverdance."

"Except blond."

"And semi-naked."

"With pierced nipples."

I had every intention of continuing. Couldn't stop if I wanted to. Our bodies moved in perfect symmetry to the routine we had won countless competitions performing in childhood.

I tried my best to remember the steps and patterns of the complicated traditional Irish stepdance we were attempting. It wasn't hard since they'd been ingrained in me every Monday afternoon for eight years of primary school. Besides, I wasn't ashamed to dance with her—even if the alcohol helped a great deal.

"Hup out that, Gibsie boy!" Johnny howled, belting his thigh with his hand to the rhythm of the music as he cuddled his snickering girlfriend to his chest. "Show us those dancing toes."

"It's dancing feet," Shannon corrected through fits of laughter. "And yes, guys! Woo! Let's go."

We completed three more sets of dancing around each other together before joining hands for our big finale.

Pulling her close to my chest, I dropped my hand to rest on her hip before leaning in close to press a kiss to the tip of her nose.

"Hey, no kissing!" Hugh roared, aiming his can at my head. "Keep your lips off my sister, fucker!"

Snickering, I deftly dodged the missile can of beer, pulled his sister flush against me, and then dipped her in glorious fashion just as the song ended.

"That was epic," Claire panted through fits of laughter as everyone around us clapped and cheered. She had the best laugh. It was so full of life and heart and sincerity. When Claire laughed, it wasn't false or pushed on, it was authentic and real. Her eyes were bright with excitement as she smiled up at me, still clutching my shoulders. "I wasn't expecting the dip."

"Yeah, well, it was either dip you or kiss you," I admitted, setting her back down on her feet. "And then I remembered I promised Kav a peaceful night." Grinning wolfishly, I added, "I didn't want to start World War III with your big brother over there."

"Liar," she teased, tipping my nose with her finger. "You chickened out and that's all there is to it."

Well, how could I argue with that?

"You guys should still be entering competitions," Shan encouraged with a clap. "I bet you'd win them all."

"Absolutely," Katie agreed, pulling Claire down to sit beside her. "I've seen all of your medals and trophies in your front room."

"We still would be if the boys hadn't poached him off me for the rugby team," Claire replied, still breathless from our earlier antics. "It's all good, though. Some of the best things in life aren't meant to last forever. That's why we cherish them when they happen. Like your favorite chocolate in a box. Or shooting stars. We don't refuse to eat the sweet because once we do, it'll be gone, or stop looking at the stars after one shoots by. We enjoy the moment because we know it's worth living in."

"Whoa," Shannon breathed. "That's deep."

"Aw, there's a wise old head underneath those curls, isn't there?" Katie teased, hooking her arm through Claire's. "Very philosophical, Baby Biggs."

8

Shits, Giggles, and Shaking Tents

CLAIRE

"I JUST MISS HIM SO MUCH." WITH HER CHEEK RESTING ON HER BOYFRIEND'S SHOUL-der, Shannon clung to him like a baby monkey would its mother. "I want him home, Johnny." Her voice was slurring and her eyes were closed as she spoke, letting me know that she was a little beyond tipsy.

"I know, baby," Johnny, who was equally drunk, soothed as he rubbed soothing circles on her back. "Joey will be home on Monday."

"I just…I love him so much," she mumbled, clawing and pulling at Johnny as if he would disappear at any minute. "Oh god, but my heart loves you most of all."

"Right back at you, Shannon like the river."

"You're really for keeps, aren't you?"

"Just try to get rid of me." Chuckling, he stood up from the sand in one swift move, taking my bestie with him. "I've got you, my little darling."

"And I've got you, Binding 13," she cooed, attempting and failing to ruffle his hair. "So pretty."

"We're going to call it a night," Johnny announced as he carried his baby monkey back to their tent and disappeared inside. "Night all."

"Night," the rest of us called back in unison.

"Jesus, they're disgustingly loved up, aren't they?" Feely mused, taking a swig of his beer.

"So bad," Katie agreed with a chuckle. "It's nice."

"It's epic," I chimed in. "And so incredibly deserving."

"And permanent," Gerard added with a nod. "Mark my words, lads, come what may next summer after graduation, we'll all be back in this town in a few years for their wedding."

"You really think so?" Katie asked.

"No thinking necessary," Gerard replied, tapping his temple. "It's already a done deal. Knowing Johnny, he already has his grandmother's heirloom engagement ring waiting in the wings for the perfect opportunity."

"Really?" My eyes widened. "Johnny has an heirloom ring?"

"Oh yeah." Gerard nodded eagerly. "The rock is the size of my fist."

"Whoa."

"I know, right?"

"I'm best man," Hugh tossed out.

"Like hell you are," Patrick shot back.

"Fuck you both," Gerard interjected. "That's my job."

"You're delusional."

"And you're shit craic," Gerard countered, catching onto my brother's bullshit bad mood, which had been present all night. "You're killing my buzz, lad. Cheer up."

"I'm fine."

"Yeah," he snorted. "What's that saying for the word 'fine,' babe?"

"Fucked up, insecure, neurotic and emotional."

"That's the one," Gerard replied, grinning. "You, my friend, are all of that and more."

"We can't all be poster boys for Prozac, Gibs."

"He doesn't take Prozac anymore," I was quick to defend.

"Thank you," Gerard replied. "My serotonin levels are back on track. Now, back to the wedding. You two are groomsmen at a push—although chances are he'll forget about you both when he goes pro." Gerard winked. "I'm the best man."

"If that's the case, then what makes you think he won't forget about you, too, smart-ass?"

"Because I'm as unforgettable as I am irreplaceable," Gerard replied with a grin. "Unlike you boring bastards."

"Jesus, that's lovely, that is."

"Yeah, Gibs, thanks a bunch."

"I speak only the truth," Gerard continued, unfazed. "I nearly died of boredom while Cap was away on tour with only the two of you for company."

"Hey!" I huffed, poking his side. "What about me?"

"Male company," he was quick to correct, leaning in to press a kiss to my cheek. "You're perfect."

"Yeah," Katie agreed with a smile. "You two have been joined at the hip this summer."

"This summer?" Hugh snorted. "Try every summer since 1989."

"Damn straight," Gerard agreed, leaning in to press another kiss to my cheek. "My little Leo."

"No lips on my sister," Hugh grumbled, but it was a defeated sound. He'd clearly consumed too much alcohol to care anymore. "Dammit, Gibs."

"Thank god for this one," Gerard continued, wrapping an arm around me. "I thank my lucky stars every day for her friendship."

"Hey!"

"I'm not even sorry," Gerard laughed. "One of you is a mute and the other is a permanent fucking rain cloud."

"I'm not a mute," Hugh argued.

"No, you're the rain cloud," Gerard replied, pointing a finger at Patrick. "He's the mute."

"Maybe if you shut your mouth every once in a while, I would have a chance to speak," Patrick drawled, stretching his legs out.

"Speak now," I urged. "Because I'm getting sick of listening to the voice in my head."

"Voice or voices?"

"My inner voice, asshole."

"Just checking."

"You guys are so mean to each other," Katie declared with a yawn. "It's terrible."

"Nah, this is just our love language," Hugh replied, draping a blanket over her shoulders. "I'd take a bullet for anyone of these assholes."

"Right back at you, brother," Gerard replied, offering Hugh the middle finger. "In a heartbeat."

"Speak for yourselves," Patrick interjected, following on from Katie's yawn with a huge one of his own. "I wouldn't piss on either one of you if you were on fire."

"Nice." Gerard and Hugh chuckled in unison.

"Boys are weird," Katie said. "Boy code is even weirder."

"Totally," I agreed. "Don't even try to understand these weirdos, chickie. I've been around these boys for sixteen years and their friendship dynamics still confuse me."

An audible moan came from a nearby tent, causing Gerard to clearly state the first thing that sprang to his mind, "So, I guess Cap's getting his hole, huh?"

"Jesus, Gibs," Patrick groaned. "I don't want to think about it."

"Yeah," Hugh agreed with a shudder. "The girl is like a sister to us."

"Ew, don't even say it like that, Gerard," I added. "'Getting his hole.'" I grimaced in disgust. "What a horrible reference to the physical act of love."

"Wow," Hugh deadpanned. "What a horrible reference to sex."

"What?" I asked. "Physical act of love?"

"Ugh." He shuddered. "That's so wrong, Claire."

"Why?" Katie laughed. "It's what they're doing, isn't it?"

"To be honest, babe, I don't want to think about what Cap is doing."

"I prefer getting his hole," Gerard declared.

"Me too," both Hugh and Patrick agreed.

"Absolutely not," Katie argued. "That's so crude."

"I have it," Gerard announced, holding a hand up. "They are *fucking* with *feelings!*"

"Fucking with feelings."

"Hmm."

"It's best of a bad bunch."

"It's genius!"

"It sounds sort of serious," Patrick mused. "To fuck with feelings?"

"I fuck myself with feelings all the time," Gerard offered up. "It's nice."

"Gerard!" I squealed.

"As you should, lad," Patrick laughed.

"Ew," Katie groaned.

"Shoot me now," Hugh muttered.

"Fucking with feelings," Gerard continued. "It's centrifugal motion."

"It's what?" Both Hugh and Patrick turned to gape at their friend. "Gibs, what the hell are you talking about?"

"Fucking with feelings," he said proudly. "It's centrifugal motion."

"Now, where in the name of Jesus did you hear that word?" Patrick asked.

"I know words," Gerard huffed, tone defensive.

"Says the fella who tried to convince the whole of fourth class that tyrant was a breed of dinosaur."

"Hey! That was an easy mistake, and you know it." Gerard shrugged noncommittally. "Could have happened to anyone."

"Funny how the things that could happen to anyone usually only happen to you, Gibs."

"Centrifugal motion," Hugh mused, scratching his jaw. "I think we covered that in science last year." He turned to look at Gerard. "Since when did you take up physics, lad?"

"I clearly didn't," Gerard huffed. "But if it's good enough for a Faith Hill song, then it's good enough for me."

Smiling to myself, I sat back and listened to their pointless rambling. Weird and dysfunctional as they were, I loved the three boys sitting around the campfire—and their captain who was nursing my drunk bestie. Every one of these stupid boys brought something to the table.

Patrick Feely, for example. He was quiet and closed off, but that's because you didn't know Patrick until you *knew* Patrick. He didn't suffer fools. He didn't bend or break or submit to peer pressure. He wasn't trying to fit in with anyone. If that made him uncool to our peers, it meant little to nothing to him. He had his secrets and his troubles, like the rest of us, but they were unspoken. In fact, I had known him since early childhood and still felt very closed off from him at times.

Then you had my brother, Hugh. Take personal sibling irks and pet peeves out of the equation, and you had another levelheaded, decent boy. And no, I didn't say that because he was related to me. He just was.

Moving on to Johnny, and you had a boy living in a man's world, body and mind. Maybe it was because of the life he led, or the fact that he'd mapped his future out before the rest of us, but he was most different. He wasn't naturally calm or reserved like Patrick but had channeled his self-control like a finely worked muscle in his body.

Seriously, the boy had some epic willpower and was able to bend his will to his favor. I'd never seen anything like it. The way he could exude power and then rein it back in with a tight iron fist.

The only person I'd ever see get under his skin was my best friend. Yeah, Shan blew that self-control to hell on her very first day at school.

Which brought me to *my* person.

Gerard was bristling with a mischievous sort of energy that emanated from him in waves. It was as enticing as it was addictive. He was the type of boy you wanted to spend all your time with, regardless of the consequences because it was instant, delayed, and prolonged gratification combined.

He had darkness in his life and so much pain, but he kept the most beautiful sunny disposition about him. It was incredibly humbling to be around the boy. To know all he had endured in his short life and that he still woke up with a smile on his face in the morning. It couldn't be easy, not with fifty percent of his family buried in the graveyard beside Shannon's parents. But he did it.

Sometimes, I wished he wasn't the one my heart had attached its flag to because he felt so far away, so unattainable, but then when we were together, everything fell into place, and all of my doubts evaporated. It was a dangerous thing to love a boy the way I loved Gerard. But I couldn't go back in time and pinpoint the moment it happened; therefore, I was resigned to loving him.

They say it's hard to get over your first love. Well, if I knew it to be true, like my heart was so insistent, I would never be getting over Gerard Gibson.

We had so much fun when we were together, but when we were with our friends, he was Gibsie. When he was with me, he was Gerard. I liked to think of them as two different people. Two very different boys. I loved them both with every fiber of my being. Sometimes I wished I didn't feel the way I did, but you can't change the heart's direction once it sets sight on its destination. And my heart's destination was hell-bent toward melding with his. Toward entwining with his and never breaking free again.

I just wanted to be with him, follow him everywhere, and never let go of the feelings he evoked inside of me. In fact, if I could bottle them up and take a little sniff every time I felt sad, that would be perfect.

Truth be told, it almost felt like a part of me was programmed to love him. It had come to me so easily. As easy as breathing. There wasn't a point in time that I could safely identify where he didn't live in my memory.

When we were little, everything was easier, less complicated, and, well, quite frankly, smoother. But with age came hormones and trauma that severed ties and fractured friendships. I suppose it was a testament to our friendship group to manage to hold the line when such trials and tribulations attacked our core. God knows many others would have thrown in the towel had they suffered similar fates.

Complications came as easy as breathing to us now, and while issues were imbedded deep within our circle, we somehow managed to hold on. To stick together. I thought that might have a lot to do with the fact that my brother and I were bringing two very different groups of people together. It wasn't as blasé as saying the boys and the girls. That wasn't it. It wasn't gender-based. It was a matter of souls connecting. From Katie and Hugh to Shannon and Johnny, to Lizzie and Patrick, to me and Gerard, there was an invisible string that connected all of us.

A little while later, when everyone was turning in for the night, I wasn't even surprised when Gerard followed me into my tent. Even though he was meant to be sharing with Patrick, we both knew it would be my sleeping bag he would end up inside. *Same as always.*

"Don't turn around," I warned as I stripped off my bikini and pulled on an old jersey of his and a fresh pair of knickers.

"Tonight was good craic, wasn't it?" Gerard mused, faithfully keeping his back to me as I changed. "To be honest, I thought it was going to go to shit when Pierce and the Viper showed up," he added, climbing into the sleeping bag. "But she kept her distance for once."

"Gerard." A heavy sigh escaped my lips. "You know I don't like it when you call her that."

Shrugging unapologetically, he yawned loudly before settling his arms behind his head. "Sorry."

"No, you're not." I laughed, climbing in beside him, while desperately trying to avert my eyes from his impressive biceps. Because Gerard had the best arms. They were delicious.

"No, I'm not," he agreed with a chuckle.

"You're so annoying."

"You love it."

"Just try be nice to each other," I instructed, rolling onto my side to face him. "For me."

"I'm always trying," he replied. "She's always pushing."

"I know." With my portable camping light switched onto the brightest setting, I took the time to study every inch of him, securing this moment in time to memory because I didn't want to ever forget this summer. Or this boy.

He was big and broad and strong, with the most beautiful sun-kissed skin. Seriously, it was as if the sun came down from the sky and illuminated this boy in the most wondrous hue of bronze. His already blond hair was bleached from the sun, making him look almost surfer dude-ish—like the boys I watched on *Home and Away* every evening on RTÉ2.

His brown nipples were pierced and adorned with itty-bitty silver hoops, and he had a tattoo on his left rib cage with the word *Resilience* in italic font that was decorated with a feather in black, and then a tiny Care Bear on his right hipbone.

I never saw other boys, never looked at them the way I looked at Gerard. He was insistently permanent inside of me, and I couldn't shake him if I tried. Not that I did much trying these days. He was comfortable and exciting and fresh all rolled into one perfect creation.

"I love you, Gerard."

"I love you, too." His lips were so close to mine that if I leaned in just an inch, we would be kissing. I wanted to. Desperately. But I held back. Knowing that my heart couldn't take the kiss. Because the kiss might be a glorious one, but it would never be accompanied by the commitment I needed from him. The relationship I needed the security of. For whatever reason, Gerard offered me his heart on his sleeve, but kept the rest of him tucked behind an impenetrable wall of mystery.

"You look sad." His voice was like an old musical box to my ears. So familiar and welcoming and soothing. He soothed me like a comfort blanket. After all, he'd been in my life long enough. I'd outgrown all my other comforters. Not Gerard, though. As my age grew, so did my desire for his company. For him, period.

"I'm not sad."

"No?"

"No." Unable to repress the full-body shudder that racked through me when he turned on his side and draped his big arm over me, I sucked in a sharp breath and whispered, "I'm frustrated."

9

Fry-Ups and Flying Off the Handle

CLAIRE

"Morning," Johnny acknowledged when I unzipped the opening of my tent the following morning and was greeted by the delicious smell of a fry-up cooking. "You look fresh."

He was right. Not only was I feeling fresh this morning, but I was looking it, too. My hair, for some miraculous reason, had decided to comply with my wishes this morning without a hint of frizz—not a usual occurrence for a girl with my texture. "That's because I'm made of steel," I explained, joining him at the makeshift firepit, where he was cooking. "Seriously, I never get hangovers."

"Because you never drink."

"I drink."

He arched a knowing brow.

"Okay," I conceded with a rueful smile, sitting down. "I've drank three times before and I've never once had a headache."

"Well, you might want to pass your secret on to your best friend." Humor filled his tone as he gestured toward his tent. "Because she's dying a small death in there."

I winced in sympathy. "Poor Shan."

"She'll be okay." Chuckling softly, he used a fork to turn the meat on the disposable grill. "Nothing a few sausages won't cure."

"Aw. You score tries *and* make breakfast." I smiled. "You're such a keeper."

"Do I smell sausages?" Clambering out of my tent, Gerard sniffed the air like a deranged Doberman. "Lifesaver, Cap," he declared, bounding over to us in his underpants. "Fucking lifesaver."

The moment my eyes landed on him; a ripple of heat ignited inside of my belly.

Johnny might be taller and ripped to within an inch of his life, and Hugh and Patrick might resemble Josh Hartnett and Ryan Phillippe with finely cut, washboard abs, but I swear I'd never seen anything quite like Gerard Gibson.

He was built and broad, with gloriously sun-kissed skin and the most amazing pearly-white smile. His eyes were like pools of gray marble you could fall into, and he was just so downright *snuggly*.

When we were little, our mothers used to refer to him as a little cherub because he was adorably chubby with blond hair and big ole gray eyes.

And sure, he was big and strong now, with muscles in all the right places, but there still was a slight softness to his physique that made him just that little bit more human.

Unlike the rest of the boys in our group, Gerard wasn't afraid to break his diet or skip the gym if he felt inclined. He did what he wanted to do when he wanted to do it and made no qualms about it.

Cheat meals and skipped gym sessions aside, he had the best ass of all the boys. Hands down, there was no competition. Gerard Gibson could fill a pair of Calvin Klein boxer shorts better than any other boy at Tommen.

Johnny, Hugh, and Patrick were all backs in rugby, which meant they needed speed and agility. On the contrary, Gerard played the position of flanker in the forwards, where physical dominance was far more vital than speed. On the team, he was a glorified battering ram and had the stocky build to match the job.

Honestly, I knew I might be biased, but Johnny Kavanagh's impressive eight-pack or Patrick Feely's adorable smile didn't hold a flame to this boy.

Not in my eyes, at least.

Because this boy had always been my favorite boy.

My favorite friend, person, human, everything.

Even when we were little, and even though he despised it, he would humor me by playing Barbies with me. Sure, he would bring along his action figures and cause as much destruction as possible to my Barbie house, but he still played with me.

It never bothered him when his other friends laughed at him for playing with a girl, and he *never* ignored me.

Not one single time in sixteen years.

Not even when it made him less cool with Hugh and the boys.

It didn't matter to Gerard.

He always made me feel like I was his first priority.

His number one friend.

From Gerard Gibson, I had been given the friendship of a lifetime that consisted of humor, loyalty, comfort, and affection.

It was for those and many other countless reasons that I found myself relentlessly clinging to the hope that we would someday take the next step.

That our friendship would progress to *more*.

Like last night for example. We had spent half of the night up talking, and the entire time I had spent mentally willing him to kiss me, and not because the bottle landed on me in a stupid game when we were kids. Because our first kiss might have been an innocent peck coerced by a spinning bottle, and I wanted more now.

I wanted him to want me, dammit.

The way I wanted him…

"Get back," Johnny warned, using an arm to guard the food from his boisterous buddy. "And put some pants on, will you?"

"I'm only trying to smell it," Gerard argued, leaning over his shoulder.

"Well, don't… Hey, back up. I'm serious, Gibs. Don't stand over an open flame like that. You're going to get your dick splattered with grease, you eejit."

"Aw," I cooed, grinning at the pair of them. "Look at you being all chivalrous protecting your best friend's willy."

"Oh, he's a true blue, alright," Gerard agreed, while he managed to swipe a rasher off the grill. "Always the hero."

"Thief," Johnny grumbled.

Snickering to himself, Gerard stuffed the crispy string of bacon into his mouth before joining me on a nearby log. "How's my little diesel generator?" He slung one big arm over my shoulders and pulled me into his side. "No need to ask if you slept well."

"Me?" I laughed, digging his ribs. "Gerard, you snore so loud it's like a cement mixer going off in bed."

"Nah, babe, that's yourself you're hearing."

"You're both as bad as each other," Johnny chimed in. "Our tent is next to yours. I could hear ye all bleeding night. Like an old married couple. Communicating through snores in your sleep, the pair of ye."

"Hey, don't judge our love language," Gerard shot back with a wolfish grin. "At least we don't keep everyone up fucking each other's brains out."

"Gerard!"

"With feelings," he deftly added, holding a finger up. "Fucking *with* feelings."

"No," Johnny agreed, not missing a beat as he turned the meat once more. "Because you're too busy cracking jokes like a pair of babies."

"At least we're not making babies, lad."

"Sure, Gibs, whatever you say." Rolling his eyes, Johnny let Gerard's teasing go clear over his head like he was immune to his banter. "Call the others, will you? Grub's up."

Twenty minutes later, the entire gang was sitting around the camp, stuffed as baby piglets after devouring Johnny Kavanagh's glorious offerings.

"Hey, guys? If we were in the dark ages, do you think we'd still be friends?"

"Huh?" Patrick mused with a chuckle. "Care to evaluate on that, Baby Biggs?"

"What I mean to say is if we were all cave people and none of today's modern technology existed." I paused to lick a tiny sprinkle of tomato ketchup off my knuckle before continuing. "And Ballylaggin was the village we all came from, do you think our friendship group would form their own tribe?"

"What did you smoke in that tent with him?" my brother accused, narrowing his eyes in suspicion. "Because this is weird, Claire, even for you."

"What?" I laughed. "It's a valid question."

"How in the name of God is that a valid question?"

"Hell yeah, we'd be a tribe," Gerard interrupted, tossing a piece of toast at my brother. "And while the rest of us were out hunting down dinner, you'd be the bitch digging holes for us to shit in."

"More like to bury you in," Hugh shot back with a smirk.

"I think we would be," Shannon offered, still looking a little worse for wear from last night's antics. Lounging on her boyfriend's lap with his hoodie swamping her small frame, she folded the sleeves up absent-mindedly as she spoke. "At least, I would hope to be in your tribe."

I smiled warmly back at her. "Always, chickie."

"I would be a nomad," Lizzie chimed in, taking a bite of her toast. "But I'd pop in every once and a while to visit."

"Oh my god, what are you *eating*?" Katie blurted out of nowhere, causing everyone to turn their attention to where she was looking. Which just so happened to be Lizzie. "What the hell is that on your toast?"

"Marmite," Lizzie drawled slowly, taking another bite.

Katie gaped in horror. "That's so wrong!"

"Maybe for you."

"Why don't you try something normal instead?"

"And what's your definition of 'normal'?"

"I don't know." Katie smiled. "Jam, or marmalade, or chocolate spread?"

Lizzie's eyes narrowed and my butt cheeks began to sweat.

Uh-oh.

Code red, I tried to send a telepathic warning to my brother's girlfriend. *Code red. Code red. Retreat now, dammit!*

"And why would I want to do that?" Lizzie asked in an icy tone. "When I *like* marmite?"

"Uh…I don't know," Katie mumbled, withering under Lizzie's forceful stare. "It was just a suggestion. Sorry."

"If I wanted suggestions from people, I would ask my actual friends," Lizzie bit out.

"Stop," Hugh intervened, taking the brunt of Lizzie's glare and meeting it head-on with one of his own. "She didn't mean any harm."

"Jesus," Pierce chuckled, clearly trying to break the tension. "Talk about becoming what you eat." Reaching over, he ruffled his girlfriend's hair. "Don't worry, babe, I love eating marmite."

"Ha. Funny," Lizzie drawled, smacking his hand away. "Touch my hair again and lose your fingers."

"I was only joking, Liz. Chill."

"And while you're at it, go fuck yourself."

"Jesus, you clearly can't take a joke anymore."

"Oh, I can take a lot of things, Pierce," Lizzie countered coolly. "I'm just choosing not to take anything from you. Not your jokes. Not your dick. Not your shit… Can you tell where this is leading?"

Oh dear.

Three. Two. One…

"Now, hold the fuck up!"

"Hey, don't talk to her like that."

"Don't defend me. I can speak for myself!"

So much for peace.

What had been a relatively quiet night in camp quickly morphed into a battle-ground before my eyes.

Sighing wearily, I rested my chin on my hand and listened as everyone argued around me. Glancing around, I locked eyes on Shannon and smiled when she offered me a sympathetic wince.

We were in the same boat.

Shan didn't want to be around this crazy drama, either.

Maybe we should make our own tribe and live in the woods.

"Why do you always look so fucking happy," Lizzie accused then, turning her attention on Gerard. "It's nauseating."

"Not half as nauseating as having to look at your sour puss," Gerard shot back, unwilling to back down or give her a pass. "Don't get your knickers in a twist with me because you're having a tiff with Lover Boy."

"Hey," Katie interjected, valiantly stepping in to try to squash their beef before it blew up like it had done a million times before. "Let's be nice today, okay? Sticks and stones, guys."

"Yeah, because stick and stones will break my bones and words will make me starve myself to death." Lizzie narrowed her eyes. "Isn't that how the saying goes?"

"Huh? What are you talking about?" I argued, brows creased in confusion. "It's 'words will never hurt me.'"

Without a word, Katie stood up and walked away from the circle, and then, with a devastated look on his face, Hugh stood up and hurried after her.

"Am I missing something?" I asked, turning to Gerard.

"No fucking clue, Claire-Bear," he replied with a shrug before retraining his attention on Lizzie. "Jesus, you are mean as hell."

"No, asshole," Lizzie snapped back, rising to her feet. "I'm just honest."

"She's not a bad person, guys," Shannon urged from the back seat of Gerard's Ford Focus. The tents had been packed away, the litter had been collected, and a temporary friendship treaty had been signed before everyone left the beach this morning, all going their separate ways until we reunited next week at school. "Hurt people hurt people," Shannon continued. "She's a hurt person. A hurt but very redeemable person."

"Nobody said she was a bad person," I answered, fiddling with the car stereo. "But she definitely pushes boundaries."

"I can agree with that," Shannon offered diplomatically. "But pushing boundaries doesn't make you bad."

"I hear what you're saying, Shan," Johnny added. "But for me, I find it really hard to tolerate Lizzie's behavior when I've seen how you carry yourself." Shifting around in the back seat, he draped a protective arm around her shoulder. "You've been hurt more than anyone I've ever known, and still you spread kindness. You wouldn't harm a fly—and certainly not intentionally."

Shan blushed bright red and ducked her face. "That's not always true."

"Yeah, it is," he countered, tipping her chin up so she looked at him. "Baby, I've watched you get stung by a bee and *not* retaliate."

"Because we need to save the bees!" Shannon urged.

"There it is," he replied, and then caught my gaze in the rearview mirror. "My point is real motion."

"Can we please stop talking about the Viper?" Gerard begged from the driver's seat. "Honestly, lads, I love the three of you, but if ye don't shut the fuck up about that girl, I'm going to open the door of this car and throw myself out."

"Then pull the car over first," Johnny replied. "In fact, do you want to just pull over now and let me drive?"

"Nope, I'm perfectly capable of driving my own car, Jonathan."

"Gibs, lad, you've coasted over the middle line three times already," Johnny tried to coax. "I really think I should drive."

"Alright." Using one hand to steer the car, Gerard reached behind him with his free hand and held his thumb up in challenge. "Fight me for it."

Johnny laughed. "By *thumb* wrestling you?"

"Are you scared you'll lose?"

"Get ready to be a back-seat bitch, Gibs." Assuming position, Johnny linked hands with Gerard and smirked. "One, two, three, four, I declare a thumb war."

"Five, six, seven, eight, I use this hand to masturbate."

"Gerard," I yelped at the same time Shannon choked out, "Gibsie!"

"And that's the end of the thumb war," Johnny muttered, abruptly dropping Gerard's hand. He wiped his hand off his shorts and shuddered. "You win."

"Who's the back-seat bitch now?" Gerard laughed, cranking up the volume of the stereo. The Offspring's "Original Prankster" blasted from the speakers, causing Gerard to bop his head like a madman, while Johnny and Shan clung to their seats in terror. I wasn't scared, though. I trusted this boy with my life. Gerard wouldn't kill me. After all, he'd promised to marry me before we both died.

Thoroughly engrossed in his drum pattern, Gerard slapped his hands against the steering wheel of his Focus, while he sang at the top of his lungs about knocking down walls.

"Lad, shut the fuck up," Johnny strangled out from the back seat when Gerard slowed at the traffic lights to serenade an elderly lady standing at the zebra crossing.

"You little hooligan," the old lady shouted back at him, shaking her fist.

"Oh my god," I laughed, twisting sideways in my seat just as the lights went green and Gerard floored it. "She's still waddling after us."

"Maybe she wants me," he shot back, winking at me.

I waggled my brows. "Maybe she needs to get in line."

"Gibs, slow the bleeding car down!" Johnny barked as he placed a protective hand over Shan's middle. "If you kill me, I swear to Christ, I'll come back and kill you!"

"How can you come back to kill me if you're already dead?"

"Where there's a will there's a relative," Johnny shot back, draping a protective arm over his girlfriend. "Trust me, Gibs, I'd find a way."

10

Back to Tommen

GIBSIE

"Now, Johnny pet, I've put a mixture of muffins and cakes in the basket, plenty for everyone, and don't forget to tell your mother to give me a call. I need the dates for the children's birthdays," Mam said on Thursday morning when Johnny stopped by to pick me up for school.

By the time I made it down the staircase to intercept her, she had already cornered my best friend in the front hallway. "I've made every one of your birthday cakes from the age of twelve and I plan to do the same for the Lynch children," Mam continued to say as she handed my best friend a gigantic picnic basket full of goods from the bakery. "She's a mighty bit of stuff is your mother."

"She's a keeper alright," Johnny agreed with a polite nod. "And thanks a million, Sadhbh. Ma will be delighted. I'll tell her to give you a buzz. She was saying that she wanted to bring you over for coffee soon."

"Oh, that would be lovely," Mam replied with a beaming smile. "I'm looking forward to meeting the newest members of the Kavanagh clan."

"The youngest two are worth meeting," I tossed out, bouncing off the last step. "But the middle fella is a demon."

"Alright, Gibs?" Johnny smirked, attention flicking to me. "Looking sharp, lad."

"Alright, Kav." I winked. "Right back at ya."

"Oh, good, you found your uniform," Mam said, retraining her entire focus on me. "Sweet Jesus, would you look at the state of you." Catching ahold of my necktie, the woman all but strangled me to death in her attempt to make me look presentable. "Now." Admiring her handiwork, she patted me down pulling and probing at the collar until she was satisfied. "You're growing more handsome by the day, Bubba."

"I know," I agreed with a wolfish grin. "I'm lovely to look at, aren't I?"

"Come on, Bubba," Johnny drawled, tone laced with sarcasm as he retreated in the direction of his car, armed with a wicker basket containing what I knew was a mountain of freshly baked goodies.

"You'll make sure Edel gets the basket, won't you, Johnny?" Mam asked, following us out to the car. "And whatever you do, don't let that son of mine anywhere near those muffins. You know what he's like with chocolate. The poor child can't control himself."

That was the thing about my mother. She might have horrible taste in men, not to mention a poorly angled moral compass when it came to upholding marital vows, but she had a heart of gold.

Contrary to my feelings toward anything with the last name Allen, I had a good relationship with my mam. I loved the woman, and I knew she loved me.

Mam seemed to know how to manage me by giving me both the space I needed when my mind went dark and the concessions required when I lost my head and screwed up. She understood that I had issues hanging over my head since childhood that I was trying to deal with myself, and she never overstepped or pushed me for more. She handled me the way I needed her to, and it was what worked for us.

"Will do, Sadhbh," Johnny replied politely, placing the basket in the boot of his car, along with a mountain of other crap. "Thanks a million."

"And you'll keep an eye on him for me at school, won't you, love?"

"Always."

"Good boy, Johnny."

"*Good boy, Johnny.*" Rolling my eyes, I tossed my bags into the boot and turned back to my mother. "Keep an eye on me? What the fuck, Mam? Am I three years old again?"

"Language, Bubba."

"Apologies, Mother." My attention flicked to the tiny brunette leaning against the passenger door when we reached Johnny's Audi, and my heart softened.

"Hi, Gibs."

"Little Shannon." I smiled. "How's my second favorite girl in the world?" She was looking a hell of a lot more put together than last weekend. Hungover at the beach and puking her guts up. "All set for fifth year?"

"Sufficiently terrified," she admitted with a nervous laugh. "And I guess we'll soon see if I'm ready or not, huh?"

"You've got this, little fighter," I encouraged, ruffling her hair when she walked over. "You're going to make this school year your bitch."

"Damn straight she is." Without a hint of hesitation, my bulldozer of a best friend hooked an arm around his girlfriend and pulled her close. "You've got this, Shan," he whispered, bending low enough to press a kiss to the top of her head. "And you've got me."

"Yeah." Releasing a shaky breath, she snaked her arm around his waist and smiled up at him. "I do."

I knew from the very beginning that what Johnny had with Shannon was permanent. I'd never seen a fella plagued more by his feelings than Johnny. He loved the bones of that girl and, yeah, it took him his usual amount of time to predict, ponder, panic, and finally process his feelings, but he had. Once his mind was set, it was a done deal.

Shannon Lynch was his endgame, and Johnny Kavanagh was hers.

Because when Johnny executed his decision, that was it. He didn't change his mind and he didn't flee I'd never seen that level of commitment from anyone, let alone someone so young, but that was Johnny. He was commitment personified. Dedication was his middle name, and he didn't go back on his word.

That's why it had hurt him so much last year when Cormac fucked him over with Bella. Because he could never do that to a friend, so it was impossible for him to conceive such a betrayal.

It wasn't the way he was programmed.

That's why he was my best friend, and I could die on a hill of fealty to him.

Because it would be returned tenfold.

After all, it was his arrival in Ballylaggin that I credited with saving my life. If he hadn't walked into my classroom that day, if he hadn't offered me that chance to reinvent myself, then I honestly didn't know where I would have ended up.

Yeah, we had shits and giggles, and banter galore, but when the cards were on the table, he had my back, and I had his. There was a permanence to that kind of friendship that soothed something deep inside of me.

I wanted to be that self-assured, but I wasn't programmed the same way he was. I didn't think like Cap or move like him. I was too impulsive and loose-lipped to ever be in control of my emotions like he was.

Unlike Johnny, rugby wasn't the be-all and end-all of my world. I played because it was fun. It was a bonus that I happened to be good at it. All my friends were playing so I joined in. What the hell else was I supposed to do at lunchtime and on the weekends? Besides, it got me out of class on numerous occasions throughout the school year. The fact that I was better than most was a nice bonus.

Apparently, physical activities were my strong point, which was a blessing considering I sure as shit wasn't going to win any awards with books.

I wanted to be smart like the rest of them. To hand in my homework and not sweat half my body weight out for fear of being called in class to read out loud or listen to the usual "Your writing is illegible" spiel. Like I didn't already know it. It was illegible because I couldn't fucking spell so it was easier to scribble the words out and make it look so messy that the teachers didn't call on me.

My thoughts weren't as clear as his, and my future wasn't set in stone. It was blurred and changing every day. I didn't know my own mind because I was afraid of it. To be in my head too much. To think too much.

So, I didn't.

I didn't think.

I refused to dwell on the past that made it hard for me to plan for the future. Because I had a feeling that in order to thrive in the future, a person had to put to bed their past.

That wasn't something I could do right now.

It wasn't something I could contemplate facing.

"What about you?" Shannon asked, snapping me back to the present. "Are you ready for sixth year?"

"You know me, little Shannon," I replied, winking when Johnny opened the passenger door for her. "I was born ready."

"Enjoy your first day, son," Keith said, joining my mother on the footpath a few moments later, coffee cup in hand. "Remember what we said about knuckling down."

An uneasy feeling settled inside of me, watching him talk to my friends. Repressing the urge to scream *I'm not your son* for the millionth goddamn time, I swallowed down my bitterness, slapped on a smile for my friends' sakes, and said, "Will do, Fa."

Mam beamed at me, thinking the word Fa was a term of endearment for the man she'd thrust into my life when I was six. In her mind, Fa was short for father. In mine, it was short for *fucking asshole*.

"How did the summer campaign go for you, Johnny?" Keith asked, steering his attention to my friend. "I heard you were offered one hell of a contract up the country."

"It was a productive campaign," Kav, ever the professional, answered in that usual tone of voice he used for reporters and media. Polite but distant. Humble but self-assured. "And nothing is set in stone yet. I still have my final year of school to complete before any decisions are made."

"But you'll eventually turn professional?"

"Like I said." Johnny glanced back at his girl before adding, "Nothing's set in stone yet."

"Well, you must have made some impression on the coaches if they wanted to sign you up early."

"I had an adequate tour."

"He was amazing," Shannon piped up from the passenger seat.

"He was fucking epic," I was quick to add, clapping my best friend's shoulder before yanking the back door open and climbing inside. "He outperformed everyone."

"That's a bold statement." Keith's brows shot up. "You have a lot of faith in your friend there, son."

"Yeah, I do," I shot back, leaning out the open window, because in all fairness, this was my best friend we were talking about. He had complete control over his body and mind, and it was something rare. Something to be envious of. To have that much self-belief. To be so self-controlled, so headstrong and fully controlled. To know your mind and go for it without doubting yourself.

Johnny Kavanagh was, at eighteen years old, one of the best rugby players in the country, and I had no doubt that given a few years, he would raise those stakes to be among the best in the world. He was *that* talented.

"My son Mark played outside center for Tommen back in the day," the asshole himself continued to say, bragging and boring us to tears. "Of course, he didn't turn professional like yourself. Went down the finance route instead."

"Probably for the best," I taunted, struggling to keep my smile in check. "All things considered." *You know, since the academy frowns on rapists that drive teenage girls to suicide and all that jazz.*

"My spin is gone. My spin is gone!" a familiar voice yelped from across the street. "Don't leave without me!"

Craning my head around, I watched as whirlwind of blond curls came hobbling down the driveway of the Biggs house, with a juice carton in one hand and a high-heeled shoe in the other.

Yeah, a high-heeled shoe as in singular. "Johnny, Gerard!" Because the other was on her right foot. "Wait for me, guys!"

"Good timing," Johnny told Claire, catching her schoolbag midair when she flung it at him.

"Oh my god, you're a lifesaver," she replied before diving into the back seat. "Hugh, the turncoat, left me behind."

"Claire-Bear." The minute my eyes landed on her, I felt instant relief. Like the button on a skintight pair of jeans had been popped, giving me space to breathe again.

"Gerard." Her smile was wide, genuine, and needed so much more than she would ever know. Leaning across the seats, she smacked a sticky, lip-gloss-tainted kiss to my cheek before turning her attention to Shannon.

"Morning, bestie," she cooed, leaning between the seats to give her an affectionate squeeze. "Oh my god, you smell *amazing*!"

"Thanks," Shannon replied, cheeks blushing. "It's the perfume Johnny brought me back from camp."

"Well, it's working for you, girl." Flopping back down next to me, Claire reached around for the seat belt, taking the middle seat, much to my delight. "This is our year, Shan. I can feel it in my bones! Autumn is a such a good season for me."

"You really think so?"

"Oh yeah," Claire cheered, fist-bumping both of us. "Here's to friendship, fifth year, falling leaves, and freaky Halloween costumes!"

"Jesus," I groaned, glum at the thought of the impending school year. "How is the summer over already?"

"No clue."

Tossing Claire's bag in the boot to join the rest of ours, Johnny rounded the car and politely waved off my mother before climbing into the driver's seat. Leaning across the console, he kissed his girlfriend before turning the key in the ignition.

The minute the engine roared to life it was accompanied by the sound of Fort Minor's "Remember the Name" as it blasted from his impressive car stereo.

Kav's playlist was always set in beast mode. It didn't matter what day of the week it was or what the occasion was, the music he played was ferocious, aggressive, and highly motivating. Seriously, after spending too long in his car or listening to his iPod, I felt like running laps and swinging fists.

The music he listened to was in direct contrast to the mild-mannered persona he presented to the world. Of course, I knew he had the ability to be a fucking demon given the chance, but the lad was just so restrained.

"I can't put my finger on it, but there's something about that man that just rubs me the wrong way," Johnny said, lowering the volume on the stereo.

That would be your good judgment, lad.

"I know he's married to your ma, Gibs, and I mean no offense," he tossed over his shoulder. "Because Keith's always been sound to me, but there's just something…"

"Sleazy about him?" Claire chimed in, adjusting her seat belt.

"Sleazy," I chuckled, draping my arm around her shoulder. "Good one, Claire-Bear."

"I know, right?" she replied, beaming back at me.

"*Yes*," Johnny said in an enthusiastic tone from the front seat. "Sleazy. That's the word. I was going to go with *off*, but sleazy hits the nail on the head."

"That's because he's a cheater-cheater, pumpkin eater."

"Claire!"

"What?" Cackling in amusement, Claire looped her arm through mine and rested her head on my shoulder, causing the smell of her strawberry shampoo to attack my senses. *Fucking perfect.* "Wife stealers are sleazy slimeballs."

"Oh my god!" Shannon squealed. "You can't say that."

"Why not?" she scoffed without a hint of remorse. "It's true."

See, this is why I loved Claire Biggs.

She saw through all the bullshit and facades.

"Ah, he's not the worst of them," I threw out there, because agreeing with Claire would open a can of worms that I had zero intention of tending to. Also, I happened to be sitting in the same car as the girl who had endured sixteen years of living under the same roof as a blood-thirsty murderer. Compared to Teddy Lynch, Keith was a lamb. *Perspective.*

"Oh my god, guys, I almost forgot!" Yelping in excitement, Shannon twisted around and thrust her phone in our faces. "You need to see this picture."

"Well, would you look at that," I whistled, snatching up the phone to get a better look at the chubby, blond-haired infant wrapped in a blue blanket and filling the screen of her phone. "I helped make him."

"You drove them to the hospital to have the baby, Gibs. Don't lose the run of yourself," Johnny filled in, pressing a kiss to Shannon's hand before settling it on his lap with his. "He's a gorgeous little fella, isn't he?"

"Drove the horror train, more like," I muttered under my breath, still feeling slightly traumatized from the noises that had come out of Aoife's mouth when she was in the throes of labor the other night. Yeah, the very night I had the misfortune of coming achingly close to seeing Joey's spawn being calved.

"Shut the front door!" Claire squealed, snatching the phone out of my hands to get a better look. "Look at that itty-bitty baby Joey."

"Joe said he has my nose," Shannon gushed proudly, clasping her hands together. "He's so beautiful, guys. And I know I haven't met him yet, but I swear that I love him to death already."

"Jesus." I blew out a breath and repressed a shudder. "I still can't believe Joey's a daddy."

"He's always been one of those, lad," Johnny said.

"True that, Kav."

"Another Lynch boy."

"He's not a Lynch, he's a Joey."

"News flash, Joey's a Lynch, Gibs."

"Nah, he's a Joey. Like Bono. He doesn't need a last name. Iconic."

"I think the term you're searching for is infamous."

"Aww." Claire continued to croon and coo at the screen of the phone. "I want one."

"You want one of those things?" I gaped at her. "Are you feeling okay?"

"Me too," Shannon admitted with a wistful sigh. "I want two."

"Two's a good number," Johnny agreed. "But three's better."

"Jesus Christ, it's contagious!" Snatching the phone out of Claire's hand, I tossed it back to Shannon. "Here, put that phone away before that baby's picture causes an epidemic."

11

I Predict a Riot

CLAIRE

OKAY, SO MAYBE I JUMPED THE GUN A LITTLE WHEN I PREDICTED THIS WOULD BE Shannon's and my year best year to date. Or heck, maybe I jinxed it. Either way, sitting across the lunch table from my sobbing best friend was not how I anticipated spending our first day back at Tommen.

We'd been back at school less than half a day, and already one of our lunch table associates had fallen prey to Mr. Twomey's dreaded suspension wrath.

Not only had Joey Lynch been suspended for pummeling Ronan McGarry, but Tadhg Lynch had taken a rap on the knuckles for his role in the altercation, too.

Apparently, Ronan was suicidal enough to call Aoife Molloy a slut to a hothead like Joey Lynch's face. Like *come on*. What the hell did he think would happen when he called the newly appointed mother of a man's child that kind of name?

Apparently, Mr. Twomey gave him a *two-week* suspension. I mean, two weeks was unheard of at Tommen. The worst I could remember since my being here was one week tops. The beating Ronan took was a severe one.

To top off all the Lynch sibling drama, Ronan had drippled blood all over my new school shoes, Katie had been sent home with period pains, and then Lizzie and Feely, of all people, had the weirdest argument at the beginning of break, which had resulted in Lizzie storming off.

Clearly Hugh was more in the loop than I was regarding what had gone down between our friends because he'd gone after Lizzie and had somehow managed to persuade her to return. She was back at the lunch table, sitting next to my brother in the chair Katie had vacated, and hadn't spoken a single word to anyone.

I wondered if Lizzie and Patrick's argument had anything to do with what Hugh said about getting Patrick to talk to Liz. Either way, all three of them were in a heated stare-down across from me.

Meanwhile, Shannon was so distraught over her brothers' suspension—plural— that Johnny had spent the last ten minutes whispering words of what I assumed were comfort in her ear, in between peppering kisses to her face.

When he tucked her hair behind her ear to kiss her temple and then trailed his thumb over the little dimple in her chin before pressing a kiss to the tip of her nose, I audibly crooned. "Aww!"

I loved temple kisses. Forehead kisses, too. And nuzzling noses were the cream of the crop. Those intimate forms of affection were my favorite, and my bestie received an abundance of both on the daily from her *lover*.

"It'll be grand, chickie," I said, trying to appease when I saw a tear trickle down her cheek. "Hey, don't cry." Reaching across the table, I snatched her hand up in mine, feeling a huge swell of sympathy for my timid friend. "Mr. Twomey did Joey a favor if you think about it." Joey clearly didn't want to be at school to begin with. His girlfriend was still in the hospital, having just given birth to their son. "At least now he gets to spend some quality time with Aoife and baby AJ."

"Exactly," Johnny agreed, giving me a grateful look. "You know his mind wasn't here anyway. He'll have a couple of weeks off to spend with his family and then he'll be back."

"Cap, you might want to tell your old man to keep an eye on Twomey." Arriving back to the table with a large wicker basket in hand, Gerard walked straight over to where I was sitting and dropped the basket down on the table in front of me. "I just saw your mam leaving the office with the Lynch brothers," he said, flipping the lid of the basket open. "And let me tell you that cranky old bastard watched her ass the entire time."

"Oooh…muffins!" I rubbed my hands together with glee when my eyes landed on the fantastic array of baked goodies, courtesy of Gibson's Bakery. "Gimme, gimme."

"Mammy K's here?" Robbie Mac piped up from further up the table. "Was she wearing the white pants suit? Oh fuck, Gibs, tell me she was wearing the white pants suit."

"The one that shows her thong print?" Pierce asked, reaching over the table to swipe a muffin out of the basket.

"That's the one," Robbie confirmed with a groan. "Jesus, that woman is immortal. Doesn't look a day over thirty-five."

"You'll be wearing the imprint of my foot up your hole if you talk about my ma like that," Johnny warned, bristling. "Pack it in."

"Hey, don't look at me," Gerard huffed. "I wasn't looking."

"Bullshit," one of the team fake-coughed, causing everyone else at the table to erupt in laughter.

"Bleeding perverts, the lot of ye."

"Boys are dogs," I groaned, momentarily standing for Gerard to sit down, and then unceremoniously sinking back down on his lap.

"It's true," Gerard agreed, reaching into his pocket to retrieve a set of car keys. "And before you even start on the lecture train, just stop," he added, tossing the keys at Johnny before reaching around me and grabbing a muffin. "I'm an emotional eater."

"Oh no, no, no, no," Hugh said with a humorless laugh as he pointed a finger at me. "There's a spare seat at the table now that Lynchy's gone. No need to sit on anyone's lap, baby sister."

"I'm not sitting on anyone's lap," I countered with a grin. "I'm sitting on Gerard's lap."

"That's me, by the way," Gerard taunted, snaking an arm around my waist, while he waved his free hand around over his head. "Hi."

"Ooh, ooh, please let me have a bite," I begged, catching ahold of Gerard's wrist when he raised the most beautiful-looking double chocolate chip muffin toward his mouth.

"Nuh-uh, bite with your mouth, babe, not with your hands," he teased, snatching the muffin back when I tried to swipe it. "Open wide."

"Claire." Lizzie broke her silence with a hiss. "Don't let him *feed* you."

"Too…ate…" I mumbled between bites. "Sorry…ugh…"

"Gibs!" Hugh joined in on the judgment. "Stop feeding my sister!"

"What?" Gerard replied, holding his hand to catch the crumbs that didn't make my mouth, while he fed me another bite of his muffin. "She wants it."

"Oh, leave it alone." Feely laughed. "What harm are they causing to anyone?"

"Pa, he *just* put his fingers in her mouth."

"No, he didn't. He put a piece of muffin in her mouth," he replied calmly. "You're overreacting."

"I bet that's not all he puts in your sister's mouth, Hughie," Danny called out, causing most of the team to laugh and snicker around us.

"A lot you'd know about putting anything in girls' mouths." Lizzie was quick to defend me. "Get back in your box, asshole."

"Doesn't look like she has a gag reflex," Pierce goaded the boys by adding. "Lucky bastard."

"Hey! Asshole!" Gerard deadpanned, turning his attention to his teammates. "Don't even go there."

"Hey, Baby Biggs," another one goaded. "Want to come sit on my lap and I'll feed you something a lot more satisfying?"

"Cocktease."

"You're a dead man, Callaghan!" Hugh snarled, shoving his chair in his rush to get out of his chair to defend my honor.

The move was a sweet one but unnecessary because Gerard had beaten him to it.

96

"The fuck did you say about my girl?" He was on his feet and lunging across the lunch table before I had a chance to register that I was no longer sitting on his lap, but the seat he had vacated. "If you ever speak about her like that again, I'll rip your fucking guts out your asshole and smear them all over your face!"

In this moment, Gerard reminded me a lot of one of those dormant volcanoes people travel to see because they look so beautiful and assume they're harmless, but raise the temperature of their core and said volcano became truly lethal.

All it took was one sexual innuendo at my expense to flip the trip-switch inside of his brain, causing him to erupt on his teammates in the middle of the lunch hall at Tommen.

"I was only messing," Danny wheezed, clearly struggling to breathe with the hand clamped around his throat that was cutting off his airways.

"Follow me, Shan," Johnny commanded, shoving out of his chair. "Come on, baby. Quickly." Tucking his girlfriend under his arm, Johnny led her out of the lunch hall and out of harm's way.

"Whoa, Gerard," I yelped, making a beeline for the boy who had not only dragged his teammate onto the lunch table, but was straddling his chest, while his fists swung into said teammate's face with a flourish.

"Gibs, don't," Pierce commanded, trying to pull him off Danny, only to be rewarded with a headbutt to the face. "Jesus Christ, Gibs." Wiping the blood trickling from his nose with his sleeve, Pierce shoved Gerard hard from behind, causing him to lose his balance and stumble. "You broke my fucking nose!"

"Hey—" Hugh barked, diving over the table and headfirst into the fray, while Lizzie remained motionless in her seat. "Keep your hands off my friend, asshole."

"He broke my goddamn nose, Hugh!"

"Pity he didn't break your neck while he was at it!"

"What's your problem, Biggs?"

"You're my problem, O'Neill!"

"Why me? Gibs is the one always stirring the shit pot!"

"Yeah, well, he's family!"

"Fucking do something, lads!" Robbie shouted, catching ahold of Gerard from behind when he lunged for Pierce. That was a bad move that ended with all five boys crashing over chairs before landing on the floor.

Seeing his best friends outnumbered three to two, Patrick Feely rewrapped his sandwich in tinfoil before rising to his feet. "Fuck my life," he muttered before joining the rumble on the floor. "Someone find Johnny."

Several other members of the rugby team joined in then, and I wasn't sure if any of them were truly trying to break up the fight. It sure looked like they were all enjoying beating seven kinds of shit out of each other. Fists were flying and blood was pumping, and they all seemed to *love* it.

Mr. Twomey and several other teachers arrived on the scene, but they were no match for twenty-plus brick-shithouse-built, testosterone-fueled teenage boys.

Too sensible to jump into the action, but too pumped to do nothing, I discreetly stamped on Robbie Mac's hand when he rolled close to where I was standing. *Ha.* Served him right for calling me a cocktease.

"That's enough," Mr. Twomey was roaring as he managed to separate two players on the team from the year below me. "I'm warning the lot of you!"

The older boys didn't bat an eyelid. Instead, they continued their hunt for blood-lust, by beating and pummeling each other viciously.

"I said that's enough," Mr. Twomey bellowed. "You have five seconds to pack it in, or I'm calling the Gards and telling them to take every last one of you to the barracks!"

"Hey!" Johnny roared, stalking back into the lunch hall minus Shannon. "He said that's enough," he snarled in a voice that was truly terrifying. "Pack it in!"

Marching right in, Johnny reached into the biggest of the pileups and dragged a deranged-looking Gerard out from the bottom. "Pack it the fuck in," Johnny commanded, keeping one arm wrapped around Gerard's waist.

"He started it!"

"Back the fuck up, Danny," Johnny warned, pointing a finger at the boy who was still trying to goad Gerard into fighting. "We both know what'll happen if I let him go."

Whoa.

Seriously, I'd never heard him sound so furious.

"Sit your holes down," he warned, using his free hand to shove Danny away from Gerard. "*Now!*"

His tone was so full of authority in this moment that I found myself dropping into my chair for fear of getting in trouble. Thankfully, I wasn't the only one to feel the pressure of the alpha's siren. One by one, his pack untangled themselves and returned to the infamous rugby table, looking bruised, bloody, and a lot worse for wear.

"Is this what I came back to Tommen for?" Johnny demanded, still keeping a firm hold on his beta. "A bunch of jumped-up little pricks fighting with each other?"

"No, Cap."

"Sorry, Johnny, lad."

"You should be sorry," Johnny sneered, tone laced with disgust as he eyed his teammates with distain. "Bleeding disgraces, the lot of ye."

"That asshole started it," Danny snapped, pointing a finger at Gerard, who had thankfully managed to calm himself down. Being around Johnny had that effect on him. "We were having the craic and he flipped the fuck out."

"You know what you did," Gerard shot back, shoulders bristling with tension. "You know what you said about her."

"It was banter, Gibs."

"Well, your banter is *shit*, Danny."

"Jesus Christ, I was trying to rise Biggs. She's his sister."

"Yeah, well, a little word of warning: you fuck with her, you fuck with me—"

"Listen, I don't give a shite who started it. I'm finishing it," Johnny barked, tone leaving no room for argument. "Whatever happened, forget it. It's done with. It's over. It ends *now*. Does anyone have an issue with that? Anyone still feeling the need to throw down? Because I'll go outside right now with any bleeding bollox on my team that has an issue to clear up."

"No, Cap."

"No," Johnny replied coolly. "Didn't think so."

"I'll take it from here, Johnny," Mr. Twomey interrupted.

I watched as Johnny's jaw ticked, but he didn't react negatively to his dismissal. Instead, he offered our principal a clipped nod before rounding the table to return to his throne. Taking Gerard with him, Johnny pushed him into Shannon's usual chair and sank down beside him, keeping his arm resting on his friend's shoulders the entire time.

"Now, I want every member of the rugby team involved in this altercation to remain seated," Mr. Twomey instructed, phone in hand. "Everyone else can return to your classrooms. Now."

12
Push-Ups and Penance

GIBSIE

"It's your fault."

"It's *your* fault."

"You started it."

"No, *you* started it."

"You took the first swing."

"Because you overstepped."

"I was having the craic."

"You were insulting my girl."

"She's not your girl, you spanner. She's my sister."

"Stay out of this, Hugh. I'm defending my intended's honor."

"Gibs, I swear to god if you don't pack that intended bullshit in—"

"Gibson. Callaghan. Biggs!" Coach barked, dragging my attention away from the heated conversation I was attempting to have with the two assholes on either side of me. "If you're able to talk, you're not working hard enough!"

"When can we stop, Coach?" Pierce called out from further up the line, writhing in pain as he tried to maintain his position. "I'm in a lot of pain here."

"We're all in pain, dickhead." Murph, another one of our teammates, bit out. "But some of us don't deserve it."

"Pain?" Coach laughed humorlessly. "I'll give you pain, you little bollox."

Pain was an understatement for the suffering Coach was inflicting on us. Twenty-five minutes in the plank position was enough to kill a horse. A few hours in the barracks would have been an easier punishment to take.

"Please, Coach. School finished an hour ago."

"I'll keep you here all night if you don't shut your holes and concentrate!"

"I hate you all," Feely muttered, a few bodies up.

"Jesus, I can't," Robbie Mac groaned, collapsing in a heap on the grass. "My arms are bolloxed, Coach. I'm dying here."

"Back in the plank position!" Blowing on his whistle like a demented lunatic,

Coach marched up and down the line, using his foot to shove any rogue asses back into position. "I want you eating grass and puking it back up, ye little bolloxes!"

Another five minutes ticked by achingly slowly before the sound of that god-awful whistle pierced the air again. "Right. I want everyone on their feet. Shake it out and then give me two hundred suicides."

"Ah, Jesus, Coach."

"I have homework."

"I have work."

"Please, God, no!"

"Make that three hundred!" Another sharp whistle sounded. "And if you're all still breathing afterward, we'll wrap up this team bonding with a technical session."

"Move, your legs, Gibs."

"I *am*, Cap."

"No, you're not."

"Yeah, I fucking am."

"Your frame is completely stagnant, lad," he continued to complain. "Lift him higher."

"Easy for you to say, back-bitch," I bit out, heaving against the pressure in my shoulders as I tried to hold my form and not drop my teammate, who I was attempting to thrust into the air for a practiced line-out.

"Don't drop me, Gibs," Danny called out. "My body's in bits."

"I've got you, lad," I grunted, all earlier issues well and truly sweated out of my system.

Ironic that the teammate I was trying to protect in the air was the same one I'd been tearing strips out of earlier.

"Extend your arms, Gibs," Johnny continued to instruct.

"I'm *trying*," I huffed. "When's the last time you had two hundred pounds of prick on your shoulders?"

"I carry your drunk ass around most weekends," came Johnny's sarcastic response and I thought I might scream.

"Fucking backs," I grumbled to myself. "You're all shit and show, hunting the glory, while us forwards do all the hard slog."

"Hard slog? You've never seen a hard day's work in your life, lad."

"I'll have you know that I spent most of my summer helping Mam at the bakery."

"Yeah," Hugh goaded, joining the conversation. "And you have the gut to show for it."

"Call me fat one more time and I'll sit on you," I warned, outraged. "I mean it, Hugh. It's called being big-boned. And yeah, so I've put on a few pounds over the summer. Big deal. I can lose the weight, but you can't lose that face, lad."

"Did you just call me *ugly*?"

"Did you just call me *fat*?"

"Pack it in, will ye. Bunch of bleeding babies," Johnny instructed, while turning his attention back to me. "Your weight isn't the problem here, Gibs. It's the smoking."

"I told you that I've cut down."

"I'm not interested in anything less than zero a day."

"What shit craic."

"Don't twist my melon."

"Don't put your melon in my face to twist."

"Focus!"

"Hold up—what the fuck is a melon?"

"He's referring to his brain, Gibs."

"Melons are brains?"

"Yours certainly is."

"I take offense to that."

"Jaysus, I'm surrounded by idiots."

"Okay, now switch," Coach Mulcahy interrupted with a bark. "Four take Seven and start again. Two, I want a clean ball. None of this crooked bullshit."

"Coach, he's not ready for the lift," Johnny began to say, but was cut off when Coach turned his glare on him. "Who's calling the shots here, Thirteen?"

Jaw ticking, Johnny retreated with more grace than I would have been able to. "You, sir."

"That's right," Coach replied, dusting the metaphorical feather in his cap at publicly scolding *our* cap. "You had a good summer with the Irish squad, but don't get too big for your boots, Thirteen."

"Too big for his boots?" I shook my head. "His boots shouldn't be anywhere near this shithole pitch. He's too fucking good for us, and you're just jealous."

"Are you questioning my authority, Seven?" Coach narrowed his eyes. "Did you not get enough grass in your lungs when you were in the plank?"

"Actually, I've built up quite an impressive tolerance to grass in my lungs," I shot back with a grin. "The trick is little and often. Every Friday night works best for me."

"Jesus, Gibs," Johnny groaned. "You just can't help yourself, can you?"

"Take a walk, Gibson," Coach roared, blowing his whistle. "And don't step foot on my pitch until you have an attitude adjustment."

"Woo-hoo!"

Thoroughly delighted with myself, I dropped Danny like a sack of spuds and hauled ass toward freedom.

"You know you just gave the lazy fucker what he wanted."

"Language!"

"Why does he get to leave early?"

"Less of the backchat, Ten."

"But he started the fight."

"Dammit, Gibson! I've changed my mind. Get back here!"

"La, la, la." Plugging my ears with my fingers, I ran faster than I had all training and legged it to safety. "I can't hear a word of it, lads."

When I reached the steps to the P.E. hall, three familiar faces greeted me. "How's my brown-eyed girl?"

"Yay!" Claire squealed, clapping her hands. "Not only did you defend my honor, but you survived Coach's boot camp of punishment to boot." Springing to her feet, she made a beeline for me, not stopping until she had her arms wrapped tightly around my neck. Reaching up on her tippy toes, she pressed a loud, smacking kiss to my cheek. "My hero."

"Nice." I laughed, catching her around the waist. "I'll defend your honor more often if it gets me this kind of attention."

"You didn't need to do it," she hurried to say, expression serious for a beat before a huge smile filled her face. "But it was *so* epic."

"Epic as in sexy?"

"Epic as in chivalrous."

"And sexy?"

"Yes, Gerard, *and* sexy." She laughed, trailing her fingertips over my swollen cheekbone. "Oh, look at your poor face."

"He'll survive," Lizzie grumbled, rising to her feet, bitch mode activated. "Congrats on getting the whole team punished, Thor. You've outdone yourself."

"Always happy to please."

"It wasn't a compliment, asshole—"

"We were watching from the sidelines," Shannon explained, standing up and thankfully interrupting the Viper. "It looked intense out there, Gibs." Chewing on her bottom lip, he glanced toward the pitch and then back to me. "Do you think Johnny's okay? He's still out there running drills."

"Are you kidding me? Cap's loving this." I chuckled, feeling the need to soothe her anxiety. "Boot camp is like an orgasm to his workaholic ass."

"Oh." Her cheeks flushed bright pink with embarrassment, but a smile quickly replaced the concerned look on her face. "Okay. Well, that's…good."

"Can someone explain to me why Joey Lynch got a two-week suspension for hitting one rugby player, yet Thor incites an entire rugby team into brawling and gets off scot-free?" Lizzie demanded, folding her arms across her chest. "Seems to me like the patriarchy is in full working order at Tommen. Rich boys looking after rich boys and all that jazz."

"You tell me, Liz," I shot back, bristling. "Twomey can suspend me if he wants to. You'll hear no complaints from me."

"Except that he won't," she shot back. "Because Tommen protects their precious rugby heads at all costs. Isn't that right, Thor?"

"Guys, come on," Shannon begged. "Please don't fight."

"I'm not fighting, Shannon," Lizzie countered. "I'm stating facts."

"You're instigating an argument." Claire cut in, releasing her hold on me to face her friend. "Stop it."

"You're always taking his side," Lizzie snapped, throwing her hands up. "Every goddamn time, Claire."

"I'm not taking anyone's side," Claire countered in a frustrated tone. "Because there's no side to take here, Liz."

"Yeah, you keep telling yourself that." Roughly shoving past us, Lizzie stormed down the steps of the P.E. hall. "Maybe one day you'll start believing it."

"Lizzie!" both girls called after her, while I mentally sagged in relief at her retreating frame.

It hurt to be around Lizzie, to be the sole soundboard for her pain. It took everything I had inside of me to *not* scream and retaliate with a ferocity that would silence her forever.

Our stories were entangled, and while I felt fucking terrible for all she'd been through, it *wasn't* my fault.

After the rumor went around about her sister's suicide note, I used to hold my breath when I saw her, waiting for her to tell the world the truth. When it didn't happen, I started to suspect that she didn't know the full story.

There was only one person at fault and it sure as shit wasn't me.

I didn't want to fall out with anyone, but I had grown weary of taking the abuse. Of being the punching bag for another person's mistakes. *I* didn't hurt Caoimhe Young. *I* didn't do that. *I* wasn't the one to blame, and somehow I'd managed to become the sole target of her sister's anger and grief.

I had zero plans on participating in this who-had-it-worse argument.

In my eyes, everyone had their own cross to carry. But Lizzie's cross wasn't put there by me. I didn't fucking hurt Caoimhe. She didn't have any of the facts. She wasn't there and she didn't know shit about what went down between them.

I, on the other hand, had the misfortune of having a front-row ticket to the meltdown. To the drama. To the beginning of the end for her sister, and I knew for a fact that Lizzie had put two and two together and come up with five. I didn't say anything because what was the point? She wouldn't believe me anyway. Caoimhe hadn't.

I desperately wanted to silence her with the *truth.*

About the real reason her sister was dead.

About what really happened that night.

But I couldn't because aside from the fact that I had never verbalized the truth to anyone still living on earth, Lizzie would never relent.

She would never say sorry.

She would never stop trying to turn our friends against me.

She would never stop *blaming* me.

Her words were poison, and if she knew my truth and used it against me, I would stop working. I knew I would.

She would use my pain as a bullet and shoot right at my heart.

She would find a way to blame me.

They all would.

That's why she didn't know.

That's why none of them knew.

That's what I had to remember to forget.

"Shannon like the river," a familiar voice called out and all three of us turned to see Johnny, Hughie, and Feely walking toward us.

"Oh, he's not limping, thank god," Shannon whispered to herself before bolting down the steps in the direction of my best friend.

"Ignore Lizzie," Claire instructed, turning to face me. "She's in her own head, Gerard. Nothing she ever says to you is personal."

That's where she was wrong.

It was all personal.

Very personal.

When her hand slipped into mind, I felt that familiar swell of relief. Claire had some magical powers in her touch because I swear to god she made me feel better. Safer. Steady. *Anchored.*

"It's all good, Gerard," she added, smiling up at me. "You're good."

No, I wasn't.

But I could pretend to be.

For her.

13
I'll Give You My Weekends

CLAIRE

"You make it look so easy," I said when Gerard put the final touches on an exquisite-looking chocolate éclair before handing it to me. It was late Saturday evening. He had closed the bakery over two hours ago, but we were still messing around in the empty kitchen, while Gerard trialed new recipes, and I tasted every single one of them. "Oh my god!" I could have wept with joy when I took a bite and the delicious combination of fresh cream and melted chocolate attacked my senses. "So…good!"

He grinned at me. "It's good, huh?"

"Better than good," I agreed between bites. "Gerard, you are seriously talented."

Chuckling softly to himself, he walked over to where I was sitting on the counter and picked me up in one effortless move before setting me back down on my feet. "No asses on the counter, babe."

"Oops," I replied, leaning against the counter instead. "Sorry, Chef." I wasn't. I didn't care, but he was so abnormally responsible when he was at the bakery that I humored him. I knew it had a lot to do with the fact that Gibson's Bakery was one of the few things Gerard had left of his father. It made me happy that Sadhbh had stepped in and kept the bakery running after Joe died. It was one of the few places Gerard still had that hadn't been infected with the Allen stamp. Because this was Gerard's legacy, and it was beautiful to know that he was finally showing an interest in claiming it.

With his blue hairnet on, and an apron that said *Never trust a skinny chef*, he looked ridiculously cute as he washed up at the sink.

"You look adorable."

"You know I love it when you stroke my ego, Claire-Bear, but somehow I don't think calling a seventeen-year-old lad adorable is a compliment."

"It is in my world." Pushing off the counter I was leaning against, I grabbed my coat and bag. "So, listen, I have a bit of a crazy idea to run by you." Shrugging on my coat, I removed the hairnet Gerard had placed on my head the moment I entered the kitchen earlier and smiled up at him. "And it might sound like it's totally out of left field, but I've been thinking about it a lot."

"Sounds like trouble," he mused, rinsing his hands with a towel. "I'm in."

"You don't even know what it is yet." I laughed, hanging my bag off my shoulder. "What if you hate the idea?"

"If it's your idea, then I won't hate it." Removing his apron, he hung it on the hook with the others and snatched his hairnet off. "Besides, you've just given me your entire Saturday by hanging out here and keeping me company at work." He pocketed his wallet and car keys before moving for the light switch. "I can give you my Saturday night."

"Oh yeah?" I replied, tone flirting. "You want to give me your weekend, Gerard Gibson?" Moments later, we were bathed in complete darkness. "Gerard!" I yelped, startled by the sudden blindness even though I knew it was coming.

"I'll give you all my weekends, Claire Biggs," His hand reached for mine, fingers entwining in that familiar way I treasured. "I'll give you my weekdays, too."

"You were right," Gerard declared later that night as we stood side by side, with Gerard in his boxers and me in a T-shirt and knickers. "I hate this idea."

I slipped my hand in his "You can do this."

"No." He shook his head. "I can't."

"You can do anything, Gerard Gibson."

"Most things," he agreed, and it broke my heart when I felt the tremor running up his arm. "But not this."

"Trust me."

"Trusting you isn't the problem here, Claire-Bear." He continued to stare at the giant, oval bathtub in my parents' downstairs bathroom like it was the enemy. "It's the sheer, unadulterated terror that's clawing its way out of my throat that's causing me a problem."

"I know you're scared," I urged, turning to look at him. "And it's okay to be scared, but you need to be able to sit in water before I can teach you how to swim. So, I was thinking the bathtub would be the best place to start. It's private and no one will see you, so you don't have to feel awkward or embarrassed."

"I don't need to learn how to swim," he strangled out, eyes wild and fearful. "Because I have no intention of putting myself in a position where I need to enforce that skill ever again."

"I have so much faith in you, Gerard Gibson." Reaching on my tiptoes, I cupped his face in my hands and stroked his nose with mine. "You *can* do this."

His hands moved to my hips, fingers kneading the fleshy part of my hips as he breathed deeply and slowly, clearly trying to self-regulate. "It's just a bath."

"Yes," I agreed, voice barely more than a whisper as I continued to stroke his cheeks with more affection than was healthy.

His breath fanned my face when he whispered, "And you'll be with me."

"Always," I vowed.

A pained groan escaped him, and he dropped his brow to rest against mine. "I've got this."

"You have," I breathed, shivering from the feel of his hands on my bare skin.

His entire frame was rigid for the longest time, and when he didn't say a word for a solid three minutes, I honestly thought this was as far as he was prepared to go, but then he surprised us both by saying, "Fine. Let's just get this over it."

"You're sure?" I asked warily.

"No, but you are, and that's good enough for me," he replied, sounding just as uncertain. The way he was eyeing the water broke my heart, but I didn't let him see. Instead, I plastered on the brightest smile I could muster and stepped into the tub.

"You've got this," I said, holding a hand out to him. "And you've got me." Always.

His gaze flicked from my outstretched hand to the water lapping at my shins. A long beat of tense silence settled between us before he finally made a move. Gingerly, he stepped into the tub, one foot at a time.

The minute both of his feet were submerged, he exhaled a ragged breath and looked at me in surprise. "I did it."

"You did it." Bursting with pride at his huge, monumental breakthrough, I beamed up at him. "Now, I need you to turn around."

"Turn around?" he repeated uncertainly.

I nodded brightly. "Trust me."

Blowing out a shaky breath, he turned around achingly slowly until his back was facing me. "Good job," I praised, resting my hands on his waist. "This is excellent, Gerard."

Asking Gerard to do this had been an extremely risky move on my behalf, because there was a very big chance that it could have gone the other way. While I couldn't relate to what he had been through, I could relate to the panic. Because I had felt that panic when I was five years old and he disappeared beneath the waves. I'd endured that helpless panic while he was in the water, and for many minutes afterward when they were trying to revive his lifeless body.

The image of seven-year-old Gerard blue and limp lived rent-free in my mind. I rarely suffered from bad dreams or nightmares, but when they came, it was always the fear of losing him twice.

"What now?" he asked.

"Now we sit."

"Nah, I'm good standing, thanks."

Fully expecting my request to be met with refusal, I lowered myself into the tub until I was in a sitting position. "You've got this," I repeated, holding my hands out for him to join me. "I'm right behind you, I promise."

"Why don't we have a shower?" he asked, twisting around to look at me. "I'm good with showers." Sounding panicked, he pointed to the chrome shower fitting on the wall. "I have no fucking problem with showers."

"Because you need to be immersed in the water," I explained patiently, watching as he bounced from foot to foot. The nervous energy emanating from him was stifling, but he had made it further than he ever had in the last ten years, and I was tenacious. "You've got this, Gerard."

"I've got this," he repeated, more to himself than me, as he reached down to grip the sides of the tub, only to freeze in a hunching pose with his back to me. "I can't."

"I'm right here," I whispered, reaching up to touch his back with my wet hand. "See? It's okay."

The muscles in his back twitched and he jerked violently. "Fuck." The sensation of water on his skin was clearly causing him emotional pain. "Fuck, okay, I… Fuck."

"I'll count you down, okay?"

"Okay."

"You've got this," I encouraged, reaching up to hold his hips. "Three, two, one… and sit."

Nope.

Nothing.

Gerard didn't move an inch.

"Three, two, one," I repeated calmly. "And sit."

Again, nothing.

Not even a twitching toe.

Dammit.

"Okay, stay right there." Shifting onto my knees behind him, I reached over the side of the tub to grab a scrunchie. "I have a plan."

"Don't fucking leave me, Claire!" Gerard choked out, hand shooting out to grip me.

"I'm not going anywhere, I promise," I coaxed, retrieving the scrunchie and dunking it into the tub to soap it up. "I'm just going to wet you."

"Wet me?"

"Uh-huh." When the bath scrunchie was wet and soapy, I gently dabbed his back without squeezing it out, letting the water trickle down his skin instead. "How's that?"

"Okay," Gerard replied, still positioned like he was about to bolt over the rim of the tub at any given moment. Seriously, he reminded me a whole lot of Brian in this moment—fearful and mistrusting.

"Your back is so long," I mused, paying careful attention to every freckle and scar on his body as I slowly washed him. "You're so tanned, Gerard. Your skin is beautiful."

"So is yours," he answered, but his tone didn't hold its usual hint of flirty banter. It had been replaced with terror.

Desperate to soothe the anxiety in him, I leaned in close and pressed a kiss to his back.

"Claire," he bit out, shivering. "Don't tease me when I'm in dire straits here, babe."

"Hey, Gerard?" Feeling devilish, I dropped the scrunchie and reached for the hem of my drenched T-shirt instead. "Want to see my boobs?"

"Do I fuck," he choked out, craning his head back to look at me. "The answer to that question is always, Claire-Bear. Always."

Laughing, I whipped the fabric over my head and tossed it over the side of the tub.

"Damn the inventor of bras," he complained, trying and failing to get an eyeful of my body. "Jesus, that was cruel."

Cackling with mischief, I reached for his hips. "Sit in the water and I'll show you more."

"Liar," he huffed, but I felt his body slowly relax. "No, you won't."

"You'll never know if you don't try," I laughed.

"Hmm." He lowered an inch, and then another one, until he was kneeling in the water, hands still gripping the sides like his life depended on it.

"Look at you," I praised, reaching up to rub his big shoulders as I shifted my legs so that I had one on either side of him. "The things you do for boobs, Gerard Gibson."

"The things I do for you, more like," he corrected.

"Okay, so I'm going to put my hands here," I explaining wrapping my arms around his waist to rest on his hard stomach. "And when you're ready, I want you to rest your back against my chest, okay?"

"You won't put water on my face?"

"I won't put water on your face," I vowed, feeling him slowly lower himself into a sitting position in the bath.

"I can keep holding onto the sides?"

"For as long as you need to," I agreed, thrilled when I watched him slowly lower himself until his back was touching my chest. "I'm right here."

"Believe me, I know," he bit out, full-body shuddering. "It's the only reason I'm doing this."

Keeping my arms wrapped around his waist, I shifted slightly so that my back was resting against the tub, and his big body was nestled between my thighs.

"It's on me," he breathed, looking panicked as the bubby water lapped against our bodies. "I don't want it on my face."

"I've got your face right here," I assured him, using my cheek to nuzzle his. "I won't let you go under."

"I'm going to hold you to that, Claire-Bear," Gerard groaned, still gripping the tub.

"Can you do something for me?" I asked a little while later, still keeping a firm hold of Gerard's waist, knowing that he needed to feel my touch to keep him relaxed in this moment. He needed to feel like he was being held up, even though he couldn't sink deeper. It was a psychological reaction to the trauma he'd endured as a child.

"Hmm?"

"Relax your arms."

"*Claire.*"

"Think of the boobs, Gerard."

"Jesus Christ, what am I doing," he muttered as he reluctantly relinquished his hold on the cast-iron bathtub and placed his hands on his stomach.

"I'm so proud of you," I whispered in his ear, using one of my hands to cover his. "You're amazing, do you know that?"

The feel of his hand in mine felt so epically right that I had to remind myself that this wasn't a romantic thing. I was trying to help my friend. That was it. We were friends. Right this moment, we were in our friendship era and nothing more. *Stem the raging hormones, Claire.*

"Why do you do it?"

"Hmm?" I mused, still nuzzling his cheek with mine. "Do what?"

Gerard turning his hand over, palm up, and entwined his fingers with mine. "Waste your time on me?"

"For two reasons," I explained, feeling my heart beat harder. "First, because I happen to believe that no time is ever wasted when I'm with you." My cheek grazed his temple as I spoke. "And second, you're my favorite person in the whole world. There's no one I would rather spend my time with."

"Really?"

"Really, but don't tell the girls."

"Never."

"Now, close your eyes, Gerard. Take in the feel of the water on your body and how safe you feel right now." Resisting the urge to press a kiss to his temple, I stroked his cheek with my nose and clamped my thighs around him instead. "I want you to replace the memory of that day with this one."

14

Summoned to the Office

GIBSIE

CONTRARY TO LIZZIE'S BELIEFS, I WASN'T ENTIRELY OFF THE HOOK AT SCHOOL. THE whole inciting a riot in the lunch hall on my first day back had resulted in a week's detention and daily trips to the office, not to mention several surprise inspections on my locker.

At my daily trip to the principal's office, I found myself interrogated by Twomey in great detail and told in no uncertain terms that he was *keeping his eye on me.* I didn't blame him. I had no doubt that I was the highlight of his professional career. After all, he was the one who told my mother that he had never met another student as *uncommon* as me in all his years of teaching.

I liked to think of that as a compliment.

Regardless of how much Twomey's attention tickled my funny bone, I couldn't hide my aggravation when I was summoned to the office at the end of last bell the following Thursday.

I had plans after school and had already dealt with his lectures and locker raiding at big lunch.

Beyond pissed off at the intrusion into my personal time, I stalked into the office, not bothering to stop the double doors from slamming shut behind me.

"Hey, stranger," a familiar voice purred from the other side of the admissions desk. "Long time no see."

Not fucking long enough. "Dee." Slapping on a smile, I strolled over to the counter and leaned against it. "Twomey's looking for me again?"

"Nope, I am."

Christ, I truly was broken.

I stared blankly back at her. "You are?"

She laughed. "Is that so hard to believe?"

No, it wasn't hard to believe but it was daring. Calling me to the office over the intercom? Jesus, that was a bold fucking move. "What can I do for you?"

"I think you know exactly what you can do for me." She slid her car keys across the counter and said, "I'll be there in ten."

Dressed in a low-cut blouse and pencil skirt, with her blond hair piled on top of her hair like a sexy librarian, the woman was undeniably attractive.

And I felt *nothing*.

Not so much as a twitch.

"No can do."

"No?" Confusion swept over her face, and I watched as she flicked through what I presumed was the schedule diary before saying, "You're not training after school."

No, I wasn't training after school, but that didn't mean that I was free for any other extracurricular activities, and certainly none that involved my head between this woman's legs again.

Jesus.

When Dee showed interest in me back in the day, I'd been reckless. It was a horrible trait of mine. Freewheeling into mischief without a thought for the consequences. It was my decision and I thrived on the feeling of being in control. Of initiating what I wanted and not the other way around. There was something very wrong in my head. I knew it. I just… I couldn't change the way I was programmed. I guess in the back of mind, I felt I had a point to prove to myself and who better to do that with than an older woman?

I could touch.

I could do that.

No fucking problem.

But being touched wasn't so easy for me because I didn't feel *anything*, so I avoided it and became what this woman liked to refer to me as her personal giver.

It was a reckless sort of urgency that took ahold of me. A need to be touched and avoided all in one breath. It was complicated and I feared delving too deep inside my head, inside my memories, to find the root of the problem. Either way, I was in total control and that was how I liked it.

When I was with her, we moved at *my* pace. She wasn't forcing me to do shit, and in turn, I had learned everything I knew from this woman. Problem was, after a while, being Dee's *giver* had begun to feel icky, and the moment she had started to push me for more, I'd quickly slammed the brakes.

When it came to this woman, I had been such a fucking eejit. I wasn't about to lie and say that piercing my dick back in fifth year didn't have anything to do with Dee. It had. It was my temporary way out of a situation that had gotten too big for me. A successful one at that, because I'd deftly managed to avoid the woman since then.

Hugh and the lads assumed I was a fuckboy without a conscience, and I let it roll because why the fuck not? They'd be surprised if they knew the real me, the person I was beneath the surface, desperate for the kind of affection that I could control.

Leaning against the tall countertop that separated the students from the staff, I felt a wave of self-loathing roll through my body. It was a feeling I'd spent my life trying to run from and somehow, I always managed to find myself back here, drowning in my disgust.

"No, I'm not training after school," I clarified, pulling my attention back to the present, to the woman looking expectantly at me. *Why are you the way you are*, my conscience demanded, furious with me for once again getting my ass caught up in a level of drama that I wasn't nearly mature enough to handle. "Listen," I said, trying a different approach. "We've had a good run of it, but I'm going to be busy with school this year."

Instead of taking my words at face value, Dee threw her head back and laughed. "Gibs, this is me you're talking to."

I steeled my resolve and said, "I'm not interested anymore."

"You're not interested." It wasn't a question, but her accusatory tone of voice assured me that she wasn't about to let me off the hook easily. "Because of her?"

Claire's face flashed through my mind, sending a whole new level of devastated guilt washing through me. "No," I bit out slowly. "Because *this* never should've happened in the first place." I discreetly gestured between us and blew out a sharp breath. "Just call it a day and walk away, Dee."

"That's not what you were saying before."

"Well, it's what I'm saying now."

"You're acting like I forced you."

"No, I'm not acting like anything. I'm telling you that it's done with."

"So, it's official?" Leaning back in her chair, she folded her arms across her chest and studied my face. "You've finally grown a pair of balls and decided to settle down with her?"

"I'm seventeen," I snapped back, beyond pissed off that she was bringing Claire into the equation. "I'm not settling down with anything."

"You don't look seventeen."

"Well, if you need a reminder of my age, then take a look at my birth certificate," I tossed back. "It's in my file."

Dee flinched like I had smacked her, and I felt like a knob. "You said it helped."

"It did," I urged, feeling my sanity slip further away the longer this conversation lasted. "But that's past tense, okay? I'm over it."

"So, I don't do it for you anymore."

"I'm just not interested anymore," I groaned, dropping my head in my hands, elbows resting on the counter. "I'm sorry if that hurts your feelings."

"Don't apologize," she snapped, tone laced with hurt, as she rolled her desk chair backwards and stood up. "And don't even think about telling your little girlfriend about this."

Trust me, if I could erase it from my mind I would in a heartbeat. "She's not my girlfriend, Dee," I shot back with a clipped nod. "But don't worry," I added, moving for the door. "I have no plans to tell her."

"She won't understand," she called after me. "How your mind works. You'll never be able to make it work with her."

"I'll take my chances."

15

Shiny Happy People

CLAIRE

"Evening, family," I chimed, strolling into Gerard's kitchen on Friday evening.

"Evening, sweetheart," Sadhbh acknowledged with a smile from her perch at the kitchen table. "How was your week?"

"It was good, yours?" Draping my coat on the back of the kitchen chair, I made a beeline for homemade pizza on the table. "Oh my god, you put black pudding on it!" I gushed, stealing a slice of cheesy goodness. "You are a queen, Sadhbh Gibson."

"Sadhbh Allen," Keith corrected with a chuckle, glancing up from the newspaper he was combing over.

"*Allen*," I forced myself to say, offering him what I hoped was a half-decent smile. Because while I had no desire to please this man, I happened to both adore and respect his wife. "Where's Gerard?"

"In his room," Sadhbh replied with a worried sigh.

"Oh?" Concern flashed through me. "He didn't come down for dinner?"

"Apparently, he's on hunger strike," Keith filled, flicking the page of his newspaper. "Which would be fine if he wasn't making such a damn racket."

"Hmm." Taking one last bite of my slice, I dropped the crust on the table and moved for the door. "I'll head up now."

"Be a good girl and tell him not to break anything, will you?"

As soon as I reached the upstairs landing, the familiar sound of REM's "Shiny Happy People" echoed loudly from the other side of Gerard's bedroom door, causing me to groan internally. The upbeat music might lure others into the belief that Gerard was in a good mood.

Not me.

No, because I knew only too well that the more upbeat or outrageous explicit music he played, the worse he was feeling. On the inside, of course. Because Gerard Gibson would rather brush his teeth with glass than admit that he was having a bad day. Problem was that a bad day made for a very erratic impulsive Gerard.

When we were younger children, Gerard's bad days resulted in him being grounded at home. Nowadays, it was full-blown suspensions and heartbroken girls in his wake. Yeah, he was a complicated little pocket of sunshine.

His current song choice assured me that he was in his head big time and that I had a job to do. A job I took very seriously.

Blowing out a breath, I rolled my shoulders and reached for the door handle.

When I stepped inside, I was greeted by the sight of the entire contents of his room, bed included, thrust into the middle of the room in a huge, messy pile.

Clothes, DVDs, his TV, his furniture…Everything he owned was piled in a giant heap on the middle of his bed.

All that had been left untouched was his coveted stereo system that rested on the huge bay windowsill, where it continued to play today's mood list of music at an obnoxious volume. Loud enough to have old Eddie Clancy from next door ringing the doorbell any minute now.

Oh, Gerard…

Sighing wearily, I placed my hands on my hips and observed his meltdown.

Oblivious to my presence and with his back to me, Gerard continued to paint—or at least I presumed that was what he was attempting to do—his bedroom ceiling the most obnoxious canary yellow I'd ever seen. Balancing precariously on a rolling desk chair, he strained his body upward to reach the ridiculously high ceiling.

When Sum 41's "Fat Lip" replaced the previous song, I finally found my voice. "Please tell me that's not what I think it is."

When he didn't respond, I shook my head and stomped over to the window. "Gerard!" Lowering the volume of the stereo to nondeafening decibels, I pushed open the window, worried about the fumes of the paint and lack of fresh air. "What the hell are you doing?"

"Claire-Bear." When he spun around to face me, his smile was wide and full of mischief. Mischief and humor that didn't meet his eyes.

It's an act, my heart reminded me. *Don't let him trick you.*

All smiles and laughter. Hiding his heartbreak. Hiding his pain. I wanted to save him from his past. I wanted to love him through it all. I just *wanted* him.

Setting down his paintbrush on top of the open can of paint, Gerard sauntered toward me, body thrumming with energy.

If this was another seventeen-year-old boy, he might be mistaken for being under the influence of narcotics. Not Gerard. Nope. This was his predisposition. His entire makeup was off-centered to the point where energy came too easily for him. He had a prescription for his condition, something I knew his mother harped on about on the regular. I wasn't sure how regular he was with taking his ADHD medication nowadays, but he'd been a disaster as a younger child.

"What's that?" I asked when the folded-up piece of paper hanging out from the edge of his bed caught my eyes. "Gerard Gibson." I feigned hurt. "Are you hiding love letters from other girls under your mattress."

"No love letters," he replied with a chuckle, quickly shoving the note back under his mattress. "I promise."

"Whatever." I rolled my eyes and looked around the room. "Care to explain why you're painting your ceiling?"

"I fucking hate that ceiling," he explained, pointing to the part that he had redesigned. The part right over where his bed was situated. "It depresses me."

"The ceiling depresses you?" I arched a brow. "Make it make sense, please."

He grinned back at me, another wolfish smile that didn't meet his eyes. *Oh boy.* "You know I don't sleep well."

"Yeah," I agreed slowly, waiting for the penny to drop.

He shrugged. "At least I'll have something to look at now."

"But it's just a giant yellow smiley face," I replied, confused by the rest of the untouched white ceiling.

"I know."

"That's strange."

"I know," was all he replied, entirely unaffected by the thought that people might think it strange that he had a giant circle painted over the part of the ceiling where his bed usually resided beneath.

"Are you redesigning the whole room?"

"I haven't decided yet. Here," he paused to hand me a paintbrush. "Make me something."

"Make you something?"

He nodded. "Something to make me smile."

"I know your game." I narrowed my eyes in suspicion. "You want to rope me into another one of your haywire plans so when it backfires on you with your mam later, and it *will* backfire, you'll have a partner in crime to take the heat off you."

"You think I'd let you get in trouble for me?" He threw his head back and laughed. "Never, Claire-Bear."

"Hah," I shot back. "Liar. You've roped me into some seriously questionable scenarios down through the years, Gerard Gibson."

LEN's "Steal My Sunshine" wafted from the stereo, and he waggled his brows before tapping my nose with a healthy dollop of yellow paint. "Give it up, Biggs."

"You're an eejit." I laughed, unable to avoid his onslaught.

Laughing to himself, he sang along to the song, shoulders relaxing with every minute we spent together.

Good job, I mentally praised myself. *You're grounding him.*

The affection my heart stored for this particular boy was borderline unhealthy, and my need to soothe his bad days was almost as strong as it was to soothe my own. I suppose that was what happened when two people spent a huge portion of their lives together.

Pondering mischief and with my playful mood activated, I moved to inspect the giant smiley face on his ceiling, the one Gerard was currently adding a joint to with permanent black marker.

"Oh, your mam is going to freak when she sees it." I laughed when he continued to draw little cloud bubbles of smoke around the face. "You know she hates it when you smoke."

"It's art," he shot back. "Art is… What's the word?"

"Subjective?" I offered with a frown.

"That's it, Brains," he praised as he balanced dangerously on the moving chair. "Now, come on and help me. Put your own stamp on my ceiling."

Kind of like the stamp you've put on my heart?

"If you think for one minute that I'm breaking an ankle participating in your skullduggery antics—ahh!"

"Skullduggery." He chuckled, pushing his head between my thighs from behind and hoisting me onto his shoulders without breaking a sweat. "And you call me strange."

"You are getting ridiculously strong," I admired, cupping his stubbly chin with my free hand as he stood up with me on his shoulders and hoisted me toward the ceiling.

Paintbrush still in hand, I tilted my head to one side, studying his artwork, before considering the first stroke of my brush. "He looks lonely."

"Who?"

"Mr. Smiley Face."

"I can see that," he agreed, hands settling on my calves.

"He needs Mrs. Smiley Face."

"He definitely does."

And that was how I spent the rest of the evening, on Gerard Gibson's shoulders, painting his world just a little bit brighter.

16

Sleeping Girls and Racing Hearts

GIBSIE

"Hey, Gerard?"

"Yeah, Claire-Bear?"

"What's it mean?"

"Hmm?"

"Love?" Rolling onto her belly, she rested her chin on her hand and beamed up at me. "What's it mean?"

Grinning, I copied her moves and rolled onto my belly, facing her. "It's what the grown-ups do when they get married."

"Hm." Her blond brows pulled together, and she licked the ice-cream off her chin before saying, "Hey, Gerard?"

"Hmm?"

"Why do grown-ups get married?"

"'Cause they get in love with each other," I explained, taking a lick from my ice cream before holding it out for her.

"But why do they get in love with each other?" she asked, taking a lick of my cone. "Is it fun?"

"It's when you live in the same house as your best friend, and you have babies and a cat," I paused to lick my cone, before continuing, "and a big bed, and…"

"And pillow fights?"

"Yep." I nodded. "And you get to eat cake in bed with the same person for ever and ever and ever."

Her eyes grew really big. "But I don't want marry anyone." Leaning closer, she licked my cone and smiled. "Except you…"

Laying on my side with my arm around Claire, I pulled my mind from the past and focused on the present.

Beautiful.

She was so fucking beautiful that it made my chest ache. Honest to God, looking at this girl for too long caused a physical ache to develop in my rib cage. Even the back of her head. That was all I could see from my current viewpoint, and still, my heart bucked wildly in response.

Even when she was sleeping, she dominated my thought process to the point where I couldn't resist the urge to shake her arm and wake her up, just so I could hear her voice.

"Claire-Bear?" I whispered in the darkness, feeling that familiar swell of anxious energy building up inside of me. "Are you awake?" Of course she wasn't. It was half past four in the morning and she was clearly sleeping like every other normal human, but I was selfish and needy. "Babe?"

"Shh, Gerard," she half moaned, half purred. "Mmm." Shifting around, she thrust her ass against me and snuggled deeper into the mattress. "Five more minutes." Reaching up, she gripped my forearm with her hand, nails digging into my flesh and then retracting like a little kitten. "I'm just resting my eyes."

I chuckled in the darkness, knowing that she was more awake than asleep.

"Shh." Twisting around to face me, she draped her thigh over my legs and snuggled into my side, using her cheek to nuzzle my bare chest. "I'm super tired."

I smiled in the darkness. "Say it again."

"Mmm, say what?"

"Super."

"Shh."

"Come on, Claire-Bear."

"No."

"Come on, just once."

"No."

"Just say it."

"Why?"

"Because it's fucking adorable."

"Fine," she huffed, reaching a hand up to pinch my nipple. "Super."

"Fuck." I couldn't stop the laugh that escaped my lips. "You're *super* cute, do you know that?"

"I was five," she grumbled, fully awake now. "I thought I was being sophisticated using the word 'super' all the time."

"Hey, the five-year-old version of you is still more sophisticated than the current day version of me." Grinning, I added, "You still make that tiny whistle noise when you say it."

"No, I don't," Claire huffed. "That whistle noise was an unfortunate temporary side effect of losing my baby teeth." Pulling up on her elbow, she smiled down at me. "See, perfectly formed adult teeth now, with zero whistling."

"You're so beautiful," I admitted because one, I had a problem keeping my mouth shut, and second, it was the truth. I'd never seen anything like her. "I swear you shine even in the darkness."

"You're such a joker."

"I'm not joking."

She studied my face for a long beat, clearly searching for the lie before blowing out a shaky breath and flopping back down on my chest. "You are so frustrating, Gerard Gibson."

"Yeah." Swallowing deeply, I draped an arm around her and nodded. "I know."

"Tell me a story."

I arched a brow. "A story?"

"Mm-hmm." Nodding, she yawned sleepily. "It's the least you can do considering you woke me from an epic dream."

"You were dreaming?"

"I dream every night."

Wow. Lucky her. "What were you dreaming about?"

"The usual," she replied, cheek resting on my chest again.

"Which is?"

"You."

My heart jackknifed in my chest. "Tell me about it."

"Nope," she mumbled. "You're the one supposed to be telling me a story."

"I can't think of a story."

"Then just talk," she encouraged sleepily. "Just talk, Gerard. I want to hear your voice."

"Talk about what?"

"Us," she whispered. "Tell me all the nice things."

"I don't have good dreams when I sleep," I offered cautiously, trying to choose the right words, something that didn't come easily to me. "But whenever I daydream, you're the star of the show."

"I am?"

"Of course."

"Keep going."

"I have a hard time concentrating," I offered, unsure if this was worth telling her, but she said talk, so I was. "But when I'm with you, I feel like I have my thinking cap on." Pondering, I folded one arm behind my head as I tried to form sentences out of my wandering thoughts. "You're the only person who can hold my attention. It shifts and wanders off on just about everyone else. But not you. Never you."

"Really?"

"You already know this."

"Maybe, but it's nice to hear you say it."

I thought about her words for a long moment before saying, "I love you, Claire."

"I love you, too, Gerard." A shiver racked through her. "A lot."

17

Babies and Basket Cases

CLAIRE

"Oh my god. Oh my god! Look at his little foot."

"Shh, Claire. Don't squeal. You'll hurt his tiny ears."

"Oops! Sorry." Slapping a hand over my mouth, I bounced from foot to foot, desperately trying to fight the urge to swipe the baby out of my bestie's arms and steal him for myself while Third Eye Blind's "Semi-Charmed Life" played on repeat on the nearby stereo. "I think I love him."

Almost one month had passed since we returned to Tommen, and all seemed to be well in the world again. Joey and Tadhg had returned from their suspensions, and aside from a few sketchy instances at the beginning of term, everything seemed to be running like clockwork for our little gang. Best of all, Gerard and I were still spending most of our time together—when he wasn't working out with Johnny, that was.

Shannon's adorable nephew was almost one month old, and this was my first time getting to meet the little guy—even though I'd been trying to get my hands on his chubby little cheeks since he came out of Aoife's womb.

"You should smell him," Shan encouraged, as she cradled her nephew in her arms. Leaning in close, she took a whiff of his blond hair and moaned. "He's got that epic newborn baby smell."

"Liz, come here!" Unable to tear my eyes off what had to be the cutest baby I'd ever seen in my life, I waved my hand around wildly, gesturing for her to join us. "He's so— Shut the front door! He's sucking his thumb."

"I know," Shannon gushed excitedly.

"Isn't that the most adorable thing you've ever seen?"

"So adorable."

"He's a baby, guys." Sounding entirely uninterested, Lizzie remained on the couch in Joey and Aoife's annex/apartment, not bothering to join us in our gushing. "That's what they do. They suck their thumbs."

"But this baby is the best baby," I added, tracing AJ's chubby cheek with my finger. "I want one."

"Me too."

"You two are disturbed."

"Thanks, girls," Aoife said, reappearing from the bathroom with a towel wrapped around her hair and a fresh pair of pajamas on. She certainly looked a lot fresher than she had when we arrived after school. What with her leaky nipples and AJ's baby puke on her back.

"I feel like I haven't showered alone in weeks," she added with a smile. "Is AJ okay?"

"Well, you sort of haven't," Shan replied. "And yep, he's just as perfect as he was ten minutes ago."

"Yeah," I agreed, offering the stunning blond a sympathetic smile. "How are you feeling?"

"She pushed an entire human being out of her body a month ago, Claire," Lizzie drawled. "How do you think she's feeling?"

"Vagina," Ollie chimed in from his perch on the couch, where he was playing Snake on Aoife's phone. "It's called a vagina."

"Hey, good job, stud," Aoife praised, ruffling her boyfriend's little brother's hair. "You are kicking ass with that speech therapist."

"Thanks," he replied, beaming up at her like she hung the moon. "When's Joe home?"

"He's working late tonight, stud."

Ollie's face fell, but like the absolute queen she was, Aoife was quick to add, "It's all good, Ols. You know he'll pop next door to say good night to the three of you before bed. Same as always."

"You promise he's still better today?" Ollie pushed, brown eyes wide and full of innocence. "He's not sick again?"

"I promise," Aoife replied, though she had to clear her throat several times before adding, "Today is another good day, Ols."

I was quite certain that I felt my heart crack in my chest. This wasn't an everyday conversation that I was listening to. This orphan child was asking for reassurance that his heroin-addicted brother was still clean. From the girl who'd given birth to said brother's baby only a few short weeks ago.

That poor kid.

That strong girl.

"Stop it," Lizzie, who had suddenly appeared by my side, whispered in my ear. Slipping a tissue into my hand, she nudged me toward the door. "Not in front of the kid."

Pretending that I had to answer my phone, I quickly pressed it to my ear and hurried outside, holding my breath the entire time.

When I had the door of the annex closed behind me, I choked out a sob and clutched my chest, as an array of different emotions battered my heart. "Oh god!"

"You alright there, Claire?" Johnny asked, appearing in the garage doorway with a look of confusion etched on his face. I knew from spending countless hours at the manor this past summer that the garage housed a state-of-the-art home gym.

"Uh-huh," I choked out, using the tissue Liz gave me to blow my nose. "It's just so *sad*."

"Sad," a little voice chimed in. It was only then I noticed the small boy clung to Johnny's legs. "Claire sad."

"Hi, Sean," I sniffled, offering a bright smile to my bestie's youngest brother. "And I'm not sad. I'm super happy."

"Claire's silly, isn't she?" Johnny coaxed, scooping him up in his arms. "Because we're not supposed to cry when we're happy, are we? Hmm? Tell her that she's supposed to laugh."

"Laugh," Sean replied solemnly, and then he did the most adorable thing ever. He reached up and pulled at Johnny's cheeks to make him smile. "See?"

Now, I did laugh. "Oh my god, you are just the cutest!"

"Do me a favor, will ya, big man?" Setting Sean back down, Johnny ruffled his curls before saying, "Run inside and ask Dellie if Johnny's dinner is ready."

With his little chest puffed out, Sean nodded eagerly before bolting off in the direction of the back door.

"I'm so sorry," I blurted out when he was out of earshot.

"You're only human," Johnny replied, watching the preschooler like a hawk until he disappeared inside the manor. "It's a lot to take in."

"It just so heart-wrenching" I admitted, following him into the garage, feeling ridiculously emotional. "How do you handle it?"

"With these," he explained, pointing to the weights and gym equipment behind him. "It gets easier."

"Usually, I'm okay," I said. "But seeing Aoife and AJ, and then knowing everything they had to go through…" My voice cracked and I had to press my tissue to my nose to stop it from dripping. "And then Ollie was asking her if Joey was better, and Aoife could only tell him that he was better today…" Choking out another sob, I batted my tears away. "And then it hit me that Joe's never going to be fully better, is he? Because there's no cure for his disease!" Sniffling, I added, "He'll always be an addict, with no promise of anything beyond *today*."

"Yeah, Claire, he will."

"But that's so sad!" I choked out, unable to stop the wail that escaped me. "He's trying so hard, with school and work and the baby! And they've been through so much! And Aoife's so brave! And they *still* don't get any guarantees for the future!"

Sighing heavily, Johnny sank down on his weight bench and patted the bench beside him. "Come on."

Wailing like a banshee, I slumped down beside him and dropped my head in my hands. "Why do bad things happen to good people?"

"I don't know, Claire," he replied, patting my shoulder. "I really don't."

"It's just so *shitty!*"

"Yeah, it is," he agreed, offering me a bottle of water. "But the fact that Shan and the boys are here today, still standing, still breathing? It's a miracle in itself. As for Joey? He's a force to be reckoned with. I've never seen a more resilient human in my life. Yeah, he'll always be an addict, but he's got a family in there worth staying sober for. A girl and a baby that not only would he fight to the death for, but that he also wants to *live* for. So, fuck guarantees and don't bet against him. He'll forge an epic future for Aoife and AJ, just like he forged a future for his siblings."

18

Rhett Butler

GIBSIE

"You know, when you asked me for an old pallet from the farm, I should have known it was for one of your hairbrained schemes," Feely declared. We were in my back garden after school, surrounded by power tools, saws, and pieces of chopped timber. "This is strange, Gibs. Even for you."

"No, it's not strange," I argued, balancing a nail between my teeth, while I hammered another one into the wooden house I'd spent most of the evening crafting. "It's the height of levelheadedness."

"Care to explain the method to this particular brand of madness?"

"It's getting cold. Reggie is going to need someplace warm to hibernate."

"You know, if you freed the poor creature, he'd do it for himself."

"Not according to our vet, he won't. He's been handled too much. Reggie doesn't know that he's a hedgehog. He was only a baby when we rescued him. He won't survive a winter in the wild."

"You know wild hedgehogs carry diseases, don't you?" Feely pointed out, leaning against the closed patio door. "You really shouldn't keep him on your lap like that, lad."

"For the last time, Reginald isn't diseased!" I snapped. "He's as clean as a whistle. Same as me."

"Same as you?" he laughed. "Is that supposed to reassure me?"

"Don't mind him, son," I grumbled, returning my attention to the task at hand, while my little buddy burrowed into the fabric of my gray sweatpants. "Daddy's going to build you a better hibernaculum than any of the other hedgehogs."

"At least use gloves when you're handling him."

"What's with the judgment, Patrick?" I snapped. "I asked you to help me because you're the best of us at woodwork and you've always been the least judgmental of the lads. Or so I *thought*."

"I'm not judging you, Gibs." He chuckled, coming to sit down on the patio beside me. "Here." Taking the hammer out of my hand, he retrieved a nail and set to work on the felt roof. "Let's make sure your *son's* hibernaculum is waterproof."

I grinned. "Thanks, lad."

"Question," he said a little while later, when the felt roof had been neatly tacked into place. "Have you noticed anything out of the ordinary with Liz?"

"Liz?" I turned to gape at him. "As in Viper Liz?"

He nodded.

"Hell no, I haven't noticed anything out of the ordinary with her. In fact, I try my best not to notice her at all," I replied, appalled that he would ask me such a question. "In case it skipped your attention, lad, that witch hates my guts."

"Come on, Gibs," he tried to reason. "Don't call her that. She was your friend once."

"Yeah, and look where it got me," I shot back defensively. "Directly in the firing line of her poisonous tongue."

"I'm not defending anything she's done to you down through the years," he said carefully. "Because she's been well out of order."

"But?" I bit out, just knowing there was a *but* to this bullshit.

"But I really feel like there's a conversation that needs to happen between you both. One that's long overdue."

I simply stared, unblinking, unable to form any words to respond to this bullshit.

"Come on, Gibs," he pushed. "Try to see where I'm coming from here."

"I can't," I replied, placing Reggie inside his little house. "Probably because I'm blinded by the sheer height of betrayal!"

"She's not a bad person," he called after me when I stood up and moved for the door. "She's just hurt."

"We're all hurt, lad," I snapped, yanking the patio door open and storming inside. "Some of us don't take it out on everyone else."

"You know what they say Mark did to Caoimhe," Feely said, following me inside a thankfully empty kitchen. "I know he's not your brother, Gibs. I know that, okay. But she believes the rumors. She thinks he's responsible and if you and Liz have a conversation about it, I think it might really help her to heal."

"Thinks!" I snapped, slamming the fridge door closed. "Last time I checked, thinking something wasn't the same as knowing something, Patrick!"

"Come on, Gibs," he tried to plead. "We've all heard the rumors, lad." Leaning against the island, he added, "Half the town thinks he raped her."

"Apparently not the half that contain the Gards," I shot back, bristling. "Because they cleared him after questioning!"

"It's hard to prove a dead girl's story."

"Agreed," I countered, feeling cold to the bone. "Especially when it's complete bullshit."

"So, you think Mark's completely innocent in all of it?" he argued. "You don't feel like he has any hand in Lizzie's sister jumping off the bridge that night?"

"I *didn't* say that," I snapped, hating the tremor in my voice.

"Exactly," he urged. "Because you know as well as she does that there's something to this. Come on, Gibs, think about it, lad. There's no smoke without fire…"

"No!" I roared back at him. "No, I won't think about it, Patrick, because I don't fucking want to, okay? Because I'm done with thinking about it. Done with being blamed for it. I'm just fucking done, okay!"

"Okay." He held his hands up, brows furrowed. "Okay, Gibs, relax. I won't bring it up again. Just take it down a notch, lad."

"Thanks for helping build Reggie's hibernaculum," I replied flatly, moving for the back door.

"Wait, Gibs…"

"You should go now," I deadpanned, closing the patio door before he could follow me outside.

"Word on the street is you threw Feely out on his ass earlier," a familiar voice said a little while later.

"Word on the street would be right."

"Care to explain?"

"Nope."

"So, you're still pissed?"

"Yep."

"Shit." Closing my bedroom door behind him, Hugh strolled over to the beanbag in my room and sank down. "He must have done something fairly terrible to get on your bad side, Gibs."

"Oh please." Rolling my eyes, I tossed my rugby ball into the air before catching it. "Don't pretend like Feely didn't rush across the street to fill you in the minute I told him to fuck off. You two are as thick as thieves."

"Kind of like you and Cap?"

"Exactly like me and Cap," I agreed. "Which is how I know he went straight to you with the drama."

It wasn't that deep with Feely. By tomorrow, the whole thing would be long forgotten about, but for now, I was still in my feels.

"I wasn't going to deny it," Hugh replied calmly. "I just figured I'd come and check on you."

"Why bother wasting your time?" I shot back, spinning the ball out once more. "I'm always okay."

"True," Hugh said in an even tone. "Except for when you're not."

I didn't have an answer to that, so I remained silent.

"Gibs." A heavy sigh escaped him. "Talk to me, lad."

"About what?"

"Maybe you could start with whatever it is that makes you shut down like this."

Pulling up on my elbow, I turned to look at him. "Do I *look* shut down?"

"Yes," he shot back without a hint of hesitation. "Given the fact that I've known you every day of your life, I would say yeah, you're clearly in shutdown mode." He kept his brown eyes locked on mine when he said, "This is about Lizzie."

My blood ran cold. "No."

"Come on, Gibs."

"Jesus Christ." Frustration filled my chest to the point where I wanted to rip the four walls off this fucking house. "Why does everything have to be about *her*?"

"It doesn't."

"According to you and Feely it does."

"No," Hugh tried to reason. "Feely told me what happened. What he was trying to do, and I get it. I know she's not been the best person to you in the past, but…"

"Listen, lad, I get that you and Pa have had this weird attachment to the Viper since forever, but I don't want a damn thing to do with it," I quickly cut him off by saying. "I'm not her friend, I'm not her punching bag, I'm not her fucking anything. So, whatever issues she's having, don't come around here projecting them onto me, because in the words of Rhett Butler, 'Frankly, I don't give a damn!'"

Hugh was quiet for a long time before finally rising to his feet. "You care, Gibs." He moved for the door. "You don't want to care, but you do," he added quietly. "Same as the rest of us."

"Same as you, more like."

He didn't deny it.

"You're a glutton for punishment, Biggs," I called after him.

"Right back at you, Gibson," he called back. "Now, hurry your ass up and get out of your bad mood. Mam's setting the table for dinner."

Instantly, my stomach was on high alert. "What's on the menu?"

"Your favorite."

"Bacon and cabbage?"

"With roast potatoes."

Dammit.

19

Slumber Parties and Sex Talks

CLAIRE

"Bestie!" Tossing my overnight bag on the floor, I pounced onto the delectable queen-sized bed that housed my pint-sized friend and an aging Labrador. "Give me a hug."

"No, no, no, don't jump on me... Ahhh!" Tangled up in a heap of flailing limbs and rogue hair, Shannon stifled a laugh. "You're in a good mood."

"I am," I agreed, rolling onto my side to give Sookie a belly rub. The old girl let out a contented groan and kicked out her legs. "You're the sweetest baby in the world," I cooed, feeling all squishy inside at the sight of her little gray beard around her snout. "She's too much, Shan."

"I know," she agreed, closing the book she'd been reading. "She's getting so stiff lately." Worrying her lip, she flicked her gaze from the dog to me. "Let's just hope she has another few years in her, huh?"

"Oh my god, can you imagine?" I shuddered in horror. Aside from the fact that I honestly didn't think the Lynch siblings could take another death in the family, I dreaded to think about Johnny's reaction on the day his faithful companion wasn't here anymore.

Johnny was a careful person. He didn't reveal a whole pile to anyone in our friendship circle that wasn't named Shannon or Gerard, so it was hard to tell what he was thinking or feeling at times, but nobody could deny his undying love for the dog I was rubbing. I'd been over to his house several times a week since the Lynch kids moved in, and it was as plain as the nose on his face that he was just as besotted with his dog as he was his girlfriend.

His commitment to Sookie gave me comfort in a strange way. His mam had younger, more active, more complexional attractive dogs, but Johnny didn't see Bonnie and Cupcake. He barely looked sideways at them. I thought that kind of devoted blind loyalty was an extremely beneficial trait.

In my mind, it meant that he wouldn't be tempted to turn his head from the brunette in front of me, either. He had a level of dependability to him that none of the other boys in our friendship circle displayed. That's how I knew they would be together forever.

What Johnny and Shannon had was permanent. They nurtured their relationship like it was of the greatest importance to both of them in equal measure. As sure as there was a cat in Cork, she would be the girl on his arm when he collected his Grand Slam medal, just as he would be the one in the crowd cheering her on when she collected her college degree.

They would do everything the right way, because that's how Johnny was structured to behave, and Shannon thrived on his ability to balance life and do the right thing.

Their moral compasses were aimed in the same direction, and their hearts were set on each other. The trust they had in each other was faultless, and I imagined them many years into the future with a house in the countryside, similar to this one, with a pack of dogs roaming through the house and a bunch of children to nurture.

And if Johnny looked anything like his dad in thirty years, then Shannon was a lucky, lucky girl.

Yeah, Daddy K, or DILF, as Lizzie and I had labeled him, was a beautiful creation of a man. I wasn't sure if it was the tailored suits he wore or the mild-mannered persona that masked the aura of a powerful man that did it, but all of us girls were sold.

Shannon's new digs sure beat the heck out of looking at mine or Lizzie's dads, that's for sure. Or worse, Hugh. *Ew.*

Joey and Aoife were another couple that I knew in my heart were endgame, but it wasn't the same. They had a fiery temperament to them, almost like a ticking time bomb. Two wildcards thrust together in a friendship fueled by affection, camaraderie, and let's face it, some seriously hot sex. You didn't have a baby together in secondary school unless the boy was a stallion. And by God was Joey Lynch a stallion. They had a volatile hue to their love that wasn't present in Johnny and Shannon's relationship, which made me long for Shannon's situation just that little bit more. After all, they seemed innocent enough. Unlike Joey and Aoife. Their relationship was like fire and ice. I knew few people, if any, who could endure what they had and come out on top.

I was so proud of Joey for all he had come through, but it scared me daily that he might relapse, so I couldn't imagine how it felt to be the mother of his child and have so much of my life invested and entwined with his. It must be really scary to live with a boy who was always tempted by drugs. I guess that's what true love was, though. It wasn't perfect. It didn't come in the perfect gift-wrapped box. It was messy and raw and pushed you to your absolute limits.

Perhaps Joey and Aoife's limits just happened to stretch a little further out of the comfort zone than Johnny and Shannon's. Who knew? Certainly not me, the girl who had kissed a grand total of two boys in her entire lifetime.

One being Jamie Kelleher.

The other being Gerard.

One was with tongues, and the other was with hearts. Well, my heart to be precise, because only Jesus himself knew where Gerard's heart was at. He proclaimed his love for me on the daily, but it was almost habit at this stage. Kind of like the way you told your mam and dad you loved them before you left in the morning. A passing comment. A nice farewell. I wasn't sure how deep it went for him, but for me, it was deeper than the ocean. I couldn't break the surface of those feelings. I'd been trying for sixteen years.

"Hey, daydreamer, where'd you go?" Shannon teased, snapping her fingers in front of my face. "You totally zoned out there, didn't you?"

"My bad," I replied with a sheepish shrug. "But I'm back now. So, what's on the sleepover agenda, bestie—and you better not say Johnny because I will be seriously miffed."

"No, not Johnny." She laughed. "He's actually going to Biddies with the guys tonight."

"He is?" My eyes widened. "They actually convinced him to go?"

"I think it was more coercion than convincing." Shannon laughed. "I heard him arguing with Gibsie." Snickering, she added, "Gibsie agreed to spend all of tomorrow working out with Johnny if he went to the pub with him tonight."

"Oh, that poor innocent fool," I mused, rolling onto my back. "Johnny's going to kill him on the treadmill tomorrow."

"Only if Gibs doesn't kill Johnny with shots tonight first."

"Girlies, while I adore your company," Aoife declared later that evening, curled up on the couch with an episode of *The OC* playing on the television, she turned to look at us, "It's Friday night and you're only young once." Smiling, she added, "Don't you guys have something more fun in mind?"

"We were trying to watch a movie," Shannon explained, waving a hand around as she spoke, "We had the popcorn ready and everything, but the boys wouldn't stop breaking into my room." After Tadhg, Ollie, and Sean's six-hundredth interruption, we had decided to escape to the annex. "You don't mind if we join you, do you?"

"No, I don't mind." She laughed, patting the couch next to her. "You know you're always welcome in here."

"Yay." Thrilled to be away from the boys, we both made a beeline for the couch, nestling under the blanket with Shannon's big sis-in-law. "You're the best."

"Where's Joe?"

"Upstairs showering," she explained, unwrapping a Rolo chocolate from the packet resting on the arm of the couch. Gesturing to the sleeping baby on her lap, she smirked. "AJ had a poonami. Joe got caught in the cross fire."

"Ew. My kittens don't have poonamis." I scrunched my nose up in disgust. "And if they do, it's in their litter tray and Gerard cleans it for me."

My response caused Aoife to throw her head back and laugh. "Yeah, well, human babies do it frequently, Claire Babe, so you might want to think about that before you partake in the devil's tango with that stud of yours."

"The devil's tango?" I stared blankly at her. "Is that a euphemism for a dance routine or something?"

"Or something," Shan replied, cheeks turning bright pink. "It a euphemism for, uh, intercourse."

"Intercourse?" I gaped. "That's what it's referred to as?"

"Oh, my sweet summer child," Aoife laughed with a mischievous twinkle in her eyes. "How much I could teach you about the world."

"Then teach me, oh wise one," I shot back with a grin. "I'm all ears."

"Okay, this could actually be fun." Aoife grinned. "The sex talk, Aoife Molloy style."

"Molloy," Joey warned, returning from his shower just in time to spoil the fun. "Whatever it is you're thinking about telling them don't. They're only in fifth year."

"What were you up to when we were in fifth year, Joe?"

"I'm not the comparison here, Molloy," he replied, breezing through his apartment in a low-hanging pair of gray sweatpants. Both of his arms were inked in an array of black loops and swivels that stopped at his wrists and disappeared beneath the sleeves of his black T-shirt.

"No," Aoife laughed, eyes tracking him. "Because you know damn well what kind of trouble you were getting into, Joe."

"I think it's pretty clear what I was getting into, Molloy," he shot back without a hint of embarrassment, before gesturing to the baby she was cradling. "Let's not encourage my baby sister and her friend to follow in our footsteps, yeah?"

"Relax, they're both being safe," she replied and then gave us both a look. "You *are* being safe, right, girls?"

"Right," Shannon confirmed while I blurted out, "I'm a virgin."

"Good," Joey approved, pointing the knife he was using to butter a slice of bread at me. "Keep that shit up, Baby Biggs."

I beamed back at him. "Thanks, Joe."

"I knew I always liked that girl," he told Shan, while pointing to me. "Keep her." He turned back to me. "Lock and key, ya hear?"

"I hear you, Joe."

"Before we even get into the fun parts of sex, I need to stress that condoms *and* birth control are a must," Aoife quickly continued. "It's not a matter of one or the other." She eyed us knowingly. "It's both, girls. It's *always* both."

"And fair warning," Joey cut in. "If you're puking on the pill, you're unprotected." Layering his bread with a slice of ham and then another slice of bread, he cut it in half. "And if you're unprotected, you're pregnant," he added, strolling over to hand Aoife one half of the sandwich. "And if you're pregnant, you're a parent."

"Thanks, stud," Aoife replied, taking a bite of her sandwich before turning back to us. "And if you think your body miraculously bounces back after childbirth, then you're wrong. You are *ruined* down there, girls. Like seriously. I tore so bad, but another mam I knew was ripped from her vagina to her butthole."

"Shut the front door!" I yelped, horrified. "Ew."

"Hand on my heart." Aoife pressed a hand to her chest, while she cradled her sleeping son with the other. "I'm telling no word of a lie here, girls. She was *maimed*."

20

Pints and Piss-Ups

GIBSIE

"Shots?"

"No."

"Fine, pints?"

"I'll have a pint of water."

"*I'll have a pint of water,*" I mimicked, thoroughly disgusted with the overgrown creature standing next to me at the bar. "You'll have a pint, and you'll be happy about it."

"Gibs."

"Not another word, Jonathan."

"Jesus Christ, fine. I'll have a pint of Heineken."

"Good man yourself." I clapped his shoulder. "Make it four pints, Mary," I told the woman behind the bar. "And we'll have four shots of baby Guinness while we're waiting."

"Gibs."

"Each," I added, slapping a fifty euro note on the counter. "We'll be over in our usual corner."

"I'm not having shots," Johnny grumbled, walking over to the table with me, while politely acknowledging half the bar as he went. Everyone wanted a piece of my best friend, but he was on my clock tonight.

"Cap, Gibs," both Hugh and Feely acknowledged when we joined them at the table.

"Lads, please remind this overgrown fucker that he is only eighteen," I said, pulling up a stool at the table. "And that he needs to do regular eighteen-year-old things because that's what this year is supposed to be about for him."

The whole reason Johnny had postponed his signing to the pros was because he felt like he had missed out on most of his youth. I was determined to remedy that. My first plan of action was Friday night pints like a normal bunch of sixth years.

"You're in better form than you've ever been," Hugh offered, smiling politely at Mary who had arrived with a tray and was setting shot glasses down in front of us. "You can take a night off, lad."

"And school?"

"The books will still be there for you on Monday," Feely added. "Not that you have to worry about academics."

"Come on, Cap," I coaxed, slapping his shoulder. "Let's make some fucking memories here. You'll be gone before we know it and then all you'll have is your regrets." Reaching for a shot, I held it up and implored him with my eyes to do the same. "Be a teenager with us."

"*Come on, Cap,*" Johnny mimicked several hours later. "*Be a teenager with us.*" Shaking his head, he blinked the bleariness away and tried to glare at me. "Why haven't I learned by now to *never* listen to you?"

"Just your good luck, I guess," I said, clinking my half-empty pint glass against his. "Bottom's up."

"No, no, no." Feely laughed, grabbing my attention. "I would use the 50/50 option on the easier questions. There's nothing worse than seeing a fellow stuck on the $64,000 question with four outlandish options to choose from."

"What's that now?" I asked, curious.

"Hugh was asking which lives I would use if I ever got called up to be on *Who Wants to Be a Millionaire* on the television."

"Well, make sure you put me down as your phone a friend," I said, tapping my temple. "I'm a whiz at that show."

Both of them cracked up, laughing in response.

I narrowed my eyes. "Well, that's fucking lovely, that is."

"Cap would be my first port of call," Hugh chimed in.

"Same here," Feely added.

"And then you, lad," Hugh said, turning to Feely.

"Right back at you, Hughie."

Betrayal.

Jesus Christ, the *betrayal!*

"It's nothing personal, Gibs," Feely tried to coax, still laughing. "Don't get the hump."

"Hey, Johnny, if you got on the show, you'd call me, wouldn't you?" I turned to my best friend. "I'd be your phone a friend if you were on the show, wouldn't I?"

Johnny stared at me like I'd grown three heads. "What the fuck are ya talking about, Gibs?"

"Those assholes would call each other if you didn't answer," I explained, pointing a thumb in the direction of Feely and Hugh. "But you'd call me, wouldn't you?"

"Of course I would, Gibs," he appeased, patting my arm. "You're my number one, lad."

It was bullshit but the fact that he had my back in public like this meant everything.

"See, fuckers," I grumbled, tossing back the rest of my pint before raising my hand to call for another round to be brought over to us.

"Hey, lads, do any of you want kids?"

I gaped at my best friend. "Kids?"

"Yeah." Johnny nodded solemnly. "Are ye planning on having some?"

"You want kids, Cap?" Hugh asked.

"Of course."

"Now?"

"No, not now, ya bleeding eejit," Johnny replied, sounding pissed as a fart. "In the future."

"Thanks, Mary," Hugh said to the ageing barmaid when she arrived at our table with another round of pints. He handed her off a twenty before turning his attention back to our captain, clearly engrossed in the horrific topic. "How many kids?"

"I don't know, maybe two or three," Johnny mused, draining the last of his pint. "Definitely not one on his own." His brows furrowed. "Wouldn't want them to be lonely."

"Girls or boys?"

"What are you doing?" I demanded, glaring at Hugh. "Stop encouraging this behavior!"

"Whatever Shan can give me," Johnny replied, ignoring the appalled look on my face. "I'll take whatever she's willing to give me." He frowned again, thinking hard about something before saying, "You know, I think I'd love a daughter." He scratched his jaw as he spoke. "I'd be delighted with sons, too, of course, but I'd love to raise a little girl with Shan." Shrugging, he added, "You know, show her how different it should've been for her."

"You'd make a good girl dad," Hugh agreed with a solemn nod.

"I know," Johnny agreed, reaching for one of the fresh pints the barmaid had set. "Fuck it, we'll see how it goes, won't we? Time will tell."

"I don't want kids," Feely mused, scratching his jaw. "I don't think I want a family, period."

"Jesus, that sounds depressingly lonely," Johnny replied.

He shrugged but didn't answer.

"I kind of like the way Claire and I grew up," Hugh offered, rubbing his jean-clad thigh. "Having a baby sister is a pain in the hole at times, but we've had a good life." He shrugged. "If I was to have a family, I think I'd like something like what my parents gave us."

"Do ye think Lynchy and Aoife will have more?"

"In a few years, probably."

"Well, if anyone wants to know the whereabouts of my future children," I interjected, holding a hand up. "I left a fresh batch of them in a tissue in my room this morning."

"You sick fucker," Feely laughed, while Hugh shuddered in revulsion.

"Filter, Gibs!" Johnny barked, elbowing my side. "*Filter*."

I shrugged unapologetically. "You know what I was just thinking?"

"No, Gibs, and I doubt we want to know either," all three of them chorused.

"I was thinking that it must be nice to know that your parents wanted you so badly that they went to the extreme lengths of having you cooked up in the lab." I patted my best friend's shoulder. "Fair play, lad."

"As opposed to?"

"Pillowing your way through a hole in a condom," I offered honestly. "I heard that, you know? When my parents were separating. Apparently, I was just such a strong swimmer that I poked a hole in the condom."

"Don't worry about it," Feely was quick to placate. "I was an accident, too. Mam was forty-six when she found out she was pregnant with me. All of my sisters were raised. She thought she was in the menopause."

"Jesus, Pa." Johnny's brows shot up. "Your ma is sixty-three?"

"That's some quick math, lad."

Johnny brushed the compliment off. "I never knew your ma was that old."

"Why?" Feely asked. "How old is your mam?"

"In her early forties," Johnny replied. "Da's a couple of years older."

"Mine's forty-three," Hugh said. "Same as my old fella."

"And mine," I chimed in. "They all went to school together."

"My old fella is closer to seventy," Feely said quietly.

"Whoa," I mused, shaking my head. "You're probably going to be really young when they die."

"Jesus, Gibs!" Johnny and Hugh both barked. "Filter!"

"Don't worry about it," Feely chuckled. "I'm well used to him." His phone chimed then, and he quickly pulled it out of his jeans pocket and tapped at the screen.

"Who's texting you?" I asked, leaning over the table to get a better look at his screen. Why, I had no clue. I had trouble reading on a good day, without a dozen pints in my belly.

"Gibs," Johnny scolded, catching ahold of my shirt, and pulling me back up. "You don't ask a fella that."

"Nah, it's grand," Feely replied, tapping a few lines of a text out before sliding his phone back in his pocket. "It's just Casey."

"Casey?" Johnny frowned. "Who's Casey?"

"Jesus, Cap, for such a smart fella, you have the worst observational skills." Hugh chuckled. "She's Aoife's friend."

"The wild one," I chimed in, waggling my brows. "Feely's been tapping her for months."

"Gibs," Feely groaned. "Don't fucking say that, will you?"

"Aoife's friend?" Johnny stared blankly. "Nope. No idea."

"That's because you've been too busy chasing rugby and Shannon to look up and see what's happening with the rest of us." Hugh laughed.

"That's not entirely true," Johnny argued. "I know plenty about what happens in your lives."

"Hah!" I clapped his shoulder. "Good one, Johnny."

"I fucking do!" Setting down his pint, he folded his arms across his chest and glared at the three of us. "You," he said, beginning with Feely. "You're eighteen, apparently in a situationship with this Casey, the youngest brother of three sisters. Your birthday is in July, and you're a closet musician with a voice better than anyone on the radio." Then he turned to Hugh. "You, you're seventeen, the oldest of two kids, your birthday's on Halloween, same as Seany's, you've been with Katie since forever, and she's your first serious girlfriend." Finally, he turned to me and said, "And you, you're the baby of the gang. Your birthday's in March. You've never had a girlfriend because you're in love with his sister since the beginning of time and have the attention span of a crème egg, and you're fucking the school receptionist." Blowing out a breath, Johnny smirked at us before saying, "Did I miss anything?"

"Only a few minor details," Feely mused, pushing his dark hair off his face. "I'm not in a situationship with anyone, but that was impressive, Cap. And to be fair, you're a million times better since you got with Shannon."

"That was dreadful," I accused, turning to gape at him. "My birthday is in *February* not March. I most certainly do not have the attention span of a crème egg, and I am not fucking the school receptionist."

"And Katie and I started going out when I was in fourth year," Hugh offered, holding a hand up. "Not since forever."

"No, no, no," Johnny argued. "I specifically remember you being obsessed with that girl back in second year." He tapped his temple. "I know because you were always missing out on training when we were younger to go chasing after her."

"Wrong girl, Cap," Feely muttered, rubbing his brow.

"The fuck?" Johnny gaped at him before turning to me. "And your birthday's not in March?"

"No, it is not in bloody March, you sorry excuse for a best friend," I huffed. "The fucking cheek of you forgetting my birthday."

"Sorry, Gibs, I could've sworn it was in March." He scratched his jaw. "Why is March in my head?"

"Because *Shannon's* birthday is in March," I growled. "You pussy-whipped prick."

"And he's not in love with my sister, either," Hugh interjected. "He just thinks he is."

"Don't you start," I warned, turning to glare at Hugh. "I might not be smooth like the rest of ye, or a fucking mathematician like Brains over there," I paused to point at Johnny, "but I have a heart that pumps and beats and grows feelings. I care. I feel. I love. And all of it is solely directed toward your sister."

"Then make a fucking change, Gibs," Hugh snapped, glowering at me. "Because I have to say, lad, if you think you're getting anywhere near my sister while you're sticking your dick in Dee, then you're sorely mistaken. Claire deserves more than to get mixed up in your twisted drama and you know it."

"Oh my Jesus. For the last time, I am not sticking my dick in Dee!" I growled, throwing my hands up in despair. "I haven't been anywhere near that woman since fifth year." Narrowing my eyes right back at Hugh, I snapped, "And I'll have you know that I would never do anything to hurt your sister. I would rather peel the skin off my bones first."

"Except that you already do a whole pile that could hurt her," Hugh urged, tone serious. "Come on, Gibs, if Claire knew about your extracurricular escapades, it would rip the heart clean out of her chest."

"He has a point," Feely added, taking Hugh's side. "Claire's in love with you, lad. Has been since we were kids. You know this. It's no hidden secret. And if you felt the same way, you'd have done something about it by now."

"Hold up," Johnny said, coming to my defense. "Nobody is saying Gibs is the only fella to put his dick in the wrong girl here. Not one of us is an angel, lads. Everyone has a past."

"True," Feely agreed.

"I haven't," Hugh deadpanned.

"So, you're a squeaky-clean virgin, now are ya?" Johnny chuckled. "Saint Hugh?"

"I've only been with Katie," Hugh replied, eyes locked on Johnny. "So, what do you think, Cap?"

"But you've been together since…" Johnny's brows shot up. "Shite."

"Yeah," Hugh snapped. "Unlike the rest of ye sick bastards, I don't spread myself around like butter."

Feely cocked a brow. "Butter?"

"Butter."

"Hey, I'm loyal," Johnny huffed. "Like a bleeding Labrador."

"Listen, it's got nothing to do with who you've been with in the past and everything to do with what you're doing in the present," Feely said, steering the conversation back on track. "All we're trying to say here is stop playing with Claire's feelings."

"Exactly," Hugh agreed, with a stiff nod. "No more of this leading her on bullshit."

"You either want her or you don't," Feely added. "And if you don't, that's grand, Gibs. Understandable. But if that's the case, then step aside and let the girl have a life. Because she doesn't have a chance of getting over you when you're standing in her way."

21

Saturday Night Vibes

CLAIRE

"I WANT A BIG, DIRTY TAKEAWAY, WITH A MINIMUM OF THREE THOUSAND CALORIES and a side order of grease," Gerard announced when he staggered into my bedroom late Saturday evening. "Seriously, babe." Clad in gray sweatpants and a white muscle vest, and with his blond hair standing on end, he looked like a broken man. "I'm fading away here."

"Oh my god?" I half gasped, half laughed, as I took in his disheveled appearance. "Who *broke* you?"

"Who'd you think," came his disgusted response as he stumbled toward me. "Quick, push over, babe. My legs are bolloxed."

"Don't you mean *Bambied*?" I snickered, using the new word I'd learned, courtesy of Joey's baby mama.

"Seriously, they're shaking so bad it feels like my kneecaps are about to dislocate from the rest of me," he groaned, causing a laugh to escape me.

According to Aoife, getting Bambied was when a boy made you orgasm so violently that your legs shook like a baby deer trying to stand up for the first time. Since moving into the annex at the Kavanagh's house with Joey and AJ, Aoife had become something of a revered, seductive goddess to the rest of us girls, doling out wisdom and knowledge that blew our minds.

Seriously, I had learned more about sex in the last few weeks I'd spent hanging out with Joey's baby mama than I had in my entire sixteen years on earth.

Aoife was joining us at Tommen after the Halloween holidays, and I couldn't wait. Aside from the fact that it was awesome to see Katie come out of her shell with her childhood friend present, what her presence did for Joey was incomparable.

"Look at those tremors," I cackled when Gerard face-planted on my mattress, narrowly avoiding Cherub, who was curled up on my lap, taking a break from the ever-boisterous Tom, Dick, and Harry—the three male kittens Mam agreed to let us keep from Brian and Cherub's adorable litter this past summer. Salt and Pepper had been adopted by cousins of ours living in Bandon, while a friend of Sadhbh's in Clonakilty had adopted Millicent.

Yeah, that had been a dark day for the Biggs-Gibson family.

"You think that's funny but it's not," Gerard groaned into the mattress. "Because that bastard fucked me harder in the gym today than he ever did little Shannon."

"Gerard, *ew*!" I grimaced, slapping at his sweaty shoulder. "You couldn't take a shower before you came over?"

"Shower?" He raised his head to gape at me. "Claire, it took everything I had in me to get back to you!"

"It couldn't have been that bad."

"He's a madman," he argued. "A sadist. I never want to see the inside of a gym again."

"Yeah, well, you agreed to go to the gym with him in exchange for pints at Biddies last night," I reminded him. "And if I recall correctly, you also asked him to train you up so that you could get a spot in the Academy."

"Train me, Claire," he deadpanned. "Not break my will."

I covered my mouth to stifle a laugh. "So, you're not sold on the professional rugby player career anymore?"

"Fuck that," he groaned and, with a great deal of effort, rolled onto his back. "I was built for comfort, not speed. I'll join the family business and become a baker."

"You are a great baker," I indulged him by saying.

"I *am* a great baker," he agreed, looking up at me with a delighted expression. "I've seriously improved."

"Hands down," I praised. "You're like a different person in the kitchen since you took the job at the bakery." Smiling, I added, "And your fairy cakes are the best I've ever tasted."

"See, this is why I love you." He reached out a hand to stroke Cherub. "You get me."

"I do get you." I laughed, gently placing my purring queen on top of his back. "Which is why I must add that this ripped version of Gerard Gibson"—I paused to trail a finger over the fabric that concealed his recently renewed abdominal muscles before climbing off the bed—"is pretty, but I like the old version best."

"You miss my love handles," he purred, carefully rolling onto his back and then setting Cherub back down on his stomach. "You prefer a little extra Gibs to keep you warm at night, don't you?"

"Maybe?" I laughed, not that he ever had love handles to begin with. "Here," I said, distracting myself from my lustful thoughts by scooping up our three mischievous kittens and carrying them over to the bed. "Say hello to your daddy."

"Dick!" Gerard cooed, snatching up the furriest of the three. "How are you, son?"

"Don't forget to give Tom and Harry some attention," I warned, climbing back onto the mattress. "You're always favoring Dick."

"But that's only because I love my Dick," he continued to coo, holding the kitten up to his face so that they could rub noses. "Isn't that right, son? You're my favorite, aren't you? Yes, you are with your little pink nose and teeny tiny paws."

"*Gerard!*"

"Alright, alright." Reluctantly setting down the beautiful ginger-haired kitten, he turned his attention to Dick's littermates. "Listen, babe, you know I love all our kids, and I know it's not their fault, but I can't look at Tom and Harry without seeing *him*."

"Gerard," I gasped in horror, snatching up Harry. "How *could* you?"

"I know," he agreed with a groan. "It's terrible, isn't it? But I can't help it. They've got his beady green eyes and that creepy white hair…"

"Brian might have fathered them, but you are their dad! And dads are supposed to love all of their children equally!"

"I know!" Throwing his hands up in defeat, he added, "That's why I wanted to keep Millicent. She was every inch her mother's daughter." He pointed to Cherub who was still snoozing on his lap. "Look at that pussy. Look at how beautiful and sweet she is—"

"Oh my god, I can't believe this!" I shrieked, scooping up the boys and stomping back to their basket. "You don't love our babies."

"I *do*! I do love our babies, Claire!" Bambied legs forgotten, Gerard sprang off the bed and hurried after me. "But that bastard Brian has given me an awful life. You know that. Remember when he snuck up on me in the shower and scratched my gooch? Or the time he bit my toe and I had to get a tetanus shot? He *traumatized* me, Claire. I can't help it if every time I look at Tom and Harry, I'm triggered!"

"This is terrible," I wailed, kneeling in front of the basket full of kittens. "Don't worry, babies, I'm as disappointed in your father as you are."

"Wait—" Snatching me up in one swift move, Gerard set me on my feet facing him. "Are we in a fight?"

"You know what, Gerard." I planted my hands on my hips. "I think we are."

"We're a team, babe," he tried to reason, wrapping an arm around my waist and pulling me flush against him. "We don't fight."

"On, no, no, no," I warned, reaching up to twist his ear. "Don't *babe* me, Gerard Gibson. You can't smooth talk your way out of this."

"Okay, ouch!" he grumbled, cupping his ear. "Was there any need for violence?"

"*Yes*," I replied emphatically.

"Everything alright, you two?" A light knock on my bedroom door sounded moments before it cracked open, and Mam's head appeared. "I thought I heard shouting."

"Gerard doesn't love all of our babies," I cried out in outrage. "He only loves one!"

"No, I love them all," he defended, looking flustered. "I just don't like looking at two of them."

"Is it Tom and Harry?" Mam asked in a sympathetic tone. "Is it because they look like Brian?"

"Yes," we both chorused in equal volumes of outrage.

"Oh dear." Pushing the door fully open, Mam walked into my room, using her hand to cover her smile. "Okay, let's have it." Walking over to my bed, Mam sat down and crossed her legs. "One at a time."

"I have spent *months* looking after our babies," I got there first by saying. Okay, by screaming. "Doing the night feeds when Cherub refused to look after them. I went without sleep for these babies when they are his responsibility, too!"

"Oh, no, no, no, don't even go there!" he warned, holding a hand up. "I have done everything I can for our babies!"

"Except love them," I spat back. "You big dick!"

"Language, Claire," Mam scolded.

"I beg your fucking pardon," Gerard choked out, eyes widening. "Who's the one who took them to his house every weekend to give you a break? And who's the one that took a job at my mam's bakery to pay Cherub's maternity bill at the vets? Or for the boys to get their pediatric neutering so they didn't fuck their own mam and have incestuous hillbilly babies?" He slapped his chest. "This big dick, that's who!"

"Language, Gibsie."

"Oh yeah, Gerard." Ignoring my mam's request to tone it down, I rolled my eyes to the heavens and shouted, "What a great weekend dad you are. Out with your wallet to make it all better. Fatherhood is about more than just money!"

"Reginald lives with me full-time!" he shouted back at me, throwing his hands up. "And I have never asked you to provide a single caterpillar in child support for him. No, because I dig up all the critters myself. *Every day*. So don't act all high and mighty with me, baby!"

"And I appreciate you doing that," I begrudgingly shouted back. "You know I hate getting my nails dirty."

"I *do* know that." Planting his hands on his hips, Gerard nodded stiffly. "That's why I never ask you to do it."

"And for financing our babies," I said, still half shouting, even though I could feel the fight leave my body. "I appreciate you being the breadwinner in our family, too."

"No problem," he countered, tone still raised and hard, mirroring mine. "It's the least I could do for you and the kids. I appreciate what a wonderful mother you are." Purposefully hardening his tone, he added, "I wouldn't want to do this with anyone else."

"And you're so much more than a weekend father," I admitted, voice softening. "And I wouldn't want to do this with anyone else, either."

"Okay then." He nodded stiffly. "Are we still fighting, or can we hug it out?"

"Hug it out," I replied, bolting straight for him. "Definitely hug it out."

"Thank Jesus," Gerard replied, wrapping me up in a bear hug. "Worst ten minutes of my life."

"What am I going to do with the two of you?" Mam laughed from her perch on my bed. "You're like an old married couple."

"I don't know, Sinead," Gibsie replied with a solemn shrug. "But whatever it is, could it revolve around food? Preferably something from the Chinese or the chipper."

"No, no, please not the chipper," I protested, stepping around Gerard to get to my mam. "We had chipper food last Saturday night. I've been dying for beef satay all week."

"Ooh, yeah." Gerard's eyes lit up. "Make that two beef satays."

"With black bean sauce."

"And egg fried rice."

"Should we get a portion of chips?" I asked, tilting my head to one side. "Or will we just have the prawn crackers?"

"Prawn crackers," Gerard confirmed with a grim nod. "Remember the last time we got the chips?"

"The salt and peppered ones?"

"No, those were fantastic. I'm talking about the soggy ones."

"Ew, yeah." I scrunched my nose up at the memory. "Good call, Gerard." Turning back to my mother, I reeled off our food order, tapping on a bottle of fizzy orange at the end.

"When I asked what I was going to do with the two of you, I was referring to your antics in general," Mam said with a sigh of amusement. "Not filling your bellies."

"Fill our bellies," I encouraged, reaching over to pat Gerard's at the same time he reached out to pat mine.

"Yes, please do," he agreed with a solemn nod. "We're fading away here."

"You two." Mam laughed. "Alright. I'll order the food. You two clean up those kittens and come downstairs and join the others."

"Others?"

"Hugh and Katie are in the living room," she explained. "I'll call the Chinese and order a delivery for the four of you before I head into work for my shift. Your father is in the office upstairs if you need him. He's on a deadline for work, and you know what that means, so please only go up if you absolutely have to."

My father, a once-upon-a-time super-successful property developer, had thrown the towel in on his corporate job ten years ago. After his best friend died, Dad chose to give up the hustle and bustle, choosing instead to lock himself away in the attic writing murder mystery thrillers. It was cathartic for him and his way of dealing with the grief that had overtaken him after Joe died. The fact his books were wildly popular was an added bonus.

"We'll be good," we both chorused, giving each other a knowing look. Because once Mam left for work, Dad wouldn't be coming downstairs to check on us. *Free house.*

"Hmm." With another shake of her head, Mam walked out of the room. "Oh, and for future reference, keep the door open, Claire."

"But what if Dick escapes and sneaks into Hugh's room again?" I called after her.

"That's not the dick I'm worried about escaping," Mam muttered under her breath.

22
Team Clibsie for the Win

CLAIRE

Two hours later, the Chinese food had been demolished right along with half of the contents of Mam's sideboard; the one in the front room she kept locked that contained the alcohol and tins of biscuits and sweets she was storing for Christmas.

Of course, Hugh and I happened to possess the "missing" spare key of said sideboard and had managed to inconspicuously outsmart Mam by taking just a little bit at a time for years. Taking enough to get tipsy and have a gorge on chocolate, but not enough to tip her off or smell a rat.

"How am I supposed to keep up when you keep changing the rules?" Gerard demanded, tossing his last card down on the coffee table and swiping up a fancy little glass filled with sherry. "Fuck the pair of you," he grumbled, taking a sip of his drink, pinkie finger extended. "I know you're cheating."

"It's Snap, Gibs." Hugh chuckled, placing a card down on the pile. "You can't cheat in Snap."

"Snap!" Slamming her hand down on the huge pile, Katie squealed in excitement. "Again."

"See?" Gerard's eyes bulged as he pointed to the enormous stack of cards in front of Hugh and Katie. "Fucking cheaters."

"Don't hate the player, Gibs," Katie snickered, leaning against my brother, who was sitting behind her on the armchair. "Hate the game."

"Nope, Johnny and Shan definitely aren't coming over," I chimed in, reading from the text message I'd just received from Shannon. "Sorry guys. We're having an early night. See you at the coffee shop tomorrow. X. X. X." Exhaling a dreamy sigh, I tossed my phone down on my lap and retrieved my bowl of ice cream mixed with Baileys Irish Cream. "Aww."

"I bet they're doing something romantic," Katie gushed.

"With candles," I replied wistfully.

"And romantic music," she agreed, taking a sip from Hugh's beer bottle.

Gerard snorted. "I bet they're fucking."

"Gerard!"

"Gibs!"

"He's right," my brother laughed, dodging the elbow Katie aimed at his ribs. "It sounds like Cap's doing more than just bulldozing Shannon's life."

"They're certainly not sitting around playing Snap," Gerard added, eyeing the coffee table with disgust. "What's happening to us, lads? It's Saturday night and we're playing card games like a bunch of geriatrics when we should be out getting off our trolleys."

"I'm only sixteen, that's what's wrong with me," I offered. "And you three are only seventeen."

"Not for long." Waggling his brows, Gerard tossed a handful of Minstrels at Hugh. "A certain brother-in-law is turning eighteen at the end of the month."

"You are so lucky to have your birthday on Halloween, babe," Katie added. "How cool is that?"

"Just think, lad, your mam and dad must have had one hell of a Valentine's that year."

"Disturbing notion, Gibs," Hugh groaned, popping a couple of Minstrels in his mouth before tossing the rest back at Gerard. "But impressive conception math."

"Speaking of." Scooping one final spoon of alcohol-laced ice cream into my mouth, I set my bowl on the coffee table and sprang to my feet. "We need to talk Halloween costumes."

"No." Hugh shook his head. "We really don't."

"Yes, we do," I argued, rubbing my hands together. "Mam's throwing a party at the house for your birthday at Halloween. It's fancy dress—and it's not optional."

"Woo-hoo." Draining his glass of sherry, Gerard stared into the empty glass before reaching for the bottle. "What are we going as this year, babe?"

Brimming with excitement, I swung around to give him my full attention. "Okay, so this year, since there's an even ratio of girls to boys in our group, five on five, I was thinking we could all go as famous couples."

Frowning in concentration, Gerard unscrewed the cap on Granny's sherry bottle and took a deep swig. "I'm listening."

"Picture this," I told him, waving my hands around animatedly. "You and me, rocking it out in PVC leather."

Confusion swept over his face. "Are we going as Motley Crue?"

"No, silly, Danny and Sandy," I laughed. "From *Grease*."

His eyes lit up. "I fucking love that movie!"

"I know. I've been working on our costumes already." Smiling bashfully, I added, "So, for Joey and Aoife, I was thinking Joker and Harley Quinn."

"Oh yeah, I can totally see that," Katie said with an enthusiastic nod. "But will she want to dress up?" Shrugging, she added, "You know, after given birth and all that?"

"Oh please, you've seen that body of hers," I shot back. "The girl is even more smoking hot post-baby than she was pre-baby."

"Agreed," Katie replied. "I would kill for Aoif's figure."

"I know, right?" I beamed. "And then for you guys, I was thinking Edward and Vivian from *Pretty Woman*."

"Huh." Frowning, Katie tilted her head to one side and asked, "Wasn't she a prostitute?"

"And didn't he have gray hair?" Hugh added, looking equally skeptical.

"You're blond, Hugh. It's close enough. Make it work," Gerard tossed out, thoroughly enjoying our granny's Christmas sherry. "Now, don't interrupt your sister's creative process, dammit." He took another huge swig from the bottle and waved a hand around aimlessly. "As you were, sweetheart."

Smiling indulgently at his adorable drunken expression, I quickly continued. "And then for Johnny and Shan, it's a no-brainer."

Katie smiled. "Romeo and Juliet?"

"Yes!"

She nodded her head in approval. "Good choice."

I beamed back at her. "I know, right?"

"Wait." My brother held a hand up. "Didn't they both die in the book?"

"She's talking about the movie version," Gerard replied with a snort. "Dumbass."

"Pretty sure the movie version met the same fate, Gibs," Hughie drawled sarcastically.

"Well, they don't die in my Ballylaggin version," I shot back before quicky continuing. "And then for Liz and Patrick, I was thinking something a little edgier like Morticia and Gomez Addams—you know, to match Lizzie's personality."

"Oh my god, I love it," Katie laughed, clapping. "Claire, you're a genius."

"I don't see it," Hugh tossed out. "First off, she's blond. Second, she doesn't do fancy dress, and third, if she does show up, she'll be with Pierce."

"Goddammit, Hugh," Gerard slurred. "Stop interrupting your sister's creative process."

"You might want to put down the sherry, Gibs," Katie chuckled. "You're getting a little feisty over there."

"No need. It's already gone." He tipped the bottle upside down for emphasis, causing one lone droplet of chestnut-colored liquid to drip onto the back of his hand. Never one to be wasteful, Gerard quickly licked it up with his tongue. "See?"

"Ah, Gibs, lad. You're going to have one hell of a sick head in the morning," Hugh said, wincing. "A sherry hangover is fecking dreadful."

"Liz already agreed to dress up as Morticia if Patrick will go as Gomez," I told my brother, feeling smug. "And according to her latest text message, she won't be going anywhere with Pierce."

"They're off again?"

"Yep." I shrugged. "If the pendulum swings and they get back together before the party, then he can go as Uncle Fester."

"Girl doesn't know where her head is at," Katie mused.

"True that," Gerard chimed in, snatching up a bowl of popcorn. "She's been blowing hot and cold for years. Isn't that right, Hugh?"

"Gibs." My brother's entire frame went rigid. "Don't."

"What did I say?"

"Nothing," Hugh deadpanned. "Keep it that way."

"Sorry, lad. Didn't mean to hit a nerve."

"You didn't."

"First love stings like a bitch, though, doesn't it?"

"*Gibs!*"

"Oh, stop trying to cause trouble." Katie laughed, reaching for another bottle of beer from the coffee table. "I already know all about it. Hugh told me when we first met."

"Did he really?" Gerard grinned mischievously and tossed a piece of popcorn at my brother "He told you *all* about it?"

"I said that's enough, lad," Hugh snapped. "Nobody wants to hear it."

"I second that," I agreed, good mood fading fast at the memory of the biggest betrayal of my childhood.

My best friend and my brother.

Yuck.

Aside from the fact that they were disgustingly close friends when we were kids, Lizzie broke the fundamental law of friendship in fourth class when she agreed to be my *brother's* girlfriend.

It didn't matter to me that it was totally innocent. In my eyes, it was a crime against girl code and had resulted in us not speaking for three whole weeks.

Never one to hold a grudge, I'd given in and resumed my post of being her friend, while I secretly counted down the days until they broke up and I got my friend back.

I had never admitted it at the time, and never would, but a lot of my anger was caused by a hefty dollop of jealousy. Not so much because Lizzie was going out with my brother. But because he had asked her, when *Gerard* never asked *me*. Hugh was

Lizzie's childhood sweetheart and Gerard was mine. Lizzie got a shot with hers, and I didn't.

"The Hizzie era was like a million years ago." Flopping down on the couch beside him, I threw my legs over his lap and sighed. "We're in the Hatie era now."

"The Hatie era." Gerard threw his head back and howled with laughter. "Oh, Claire-Bear, that sounds fucking terrible."

"What?" I slapped at his arm. "It's better than the Kughie era."

"Kughie!" The term only caused Gerard to laugh louder. "I can't… I can't…"

"Oh, shag off, Gibs." Hugh chuckled, tension easing from his shoulders. "Like yours is so much better."

"Yeah," Katie snickered in agreement. "Clibsie."

"Whatever lad, I'd take Clibsie any day over Kughie."

"Is that so, Glaire?"

Gerard choked out another laugh. "Glaire's still better than Hatie."

"Team Clibsie for the win," I teased, fist-bumping Gerard. "Unlucky, guys."

"Okay, Team Clibsie," Katie giggled. "Care to put your money where your mouth is and find out who the superior duo is?"

"My money's upstairs," Gerard replied solemnly. "Walking around on four legs."

"I was joking," she chuckled, clearing off the coffee table. "Let's play a game. Team Clibsie versus Team Hatie."

"Hatie," Gerard snorted.

"How about losers clean the kitchen after takeaway night," she offered with a smirk. "Every Saturday night for a *month*."

"Make it two months, and you've got yourself a deal," Gerard counter-negotiated, attention piqued.

"Two months it is," she challenged. "Do you accept?"

"Oh, it's on like Donkey Kong," Gerard replied, fully invested now. "You're going down, Hatie."

"What kind of game?" I asked, curious.

"What about Scrabble?" Katie offered. "You guys have a board, right?"

"Phone another friend there," Gerard shot back with a big fat thumb's own. "Because it's a no deal from me."

"Monopoly?"

"No, I can't be dealing with any board games with words on them."

"Poker?"

His eyes lit up with mischief. "Strip poker!"

"Ew, Gerard!" I balked. "Gross."

"Uh, hello?" Hugh gaped at him before gesturing between us. "Full-blood relatives in the room."

"Ah come on, lad," Gerard begged. "Take one for the team."

"Hard pass," Hugh deadpanned. "Move along, perv."

"Ooh, ooh, I've got it." Quickly standing, Katie made a beeline for the kitchen, returning a few moments later with a bottle of Dad's Jameson and four shot glasses. "Let's play Never have I ever."

"Ooh, this could be dangerous." Rubbing his hands together with glee, Gerard reached for the bottle. "Let's do it."

23

Below the Belt

GIBSIE

WHAT STARTED AS A GOOD-NATURED GAME OF NEVER HAVE I EVER HAD MORPHED into something that resembled a warped episode of Jerry Springer. Maybe it was the whiskey flowing in his veins, or maybe it was payback for bringing up the whole Lizzie fiasco, but Hugh was on *fire* with his questions.

"Never have I ever fingered Bernadette Brady against the wall at the Boiler Room disco in second year."

Harsh.

"Anyone?" Hugh continued to goad; eyes narrowed on me as he held up his full shot glass. "Anyone at all?"

Bastard.

Drunk or not, I was acutely aware of the girl sitting beside me. This was a dangerous fucking game, and his question was below the belt. Regrettably, I raised my glass to my lips and tossed it back.

When Claire stiffened beside me and croaked out the word, "*Ew*," I was filled with self-loathing.

"Okay, guys," Katie slurred, three sheets to the wind right along with the rest of us. "Maybe we should call it a night?"

Yeah, fuck that. "My turn." Snatching up the almost empty bottle of whiskey, I clumsily refilled my glass and raised it up. "Never have I ever gotten caught kissing my girlfriend in the tree house by my mam?"

When Hugh raised his glass to his lips, Katie shook her head in confusion. "Sinead never caught us in the tree house, Hugh."

Take that, fucker.

With a guilt-ridden expression on his face, Hugh tossed the shot of whiskey back his throat, causing his girlfriend to whisper the word, "Oh."

"My turn." Furious, Hugh used the last drop from the bottle to refill his glass, clearly seething. "Never have I ever fucked an older woman."

I glared back at him, equally seething.

"Drink up, Gibs," he bit out.

"No can do, lad."

"This is a truth game."

"I know," I deadpanned.

"Then take the fucking shot."

My jaw clenched. "*No.*"

"Guys, I think we need to stop," Katie tried again, placing her hand on her boyfriend's shoulder. "It's getting way too deep between you guys."

"How about I rephrase the question to never have I ever stuck my dick in a member of the school administration," Hugh pushed, ignoring his girlfriend's plea. "Bottoms up, lad."

Unblinking, I raised the glass to my lips but stopped short at the final second and tipped my glass upside down instead, not giving two shits when the whiskey seeped into the fabric of my sweats.

"You broke the rules." Hugh folded his arms across his chest. "We win."

I shrugged nonchalantly. "If you say so, lad."

"You guys are on cleanup duty."

"For two months."

"No, no, no…" Yawning loudly, Claire burrowed her way under my arm and snuggled closer. "Night, guys. No cleaning for me tonight."

"No…" Katie wailed, crawling onto the couch to pull at Claire's arm. "Don't leave me on my own while these two have their pissing contest."

"But I'm *drunk*," Claire half whispered, half slurred, somehow managing to clamber onto my lap. "And so…sleepy." Inhaling deeply, she loosely hooked an arm around my neck. "Mmm…" Nuzzling my chest with her cheek, she fisted my shirt with her free hand before whispering, "Take me to bed, Gerard."

In any other circumstances, hearing her say those words would have sent a thrill through me. Instead, a huge swell of guilt rose inside of me, so much so that it was sobering me up.

"The ground's spinning, Gerard," she hiccupped. "Mmm… Don't let me fall."

Jesus.

What the hell was I thinking, letting her drink whiskey?

"I've got you, Claire," I coaxed, making a conscious effort to sober myself the hell up as I stood up, taking her with me. "You're safe with me, babe."

"I know," she agreed with a contented sigh, eyes still closed. "My bestie."

Ignoring Hugh who was stilling glaring daggers at me, I proceeded to walk in an impressively straight line, all things considered, toward the staircase. I was far from a responsible drunk. Usually, I was the friend in the group that needed to be taken care of.

But tonight was different.

Tonight, I had to man up.

Because this was *Claire.*

"Nearly there," I coaxed when we reached the top of the landing. "A few more feet"—I paused to kick her door open—"and you can sleep in your nice warm bed."

"With you."

"If that's what you want," I replied, sitting her down on the edge of her bed.

"That's what I always want," she slurred, swaying from side to side.

"Then I'll stay," I confirmed, quickly ushering Cherub and the babies back to their own basket. "I'll be right here with you."

"Good," she hiccupped. "Because I'm super drunk."

"Yeah, babe, I know." Drowning in my guilt, I returned to her side. "You'll be okay." Reaching for her feet, I gently peeled her Ugg boots off before tossing them in her shoe-box. "Right as rain in the morning." Walking over to her dressing table, I retrieved the headband I knew she wore to bed each night. "And I'll cook you up a nice, crispy fry-up."

"I might puke," she confessed. "My stomach's rolling."

"I'm good with puke. Just don't bleed on me and we're golden," I replied, sitting down beside her. "Now, how do we put this thing on?" Concentrating as hard as I could, I carefully placed the headband on just like she would if she could.

"Tie it back please," she instructed in a weak tone, leaning heavily against my shoulder. "In case I"—a hiccup escaped her before she could finish—"puke."

"Ah, shit, Claire-Bear." Retrieving the thick fabric scrunchie from her wrist, I attempted to pulls her curls into a haphazard ponytail. "You're putting me to the pin of my collar here."

"You're always my hero," she half slurred, half laughed. "So pretty."

I waggled my brows at the compliment. "Why, thank you."

"You are," she offered, tone serious as she reached up to trail a finger down my cheek. "You're so pretty."

"I've been told I have a certain boyish charm that chiseled abs and strong jawlines can't absorb."

"And silly," she slurred. "*Super* silly."

"I love you." The words flew out of my mouth of their own accord. Forcing a smile, I gave her cheek a playful squeeze before adding, "My little snuckle-bunny."

"Why thank you very much"—she paused to hiccup—"my little spud monkey."

"Spud monkey?" I laughed. "That's all you could come up with?"

"Yep." She laughed and then quickly contorted in what looked like physical pain. "Oh god, *no*!"

"What?" I demanded, startled by her sudden switch in mood. "What's wrong?"

"I'm so sad, Gerard."

My heart seemed to both stop and speed up at the same time when those words came out of her mouth. "You're sad?" Instantly, I had this primal urge to make it better. *To make her happy.* "Why are you sad, babe?"

"Ugh." Groaning in discomfort, she covered her hands with her face and leaned forward. "Forget it."

"Hey...*hey*, look at me, Claire." Crouching down in front of her, I pried her hands away and forced her to look at me. "Talk to me."

Her brown eyes locked on mine, hazy and unfocused for a long beat before finding traction in our stare. "Because."

"Because?" I coaxed, still cupping her face.

"Because you don't love me the right way," she whispered, leaning into my touch. "The way I need you to love me." She reached up and covered my hands with hers. "The way I love you."

If I thought my heart was breaking earlier, it fucking shattered in my chest when I heard her vulnerability.

"I do," I replied, roughly clearing my throat. "I love you in so many ways."

"Then *why*?" she slurred. "Why won't you just kiss me?"

Because I'm terrified. "Claire."

Exhaling a shaky breath, she leaned in close.

"Don't do it," I begged when her mouth was a hairsbreadth from mine.

"Don't do what?"

"You know what," I strangled out, resting my brow against hers as my chest heaved and my body trembled with a mixture of lust and sheer fucking terror. "It'll change everything."

"Would that be such a bad thing?"

How could I explain it to her when I couldn't explain it to myself? The desire to feel affection and the urge to run from it both in one breath. Fuck, maybe Mam was right, and I needed more sessions with Anne because I sure as shit wasn't winning at life tonight.

"Yes," I finally admitted, heart bucking wildly in my chest. "For you."

"I can't wait forever, Gerard," she whispered, her tone laced with sadness as she slowly withdrew. "It hurts too much."

Pain.

It was everywhere in this moment.

"I know," I forced myself to say, while my heart screamed at her heart to *hold on just a little bit longer.*

24

All Aboard Jacob's Ladder, the Work Ladder

CLAIRE

"I'M STILL WAITING, GUYS," I CROONED, AS I SET THREE DISPOSABLE CUPS OF HOT chocolate down and joined my friends at the table they had managed to snag in our favorite coffee shop the following afternoon. "Tell me you're super proud of me."

"Super?" Lizzie rolled her eyes and reached for her mug. "What are we? Five years old again, Claire?"

"Nope, we're all sweet sixteen and never been kissed," I chirped back, feeling better than I deserved given last night's antics. Apparently, I had the stomach of a horse and the immunity of a demigod. *Hangover who?*

"Speak for yourself," my dry-witted friend shot back with a snort. "Isn't that right, Shan?"

"Liz." Shannon choked out a laugh. "Don't be bad."

"Okay," I drawled. "Let me rephrase that to *I'm* sweet sixteen and never been kissed. You two are modern women of the world, all loved up and married off to your rugby studs."

Shannon beamed, while Lizzie gaped at me in horror. "First off, I'm closer to seventeen than both of you. And second, I would rather shit in my hands and clap than marry anyone," she deadpanned. "Much less *Pierce*."

"What?" My mouth fell open. "You *just* texted this morning saying it was back on."

She shrugged uncommittedly. "I spoke too soon."

"Poor Pierce," Shannon mused. "He really likes you, Liz."

"Oh, please, Shan. He really likes my tits."

"Lizzie!" she squealed, slapping a hand over her mouth to bury the snort that escaped her.

"What?" Lizzie shrugged uncommittedly. "It's true. And as for you, Miss Sweet Sixteen…" She paused to point a finger at me. "You've been kissed." Winking, she added, "Twice."

"Oh *yeah*." Shannon's eyes lit up. "Jamie Kelleher at the school disco in second year, wasn't it?"

"Ugh. Don't remind me," I groaned, burying my head in my hands. "That was a horrendous ordeal I would sooner saw my arm off than repeat."

"And don't forget Thor," Lizzie added, expression laced with disgust. "He came first. Claire let that creep put his mouth on her during a game of spin the bottle long before Jamie ever came along."

"Hey," Shannon and I both said in unison. "He's not a creep."

"No, he's just related to one," Lizzie shot back, tone laced with venom.

I narrowed my eyes in warning. "Liz."

"Which makes him a creep in my mind."

"Oh my god, you are like a broken record!"

"Okay, okay, let's change the subject, guys," Shan was quick to interject before another full-blown argument ensued. After all, it wouldn't be the first time.

Lately, Lizzie's moods had been turbulent to put it mildly, while my patience with her bad attitude was running thin. When I had tried to talk to her about the cut on her leg, she'd all but taken my head off. When I told her that I was going to talk to her mother, she flipped out even more. Then, after giving me the cold shoulder for a week, Liz had told me that I was, in no uncertain terms, to keep my nose the hell out of her business if I valued our friendship.

Apparently, it was okay for Shannon to broach the subject, though, because she received no such response when she tried.

I got that Lizzie had an issue with Gerard, but it was a completely irrational and unfounded one that I, quite frankly, had enough of excusing. I was getting tired of being pounded on, too. I was always the punching bag. Never Shannon.

"I'm super proud of you," Shannon offered then, smiling across the table at me. "For getting the job. It's amazing news, Claire."

"Thanks, chickie." I beamed, momentarily appeased as a wave of pride rolled through me. When time passed by and I didn't hear back from Hugh's boss, I assumed I'd been unlucky. However, Kim called this morning to say that I could start during midterm break. It wasn't big money, and the shifts were every second weekend, but it was a start. "Your girl here is officially on the work ladder."

"Courtesy of our girl here's brother," Lizzie reminded me before taking a sip of her hot chocolate. "Hugh is always bailing you out."

"So?" I batted the air with my hand, refusing to let her goad me into another argument. "That's what big brothers are for."

"Sinead is going to be thrilled," Shannon offered, attention flicking between my face and the phone she was discreetly glancing at under the table. No prizes for which particular rugby player was sending her sneaky sex texts. Number 13. *Cough, cough.* "She's been wanting you to get a job since your birthday, hasn't she?"

"Oh yeah, she's been tormenting me since August." I nodded in confirmation. "Mam's always been very serious about both Hugh and I making our own way in life. She's like 'Just because you two are in the fortunate position to not have to work until you finish school doesn't mean that you shouldn't.'" I took a sip from of chocolatey goodness before continuing. "Hugh got a job as soon as he turned sixteen as well."

"Lifeguarding, too, right?"

"Uh-huh." I nodded eagerly. "We're both fully trained and qualified."

"Wow." Shannon leaned back in her chair with an impressed expression etched on her face. "I knew you volunteered at the pool, but I didn't know you were an actual qualified lifeguard."

"Yep, I took the test the day after my birthday."

"Whoa."

"Meh." I shrugged and offered her a wink. "Some families produce hurlers."

"And some produce swimmers," she filled in with a smile.

"It's because of what happened when they were kids," Lizzie said, eyes locked on the rim of her mug. "Because of what happened to *him*."

"Gibsie and his family?" Shannon asked in a soft tone.

Lizzie nodded stiffly, but thankfully had the good grace to not toss a mean comment out in this moment.

"It was his First Holy Communion Day, wasn't it?" Shannon's blue eyes widened. "You guys were all there?"

"Not me," Lizzie replied. "Claire and Hugh were."

"After the accident, Mam put us straight into swimming lessons," I explained, feeling the familiar wave of sadness settle heavily on my shoulders at the memory. "Dad's an amazing swimmer, and Mam's not too bad herself, but she wanted to prepare us." Repressing a shudder, I tucked a curl behind my ear and smiled across the table at both of them. "It's an essential life skill to have, and it kind of feels like giving back, you know?"

"Which is why you volunteer at the public pool?"

I shrugged. "Not every family can afford to send their children to swimming lessons," I explained. "It's expensive, and you would be horrified if you knew the statistics on accidental drowning in Ireland."

"Well, we do live on an island."

"Which is *why* the government really needs to do something about it," I urged, drumming my fingers on the table as I spoke. "Swimming should be a compulsory course in primary schools across the country. I mean, algebra won't save your life, but the breaststroke might. I've been writing to the board of education about this since fourth class, but I've never gotten a decent response," I added, scrunching my nose up in disapproval. "Just the usual 'It's at the discretion of each individual school' spiel they've been feeding me since forever."

"I *am* proud of you for that," Lizzie interjected, reaching a hand over the table to cover mine. "You must have written at least seventy letters since fourth class." Smiling, she added, "Your tenacity is admirable."

"Thanks, Liz," I replied, giving her hand an affectionate squeeze, earlier tension forgotten, as a momentary glimpse of the girl I'd grown up with shone through the dark cloud that followed her around.

At that exact moment, the glass door of the coffee shop swung open, and in came a familiar face.

"Hey, stranger!" I called out with a wave as my brother's bestie took in his surroundings with his usual thoughtful blue-eyed gaze before scanning our table and strolling toward us. "I feel like we haven't seen you in forever."

"You saw me at school yesterday," he replied with a smile.

"But you haven't been over to the house lately."

"Yeah, sorry about that. It's been manic on the farm," Patrick explained. He looked ridiculously hot for a boy dressed in wellies, faded blue jeans, and an old, half-torn white T-shirt. And the rustic wine-pleated overshirt he had on was the perfect icing on a very delectable cake. He was all dark hair, shy smiles, sun-kissed skin, and soulful blue eyes. The perfect recipe for teenage heartbreak. "Hey, Shan. Liz."

"Hi, Feely."

"Patrick."

"You look good, Pa," I decided to tell him, waggling my brows with mischief. "Super handsome."

"Jesus." Lizzie rolled her eyes. "Again with the word 'super,' Claire?"

"What?" I held my hands up. "He does."

I wasn't the only one to notice, either. Several girls at other tables littered around the café had all turned their heads in his direction. Heck, even Lizzie was looking.

"Thanks." He chuckled with a shy smile, reaching into his back pocket to retrieve his wallet. "Want anything from the counter, girls?"

"Nah, we're good," I answered for all of us, and then watched in amusement as Lizzie's eyes tracked him all the way to the counter.

Oh, yeah, she was *definitely* looking at Patrick.

The only one immune to his sexy stable boy attire was Shannon, who was too busy blushing at the screen of her phone to give him a second glance.

"He does look good," Lizzie surmised, finally turning her attention back to us. "He'll do Gomez Addams justice next Saturday night."

"Oh my god, Liz!" I squealed, unable to stop myself from bouncing in my seat. "You *like* Patrick." Clapping my hands in pure unadulterated joy, I twisted around in my seat to get a better look at how good his ass looked in those jeans. "Yes, girl, *yes*! I approve of the upgrade."

Lizzie gaped at me. "What are you talking about?"

"And did you notice that he didn't even smell bad?" I hurried to add, truly gleeful now. "He's been working on the farm all day, and there's not a whiff of cow poo off his wellies. Just freshly cut silage and a little petrol." Grinning, I added, "He's a keeper, Liz. Pa's amazing. Much better than Pierce, if you ask me." I scrunched my nose up in disgust when I added, "And I bet he doesn't take girls' v-cards in the back seat of his car at the GAA grounds, either."

"You like Feely, Liz?" Shannon asked, with a wide-eyed expression, when she finally decided to put her phone away and give us her attention. "How did I not know this?"

"Ah, maybe because it's not true," Lizzie deadpanned. "He looks good, I noticed, and now Claire's planning the bridal party."

"So, you *don't* like him?" Shannon asked, sounding confused.

"No, I *do* like him," she began to say but I cut her off with an enthusiastic "Yay. This is the best news ever!" before she could continue.

"As a friend," Lizzie clarified slowly. She turned to Shannon and repeated the words, "As a *friend*."

"Oh." To give her credit, Shan looked almost as disappointed as I did about it. "Well, he's a really nice person," she offered, tone hopeful. "And gentle, and kind…"

"And *perfect* for you!" I threw my two cents into the mix and added—again, maybe a little overly enthusiastically.

"Jesus, say it louder, Claire," Liz growled. "I don't think the old biddies at the table in the corner heard you."

"Sorry," I replied with a sheepish wince. "But all I'm trying to say is that I think you two would be perfect together."

"Oh my god." Lizzie turned to Shannon. "Can't you do something with her?"

"Like what?" Shannon laughed.

"I'm serious." I continued to plead my case. "You and Patrick make so much sense." I was almost disappointed in myself for not thinking about the two of them sooner, but now that I had, I couldn't get the idea out of my mind. "He's the perfect amount of calm to your storm!"

"Put a muzzle on her or something," Lizzie said, ignoring me entirely.

"Whatever." I rolled my eyes. "You two are perfect for each other, but don't take my word for it."

"Who's perfect for each other?" Patrick asked, sliding onto the bench seat next to Shannon. "Or am I safer not knowing?"

"Uh…this is definitely one of those better-off-not-knowing scenarios," Shan replied as she scooted over on the bench and gulped down another mouthful of hot chocolate.

"Hey…*Patrick*?" Smiling, I leaned across the table, giving him my full attention.

"Hey…*Claire*," he humored me by drawling, while he cracked open a can of fizzy orange and took a sip.

"Are you seeing anyone at the moment?"

"Seeing anyone?"

"Yeah." I nodded eagerly. "Like a girlfriend or something."

"Oh god," Shan choked out before practically diving for her mug.

Patrick stared blankly at me for a long beat before arching a brow. "What are you up to, Baby Biggs?"

"Ignore her," Lizzie growled, and then forcefully kicked me under the table. "She didn't take her meds this morning."

"Actually, I did," I shot back, and then added, "I take a daily multivitamin," for clarification.

"Pity it wasn't Valium," Lizzie grumbled. "Or a very strong tranquilizer."

"So do I," Shannon offered up. "Take multivitamins, that is. Although, I take, like, three different ones. Edel buys a ton of health products for me and the boys." Smiling sheepishly, she added, "I guess I was lacking in a few vitamins."

It was beautiful to see, to finally know that my friend was receiving the maternal love she always deserved. Because in all honesty, no one deserved a better life than Shannon Lynch and her brothers.

"Not anymore," Lizzie replied protectively, giving our friend a reassuring smile. Yeah, it was safe to say that our entire friendship group was more than a little protective of her. "You're kicking ass now, Shan."

"Yeah." Her cheeks flamed with heat. "I am."

"So, who's the other drink for?" Lizzie asked then, pointing to the spare can of fizzy orange on the table. "Or are you parched with the thirst?"

Patrick opened his mouth to respond when the café door flew open.

"Gibsie!" Shannon said with a huge smile on her face, while Lizzie bit out the word, "Thor," like it was poison on her tongue.

"About time," Patrick said, tapping on his watch. "What happened to I'll park up and follow you right in?"

"Don't blame me, lad. The traffic is fucking mental in this town," Gerard declared, taking up the whole room with his larger-than-life presence. "I've been circling around for a parking spot since I left you."

He was wearing faded blue jeans and a white T-shirt that was molded to his body, emphasizing those impressive biceps he'd spent most of his teenage years accumulating.

"Pity you didn't circle off the face of the earth," Lizzie caught my attention by saying, and I internally groaned. *Here we go again.*

"Don't even start with me, Viper," Gerard warned, strolling over to our table. "I've had a very pressing day, and I'm in no form for your antics."

"Asshole, you wouldn't know the meaning of a pressing day," she countered. "Although, you could make my day a lot better by disappearing."

"Is that right?" Gerard replied, eyes wide and tone dripping with sarcasm. "Well, in that case, I better pull up a chair and get comfy."

Lizzie narrowed her eyes at him. "Drop dead."

"You first," Gerard shot back before reaching over to ruffle Shannon's hair affectionately. "Keep that head up, little Shannon." He offered her a reassuring wink. "Everything's grand."

"Hi, Gibs," Shannon replied, clearly embarrassed by Lizzie's outburst.

It wasn't a nice place to be when she erupted on him, but it didn't make me feel embarrassed anymore.

Just tired.

Looking uncertainly between the pair of them, Shannon glanced from Lizzie to Gerard before asking, "Are…you okay?"

"I'm always okay," he replied warmly, and then he turned his megawatt smile on me, causing every bone in my body to turn to jelly. "Claire-Bear."

"Hey, Gerard," I replied, desperately trying to sound nonchalant, even though every nerve ending in my body sprang to life when he slid onto the bench next to me.

Most of last night was a blurry haze, but when I woke up in his arms this morning, it felt different.

Deeper.

"You doing okay?" Ignoring the rest of our friends, Gerard leaned his forearm on the table and angled his body toward mine, giving me his undivided attention. "How's the head?"

Sometimes it was hard to know where I stood with Gerard because sometimes I wasn't sure which version of Gerard I was getting. When we were alone at night, the vulnerable boy I'd spent my life adoring made an appearance. When we were with friends, it was the confident, no-fucks-given version of him that become dominant.

And that particular version, no matter how infuriating at times, was undeniably sexy. Like seriously *hot*.

"I feel grand," I responded, feeling myself melt under the heat of his stare. It couldn't be helped. It was impossible not to wilt when a boy stared this intensely into your eyes. "Never better."

"So, we're okay?" he asked, keeping his big gray eyes locked on mine.

When he reached up and tucked a rogue curl behind my ear I swear, an audible puff of air escaped my lips, which, I had to begrudgingly concede, wasn't as embarrassing as a moan.

And there had been times I had moaned.

Many times.

"Huh?" I asked, dragging myself from my thoughts, when I realized he was clearly waiting for me to speak. "Why wouldn't we be okay?"

"You tell me."

"I have no idea," I breathed, repressing a shiver.

"Okay then." A small smile tugged at his lips. "That's all I needed to know."

Confused by where the conversation was leading, I blurted out the first thing that came to mind "I got a job!"

"A job?"

"Yep." Finding my composure, I cleared my throat and smiled. "Remember that interview I went for back in the summer? The one for part-time lifeguard at the hotel with Hugh? Well, his boss called this morning." Shrugging, I exhaled another shaky breath and forced a smile. "She hired me."

"She did?" The smile Gerard was sporting grew to epic proportions. "Fuck yeah, my little mermaid!"

"Yep," I breathed against his chest when he pulled me in for a massive bear hug. Unable to stop myself, I inhaled deeply, filling my senses with his delectable signature scent. I didn't care if it was creepy or not. The boy smelled *delicious*. "I start during midterm break."

"You're amazing." He chuckled, pulling back to look at me. "Do you hear me, Claire-Bear?" Cupping my cheeks with his big hands, he leaned in close and pressed his forehead to mine, while excitement and pride danced in his eyes. "I'm so fucking proud of you."

"Oh, cop on." Lizzie gagged from across the table. "She got a part-time, Thor. She didn't make partner in a law firm. A little clarity, please."

"It *is* a big deal," Gerard argued, taking her bait, as he twisted back to face the rest of our friends. "It's a huge fucking deal, actually."

"*Sure*, it is."

"Just leave it alone," Patrick instructed calmly, twisting the metal topper on his can back and forth. "If you two can't be civil to each other, then do us all a favor and ignore each other."

"What?" Lizzie protested in a defensive tone. "He's acting like she won the lotto."

"And that pisses you off because?" Gerard demanded. "What's your problem, Viper? Why can't you be happy for her?"

"Gerard," I growled, digging him in the ribs. "Don't call her that."

"I *am* happy for Claire," Lizzie spat out. "But you're putting on a full-blown act in the hopes of getting in her knickers. It's bullshit, and I'm onto you, asshole."

"You're delusional."

"And you're a useless prick."

"Actually, I have a job, so I'm not completely useless."

"Yeah." She snorted. "A pity position at your mammy's bakery."

"Where's your job at, Liz?" Gerard demanded. "Huh? The fuck are you doing with your life?"

"Actually, we've been babysitting," Shannon offered up, clearly trying to diffuse the situation.

"Babysitting?" Gerard arched a brow. "Together?"

"Uh, yeah," Shannon explained, cheeks turning bright pink. "It's a little business venture we started working on during the summer." Smiling, she added, "It's really starting to take off."

"Got a problem with that, Thor?" Lizzie was quick to ask, glaring at him.

"With Shannon babysitting?" He shook his head. "Not a one. She's perfect for the role."

"So, it's just me you have an issue with?"

"It's just you."

"Guys," Shannon groaned, placing her hand on Lizzie's. "Please don't."

"Care to evaluate?"

He leaned back in his seat and folded his big arms across his chest. "I wouldn't leave you in charge of my hedgehog, let alone a child."

"Because?"

"I'm a good judge of character."

"Meaning?"

"Meaning exactly that."

"So, you don't think I'm capable of looking after a child?"

"Nope."

"If I recall correctly, my sister babysat you an awful lot when we were kids."

"Thanks for the trip down memory lane."

"And you liked it when she babysat you."

"Did I?"

"Oh my god, guys!" I snapped, throwing my hands up in frustration. "Just stop it, will you?"

"You stop it," Lizzie snapped back, meeting my glare head-on with an even angrier one of her own. "Stop letting that asshole walk all over you."

"He's not," I groaned, imploring her with my eyes to hear me.

"Yes, he is!"

"What in the name of Christ are you talking about?" Gerard snapped, running a hand through his hair. "I congratulated *our* friend on getting her first job. Yeah, *our* friend. Last time I checked, that wasn't a method of seduction. But you still somehow manage to fly off the handle!"

"Don't try to make out like I'm crazy, Thor," Lizzie spat back. "We all know what you're doing here. I'm just the only one with the balls to say it."

"I'm not trying to make you out to be crazy, Lizzie," Gerard shot back, eyes bulging. "I don't need to, because the whole fucking world can see it plain as day."

"Gibs!" Patrick snapped. "That's too far, lad."

"No," Lizzie countered heatedly. "What would be going too far is telling him that Peter Biggs saved the wrong child from the wat—"

"La, la, la!" Shannon sang out in a frantic tone as she reached over and clamped a hand over Lizzie's mouth. "Words stick, Liz. Please don't say it."

"Let her," Gerard demanded, while he leaned back in his seat and glared at her. "Come on, Viper. Finish what you were going to say. Get it off your chest."

"Don't," the rest of us begged in unison and then simultaneously held our breaths, waiting for all hell to break loose.

"I don't need to say it," Lizzie finally replied, eyes locked on Gerard. "From the look on your face, you already know it's true."

Shannon groaned, and Patrick dropped his head in his hands. Meanwhile, my jaw damn near hit the floor.

"You did *not* just say that, Lizzie Young," I whisper-hissed. "Tell me you did not just say that!" When she made no move to respond, I turned to the boy sitting beside me. "Gerard." The boy that was climbing to his feet. "No, Gerard, don't… Just wait a minute, will you?"

He didn't wait.

He didn't respond, either.

Instead, he stood up quietly and walked out.

He didn't even slam the café door behind him.

"That was bad," Shannon groaned, still covering her head with her hands. "That was so bad."

"Yep," Patrick agreed calmly. "A total shit show."

"You need to apologize," I snapped, glowering across the table at Lizzie. "You need to go out there and apologize to that boy."

"When hell freezes over."

"I mean it, Liz," I pushed, feeling furious. "Right this second."

"I'll tell you what, Claire," she shot back heatedly. "I'll apologize to him for his sister dying when he apologizes to me for mine!"

"Oh my god." I wanted to scream. "Caoimhe has *nothing* to do with how you spoke to him just now."

"Caoimhe has *everything* to do with everything," Lizzie choked out, tears filling her eyes. "*Everything.*"

"You and Gibsie have both lost your sisters," Shannon tried to reason with her by offering. "You know how bad it hurts, Liz. It cripples you daily. That's how Gibsie feels, too."

"Maybe," she conceded, but her tone was still fully loaded with venom when she spat out, "Difference is I had nothing to do with his sister's death and he had everything to do with mine!"

"How?" Shannon urged. "He was just a little boy when Caoimhe died, Liz. A little kid like the rest of us."

"Ask his brother."

"Stepbrother," Feely interjected calmly.

"Fine," Lizzie seethed, teeth grinding. "Ask his *stepbrother.*"

"Mark?"

"And while you're at it, ask why that monster was involved with my sister in the first place!" Nostrils flaring, she spat out, "Ask whose fault was *that.*"

"Nope. I can't." Shaking my head, I threw my hands up in resignation and slid out of my seat. "I honestly can't do this with you anymore. I know you're a good person, Liz, or at least, I know there's a good person in there somewhere, but I'm tired of being on the front line defending your actions when I don't agree with them."

"I never asked you to do that for me."

"You didn't have to, because that's what friends do, but it's getting old and I'm growing up."

"Claire, wait," Shannon called after me. "Don't go. Let's just sit down and talk this out."

"No, you can talk to her. I need to not be near her right now, Shan," I called over my shoulder as I made a beeline for the exit. Because if I didn't get away from our friend, I would explode. "I'll call you later, okay?"

25

I'm Always Okay

GIBSIE

What would be going too far is telling him that Peter Biggs saved the wrong child from the water that day.

The wrong child drowned.

The wrong child was saved.

Body rigid, I sat in the driver's seat of my car, hands gripping the steering wheel, eyes staring into the past as I fought against the wave of memories threatening to drown me.

Lizzie hit the nail on the head with everything she said—and everything she didn't say. The bare bones of it came down to the fact that Bethany died that day when it should have been me.

Lizzie didn't say anything I didn't already know.

Wrong.

Wrong.

I was all fucking *wrong!*

My sister had fallen overboard because of me.

Because I'd been teasing her with a stupid toy laser that I'd snagged that morning from a lucky dip bag.

I could have just let her play with the damn laser. It wasn't even a good one. Just a cheapie I could have replaced in the pound shop for 50p. I'd made enough money that day. Over two hundred pounds in the cards I'd opened. Cards that had meant so much to me that morning only to mean nothing at all that night. I could have given Beth a turn. I could have bought her a lucky dip bag of her own. But I didn't.

No, because I decided to show off with Hugh instead.

I didn't have to shine the red laser at the dolphin chasing the boat, and I did.

I did that.

Me.

When she fell overboard chasing the stupid red light, protective brotherly instincts caused me to jump straight in after her. I didn't think about what I was doing, or the fact that I couldn't swim. I didn't realize the danger I was putting my entire family in. I just saw my sister go overboard and reacted on instinct.

If I had used my brain and stayed in the boat, Dad would have been able to pull Bethany to safety without the distraction or exhaustion of trying to save me, too. Instead, I made the biggest mistake of my life and, in turn, caused the death of not only my baby sister, but my father, too.

It was, by far, the worst day of my life because I *knew* that I was responsible. I was responsible for my sister falling overboard. I was responsible for my father exhausting himself in the water trying to keep two children afloat. I was the one who slipped out of his arms, causing him to let go of Bethany.

Me.

I missed my dad to the point where it was hard to breathe sometimes, and I often felt like I was still in the water with him. At night, I thought a lot about how his hand felt the last time it had touched mine. His grip. His touch. The cold. The slippery feeling as he let go and I was forced to the surface. That was it. He went under and I went up. It wasn't fair. He was a better person than I could ever be.

As for Bethany? I tried not to think about her at all. The pain was too severe. When I let her enter my mind, when I unleash the memories of my beautiful toddler sister to play on loop in my head like some black-and-white movie from the fifties, the guilt trip that followed left me paralyzed in bed for days.

If I had one wish in life, it would be to go back in time. To have the ability to change the course of that day. To go back and refuse point-blank to get on that fucking boat. To throw away that goddamn lucky-dip laser.

To change the past so that I could fix the present and make a future worth remembering.

Since God didn't grant wishes, and I didn't have a magic lamp or a blue genie at my disposal, I did the next best thing and forced myself to forget.

To not remember any of it.

Not what happened on the boat that day.

Not what happened afterward.

None of it.

I channeled every ounce of energy I had into erasing my memories. If I couldn't change the past, then at least I could force myself to forget it.

"Gerard!" Claire's familiar voice called out then, dragging me from my thoughts and bringing me back to the present with a bang. "Wait up!"

Her voice cut through my senses like a wrecking ball, causing the poisonous fog of my past that had been lapping at my heels to reluctantly retreat. I didn't turn to greet her, but I didn't drive away, either.

I couldn't.

Instead, I reveled in her presence; like a blazing bolt of sunshine chasing the darkness away.

"It's not true," she announced breathlessly when she climbed into the passenger seat a few moments later. "What Liz said back there?" Gulping in several deep breaths, she turned sideways to face me. "Not one word of it is the truth."

Yeah, it is.

"It doesn't matter—" I began to say, but she quickly cut me off.

"It *does* matter." Her eyes were bright, her cheeks flushed from the exertion it had taken to sprint across town from the café. "It matters because you matter, and I know you like to get stuck in your head every now and again, but promise me that you believe me when I tell you that she was talking shit back there."

"What Lizzie says doesn't hurt me."

"Well, you're a stronger person than I am, because it hurts me."

"It's all good, Claire-Bear," I replied, forcing myself to smile while I internally battled to get a handle on my emotions. "I'm okay." Licking my lips, I reached for the key in the ignition, but my hand was shaking too hard to function. "It's, ah…" Blowing out a shaky breath, I balled my hand into a fist to steady the tremors before trying again. "It's all good." This time, when I turned the key in the ignition, the engine complied by roaring to life. "I'm *okay.*"

"Gerard." Her tone was soft, too fucking soft to handle in this moment, and when she covered the hand I had resting on the gear stick, I almost lost it. "It's okay to not be okay."

"Well, I *am* okay," I repeated, keeping my attention locked on the road ahead as we pulled into Ballylaggin afternoon traffic. "I'm *always* okay."

"I know, Gerard," she replied sadly, entwining our fingers. "I know."

Fuck, I didn't deserve her friendship. She knew what I was about. She'd been there that day, right on the boat, watching as my world imploded around me. She knew as well as everyone else on that boat that I was responsible, and she *still* held my hand.

"Do you know what I think this day calls for?" Claire asked, finally breaching the silence when we pulled into the driveway of my house a little while later.

"I don't know, Claire-Bear," I indulged her by answering. "What does today call for?"

"The couch, a blanket, a big bowl of popcorn"—she paused to grin at me—"and a rerun of Johnny and Baby."

"Oh, no, no, no," I shot back with a shake of my head. "Not fucking happening."

"Oh yes." Her grin widened and she nodded eagerly. "It's happening."

"No, it's not." I shook my head just as emphatically. "My brain can't take another rerun of *Dirty Dancing*. It'll explode."

"Oh, don't be so dramatic." She laughed, slapping my arm. "We've only watched it a couple of times."

"Claire," I growled, unable to mask the outrage in my voice—because her obsession with Johnny Castle was a lot like her obsession with Johnny Depp: unhealthy as hell and getting worse by the day. "I've watched that film so many times with you that I can recite the bastard thing word for word." I shook my head again. "No, I'm sorry. I can't."

"As opposed to your obsession with *The Shawshank Redemption*?" she countered, sounding equally frustrated with my refusal to bend to her will—something we both knew I would end up doing. "If I have to listen to another one of your Morgan Freeman voiceovers I'm going to cry."

"Claire." I gaped at her in horror. "You can't possibly compare those two movies." Narrowing my eyes, I added, "And I do a *wonderful* Morgan Freeman impression."

"Yeah," she snorted. "Wonderfully bad."

"Ugh!" I sucked in a sharp breath. "You said you loved my Morgan Freeman impression."

"Yeah, well, I lied." She cackled, reaching across the console to poke my stomach. "You get a big fat F."

"F for fantastic?"

"F for bad."

"Shouldn't I get a B for bad?"

"Only in your world, Gerard." She laughed. "Of course, I might be open to improving your grade if you give me what I want."

"Oh, Teacher," I purred, tone playful now that the mood had significantly lightened between us. "Tell me how."

"An afternoon snuggling on the couch, stuffing our faces." Batting her big brown eyes up at me, she smiled angelically and added, "With the kittens on our laps, and Johnny and Baby on the flat screen."

"Jesus." I shook my head in resignation. "Okay, fine, fine! But this is the last time, Claire."

"Yay!" she cheered gleefully, clapping her hands together. "See? I knew you'd come around to my way of thinking."

"Yeah," I huffed. "Like I have much of a choice."

"Oh, stop it," she teased, leaning across the seat to press a kiss to my cheek. "You know you love me."

Yeah, and I had a feeling the whole world knew it.

"Yeah, so this isn't going to work for me." With my hands on my hips, I stared dispassionately at my reflection in the mirror. I'd watched the rom-coms, ate the popcorn, and basically did everything she told me to all evening, but I had to draw the line somewhere, dammit, and I had feeling dressing me up might be it. "I can pull off many things in life, Claire-Bear, but PVC leather clearly isn't one of them."

"Don't be silly, Gerard," Claire replied from her perch on her bedroom carpet. With a sewing needle pursed between her lips, she tugged on the waistband of my pants, trying and failing to close the damn button. "You look great."

"Great? Look at me, babe!" I demanded, gesturing to the horrendous outfit she had somehow managed to sew me into. "I look like the love child of Jon Bon Jovi and the Michelin Man!"

"Honestly, Gerard, you look great," she continued to coax, setting aside her needle and thread so that she could use both hands to wrestle me into my pants. "Super sexy."

"Yeah, fucking right," I huffed. "You can see the stem of my cock, Claire!" Eyes bulging, I pointed to the very obvious *mishap* in her design. "I know you can't see the full shaft, but you can see my pubes and that's not supposed to happen, right?"

"No, it's not supposed to happen," Claire agreed with a bite to her tone as she continued to wrestle with the button on my pants. "But I'm trying to fix it, so quit being a baby and suck in your belly, dammit!"

"Do you want me to die?"

"I want you to suck in your waist so I can tie this bloody button!"

Releasing a furious growl, I begrudgingly obliged and sucked in my breath. *Again.*

"Dammit, it won't close," she cried out in frustration.

"I know," I shouted back. "Because I have a cock and balls that you clearly didn't plan for when you designed these cockless Ken pants!"

"Ew, Gerard, don't use the word 'cock.'"

"Is 'dick' better?"

"Ew no, that's our son's name. Say 'willy.'"

"Fine," I snapped, glaring down at her. "Willy."

"Ahhh!" Releasing a high-pitched scream, Claire climbed to her feet and stamped her foot. "It's pointless." Pressing a hand to her forehead, she stalked over to her bed and face-planted on the mattress in dramatic fashion. "I failed."

"No, no you didn't," I grumbled, as I penguin-walked my ass over to the bed to comfort her. "It's my dick's fault."

"Willy."

"Willy," I corrected, sinking down on the bed next to her. The loud tearing sound followed by a sudden gust of cold air that hit my bollocks assured me that sitting down in cheap PVC leather was a terrible decision. "Ah crap. I think we have a code blue balls, Claire-Bear."

"Just forget it," Claire wailed into her duvet. "Take them off and burn them. We don't need to dress up this year."

"You know, I could just wear regular black pants," I offered. "Like he does in the movie." Rolling onto my side, I traced the curve of her spine with my finger. "Come on. Don't be sad."

"Yeah, but I've been working so hard on these costumes."

"I know," I coaxed, settling her hair over one shoulder, revealing one perfectly shaped ear with three tiny stud piercings on the lobe. "Come on, Claire-Bear. Look at me."

"I just wanted it to be perfect." Sniffling, Claire peeked up from her facedown position. "That's all."

"I'll figure it out," I heard myself say, needing to make it better for her. "I'll bring the pants over to Mammy K and she'll work her magic on them."

"Really?" Big brown eyes full of unshed tears greeted me. "You'd do that for me?"

"Of course." Using my thumb, I wiped a rogue tear from her cheek. "I'd do anything for you."

"Thanks." Snatching my hand up in both of hers, she closed her eyes and leaned into my touch. "Bestie."

"Anytime." I could feel my heart accelerate to a thousand beats a minute, because while I might be cradling her face in my hand, she was holding my life in hers. "Bestie."

26

Gossips and Gobshites

CLAIRE

"O̲ka̲y̲, ̲s̲o̲ ̲y̲ou̲'l̲l̲ ̲ne̲v̲er̲ ̲gu̲es̲s̲ ̲wh̲at̲ ̲I̲ ̲ju̲st̲ ̲he̲ar̲d," L̲iz̲zi̲e̲ ̲de̲cl̲ar̲ed̲ ̲wh̲en̲ ̲sh̲e found me in the sixth-year common room the following Monday morning. "It's a good one. You're going to love it."

Now, I knew the sixth-year common room was strictly out of bounds for all of us fifth years, but they had the *best* facilities out of all six years at Tommen. When I was dropped off at school this morning at the crack ass of dawn due to Coach's manic rugby training schedule, I had taken one look at the fifth-year common room and turned on my heels.

Both Gerard and Hugh, my usual spins to school, were currently running drills on the pitch, while I was taking full advantage of their fancy-pants digs.

The sixth years had the biggest common room, with the best plush leather couches, the best kitchenette, a bathroom with shower facilities, and they even had a flat-screen television in here.

Sure, most of my friends were day-walkers since Tommen College was predominantly a boarding school, which explained the extra home comforts littered throughout the grounds, but *come on*. This took extravagance to a whole new level. *No wonder the enrollment fees cost an arm and a leg.*

Glancing up from where I was smearing butter on a slice of toast, I arched a brow. "Is this your version of an apology for yesterday?" Purposefully keeping my tone void of emotion, I added, "Because you owe a few of those around the place, Liz."

"Ugh. You know I hate that word. Besides, I've got something so much better than an apology." Tossing her schoolbag on one of the couches, she made a beeline for the kitchen area. "Some juicy gossip." Leaning against the counter that separated the kitchen area from the rest of the common room, she smirked. "About a certain curly-haired firecracker."

"*Me*?" I squeaked. So much for my cool demeanor.

"You," she confirmed with a smirking nod.

Tilting my head to one side, I studied her flushed cheeks and the rare smile that was plastered to her face. "Okay." Setting down my butter knife, I jokingly fake-bowed down to her with my hands. "You win, Medusa."

Grinning victoriously, Lizzie snatched up a piece of toast and strolled over to our favorite blue couch. "So, when I was coming out of the bathroom in the sixth-year wing, I dropped my phone by the lockers and overheard a conversation between two lads," she explained, taking a bite of buttery toast as she folded her legs crossways beneath her and got comfortable. "You have an admirer, Baby Biggs."

My eyes widened. "I have?"

"Uh-huh." Chomping down on another bite of toast, she plucked at a rogue thread on her navy school trousers. "Or should I call him an old flame?"

"Huh?" Confusion and curiosity sparked to life, and I made a beeline for the couch opposite her, toast forgotten. "I have an old flame?"

"Apparently so."

"Oh my god. Who?" Excitement bubbled inside of me, causing my entire frame to squirm with anticipation. "What did you hear?"

"I'll tell you when you close your legs, you big eejit," she shot back, gesturing to where I was sitting cross-legged on the couch. "You're in a skirt, Claire. The whole world can see the color of your knickers when you sit like that."

"Oh please, we're alone and I'm wearing black tights," I grumbled, but begrudgingly complied. "How would anyone know?"

"True," she agreed, polishing off the last bite of toast. "They're pink—but true."

"Come on, Liz!" I whined, drumming my hands on my lap. "Tell me what you heard."

"Jamie Kelleher is planning on asking you out again."

I stared blankly at her. "Come again?"

"Jamie Kelleher," she repeated in a slow drawl. "Wants to go out with you again."

"He does?" My eyes widened. "Who said?"

"He said," she replied. "He told his friend right outside by the lockers that he's planning on asking you to the cinema."

"Shut the front door!" I screamed, throwing my hands up. "Oh my god, *why*?"

"Maybe he wants a repeat performance," she offered with a smirk. "One that Thor doesn't sabotage."

"But that was all the way back in second year. We were practically babies then." A wave of mild hysteria washed over me. "And isn't he going out with Chitra Govindarajan since last year?"

"Not anymore," Lizzie explained. "She left for the University of Brighton at the end of the summer. They ended on good terms, though, which shows us that he knows how to treat a girl and isn't a complete dog like the rest of them."

"Except for when he tried to put his hand under my dress at the disco in second year," I huffed, folding my arms across my chest. "And Gerard didn't sabotage anything that night. He *saved* me."

"Okay, well, like you said, that was a million years ago, and Jamie's done a lot of growing up since then."

"Oh, I don't know, Liz," I muttered, worrying my lip.

"He's smart, he's attractive. He's single." Beaming, she rubbed her hands together. "And best of all, he's not a rugby player."

"Doesn't he play chess?"

She stared blankly back at me. "So?"

"Well, I don't know anything about chess," I blurted out, eyes widening. "Our friends play rugby."

"Chess is a far superior skill."

"But I don't understand chess, Liz," I tossed back, feeling flustered. "I understand *rugby*."

"He's a good egg, Claire," she pushed. "And when he asks you out, I think you should go out with him."

"Ew, no," I strangled out, feeling my heart buck in protest at the mere thought. "I can't go out with *Jamie*."

"Why not?"

"Because I..." Words failing on me, I tried again. "Because I'm..."

"Waiting for *him*?" Lizzie shook her head. "You need to start living your life, Claire."

"I live," I started to defend myself when the door of the common room flew inward, and a familiar face stalked inside.

"Speaking of another good egg who doesn't buy into the patriarchy," Lizzie acknowledged when Joey Lynch walked in, deep in conversation with two of his siblings—one of whom he was physically steering into the room by the scruff of the neck.

"What did I tell ya, kid?" he was growling. "Steer clear from Twomey."

"Exactly," Shannon added, hurrying along beside her brothers. "Don't give him another reason to suspend you."

"Listen, it's not my fault that prick's on our radar, Joe." Looking like an incensed baby lion cub in the clutches of his alpha father, Tadhg broke free of his big brother's hold and scowled up at him. "He's clearly got it in for us."

"That's the cost of our last name, kid," Joey shot back. "Get used to it."

"It's true," Shannon agreed, nodding eagerly. "It's not fair, but it's the way life is for us at this school."

"Not just at this school," Joey offered evenly. "His name is going to follow you everywhere, kid, so you can either make peace with it, or do something about it."

"And when he says do something about it, he doesn't mean using your fists to do it," Shannon added, worrying on her lip. "Fighting solves nothing, Tadhg."

"*Fighting solves nothing.*" Bristling with barely concealed tension, Tadhg stalked over to the couches and sank down on the one next to me. "Don't fucking patronize me."

"Morning, Lynch family. How's my favorite sibling trio?" I chirped with a grin. Digging Tadhg's side with my elbow, I winked at him. "How's your day going, troublemaker?"

Tadhg grinned back at me. "A lot better for seeing you, blondie."

"Sorry about bringing him in here, guys, but we didn't have a choice." Worrying her lip, Shannon rounded the couches and flopped down next to her brother. "Apparently, trouble follows him like a magnet."

"Sounds familiar," Lizzie drawled. "How's it going, Joe?"

"Morning," Joey acknowledged. Chewing on a hard-boiled sweet like a madman, he dropped his bag down on the couch next to Shannon before making a beeline for the kitchen area.

I didn't have to look over to know what Joey was doing. He'd performed the same routine every morning since he arrived at Tommen. Boiling the kettle, he prepped his morning fix of coffee, adding three huge spoons full of instant granules to a mug right along with half a bag of sugar. No milk. No cream.

Returning to the couch with his mug, he sank down on it next to Lizzie and stirred his coffee with a ferocity that assured the rest of us that he was privately battling another craving.

It wasn't nice to know that Joey ached so badly on the inside, to witness him battling the demon of addiction that almost destroyed him, but it was incredibly fortifying to see him kicking said demon's ass daily and coming out on top.

I'd quickly learned that when it came to addiction, the future was never set in stone, but Joey was winning the war against his mind one day at a time, and that's all anyone could hope for.

"I'd be a lot better if I didn't have to constantly watch that hothead's back."

"Oh, please," Tadhg snorted. "Like you're in any position to judge me."

"It's *because* of my position I *can* judge you," Joey countered evenly. "Don't be me, kid. Be better."

That seemed to quiet Mister Attitude because instead of tossing back a sharp comeback, Tadhg folded his arms across his chest and scowled at the floor, clearly deep in thought.

"How's the fam, Joe?" I asked, steering the conversation to safer waters, while offering Shannon's superhot brother a bright smile.

"All good."

"Any new pics of the main man?"

"Oh, I have loads," Shannon blurted out and then thrust her fancy-pants phone into my face. "See his little smile in this one?" she gushed, pointing to an angelic-looking cherub with a huge gummy smile. "Isn't he the most beautiful creation your eyes have ever seen?"

"Definitely," I agreed eagerly.

"He clearly gets it from his mam," Lizzie drawled.

"Clearly." A faint smile teased Joey's lips, but it was almost impossible to see because he had the ultimate poker face. He didn't show emotion. He didn't divulge information, either. Gerard might have walls erected around his heart, but Joey Lynch's walls were built from the blueprints of the Great Wall of China.

Regardless, he seemed to have a strange camaraderie with our angsty friend. They probably bonded over their mutual hatred of all things human.

"Yeah," Tadhg chimed in with a grumble. "Because his dad looks like shit."

"Oh, shush you," Shannon scolded.

"I could say the same to you," Tadhg clapped back with a scowl. "All I fucking hear these days is your voice."

"Tadhg."

"*Johnny, oh Johnny, yes,*" he mimicked his sister's voice. "*I love it when you rub your big oval rugby balls all over my face.*"

"Tadhg!"

"So, when's baby AJ's christening?" I threw my bestie a lifeline by asking.

"No idea."

"You don't know?" I gaped at him. "Joe, he's almost two months old already."

"Yeah," Shannon agreed. "And Nanny Murphy told us that babies should be christened before they are four weeks old." Shrugging, she added. "Just in case."

"So?" Lizzie was quick to defend. "Not everyone buys into that crap, girls."

"Into what crap?"

"The church."

"Oh my *god.*" I gaped at her. "You did *not* just say that."

"I did," she replied breezily. "And would you look, I haven't been struck down by fire bolts, either. Funny that, huh?"

"Nice." Tadhg chuckled in clear agreement.

"Well, I believe," I declared.

"Good for you. Believe in whatever you want. Just don't ram it down my throat and we'll be golden," Lizzie countered. "Besides," she continued, clearly irked with something I said, "in my humble opinion, it's a lot easier to believe in God when you haven't been faced with a reason not to."

"Jesus, I'm so glad I have a son," Joey muttered under his breath. "Teenage girls are a whole different life force."

"You sure about that, Joe?" Tadhg teased. "He might turn out like me."

"Wouldn't be the worst thing," Joey replied breezily. "You were a dream to toilet train."

Tadhg's face turned bright red. "You did *not* fucking say that in company."

"There's no talking me down this time, lads. I mean it. I quit," Gerard's familiar voice filled the air moments before he barreled into the common room, freshly showered and kitted out in his school uniform, minus the jumper. "I refuse to partake in another pukefest of a training session at the hands of that sadist."

"Oh great," Tadhg deadpanned "Fatty's here."

"What did I tell you about calling me fat," Gerard shot back, not missing a beat. "I'm big-boned, you little shit."

"Don't fight with the first-year, Gibs." Johnny, who was also missing his jumper, sauntered in after him. "And cool your jets on the whole resignation saga, you gobshite. Training wasn't that bad."

"Great," Lizzie muttered, folding her arms across her chest. "Captain Fantastic and his freak-show sidekick."

"Wasn't *that* bad?" Tossing his schoolbag on the floor, Gerard turned to gape at his friend. "I'm *chapped*! Down there, *Jonathan*. My ball sack is chapped, I tell you!"

"I told you not to pierce it, *Gerard*, but did you listen to me? No. No, of course you didn't. Instead, you went right ahead and pierced it three more bleeding times!"

"I was completing my ladder."

"Your ladder is a *liability*!" Johnny shot back, sounding just as invested in their conversation as Gerard was. "And what did I tell you about using the talcum powder? The medicated one I had after the surgery. Use generously. Before and *after* training, Gibs. Every session."

"It makes me sneeze, Cap."

"You're not supposed to *smell* it, Gibs. You're supposed to pour it on your groin and thighs."

"You don't smell it?"

"No, lad, I don't smell my balls," Johnny deadpanned before walking over to the couch and sinking down next to my bestie. "Hi, Shannon," he said in a much softer tone as he leaned in to press a kiss to her cheek.

"Hi, Johnny," she replied, cheeks turning bright pink.

"No, not your balls," Gerard continued animatedly as he climbed over the back of the couch and flopped down beside me. Ruffling my curls, he draped an arm over my shoulder before continuing. "The *powder* before you put it on your balls. Don't you smell the powder?"

"Jesus Christ, give it a rest, will ye?" Patrick growled, strolling in behind them with my brother. "I feel like I know more about the two of your bollocks than I do my own."

"That's because you don't have a clue what to do with your own bollocks."

"That's not what your mother says."

"Don't even think about bringing my mother into this."

"Can we not?" Hugh snapped, joining everyone at the couches. "For one damn morning, lads?"

"I complained about my genitals *one* time, Patrick," Gerard huffed. "I didn't make a big hullabaloo out of it like a certain captain we all know."

"True that."

"But it was a good night in Dublin."

"It was eventful to say the least."

"Hey!" Johnny snapped. "That wasn't my bleeding fault."

"Then whose fault was it, Kav?" Gerard demanded. "Mine?"

"Yes," both Hugh and Patrick chorused.

"And you think I have problems," Tadhg drawled sarcastically. "Tell you what, Joe. I'd rather be a Lynch than a bitch any day." With that, Tadhg hitched his bag over his shoulder and sauntered out of the common room, flipping the bird as he went.

Gerard turned to look at me. "Did he just call us bitches?"

"I think so," I replied, stifling a laugh.

"The cheek," he huffed before standing up and prowling toward the fridge. "Jesus, I'm starving."

"You're in trouble with that one, Lynchy."

"Don't I know it," Joey muttered, popping another hard-boiled sweet into his mouth.

"That's not your food, Gibs," Johnny called out.

"Possession is nine-tenths of the law, Johnny," Gerard replied as he busied himself with peeling the name label off a tinfoil-covered bread roll. "Unlucky, Robbie, lad… Ah, score! Chicken and stuffing!" Grinning in delight, he ripped the tinfoil off and took a huge bite. "Get in my belly."

"You're lucky you're in Tommen, lad," Joey stated, looking mildly entertained. "Because if you pulled that stunt at BCS, they'd take your life for it."

"They'd take my life for a chicken and stuffing roll?"

"They'd take your life for just thinking about it, lad."

"So, you never took something from the fridge at BCS that wasn't yours?"

"Fridge?" Joey snorted. "We were lucky to have lunch boxes, never mind fridges."

"Jesus."

"Guess who has an admirer," Lizzie offered then, causing all heads to turn in her direction.

"Who?" everyone chorused in unison.

"Claire."

"Wow, Liz, thanks." I groaned, feeling everyone's eyes land on my face. "This is all according to Lizzie," I was quick to explain, feeling my cheeks flood with heat.

"And no, before any smart-ass says it, it's not Thor," she continued, enjoying this way more than necessary. "It's Jamie."

"Jamie?" Hugh was quick to ask, brotherly detective skills activated. "Who—"

"The fuck is Jamie?" Gerard filled in, turning to stare expectantly at me.

"Jamie?" Shannon asked, looking momentarily confused before her lips formed the perfect O shape. "Oh…*that* Jamie."

"Jamie Kelleher?" Johnny furrowed his brows. "From our year?"

"No clue, lad," Joey replied, sounding entirely uninterested in the conversation as he stuffed a rogue pacifier back into his pocket and retrieved a hard-boiled sweet instead.

"Hold the phone!" Hugh's brows shot up as awareness dawned on him. "Jamie Kelleher! As in the same Jamie you went out with for like a day in second year?"

"It was two weeks, and yep," Lizzie replied with a smile. "Apparently, he's planning on asking your baby sister to the cinema."

"*Jamie,*" Gerard reiterated, unsmiling, as he bore holes into the side of my face with his steely gaze. "Jamie the handsy prick I had to put in his place at the disco?"

"No one asked you to do that, asshole," Lizzie spat out.

"She did," Gerard countered, pointing a finger at me as his eyes danced with unconcealed frustration. "*She* asked me to."

He was right. I *did* ask him to save me that night.

"Don't even think about ruining this for her," Lizzie warned. "I'm telling you now, Thor. I will rain *hell* down on you if you pull any tricks—"

"Jesus Christ, stop talking to me, will you?" Gerard shot back, holding a hand up. "I'm trying my hardest to follow the rule here."

"The rule?"

"Yeah, the rule," he snapped back. "The 'If you have nothing good to say, say nothing' rule." Bristling, he pushed a hand through his blond hair before adding, "Trust me when I say that I have *nothing* good to say about you, Viper, so just let me eat my stolen food and ignore you in peace, dammit!"

"Oh my god, guys, stop," I interjected with a nervous chuckle. "He hasn't even asked me yet."

"Yet," Gerard bit out, still staring at me.

"I mean it, Thor," Lizzie argued. "Don't even think about making her feel bad for this."

"*Again*?" a familiar voice groaned, and I turned to see Katie strolling into the room. "Do you two ever stop fighting?"

"That depends," Lizzie countered, turning her dagger on my brother's redheaded girlfriend. "On whether or not I have another opponent."

Katie looked around in confusion before pressing a hand to her chest. "Me?"

"Are you offering?"

"No, she's not," Hugh cut in, moving to intercept his girlfriend before trouble found her. "Stop it."

"Too bad," Lizzie replied breezily.

"Are you honestly considering going out with that eejit?" Gerard asked, recapturing my attention once more. His tone, for once, was serious, and his gray eyes held none of their usual twinkling mischief. He took another wolfish bite of Robbie's roll before adding, "I mean, seriously?"

"He hasn't even asked me," I said, trying to placate at the same time Lizzie shouted, "Yes, she is!"

A perfectly aimed sweet smacked Gerard upside the head, and I turned just in time to see Joey offer Gerard what looked like a coded wink. "Come on, Gus," he said, standing up. "Let's get some fresh air."

"Good fucking plan, Lynchy," Gerard huffed, dropping his food onto the counter, and stalking off in the direction of the door. "Good plan indeed."

"Oh no, no, no! Don't even think about it." Springing to his feet faster than any boy his size should be able to, Johnny chased after them. "I know what your version of fresh air is and I'm telling you now, Gibs, I will make you pay for every one of those filthy cigarettes on the pitch."

27

Counsel and Cougars

GIBSIE

RAGING. I WAS ABSOLUTELY *RAGING* AND NO AMOUNT OF FRESH AIR IN THE SCHOOL car-park with Lynchy or coddling from Kav could bring my mood out of the darkness.

"Just walk away, Gibs," Johnny instructed for what had to be the fiftieth time as he hung slightly back from where I was standing and barked orders like the dutiful captain he was. "Whenever that girl tries to start drama with you, lad. Don't react and walk away."

"I can handle the Viper, Kav," I shot back, taking a furious drag of my cigarette. "She's the least of my worries right now."

It was the truth. Nothing Lizzie ever said or did could prepare my body for the punch to the solar plexus it received upon hearing the *good* news.

"Fucking Jamie Kelleher," I bit out, still reeling, as I tried to get a handle on my emotions, only to fail miserably. "I hate him, Cap. I really fucking hate that spotty-faced swat."

"I know you do, Gibs," Johnny soothed in agreement. "Me too, lad."

"Good-for-nothing brainiac," I continued to rant, growing more incensed by the second. "Why her?" Anger bristled inside of me as I allowed my mind to linger and dwell. As I drove myself mental from overthinking. "*Why*?"

Jamie didn't know Claire. Not really. Not at fucking all. He didn't know a damn thing about her love of fashion or her prized collection of stuffed animals. He had zero insight into her obsession with Johnny Depp, nor had he any inclination of the letter she wrote to Leonardo DiCaprio when she was seven, asking him to visit Ballylaggin.

I was the one who knew her small parts, the insignificant oversights that made up the best parts of her personality. I was also the one who rescued her from that noisy bastard of a bull in the field behind Johnny's place when we were kids. I was the one that took the shocks off the electric fencer so she didn't have to. I was the one who spent every waking hour of my life not only adoring her but protecting her with my life. Not Jamie fucking Kelleher!

Leaning against an expensive-looking parked Mercedes, Joey took another drag of his cigarette, observing my meltdown unfolding around him like a caged lion would: slightly bored and momentarily contained, but absolutely lethal if provoked.

I knew he wasn't much older than me, but I never felt like I was on the same playing field as Shannon's brother. He had an old head on his shoulders, a lot like my bestie, but he had a jaded element to him that wasn't present in Shannon or the younger boys. Christ, it didn't even seem to be present in Darren. An element that expressed that he had felt every one of his eighteen spins around the sun, and it had weathered him to the point that he was an old man in a teenager's body. I mean, he was a father, dammit. He was an actual dad to an actual human being. That alone blew my mind.

"What I don't understand is why you're not with her already," Joey finally joined in the conversation by saying in a lazy tone.

"Who?" I gaped at him in horror. "*Lizzie?*"

"Yeah," Joey replied, tone laced with sarcasm. "Because that makes sense."

"He was referring to Claire," Johnny interjected with an expectant look. "And don't waste your breath, Lynchy, because I've been saying the same bleeding thing for years, and it's still falling on deaf ears."

"Because it's not the right time," I ground out, feeling my body break out in a cold sweat at the thought. "I've already told you a thousand times, Kav, not everyone wants to settle down in secondary school."

"Except that you do," Johnny pointed out in the know-it-all tone of his.

"How'd you figure that one?"

"With her, you do," he stated calmly. "Because you love the bones of that girl, and this sour mood that you're sporting is directly related to the fact that another fella is planning on asking her out."

Hit the nail on the head, why don't you?

"Give it a rest, Brains," I grumbled, tossing my cigarette butt away.

"And you're in serious risk of losing said girl if you don't pull your finger out of your hole and start grafting," my best friend continued, not giving an inch.

"Agreed," his future brother-in-law offered with a shrug. "From where I'm standing, she's yours to lose, Gussie."

"Exactly," Johnny confirmed, throwing his hands up in exasperation. "Because whether you want to acknowledge it or not, she won't wait around forever, Gibs."

"True that," Joey offered with a grimace. "You don't want to be the third wheel, lad."

"So, my advice to you, as your best friend, is to go for it," Johnny pushed, blue eyes locked on mine. "Come on, Gibs, you've never been one to worry about throwing caution to the wind in any other aspect of your life."

No, because no other aspect of my life was as important as *her*.

"Just get your girl, lad, and be happy," he urged, closing the space between us to clamp my shoulders. An act of enthusiasm, no doubt. "What have you got to lose, lad?"

More than you know.

More than I can bear.

"Because I'm not in a hurry!" I tossed back, knowing my argument was weak as shit, but I didn't have anything else. They didn't get it. How the hell could they? "We don't all bulldoze, Jonathan! And we don't all mark our turf with a baby, Joseph." I cast a knowing glance at the pair of assholes doling out words of wisdom like they were the messiahs of pussy. "Some of us take our time when making life-altering decisions!"

"You're so *lazy*!" Johnny challenged, sounding just as frustrated with me as I was with the conversation. "Claire is going to move on, Gibs, and you're going to lose your shot, lad."

"Don't give me that judgy look," I warned, breaking out of his hold to point a finger in his face. "I don't need anyone else's opinions on my love life, thank you very much."

"Morning, boys," an achingly familiar voice purred. I turned around to see Dee locking the driver's side of her car nearby, and I swear to Christ, I could have wept. *What bloody timing.*

"Morning, Dee," Johnny acknowledged politely, while he not so discreetly elbowed me in the ribs as if I wasn't already fully aware of the woman. "Nice weather."

"Not as wet as I like," she tossed back with a heavy dollop of flirtation. "How are my favorite boys?"

"The fuck?" Joey whisper-hissed, clearly noting how inappropriate her behavior was. "Isn't she office admin?"

"Yep, and yep," Johnny replied, nudging me again. "She's the school's receptionist."

"It's a long story," I muttered under my breath, covering my words with an exaggerated cough. "I'll tell you later."

"Don't think I want to know, Gus." With a shake of his head, Joey pushed off the car he was leaning against and headed back toward the main building. "Not my monkeys. Not my circus."

Wise decision.

Wise fucking man.

With a stack of paperwork in her arms, Dee shimmied toward us, all shaking hips and bouncy tits.

Again, I felt nothing.

Fuck.

"How was your weekend, boys?"

"All good," Johnny replied, taking a safe step back from who he privately referred to as *Cougar Dee*. "How was yours?"

"Boring," she replied, taking a step closer, blue eyes locked on my face. "I was alone in my house all weekend."

"Yeah, that sounds pretty boring," Johnny answered for both of us. Catching ahold of the back of my shirt, he pulled me backwards with him. "Well, we better be getting to class," he said, tone as polite as ever as he hauled me out of harm's way. "Have a good day, Dee."

"Bye, boys," she called after us. "Don't be afraid to pop into the office if either one of you need anything."

"Will do," he tossed over his shoulder as he steered us both toward the main entrance at lightning speed.

"Jesus, where's the fire?" I huffed, breaking out of his hold before I had to break into a run to keep up with the overgrown bastard. "Slow down."

"We need to talk about that."

"What?"

"Cougar Dee," Johnny whisper-hissed as he yanked the door open and shoved me inside. "What's happening there?"

"You mean today?" My brows shot up in surprise. "I just saw her in the car park, same as you."

"You know that's not what I mean," he growled. "Christ, Gibs, she's almost thirty, lad."

"Actually, she's more like twenty-four."

He paused in the doorway to gape at me. "No fucking way."

"Hand on heart. She was in the same year as Caoimhe Young," I offered with a nod. "It's the makeup—and the sunbed."

"More proof that sunscreen is invaluable," he grumbled, pushing us both inside. "Whatever. Listen, I think we need to have a proper talk about her. I should have said something about this a long time ago," he continued, walking us through the corridor. "But to be honest, I was so stuck in my own head that I didn't give it a second thought."

"Give what a second thought?" I asked, letting him lead me into the empty lunch hall. "What in the name of God are you on about, Kav?"

"I've been doing a lot of growing up since Shannon and the boys came to stay with us, and it got me thinking about right and wrong." Taking his seat on his throne at the end of the rugby table, he drummed his fingers on the table, clearly unnerved. "And this is wrong, lad. So fucking wrong."

"Care to fill in the blanks here, Cap?" I asked, dropping into my usual seat opposite him. "Because I'm kind of stumped."

"Dee, lad," Johnny repeated, pushing his hands through his hair.

"Yeah," I drawled slowly. "What about her?"

Bristling with tension, I looked around us before leaning in close and whispering, "I think she's been grooming you, lad."

"Grooming me?"

"Yes." Eyes wide, he nodded eagerly. "Grooming you."

I stared blankly at him for a long beat before bursting out laughing. "Get a fucking handle on yourself, Johnny."

"Gibs," he urged. "I'm being serious here."

"So am I." I laughed. "Don't get all high and mighty with me because you've got a girlfriend now."

"That's not what I'm doing, lad."

"And don't fucking judge me," I added, sitting up. "I've done a lot of favors for you that resulted in me owing *favors* to that woman."

"That's what horrifies me," he snapped. "It's wrong, Gibs. This is all wrong. It's a consent issue."

I gaped at him. "Consent?"

"Gibs," he snapped, leaning over the table. "That woman has been fucking around with you since we were fourth year." Shaking his head, he bit out, "Since you were *fifteen.*"

"Now, hold the hell up," I snapped, feeling myself bristle with defensiveness. "First off, I haven't touched that woman since I got my ladder piercing back in fifth year—not that it's any of your business, but I haven't. Not one goddamn time. And, again, not that it's any of your business, but I have no plans to change that."

"Good." His visibly sagged in relief. "At least that."

"And second," I continued, feeling pissed. "I never once forced her to do anything, if that's what you're getting at." Panic clawed at my gut as I glared at my best friend. "I would never *force* anyone!"

"I'm not talking about *her* giving consent, Gibs," Johnny argued, dragging a hand through his dark in obvious frustration. "I'm talking about *you*, lad."

I stared in confusion, trying and failing to absorb the meaning behind his words. "*What*?"

"Sex, Gibs," Johnny groaned, looking comically distressed. "You know if she fucked you back then, it's classed as statutory rape."

"What in the…" I shook my head and pressed a fist to my mouth, trying my hardest to find the words to deal with my best friend's latest theory of madness. Dee was exactly what I needed in a time when I didn't know what I needed, but there was no point in trying to explain that to Johnny. Because in all honesty, how could I expect him to understand when I didn't understand it myself? "No. Nope. No. I cannot deal with your overthinking—not to mention *hypocritical*—brain this early on a Monday morning."

"Gibs…"

"How many older women did you fuck when you weren't supposed to?" I demanded. "Before you decided to hang up your boots and throw your cards in with little Shannon."

"Too many," he wholeheartedly admitted. "Too goddamn many, and that's what I'm trying to say here, Gibs—"

"Well, that's one more than me!" Throwing my hands up in defeat, I shook my head and fought the urge to both laugh and scream. "Because I never fucked her, Johnny!" Huffing out a breath, I begrudgingly added, "I just canoodled her."

"And canoodling in your worlds consists of?"

"What does it mean in your world?"

"Humor me, Gibs."

Everything for her and nothing for me. I folded my arms across my chest and shrugged. "Listen, it was oral, okay, just a little oral and heavy petting. Fucking sue me for taking the chance of a lifetime."

"You swear nothing else happened?"

"Yes."

"And you swear to me that it will never happen again?"

"Yes, Johnny, I swear."

My best friend exhaled an audible breath. "I know I probably sound like an awful hypocrite to you, given my previous behavior, but I worry about you, Gibs." His shoulders sagged in defeat, and he dropped his head in his hands. "I've been thinking about it for a while now, and when I saw her looking at you like that, it suddenly clicked into place for me."

"No need to worry about me, Johnny lad," I tried to appease. "I'm always okay."

"I can't bleeding help it," he admitted with a rueful smile. "Despite my best efforts, I've grown regrettably attached to you." Smirking, he added, "And all of your sixteen other personalities."

"Aw, shucks." I grinned back at him. "Is this your way of telling me you love me, Cap?"

"Whatever floats your boat, Gibs."

28
Lunchtime Propositions

CLAIRE

LIZZIE'S EAVESDROPPING SKILLS WERE PUT TO THE TEST AT BIG BREAK WHEN I WAS abruptly stopped in the school corridor on my way to the lunch hall. "Claire, can I have a word?" Jamie asked, surprising me by stepping in front of me midrun and causing me to crash into his chest with a loud *oof*. "Jesus, sorry about that," he grunted, hooking an arm around my waist when I staggered backwards from the force with which we collided. "Are you alright?"

"Yep, yep, all good," I replied with a nervous cackle, quickly steadying myself before stepping out of his hold. "I was just racing to make sure all the chili wasn't taken by the rugby team." Blowing a rogue curl out of my face, I smiled up at him and asked, "What's up?" even though I knew full well what was *up*.

"Oh shit, if that's the case, do you want to talk as we walk?" he offered, gesturing toward the lunch hall. "I don't want you to lose out on your lunch."

"Thanks," I replied with a smile, falling into step beside him, all while trying my best not to be weird. God only knew why but I had the strongest urge to make farm animal noises in this moment. Probably because I was epically nervous and had no clue how to navigate these unknown waters.

"So, listen, I was thinking about it a lot lately, and I was hoping I might be able to take you out again sometime."

And there it was.

Lizzie was dead on the money.

Jamie did want to go out with me again.

Aw, crackers.

"Take me out?" I asked, trying to sound as nonchalant as possible when we entered the lunch hall. *Baa. Baa. Baa.* Dammit, why couldn't I stop thinking about sheep noises? "Out where?"

"The cinema? Or maybe for a drink? Whatever you want," he offered, joining the queue for hot food with me. "I know it didn't exactly end well the last time, and I was a fucking eejit back then, but I really think we could have something good."

Purposefully keeping my attention off the rugby table, I focused on the boy speaking to me instead. "Something good?"

"Yeah." Jamie nodded and smiled. "If you're willing to give me another chance."

It was a cute smile.

He was a good-looking boy with dark hair and pretty brown eyes. He was tall enough to have a couple of inches on me, and he smelled fantastic, which was always a huge bonus in my eyes. He even had a tiny dimple in his chin and an adorable crooked smile.

But he wasn't Gerard.

Feeling hesitant and uncertain, I opened my mouth to respond, but Lizzie got in there first.

"She would love to!" Joining us in the lunch line, she draped an arm around my shoulder and beamed. "Isn't that right, Claire?"

"*Lizzie*," I whisper-hissed, flicking an anxious glance in the direction of the rugby table. Immediately, my eyes sought Gerard out, and when they locked on his, I could feel the tension emanating from him.

Aw, crap.

"Listen, if you still have something going on with Gibson, that's fine," Jamie said, quick to catch on. "Just tell me now because I don't want to step on anyone's toes here."

"She doesn't," Lizzie responded before I could. "They're just friends." Tightening her arm around me, she smiled harder. "Isn't that right, Claire?"

"Uh…" I glanced back to the table once more, but this time Gerard wasn't looking at me. In fact, he had his back to me, giving Johnny his full attention. "Right?"

"Okay, good." Jamie sighed in relief, smile reappearing now the coast was apparently clear. "So, what do you think?"

"About what?" I asked, distracted by the table behind me. Namely the boy sitting at said table.

"Going out with me sometime?"

"She'll have to think about it." Appearing out of thin air, Shannon slipped under Jamie's arm and caught ahold of my hand. "Thank you so much for the offer," she added, pulling both Lizzie and me away. "It was very thoughtful. Claire will get back to you in the next five working days."

Jamie frowned in confusion. "Uh…okay?"

"Bye," Shannon called back.

"Yeah, bye," I laughed, waving after him as I let my little friend lead me away.

"The next five working days?" Lizzie huffed, trailing after us. "What the hell, Shan?"

"It was all I could think of," Shannon squeezed out, red-faced, as we hurried over to the table we used to sit at for some girl talk before we joined the rugby table. "Claire looked so uncomfortable back there, and I just, I don't know, I felt like I needed to buy her some time."

"That was epic," I choked out through fits of laughter, thrilled with her intrusion. "*Five working days.*" I snorted. "You sounded like my personal secretary."

"So, you're not mad at me?" Shannon asked, looking up at me with nervous blue eyes. "I didn't overstep?"

"Are you crazy?" I reached across the table and snagged her hand. "Shan, I'm beyond grateful. That was so awkward."

"Really?"

"Really, really."

"Oh." My bestie sagged in relief. "Thank god."

"I'm mad," Lizzie chimed in, holding a hand up.

"You're always mad?" I rolled my eyes. "What's new?"

"Claire, that was your perfect chance." Leaning back in her chair, Lizzie folded her arms across her chest and glowered. "Jamie's a nice boy. You could do a lot worse."

"Then you go out with him," I shot back.

"I don't want to go out with him."

"Yeah, well, neither do I." I laughed, completely unaffected by her incessant probing.

"Only because you're wasting your life waiting around for *him*," she grumbled, gaze flicking to the rugby table. "Oh, for Christ's sake, what is wrong with the big eejit now?"

"I think he saw Jamie asking Claire out," Shannon offered, gesturing across the room to where Gerard was glaring at his uneaten lunch like it had mortally offended him. "He looks so sad."

"He's not sad, Shan," Lizzie explained with a frustrated sigh. "He's sulking."

"Sulking?" I turned around in my seat and watched as Johnny tried to coax Gerard with a spoon of yogurt. "Oh god, he *does* look sad."

"Yeah," Lizzie agreed hotly. "But only because another boy dared to play with his toy."

"Hey," I warned, smile fading. "Don't call me a toy."

"Why not? That's exactly what you are to him."

"As opposed to you using me back there to hurt him?" I shot back, feeling a surge of heat rise up in my belly. Contrary to my appearance, I was no doll, and I had no intention of being used in Lizzie's game to get up on her nemesis. "Because I know what you were trying to do back there."

"I was trying to *help* you."

"Don't fight, guys," Shannon admonished quietly. "Come on. We're all friends here."

"I don't need you to help me," I argued back, ignoring Shannon's attempt to diffuse the situation. "I'm perfectly capable of navigating my own love life, thank you very much."

"Fine." Lizzie rolled her eyes unapologetically. "Do whatever you want, Claire."

Sometimes, I wished I never started speaking to her after she got with my brother. At least that way, when they ended it would be over. But I felt horrible for thinking that way. Especially when the girl I'd grown up with from the age of five to thirteen had been so amazing. We had eight years of pure friendship before everything went to hell. I couldn't erase that, and I didn't want to.

"Thank you," I replied with forced cheer in my tone. "I intend to."

29

I Can't, But Can You?

GIBSIE

I DON'T KNOW HOW TO MAKE IT RIGHT.

With my head bowed, and my shoulders rigid with tension, I stared down at the crumpled letter in my hands later that evening.

Why I chose to always focus on that particular line, I would never fully understand, nor did I want to. Reading these words didn't make anything better. It never had. But I didn't need to hold the letter in my hands to remember what was written in the lines. Every word was scored on my conscience.

"Where have you been?" a familiar voice demanded, storming into my room and almost giving me a goddamn heart attack in the process. "I have been waiting all night for you!"

"Jesus Christ," I strangled out, quickly shoving the letter under my mattress. "Claire! What a fucking fright to give a lad."

"Oops." Grimacing, she closed my bedroom door and padded over my bed, draped in an oversized Liverpool jersey she had clearly stolen from my wardrobe. I knew it was mine because her brother supported United, while her dad was a die-hard Gunner. "I wasn't trying to frighten you." Climbing onto my bed, she sat cross-legged facing me. "I was looking for an explanation."

"An explanation?" I stared blankly. "I'm not following you, babe."

"Okay, so I know you saw what happened in the lunch hall today," she blurted out, reaching for my hand. "And I'm guessing that's why you didn't call over after school."

She was dead on the money, but I couldn't verbalize it, because in all honesty, I didn't have a leg to stand on.

"Jamie asked me out."

Yeah, I got that. "Claire." Training my attention on her small hand covering mine, I let out a sigh. "It's okay. You don't need to explain anything to…"

"I didn't give him an answer!"

My heart bucked wildly. "You didn't?"

"No, Gerard." She shook her head slowly. "I didn't."

"Why?"

"You know why."

"Yeah." Exhaling shakily, I kept my attention trained on our entwined hands.

My life consisted of this girl. Of the perfume she wore. Of the smiles she offered. The clothes she chose on a particular day. The colors she painted her nails. She was tattooed inside of me, and I was hooked.

Claire was my safe place.

If I had a shred of anything about me, I would open my mouth and talk to this girl. Tell her how I felt. Show her how highly I valued her as a human. Love her the right way. Switchfoot's "Only Hope" was as accurate as a song could be if I had to explain my feelings for her, but I would never play it for her.

I could see my friends settling down around me and I was still playing the boy card. Still protecting myself from demons that shouldn't get to me anymore but still did.

Sensing my sudden decline in mood, Claire sighed dramatically before setting her face in a comical-looking frown. "Gerard Gibson."

Smirking, I pulled a face in response. "Claire Biggs."

She waggled her eyebrow like the Rock. "Spud-monkey."

Indulging her playfulness, I crossed my eyes until they turned inward. "Snuggle bunny."

She poked her tongue out and rolled it. "Baby daddy."

I pulled my cheeks until I looked sufficiently disfigured. "Baby mama."

Cackling with mischief, she scrambled onto her hands and knees and pounced. "My germs," she snickered, and then proceeded to lick the side of my face.

"Oh, it's like that, is it?" I laughed, wrestling her onto her back.

"Yep." She giggled from beneath me.

I arched a brow. "Oh, yeah?"

"Uh-huh," she goaded in a mocking tone. "What are you going to do about it, *Gibsie*?"

Feeling mischievous, I leaned in close and trailed the tip of my tongue from the curve of her jawline, not stopping until I reached her cheek. "My germs," I teased before pressing a kiss to the adorable apple of her cheek. "Mine."

Her breath hitched in her throat, and I momentarily panicked, fearing that I'd taken it too far. But then her hands were in my hair, and her nose was brushing against mine, as her warm breath fanned my lips. "Gerard."

"Claire," I croaked out, feeling my entire body ignite in white-hot heat as my brain failed to enforce the many reasons why I *shouldn't* be doing this.

Because this was so bad.

She was too close.

I was too fucking broken.

"Gerard."

I blew out a pained breath. "Claire."

She pressed a lingering kiss to my cheek. "Hi."

"Hi." Feeling my resolve weaken when her lips brushed the curve of my mouth, I sagged forward, buckling under the pressure of my feelings for this girl. "Wait, I need to tell you something…"

A loud knock on the other side of my bedroom door had my body levitating out from beneath her. "Yeah?" I called out, scrambling to intercept the person on the other side of my door—and to put some much-needed space between our bodies.

"Yeah?" I repeated when I opened my door a crack and peered out.

My mother's concerned face greeted me on the other side. "It's almost half eleven."

"So?"

"So, I could hear you pacing around in here all evening." Sighing heavily, she added, "Gibs, pet, you need to try to get some sleep."

"Yeah, that's what I was just about to do," I replied, and then I flicked off the big light for emphasis, stifling her view of my room. "Night, Mam."

"Night, pet," she replied. "And if you wake in the night, just come and get me okay? No need to go wandering across the road. I'm here for you, too, you know. Always."

Like hell you are. "Okay." Offering her a half-hearted smile, I closed the door and sagged against it. *Fuck.*

"This is nice," Claire announced when I finally turned around to face her. She was already under the covers and making herself comfortable in my bed. "What's the saying; a change is better than a rest?"

Panic clawed at my gut. "You want to sleep in here?"

"Well, I think it's only fair considering you hog my bed most nights."

Well, shit.

How could I argue with that?

Blowing out a ragged breath, I walked back to my bed and drew back the covers. "This is confusing," I added, climbing in. "I don't know how I feel about this."

"What?" she snickered, rolling onto her side to face me. "Because I'm on the right side of the bed when you usually are?"

"Yes," I replied emphatically. "It feels all fucked up."

"Well, suck it up, buttercup, because I'm the big spoon tonight," she cackled, draping an arm around me. "Now, give me your back and let me snuggle you."

"There's a word for this," I grumbled, while complying with her request by rolling onto my side and assuming the little spoon position. "I heard Johnny say it before. He called it emasculation."

"I would never emasculate you, Gerard," she whispered, fingers trailing over my bare stomach. "I don't even know what that means."

"Neither do I." I chuckled, snatching her wandering hand up in mine when it trailed precariously low to the waistband of my boxers. "Behave yourself, Miss Biggs."

"Gerard?"

"Hmm?"

I felt her lips on my back. "Hi."

"Hi," I replied, my body shifting as a wave of pained pleasure washed over me. "Claire…"

She kissed me again, but this time she slipped her hand out of mine and trailed it down my stomach, not stopping until her fingers grazed my inner thigh. "Gerard."

Jesus Christ. My heart was beating so hard in my chest that I thought it was going to implode inside of me.

"Don't," I croaked out, snatching her hand back up when her fingertips slid under the elasticated waistband of my boxers.

Unable to repress the shudder that racked through me, I rolled around to face her. "Claire," I whispered, cupping her face with my hand, while trying to regain some composure. "What are you doing?"

Instead of responding with words, she leaned in and pressed a kiss to the inside of my wrist. "I don't want Jamie Kelleher," she whispered, shifting closer so that our chests were flush together. "I don't want anyone else."

Her hand slid beneath the covers once more, and I couldn't stop the pained groan that escaped my lips when her fingers grazed the fabric that contained my raging hard-on.

Jesus Christ.

Everything inside of me was demanding I reciprocate her advances and finally claim this girl for my own.

Let her do it.

Just let her touch you.

"No." Shuddering, I shook my head and snatched her hand back up. I knew what she wanted, and I couldn't get out of my head long enough to give it to her. "You can't."

Big, innocent, brown eyes looked up at me. "I can't."

I shook my head slowly and held my breath, preparing for the wave of devastation that would floor me when she climbed out of my bed and stormed out. Because like the habit of a lifetime, I had once again failed this girl.

But it didn't come.

She didn't leave.

"Okay, *I* can't," Claire replied, words barely more than a breathy whisper. "But…" Taking my hand in hers, she placed it between her legs. "Can *you?*"

"*Claire.*"

"Please, Gerard," she breathed, chest heaving, as she adjusted my hand so that I was cupping her over her underwear. "*Please.*"

30

This Is What It Feels Like

CLAIRE

I COULDN'T MOVE AN INCH.

I didn't dare breathe.

My body had been taken over by hormones, and I was currently at the mercy of the only boy I had ever loved. His hand was between my legs, where I had put it, and he was staring at me with a heated expression.

Repressing the urge to push Gerard onto his back and mount him, something my body assured me it would very much enjoy, I remained perfectly still, with my hand covering his and my eyes willing him to touch me.

Because the sad fact of the matter was that while I had zero experience with boys in bedrooms, *this* particular boy could do whatever he wanted to me, and I would gladly participate. That's how desperately my body craved his touch.

A million different emotions flashed in his eyes as I watched him watch me until I thought I might cry out in frustration.

Finally, when I decided that all hope was lost, I released his hand and rolled onto my back, but then he came with me and flexed his fingers.

Oh god.

My breath hitched in my breath, and I felt my body grow lax when his hand slid into the waistband of my knickers. "You want this?"

I nodded eagerly, mouth falling open when his fingers trailed over my untouched skin.

"Say it," he instructed, pulling himself up on one elbow next to me. "I need the words."

"I want this," I encouraged, letting my thighs fall open.

"Say it again." Gerard's eyes flamed with heat. "One more time."

"I want this," I repeated, breath hitching when his fingers trailed over me. "I want you."

Gerard traced his bottom lip with his tongue and leaned in close so that his lips were brushing my ear. "I'll make it good for you," he whispered, nuzzling with my cheek with his nose. "I promise."

"I trust… Ohhh…" My entire body jolted when he pushed his finger deep inside of me. "Oh…Oh god!"

His movements were effortless to him but were wreaking havoc with my internal wiring. Every crook of his finger and every slow grinding push of his hand ignited my senses. When his thumb grazed over my tender flesh and found *that* spot, I felt my back begin to bow as tiny electric currents spiraled around inside of me, igniting a dull ache deep in my belly.

Unable to stop myself, I reached a hand between my legs and pushed against his hand, needing him to stop and keep going all in one breath. "Oh god…" I cried out when I felt him push another finger deep inside of me. My body writhed against his hand, and I felt incredibly exposed and vulnerable. But I *liked* it. I *wanted* to be vulnerable with him. I wanted him to have me, I realized. "Gerard."

I could feel his erection stabbing my thigh as he lay on his side facing me, propped up on his elbow like some Greek god. "Hmm?"

"I love you," he whispered, fingers still moving expertly inside of my body, as he evoked feelings from my body I never knew existed.

"I love you, too."

"Oh god!" Madness. This was utter madness, and I was reveling in every moment of it. I wanted to strip every layer of clothing from my body and lie naked beneath this beautiful boy. I wanted to feel more than just his fingers inside of me. I wanted him to be inside of me, but the fact that he still hadn't kissed me was concerning.

"Kiss me…" Breath hitching, I gripped at the sheets beneath me and stifled a cry as the pressure building up inside of me caused my body to tingle and jolt. "Please, Gerard…oh god…"

"It's okay," he coaxed, head bowing like he was in physical pain as his fingers worked me into a frenzy. "Fuck, you're so tight."

Of course I was. Not even a tampon had managed to cross the fortress of my knickers in sixteen years. I held on to my virginity tighter than Johnny held on to his dreams of the pros. Problem was, when it came to Gerard Gibson, I was only too willing to veer off path and loosen my grip.

"Gerard!" Head thrashing in pleasure, I reached blindly for him, not stopping until I was cupping the back of his neck. "Please…"

"I've got you." He rested his brow against mine, lips still not touching. "You're safe, I promise."

I never felt for one moment like I wasn't. Safety was a given when I was in this boy's arms and having him touch me in my most intimate place only solidified that fact. Because not only was my body assuring me that this boy was *the* boy, but my heart was in no doubt, either.

And then his hand was moving faster, his fingers pushing in and out of me in a delicious, merciless rhythm that caused me to make peace with the fact that I was about to die right here in his arms.

"Gerard…" It had to be death waiting on the other side of these full-body convulsions, and I could think of no better way to go. "I don't…" My heart tried to beat its way out of my chest. "I can't…" My eyes rolled back in my head. "What's happening…" The dull ache had grown to such a force beyond comprehension and was now causing explosions inside of me. "To me…"

"It's okay, Claire-Bear." Gerard came to my rescue and explained in a strained tone. "This is what coming feels like."

"I-it is?" Every muscle in my body coiled tight to the point that I felt like I was spasming uncontrollably. Shuddering helplessly beneath him, I continued to hold his hand in place, not daring to move so much as my pinkie finger for fear of chasing off this wondrous feeling. "Oh…g-god."

Obliging my neediness, Gerard continued to gently crook his finger inside of me until the last of the delicious lightning bolts drained from my body. Only then did he remove his hand from between my legs and reposition my underwear back in place.

The moment he did, I suddenly felt panicked, unsure of what would happen next. But then he rolled us both into our usual sleeping position, and I felt myself relax.

Hooking an arm around my waist like he had every night since we were children, Gerard pressed a kiss to my shoulder and whispered, "Night, Claire."

Reeling in the darkness, I clutched his forearm, holding on for dear life, and strangled out the words, "Night, Gerard."

31

What Have I Done?

GIBSIE

WHEN THE SUN CAME UP ON TUESDAY MORNING, CLAIRE WAS STILL IN MY BED. WITH her wild curls strewn over my pillow and her adorable kitten-like snoring filling the silence.

Body rigid, I kept a firm arm wrapped around her waist, too afraid to move an inch. The memory of last night's antics had tormented me to the point where I hadn't closed an eye all night. I supposed the plus side of not sleeping meant that I hadn't wandered off on any late-night adventures, but it didn't give me much comfort.

Because I had fucked up. Because I'd tainted her. This beautiful, willful, loyal, and innocent girl. I'd put my hands on her when I had no right to and crossed the point of no return. Still, as guilt-ridden as I felt, there was no denying that her presence was stabilizing me in a way I'd never felt in this house. Not since my dad moved out, at least.

The sound of my phone vibrating on my nightstand had my heart leaping in my chest, and I quickly reached over to snatch it up.

"Cap," I whispered when I answered the call, feeling a huge sense of relief come over me. "What's up?"

———————————

"I have to say, lad," Johnny mused forty minutes later. "I've never seen you get ready so fast for the gym," Standing above where I was perched on the weight bench, he continued to spot me. "Usually, I have to drag you from the bed kicking and screaming."

"Hmm," I replied, unable to find it in me to toss a lighthearted comment out. Nothing about me felt light this morning. Especially when my conscience was weighing me down so heavily. Ignoring the bead of sweat that was trickling down my neck, I focused my attention on bench-pressing the 120kg barbell upward.

"Christ, Gibs, did you wake up in beast mode?" With his brows raised, my best friend continued to spot me. "You've gone up an entire weight bracket overnight."

Because I'm mad, Johnny. Because I'm fucking furious with myself, and if I don't burn some of this tension out of my body, I'm going to scream.

"You okay, Gibs?"

"I'm always okay, Cap."

"You sure?"

"Yep."

"You're awfully quiet."

"It's all good," I forced myself to say. "Just full of beans this morning."

"Well, save some of those beans for St. Andrews tomorrow." he chuckled, catching ahold of the barbell and setting it into place. "Because they have a serious forward pack, and I heard their number 13 is talking shite about how he's going to end my career before it starts."

"Not on my watch," I bit out, standing up for him to take my place on the bench. Moving into position to spot him, I added, "I'll take the head clean off the bastard if he even looks at you sideways."

Johnny chuckled and reached for the bar. "Never doubted you for a minute, buddy."

32
You Let Him Do What?

CLAIRE

WHEN I WOKE UP ON TUESDAY MORNING IN GERARD'S BED, THE SIDE OF THE MATTRESS he'd slept on was vacant. In his place was a haphazardly scribbled note on his pillow that read, *Early morning training x* in his handwriting.

I'd somehow managed to ninja-sneak my way across the street without getting caught by either set of parentals, but when I found my brother in the kitchen eating breakfast before school and *not* training like Gerard's note had suggested, I felt a wave of uneasiness sweep through me.

Surviving Hugh's in-depth interrogating, I had made it to school with my dignity intact, but that wave of uneasiness continued to fester and grow with every class that passed.

I knew the boys had a rugby match tomorrow afternoon against St. Andrews, and before game days, it wasn't uncommon to not hang out together, but the fact that I hadn't managed to snag one single opportunity to talk to Gerard all day gave me the distinct impression that he was avoiding me.

The straw that broke the camel's back was his absence at big lunch. When Johnny arrived at the rugby table without sight or sound of Gerard, I hit my limit. Because if Mister Serious Captain had time to eat lunch with his girlfriend, then that was all the evidence I needed. Gerard's absence had nothing to do with scoring tries and everything to do with scoring girls.

This girl.

Me.

Oh god…

"I need to talk to you!" I blurted out, eyes locked on Shannon, who was laughing at something her boyfriend had whispered in her ear. "It's an emergency!"

"You do?" My bestie's attention flicked to me. "It is?"

"I do, and absolutely." Shoving my chair back, I leapt up, body bristling with nervous energy. "Like right *now*, Shan."

Without a word, Shannon rose to her feet and moved to my side, clearly understanding the assignment.

"It's so bad, Shan," I strangled out, catching ahold of her hand before dragging her off in the direction of the girls' bathrooms. Pushing the door inward, I hurried inside and instantly began to pace the empty bathroom. "Like so, so bad, chickie." Cracking my knuckles, I pushed at the sleeves of my jumper while I considered how to verbalize last night's events to my bestie.

"Oh my god, Claire, what is it?" Shannon's voice was laced with concern, and her blue eyes were wide in horror. "What happened?" Closing the space between us, she reached up and touched my brow. "Are you sick? Because I thought you looked flushed this morning when you arrived at school."

"Yes and no," I admitted with a grimace. "As in, yes I'm flushed but no I'm not sick—unless of course you take into account what happened last night." Whimpering, I chewed on my nails before adding, "In that case, I suppose I would be considered 'sick' in several different constitutions where promiscuity is frowned upon."

"Okay, you're rambling." She reached up and grabbed my arms. "Just take a breath and talk to me, Claire."

"Yes, I am rambling, Shan," I squeezed out. "I'm rambling because I am freaking the hell out!"

"Why?"

"It's Gerard!"

"What about him?"

"He and I… Last night he…" Nope. I couldn't do it. I couldn't verbalize last night's debauchery out loud. "Oh god, I can't say the word!"

"Say the word?" Shannon gaped at me in horror. "Claire, did Gibs do something to hurt you?"

"Oh my god, no." I shook my head. "Gerard would never hurt me. Not in a million years." Swallowing deeply, I whispered, "He did the opposite of hurting me."

Shannon continued to frown up at me for a long beat before her eyes widened in understanding and her mouth formed a perfect little O shape. "Oh."

"Oh," I confirmed with a whimper, while nodding my head enthusiastically to let my bestie know just how big of an O it was.

"You let him do what?" Lizzie demanded, standing in the bathroom doorway, clearly having heard every word. "You let that piece of shit into your knickers? Are you completely insane?"

"Oh my god, Liz, keep it down, will you?" Shannon whisper-hissed, dragging our friend into the bathroom and closing the door behind her. "Jeez."

"Okay, you need to not judge me right now," I snapped back, glowering at her. "Because first, I didn't sleep with Gerard last night, and second, I never once judged you when you *actually* slept with Pierce."

"Why *would* you have a problem with me and Pierce?" Lizzie snapped back. "It's not like he's related to the fucking monster that ruined your family." Her eyes were full of hurt when she said, "And it's not like I purposefully chose to betray my friend by getting with him."

"You seriously want to talk to me about betraying friends with boys?" I narrowed my eyes and glared back at her, unwilling to back down this time. "One word, Liz: *brother*."

"Whoa, girls. Just stop, okay?" Shannon interjected, holding her hands up. "Let's just take it down a notch here."

"So, I take it you're with him now?" Ignoring Shannon's attempts to play peacemaker, Lizzie folded her arms across her chest and glared. "You and Thor. You're a thing now, right?"

"*No*," I replied in a hard tone. "We're not, but you would already know that if you stopped throwing around accusations and actually listened for a change."

"Okay, shush!" Reaching up, Shannon clamped her hands over both of our mouths. "No more fighting, okay?" Her attention flicked between both of us as she spoke. "I know this is a delicate situation for both of you, but this isn't good , guys. It's hard enough to be a girl in this world without turning on each other. Especially since we've been friends since primary school." Blowing out a breath, she took a step back and gestured to me. "Okay, Claire, tell us everything." She then walked over to Lizzie and squeezed her hand. "And we'll listen."

I held my breath for a moment, waiting for Lizzie's comeback, but when it didn't come, I exhaled slowly and explained last night's shenanigans in explicit detail.

"And then Gerard did something with his thumb and pointer finger," I added, using my own hand to give them a detailed visual rundown. "And that was it." I threw my hands up in despair. "I was *dead*, I tell you!" Planting my hands on my hips, I looked at both of them expectantly. "Well? Any ideas?"

"He made you come," Lizzie replied flatly. "Congratulations."

"Oh my god," Shannon gushed between fits of laughter. "I'm so happy for you guys."

"Don't be," I was quick to warn. "He was gone when I woke up this morning, and he's been avoiding me like the plague ever since."

"Sounds about right," Lizzie deadpanned. "The typical MO of a fuckboy."

"Stop it," Shannon scolded, still smiling. "Gibsie is not one of those."

"Except that he is," Lizzie challenged dryly. "And Claire is just one more in a long list of Thor's conquests." With a despondent look etched on her face, she looked at me. "You're such a fool." Lizzie shook her head. "He's going to ruin you."

My hackles were immediately up, and I was instantly on the defense. "Like you're in any position to judge me."

"What's that supposed to mean?"

"Guys, stop, please…"

"You know exactly what that means," I shot back. "So just think about it before you start name-calling."

"Claire," Shannon tried to interject, begging me with her eyes not to feed the fire. "Just take a sec, okay." Turning to Lizzie, she added, "Nobody knows how Gibsie's feeling except *Gibsie*, so please let's just give him the benefit of the doubt here." She forced a smile before saying, "He clearly has feelings for Claire."

"Thanks, Shan," I said, needing her reassurance in this moment.

"It's true," she hurried to soothe. "That boy worships the ground you walk on, and the entire school knows it. I bet you any money there's a perfectly plausible reason for him missing lunch today. In fact, I could almost guarantee that if I walked out there and asked Johnny, he would more than likely say that Gibs has detention for some disastrous prank or other." She offered me a supportive smile before adding, "Trust me, Claire, there isn't one single believable scenario where that boy would choose to ignore you. He couldn't if he tried."

"But what if he regrets what happened between us?"

"He *doesn't*."

"But what if he *does*?"

"That's *not* going to happen."

"But what if…"

"Oh please," Lizzie cut in, voice trembling. "You'll be a couple by the end of the week."

My heart hammered excitedly. "You really think so?"

"Of course," Shannon agreed with a smile.

"And if that's what you want, then go for it," Lizzie added in a trembling voice. "I clearly can't stop you. But don't expect me to stick around to watch it." Sniffling, she shook her head and moved for the bathroom door. "You've made your choice and it's clearly him!"

"Lizzie, wait!"

She didn't wait.

Instead, she stormed out of the bathroom, letting the door slam shut behind her.

"She'll come around," Shannon offered, chewing on her lip nervously. "Give her some time. You'll see."

33

Keep the Head, Lad

GIBSIE

"Biggs give you an answer about the cinema yet?" I heard Donal Crowley whisper during religion class on Tuesday afternoon.

"Nah, but I'm not worried about it," Jamie Kelleher whispered back.

"She's just playing hard to get."

"You think?"

"Yeah, lad, she's obviously going to say yes."

"You sound sure of yourself."

"Why wouldn't I be?"

Rage. It was bubbling up inside of me at a rapid rate. Taking ahold of my mind in ways that I never knew it could, morphing me into what I could only compare to a ticking time bomb.

"You know, even if she agrees to go out with you, you'll be hard pushed to get a kiss on the cheek from that one. Pretty sure she's one of those pioneers, lad. You know the ones that take the pledge during their confirmation to abstain and all things before marriage."

"Not for much longer."

"Gibs," Johnny whispered hissed from the chair beside me. "Breathe."

I was trying, really, I was, but the more the two pricks at the desk behind us continued to gossip, the angrier I grew.

"I don't know, lad. She seems like a good girl."

"Yeah, but that's even better, lad, because good girls can be trained."

"*Breathe*," Johnny repeated, pushing down hard on our shared desk to stop it from shaking. "You've already had lunchtime detention for fighting with Murph," he whisper-hissed. "Don't get yourself locked up for the rest of the week."

How? *How* was I supposed to take a fucking breath? My entire body was thrumming with barely contained energy. My knees were bopping so violently, the desk was shaking. I wanted to maim something. Correction, I wanted to maim the bastard sitting behind me.

"So, what's the plan? Wine and dine her to get to the fun part?"

"Pretty much, lad. I'm going to take her on a few dates and get it out of the way so we can get to the fun part..."

And that was all I could take. Fuck detention. I would gladly park my ass in the bold chair for the week if it meant that I got to shut these bastards up.

"You're a dead man!" I roared, losing all control of my body. My desk went flying at the same moment I lunged for Jamie and Johnny lunged for me. "I'm going to rip your fucking tongue out for that..."

"He has a concussion, sir!" Johnny shouted louder, intercepting me before I could get ahold of Jamie. "He took a knock to the head during training this morning and hasn't been himself since," he added, addressing our teacher, while physically wrestling me toward the classroom door. "I better take him to the office to get checked out."

"You do that, Kavanagh," Mr. Gardener replied, looking unconvinced, but too lazy to argue about it.

"Will do," Johnny called out his shoulder as he yanked the door open and pushed me into the empty hallway.

"Did you hear him back there?" I demanded in outrage. "Did you hear that motherfucker?"

"Yes, I heard him, but I need you to keep the head," Johnny instructed calmly, keeping ahold of the back of my jumper. "Do you hear me, Gibs?" he continued to coax, steering me in the direction of the sixth-year locker area. "Just keep the head and *don't* react."

"Don't react?" I gaped at him. "After what I heard those assholes say about Claire?" I shook my head in disgust. "Yeah, fuck that."

Turning on my heels, I stalked back in the direction of the classroom we'd just exited. Well, I attempted to at least, but the death grip Johnny had on my school jumper thwarted my plans. "Calm down, Gibs."

"Don't be a hypocrite," I snapped. "You would lose your ever-loving shit if you heard anyone say that about Shannon."

"Yes, I would," he agreed calmly, walking me down the corridor like a dog on a leash. "But if the shoe was on the other foot, I would hope that you would step in on my behalf before I got myself expelled."

"Am I Sookie?" I snapped, breaking free from his hold, only to make a burst for the religion classroom. "You don't need to walk me, Johnny!"

"Get your arse back here," he ordered, spoiling my break for freedom by fisting my jumper once more. "Listen to me, will you? I'm as annoyed as you are, but use your head, Gibs. We don't throw down in class, lad. That's not how it's done."

"That's how it's done in my world," I shot back, too pissed off to think clearly. "He's not getting away with talking about her like that, Johnny. Over my dead body."

"Agreed," Johnny said calmly, pushing open the door of the sixth-year common room and pushing us both inside. "But we need to be smart about it. Fighting in class isn't going to do us any favors, Gibs."

"Who are we fighting?" a familiar voice asked, and we both turned to find Joey sprawled out on one of the couches with a coat draped over him.

"So that's why you weren't in religion class," Johnny accused. "You were taking a bleeding nap."

"Come and talk to me when you have a colicky newborn feeding on demand at home," Joey replied, standing up. "Back to my question." He stretched his arms over his head and cracked his neck from side to side. "Who are we fighting?"

"No one. We're not fighting anyone," Johnny was quick to rebuff. "Because *I* am in contract. *You* are on a warning," he added, pointing at me before turning his attention to Joey. "And *you* are on probation."

Ignoring Johnny's words of warning, Joey looked to me and repeated, "Who are we fighting, Gussie?"

"This is so bleeding bad," Johnny declared twenty minutes late, as he paced the student car-park like a man waiting on death row. "Jesus Christ, I can't believe I'm going along with this."

Meanwhile, I watched, both fascinated and engrossed, as Joey Lynch unlocked the door of Jamie Kelleher's car.

Who knew a putty knife and clothes hanger from the art room could unlock a car without damage?

Lynchy, apparently.

Once the button clicked up, Joey opened the driver's door, cigarette balancing between his lips, and reached inside. Another clicking noise sounded a moment later, and he called out, "Do you have the sugar, Gus?"

"I sure fucking do, Lynchy," I replied, handing him the bag and spoon.

"Oh god," Johnny groaned, covering his eyes with his hands. "I can't watch."

"Then don't." Without a hint of hesitation, Joey climbed back out, took the bag from me, and then walked around the side of the car. Opening the petrol cap of Kelleher's car, he proceeded to dump the sugar inside, one spoon at a time until the bag was empty.

Afterwards, he neatly screwed the cap back on and relocked the car. "Let's see this Kelleher prick take anyone to the cinema now."

"My da's going to kill me." Biting down on his fist to stifle a whimper, Johnny shook his head and walked off in the direction of his car, looking like he was close to passing out. All six foot five of him. "I'm a bleeding criminal."

"I used to think Podge was highly strung," Joey mused, quite literally leaning against the scene of the crime, finishing his cigarette. "But Kav takes the cake."

"That was fucking genius." I grinned. "I owe you, lad."

"Nah." Taking one final drag of his smoke, he tossed the butt away and pushed off the car. "Seems to me it was the least I could do."

"Oh?" I fell into step beside him. "How'd you figure?"

"Aoife," he explained, shoving his tools back into his schoolbag. "She told me what you did for her."

"I'm not following."

"Don't piss down my back and tell me it's raining, Gussie." He stopped short before we reached the main building. "I know you paid off my drug debt." Clear-eyed and sober, Joey stared right at me. "I owe you a lot more than this."

"You don't owe me anything, lad," I replied, feeling weirdly emotional. Claire once referred to Joey Lynch as the comeback kid, and I couldn't think of a better definition. Grinning, I added, "Although, if you *really* want to thank me, you could always make me AJ's godfather."

His lips twitched in response. "Don't push it."

34
Hello, Darkness, My Old Friend

CLAIRE

BY THE TIME SCHOOL ENDED, MY ARGUMENT WITH LIZZIE HAD FESTERED AND STEWED inside of me to the point where I was feeling terrible about the whole thing. I hated fighting with her, and lately that's all we seemed to be doing. I wasn't a naturally argumentative person, and while Lizzie could fight with a pillowcase, she *never* used to project her fury on me.

All of that was changing, and I could feel the shift.

I didn't like it.

Not one bit.

It almost felt like we were traveling down a broken track line with only one destination in sight.

Destruction.

Every day, we seemed to wallpaper over one crack in our friendship only to end up exposing another.

The worst part of it all was the fact that she continued to shut me out, making it impossible to help. I knew she was confiding in Shannon—well, as much as Lizzie confided in anyone, and it hurt me to know that I was on the outside of her inner circle. It hurt because I was trying to do the right thing by two people I loved and was being castigated for it.

I had the same helpless feeling in the pit of my stomach that I had last year with Shannon. Just like back then, I could sense the trouble. I could feel it in my bones, but instead of jumping into action, I froze.

I was *still* freezing.

Making the conscious decision to *not* let another one of my friends down, I snuck off from Tommen as soon as the last bell of the day signaled, making the two-mile walk to a street I rarely visited anymore. I chose to walk to the Young's house because asking Gerard to drive me over just seemed wrong, given all that had happened between their families.

Knowing that Lizzie was with Shannon at the manor meant that this was my best opportunity to…well, to basically betray her. She'd hate me for it, of course she would, but my need to be liked wasn't a good enough reason to not intervene in this instance.

This is bad.

This is a mistake.

Turn back.

Oh god, what was I doing?

I had hockey after school on Wednesdays.

I loved hockey.

I didn't skip.

But this was more important.

She was more important to me.

When I rounded the familiar stone-pillared entrance that surrounded the Youngs' impressive property, I felt a pang of sadness hit me square in the chest. I didn't enjoy coming here anymore, not since Caoimhe passed away.

The house was sad, the people residing here reminded me a lot like ghosts, and I wasn't nearly masochistic enough to spend any deal of time here.

Knocking on the door, I waited with bated breath for someone to answer it.

When the door finally swung inward, and I was greeted by Lizzie's mam, Catherine, I felt my heart crack in my chest. She looked so weathered, like the last few years had aged her rapidly.

"Hello, Claire." She offered me a small smile that didn't meet the haunted look in her eyes. "Lizzie's not home from school yet."

"Oh, yeah, I know, Mrs. Young," I replied, offering her a bright smile, while my palms sweated profusely. "Liz is at the Kavanaghs' house with Shan." Clearing my throat, I wiped my hands against the fabric of my skirt. "I was actually hoping to see you."

Surprise filled her blue eyes. "Me?"

"Yes." Panic filled me at a rapid rate, causing me to stretch my smile out further, feeling the pressure in my lungs before I uttered a single word. "Can I come inside please?"

"You can," she answered warily, swinging the door inward. "Is everything alright?"

"Oh, everything's fine," I hurried to say, feeling a desperate urge to soothe the worry lines on her face, as I followed her into the house that I had spent so much of my childhood in.

"I feel like I haven't seen you in forever," Lizzie's mam said as she led us into the kitchen. "Take a seat."

"Yeah," I replied, slipping off my coat. "I'm sorry I haven't been around much."

"No need to explain, Claire," she said softly, moving to fill the kettle. "Tea?"

"Yes, please."

"Two sugars?"

I beamed. "You remembered."

She smiled over her shoulder. "How's that brother of yours keeping?" Turning off the tap, she walked over to the counter, kettle in hand, and switched it on. "He's a good one, that boy. He was such a rock to this family after Caoimhe's passing." She shook her head sadly. "Such a pity he doesn't come around anymore."

"Hugh's grand," I replied, taking a seat at the familiar kitchen table. The one I had carved my initials into the underside of when I was six. "He's doing his leaving cert this year."

"My god," she whispered, more to herself than me. "The years are just slipping away, aren't they?"

"They sure are," I replied, feeling sad.

"Still playing the rugby?"

"He sure is," I replied. "Still living and breathing for it."

"I meant to thank your mother for the beautiful wreath she laid for Caoimhe's anniversary," Mrs. Young said, returning to the table with two mugs of tea. "I must have lost track of time."

"Oh, it was no trouble," I hurried to say, accepting the mug she held out to me. "She lays one every year. On her birthday and at Christmas, too." Taking a small tip from my mug, I mulled over my next sentence before finally saying, "You know, I'm sure Mam would love you see you again."

Mrs. Young smiled politely but didn't respond, just like I knew she wouldn't. "It's been a really long time since you caught up, right?" I pushed in as gentle a tone as I could muster.

Six years, to be precise.

Since her daughter passed away and lines were drawn in the sand.

"My door is always open for your mother," Mrs. Young replied. Meaning that she had no intention of coming anywhere near our house because of who our neighbors were. "I'm so glad you called," she continued, reaching across the table to pat my hand. "You're like a breath of fresh air, Claire Biggs."

She wouldn't think that once she knew the true intent of my impromptu visit. "Is Mr. Young home soon?" I asked, shifting in discomfort when I locked eyes on the family portrait hanging on the wall of the kitchen. The one that contained two smiling sisters with their casually smiling parents. *Oh god.* "It's just what I wanted to talk to you about should probably include Lizzie's dad, too."

Mrs. Young stared at me for a long moment, confusion etched on her face. "Didn't Lizzie tell you?"

"Tell me what?"

"We've separated."

I gaped at her. "You've *what?*"

"Lizzie's father moved out last Easter."

"He did?" My mouth dropped, right along with my heart. "Mike moved out?"

"He's in Tipperary since January," Mrs. Young explained, pausing to take a sip from her mug. "Took a job in Thurles. He comes down every few weeks to visit Liz."

"Are you *serious?*"

"I'm surprised she didn't tell you."

"Yeah," I whispered. *Me too.*

"So, I'm afraid I'll have to do," she added gently. "Now, what was it you wanted to talk to me about, pet?"

"It's Lizzie," I forced myself to say, wishing like hell I had taken the coward's way out.

"What about her?"

Aw, crackers.

"Claire?"

Blowing out a pained breath, I forced myself to look her mother in the eye when I said, "I think Lizzie is cutting again."

35
My Rodeo Romeo

GIBSIE

"That's it," I announced, storming into Claire's bedroom later that evening. "I can't take another second of this tension."

"Gerard!" she yelped, diving behind the open door of her wardrobe. "Ever heard of knocking?"

My eyes took in the towel at her feet and her damp curls. "Oops." I quickly slapped my free hand over my eyes. "You were in the shower. My bad, Claire-Bear."

"Did you actually just storm into my room saying that *you* can't take another second of tension?" The sound of clothes hangers rattling filled the air. "How do you think I feel, Mister *I like to leave notes on girls' pillows*?"

"Clearly, I panicked," I replied, using every ounce of self-control inside of my body to *not* drop my hand and peek. "And I didn't lie in the note, babe. I really was at the gym with Cap."

"Only because you were too chicken to face me," she hit the nail on the head by stating. "I mean honestly, Gerard, could you be more transparent? When have you *ever* chosen the gym over sleeping in?"

"When I put my fingers in my best friend, that's when!" I shouted back, throwing my hands up in despair. "I am so fucking sorry about that, by the way, Claire-Bear."

"Oh my god, why did you bring Reggie over here?" she demanded then, veering off topic. "You know Mam will go mental if she knows he's in the house. You heard her the time we brought home that ferret, Gerard. Any more strays and the kittens have to go."

Huffing out a breath, I turned around and stalked out of her room, not stopping until I was in her brother's bedroom. "Here you go, my little angel." Grabbing Hugh's duvet off the bed, I tossed it on the floor and placed Reggie down on it. "Daddy will be back in a jiffy."

"Why?" Claire demanded when I returned to her room. The minute my eyes landed on her standing in front of me in an oversized T-shirt, my dick shot to attention. *Steady down, lad.*

"I don't know, Claire," I shot back. "Maybe because I have a heart and wanted the poor fucker to see his mother before he turns in for the winter."

"No, not Reggie." She batted the air around her. "Why are you sorry for what happened between us?"

Her question stumped me, and I blanched. "Because!"

"Because?" she pushed. "Was I bad or something?"

"What are you *talking* about?"

"Last night." Her hand was on mine then, peeling my fingers away from my eyes. "Did I do something wrong?"

"What? No, Claire, you didn't do anything wrong. You were perfect." I pressed a hand to my chest. "I was the one in the wrong last night."

"Why?"

"Who the hell knows? Maybe it's got something to do with that chemical imbalance in the brain like Anne is always harping on about. Or maybe I was dropped on the head as a baby," I admitted, throwing my hands up. "It would certainly explain why I seem to have the self-control of a toddler in a sweet shop." I shook my head to clear my thoughts before they took me on a little wander. "Either way, I'm the one in the wrong here, okay? Not you."

"No." She shook her head and looked up at me. "I mean, why does it have to be wrong?"

"Because…" My words trailed off as I watched her watch me. There were a dozen different answers to that question, but could I think of a single one? Nope. *Fuck my life.* "Because I shouldn't have touched you," I finally settled on, heart thundering so hard in my chest I thought I might end up with a hematoma on my chest muscle. I knew all about hematomas. I'd had one on my back when I was thirteen. Never had one on the heart, though. Not until now, at least.

"But what if I wanted you to touch me last night," she blew my world by saying. And then she fucked me over even further by catching ahold of my hand and backing up in the general direction of her bed, taking me with her. "What if I still want you to?"

Jesus. I had no answer to that other than to warn her, "That's a really bad idea, Claire-Bear."

"Shh," she purred, reaching up to press a finger to my mouth, and then, because she seemed to be hell-bent on tormenting me, she reached for the hem of her T-shirt before swiftly whipping it over her head.

Oh shit.

Standing in front of me in nothing but a white bra and pink polka-dot knickers, Claire reached for my hand again, encouraging me to close the space between us.

I could only presume that the move was meant to be a seductive one, but when she miscalculated her step and landed in a heap on her bedroom floor instead of her mattress, I couldn't stop the laugh that escaped me. "Nice."

"It's not funny, Gerard," she croaked out from her perch on the floor. "Omigod." Draping an arm over her face, she wailed in despair. "I was trying to be sultry!"

"Are you wearing Barbie knickers?"

"So not the point right now." Groaning dramatically, she shook her head. "You can leave now."

Smothering my laughter, I sank down on the carpet and reached for her hand. "Come on, don't be hiding from me."

"That was *awful*," she complained, peeking up at me through her fingers. "I am so not sexy."

"You so fucking are," I corrected, pulling her hand away from her face once more. "But you're even more adorable."

She narrowed her eyes in disgust. "Kittens are adorable, Gerard."

"Then you're my little kitten." I laughed, flopping onto my back next to her. "I like your ceiling," I offered then, pointing to the ivory-colored plaster, as I reached for her hand. "It's so much warmer than mine."

"Your ceiling is the same color," she sighed, entwining her fingers with mine. "At least it used to be."

"Hmm."

"Gerard?"

"Yeah, Claire-Bear?"

"I'm embarrassed."

I turned my head to look at her. "Don't be."

"Yeah, *okay*." She rolled her eyes. "Oh look. I'm cured."

I smiled. "What can I do?"

"Uh, let's see…" She pretended to ponder for a moment before saying, "How about you try to seduce me and fall on your ass instead?"

"Okay."

"Get real, Gerard."

I grinned. "You think I won't?" Not giving her a chance to respond, I sprung to my feet and made a beeline for her stereo.

"Oh my god." Claire laughed, hurrying onto her bed, when I whipped off my T-shirt and reached for her pink feather boa.

"You better make yourself comfortable, sweetheart," I purred, flicking through songs and settling on "5, 6, 7, 8" from Steps. Snatching her sparkly pink cowboy hat off the dresser, I perched it on top of my head and winked. "Because you're in for one hell of a treat."

"Omigod, you look like one of those Chippendale strippers," Claire snickered, clapping her hands together in delight. "Let's go, cowboy!"

"Yee-fucking-haw." Throwing shapes like I was fucking the air around me, I flexed my hips, shook my tits, and dry-humped her desk chair like my life depended on it. In a weird way, it did, because this girl *was* my entire world, and making her feel better was my only priority.

I was certain Johnny and Hugh had far more superior methods of persuasion when it came to making their girls feel better, but I had all the experience of a carrier bag in this department. What I *did* have at my disposal was a lack of shame, the enthusiasm of a puppy, and hips that rivaled Elvis.

Unable to quit while I was ahead, because I clearly lacked boundaries, I pushed it up a notch and pulled Claire into my arms, dancing her around the room like I was her own personal horse.

"Oh my god," she laughed, clinging to my shoulders. "Stop, stop, stop, Gerard. I'm going to pee."

"How dare you!" Lizzie's furious voice filled the air a moment later, followed by the sound of a door slamming. "How fucking dare you talk to my mother about me!"

"Liz!" Claire yelped, scrambling off my back and rushing over to turn off the music. "What are you…"

"What am I doing here?" Lizzie cut in, picking up a rogue hockey stick and then tossing it against the wall. "What are you doing, more like. As in what are you doing talking shit about me behind my back?"

Whoa.

"That's not what I was doing! And I wasn't talking shit, Liz, I swear. I was just…"

"You were just sticking your nose in where it doesn't belong," Lizzie spat out, roughly shoving Claire away when she tried to hug her. "How fucking dare you tell my mother that! What the hell were you *thinking*?"

"I was trying to help you!"

"Well, you didn't help, Claire. In fact, you just made my life a million times worse."

"Liz, please!"

"No, don't touch me."

"I didn't mean to make it worse for you, I promise. I was just trying to help…"

"Well, congratulations because all you managed to do was make an already grieving mother's life harder."

"Liz, please…"

"No! Stop. Dammit, Claire I don't want a fucking hug right now!"

"Hey! Hold the fuck up!" I warned, feeling my hackles rise when Claire staggered backwards from the force of being shoved backwards again. "Don't put your hands on her."

"Stay out of this, Thor!"

"Gerard, it's fine."

"Like hell it's fine," I snapped, moving to stand between them. "Take all the swipes you want off me but keep your goddamn hands off her!"

"You'd love that, wouldn't you?" Lizzie spat out. "Good old gallant Gibsie taking another one for the team? Well, fuck you, asshole! I wouldn't give you the satisfaction."

"You're a bitch," I hissed, pushing Claire behind me. "Do you hear me? You are a fucking head case!"

"I'm so sorry," Claire continued to say, using the back of her hand to wipe her cheeks. "Liz, I swear I was just trying to help."

Lizzie laughed humorlessly even though tears were trickling steadily down her cheeks, matching the ones falling from Claire's eyes. "You have some nerve to speak to me like that."

"Like what?" I demanded. "Like I'm not sorry for you? Well, guess the fuck what, Liz? I'm all out of pity. The well ran dry a long time ago."

"Yeah?" she sneered. "Well, I'd rather be a bitch than a rapist any day!"

"I'm *not* a fucking *rapist!*"

"Nah, you're just related to one."

That was it.

That was fucking it.

I couldn't take this anymore.

"He is *not* my brother." My entire body trembled and shook as I glared back at her. "That asshole is *nothing* to me. He's *not* my blood. He's *not* my brother. He's not my goddamn anything, so don't you dare keep throwing him in my face!"

"He killed my sister!"

"Do you think you're the only person to ever lose their sister?" I roared, throwing my hands up in frustration. "I lost my sister, too, Lizzie! I buried my sister *and* my father!"

"They drowned," she spat out. "Accidentally. It's not the same thing. Nobody *hurt* them. Not like *my* sister or Shannon's mam."

"Oh, I'm so fucking sorry my family didn't die in more gruesome circumstances," I choked out, trembling. "Shit, maybe Beth should have drifted into the motor of the boat after she drowned, at least then we'd have a little blood and gore for the sob story."

"You know I didn't mean it like that."

"You don't know what you mean, because you haven't thought clearly a day since she died," I shot back. "You're programmed on pain and bitterness. I've tolerated your bullshit for years because I knew how you felt. Because I *know* how it feels. But you crossed the line coming in here and pushing Claire around. Now, the rest of our friends can keep handing out hall passes for your horrendous behavior, Lizzie, and I'm not taking it anymore. Do you hear me? I am *not* walking this line with you another day of my goddamn life!"

"Jesus Christ, what's going on in here? I can hear you from the street," Hugh demanded, storming into the room. "Why are you in your underwear?" he asked, glaring at his sister. "And what the hell are you wearing?"

"Don't look at me like that," I huffed when his accusatory gaze landed on me. "I was in the middle of a performance." Ripping off the boa, I pointed a finger in Lizzie's direction. "If you want to know what's wrong, ask *her.*"

"No, no, no, this is on me, guys. This is all my fault," Claire blurted out as she quickly threw on her pajamas. "I shouldn't have gone to her house." Turning to Lizzie, she said, "I'm so sorry, Liz. You're right. I shouldn't have gone to your house."

"You went to her house?" Hugh frowned in confusion. "Why?"

"Not me," I huffed, appalled that he would even think such a thing. I hadn't been to that house in almost six years, and I never planned to step foot inside the door ever again. Not that I would be welcome either way. "Claire."

"Why?"

"How the fuck would I know?" I threw my hands up. "She just barged in here all guns a-blazing." Shrugging I added, "This is the first I'm hearing of any of this."

"I thought I was doing the right thing," Claire continued, ignoring her brother as she gingerly approached her furious friend. "I'm so sorry if I made things worse for you."

"He didn't even apologize," Lizzie strangled out, entire body heaving with shudders, as her emotions got the better of her. Collapsing in a heap, she stared aimlessly at the floor. "Mark Allen raped his girlfriend. His girlfriend who was *my* sister. He raped her, and then she *killed* herself because of it. Because she couldn't live with what *he* did. And then he got to walk away and live his life while my sister's defiled body rots in the ground." Tears trickled down her cheeks when she looked up at me. "She'll never get to grow up. She'll never turn nineteen. She'll never get married and have children. She'll never do any of the things he gets to do, and *he* never even said *sorry!*"

Frozen to the bone, I absorbed her words like knives to the heart. Because they hurt. They fucking tortured me. Her narrative might be worlds apart from mine but there was no disputing the sincerity in her tone when she spoke her truth. Because she believed her version of events. Meaning nothing I could ever say or do would change or make it better for her.

As she sobbed like a small child on the floor, I felt my beating heart crack and splinter.

There was no fixing this.

Nothing would ever improve between us.

There would be no white flag.

Because Lizzie had her version of events, and I had mine.

She had the horror story versed off by heart, the one that made Caoimhe the victim and him the monster, while all I had was a crumpled-up letter under my mattress and the truth.

"I'm sorry," Claire pleaded, as she hovered around her friend, petting and coddling her like a mother would a small child. "It's going to be okay."

Unlike earlier, Lizzie didn't push and shove at Claire's attempts to comfort her. Instead, she just sat on the floor with her arms wrapped tightly around my knees and sobbed quietly.

"Gibs," Hugh said, clearing his throat. "Maybe you should…"

Yeah, I didn't need him to finish the sentence. Not when I already knew that I was no longer welcome.

She won.

Again.

Refusing to bow my head in shame, I walked out of the bedroom with my last shred of dignity in tatters and didn't stop moving until I was on the other side of the street.

"Don't start," I warned the minute I stepped inside and was greeted by a tall figure in the front hall. Reaching up, I swiped Claire's cowboy hat off my head. "I'm in no form for another lecture—"

"How's it going, little brother?"

My blood ran cold at the sound of *his* voice, and I momentarily froze, hands clutching the door handle as a wave of pure, undiluted panic washed over me.

"Gibs? Is that you?" Mam appeared from the kitchen doorway, all bright smiles and full of bubbliness. "Look who flew in a week early from Mumbai to surprise us!"

"You're back."

My stepbrother stood in the middle of the hallway with his big arms folded across his chest, looking far less formidable to the seventeen-year-old version of me than he had the seven-year-old. "I'm back."

Meanwhile, Keith appeared behind her with a stack of photographs in his hands.

"Gibs, son, take a look at this beauty," he said, thrusting a picture in my face. "This is Mark's wife, Meera, and their son, Yash."

My eyes took in the sight of the petite Asian woman, with a toddler on her hip.

He had a son.

A little boy.

"Mark's been offered an overseas transfer with work. He and Meera are considering a permanent relocation," Mam gushed, draping her arms around her husband's adult son. "Isn't it wonderful, Bubba?"

I could feel the ground shifting beneath me and my world fucking ending. "Relocation?"

"That's right, son." Keith nodded in agreement as he wrapped an arm around my mother's shoulders. "The whole family will be back together soon."

36
Big Brothers Mend the Best Fences

CLAIRE

Guilt-ridden didn't even tip the scales of how dreadful I felt as I sat across the kitchen table from a distraught-looking Lizzie.

My head was in a spin from the crazy twists and turns this day had taken. It had been one wild roller-coaster that had left me sitting in the middle of the consequences of my actions, responsible for upsetting my friend to the point where she had collapsed in a heap on my bedroom floor.

The only reason Lizzie was sitting upright in my kitchen now was the boy placing two mugs of hot chocolate on the table in front of us. Hugh had somehow managed to console her to the point where she agreed to come downstairs and talk it out with me. Thank god because if she had left without clearing the air, I thought I might join her on the floor.

"I'm sorry, Liz," I offered for what had to be the fiftieth time. But it was the truth. I *was* sorry.

From what I could gather from Hugh, my disclosure this afternoon to Mrs. Young, no matter how well intended, had upset the woman so badly that she had ended up at the out-of-hours doctor with chest pains. Chest pains that were directly linked to the fear of losing her one remaining living child.

I didn't mean to cause the woman any pain. I would never intentionally harm another human being. All I had been trying to do was be a proactive friend who acted in her friend's best interests *before* disaster struck instead of afterward.

Whether or not I was right or wrong to tell her mother might still be up for debate, but there was no denying the sheer level of upset my tactless admission had caused.

Gerard had stormed out ages ago, clearly reeling from taking the brunt of Lizzie's anguish, which, to be fair, wasn't anything new.

I desperately wanted to rush across the road to check on him, but I had a horrible feeling that my friendship with Lizzie was resting on tenterhooks right now.

I couldn't bail.

I had to see this through.

Make it better somehow.

"Liz?" Clearing my throat, I reached for my mug of hot chocolate and curled my hands around the ceramic, glad to feel the heat caress my fingertips. "Why didn't you say anything about your dad moving out back in March?"

"Mike moved out?" Confusion swept over my brother's face as he pulled out the chair next to Lizzie's and sank down. "Liz?"

"Because it didn't seem important," she bit out, attention glued to the untouched mug in front of her. "At least not in the grand scheme of things."

"When your friend's parents separate and her dad leaves the county, I'd say is pretty important in any scheme of things," I replied. "Liz, you never said a word."

"How could I say anything?" she snapped back, body rigid with tension. "Shannon was going through everything with her family back then."

Aw, crap.

Guilt swirled inside of me.

"You still could have come to me, chickie," I strangled out, voice thick with emotion. "I could have tried to help you."

"Kind of like how you tried to help me today?" came her angry response. "I *told* you what happened, Claire. I fell. Over a fucking gate and landed on barbed wire. If you didn't believe me, you could've asked Patrick. It was on his farm that it happened. You didn't have to run to my mam and traumatize her worse than she already is." Tears filled her eyes as she spoke. "You have no idea how tough this year has been on us, and you just went and made it so much worse."

"Oh god." My shoulders slumped in defeat. "I'm so sorry."

"You could have come to me."

Lizzie's gaze immediately flicked to my brother, and she choked out a pained breath. "Yeah, because that would have gone down really well."

"You could have come to me," Hugh repeated, eyes locked on hers in what felt like a blazing stare-down. "You can *always* come to me." He swallowed deeply, Adam's apple bopping before whispering, "No matter what."

"No matter what," Lizzie repeated, whispering the words to herself, as she retrained her attention on her mug.

After a great deal of groveling and a whole heap of holding my tongue, I thankfully managed to worm my way back into my friend's good graces. Lizzie still wasn't my number one fan, but when she climbed into the passenger seat of Hugh's car a little after nine o'clock, she did offer me a half-hearted wave before he drove her home.

I was taking that as a huge win.

The moment my brother's car was out of sight with Lizzie safely tucked inside, I wasted no time in scampering around the street to check on my other bestie.

I wasn't entirely sure what I expected to find when I let myself inside Gerard's house, but a huge stack of suitcases and travel luggage camped out in the front hallway was not it.

"What the…" Brows creased in confusion, I wandered through the downstairs, checking each room in my search to find the culprit of said luggage. "Gerard? Sadhbh? Keith?"

Aside from Brian snoozing in the living room armchair, the house was empty. Which was super weird because the front door was unlocked.

"Gerard?" I called out again, backpedaling into the hallway before clambering up the staircase. "You here?"

More silence.

Feeling foolish for not checking for his car in the driveway first, I hurried over to the front landing window and peered outside.

Dammit, the Allens' driveway was minus one silver Ford Focus.

Feeling oddly bereft, I padded into his bedroom and flicked on the light.

"What the…" My words trailed off when my eyes took in the carnage.

Gerard's room was trashed.

I mean, seriously trashed.

Every poster and picture frame that had once adorned his bedroom walls were now littered around his floor.

His nightstand had been turned over, his mattress had been toppled onto its side, and everything that was once housed in his wardrobe was currently sprawled, well, *everywhere.*

"Time only matured him on the outside, huh?" a male voice said from behind me. "He's still every inch the tantrum-throwing child he was six years ago."

"Jesus!" I yelped, springing around. "You almost gave me a heart attack."

"My sincerest apologies," a dark-haired man chuckled, looking suave in a crisp white shirt and expensive-looking tailored suit pants. "Blond curls. Doe eyes. Skulking in Gibsie's room. It can't be little Claire Biggs my eyes are seeing?"

Nodding warily, I eyed the man standing in Gerard's bedroom doorway. "How do you know my name?"

"I suppose you were only little when I moved out." His smile deepened and it caused a wave of eerie familiarity to wash over me. "I can't be too insulted that you don't remember me."

"Wait…" My breath caught in my throat and my eyes widened to saucers. "*Mark*?"

"The one and only."

The one and only? He said that like it was a good thing. It *wasn't*. Not for Lizzie, at least. Or Gerard. When he left town six years ago, everyone I knew had breathed a huge sigh of relief. Because he was trouble. Big trouble. "What are you doing back in Ballylaggin?"

"Am I not allowed to visit my family?"

Technically yes. But morally absolutely *not*. Instead of verbally answering, I offered him a shrug.

"I'm considering relocating my family," he explained, flashing the gold band on his left hand at me. "Meera has never been to Ireland and our son is almost two. I've been given a job opportunity, so I flew back to scope out the property market before making any decisions."

Ew. "Oh," I managed to say instead, though it was a challenge because this boy— now man—had always made my skin crawl.

The strange thing was my reservations about Mark Allen had little to do with the rumors that had gone around town about his relationship with Caoimhe Young and everything to do with what a huge jerk he had been to Gerard when we were little.

From the moment he was injected into our lives, Mark had made it his mission to make Gerard miserable. He was more than just an asshole stepbrother. He was a bully and a mean one at that.

The fact that someone as sweet and amazing as Caoimhe went out with Mark in the first place was beyond my comprehension. Past tense and present. I didn't understand the attraction when I was little, and I understood it even less now.

"Where's Gerard?" My tone was less than polite, but showing any sort of kindness to this man was abhorrent to me. Especially since I'd spent the last several hours watching one of my oldest friends in the world break down because of his actions.

While I was fully prepared to die on my hill of fealty to Gerard Gibson when it came to his and Lizzie's feud and was willing to defend Gerard's good name to the bitter end, I was under no such obligation to the man standing in front of me.

Because, sure, the authorities might not have been able to pinpoint him to the crime the Young family was so insistent he committed against their daughter six years ago, but there was no smoke without fire, and Mark Allen was definitely guilty of *something*.

"Dad took Sadhbh out for dinner in town," he replied in a breezy tone, not bothering to answer my question. "I figured I'd hang back for tonight." He smiled again. "It was a long flight."

Yeah, right.

All this proved was that Mark didn't want to bump into the wrong people in town and be told what a scumbag he was.

"And Gerard?" I pushed, eyeing his mobile phone on the bedroom floor. "Where is he?" I gestured to the carnage around me. "What happened to his room?"

"You know Gibs," he replied breezily. "Spat the dummy and stormed off hours ago."

"Where did he *go*?" I bit out, enunciating my words clearly. *What did you do?*

"You tell me, Baby Biggs," he replied with a chuckle. "You were always the one who could find his hiding places."

"Hugh?" I called out from the landing when I heard the front door open and close later that night. "Is that you?"

"Yeah, it's only me," I heard my brother call back. Moments later, he appeared on the staircase. "What's up?"

"What the hell took you so long?" I demanded, leaning over the banister. "I have been freaking out on my own for two hours, Hugh!"

"Why?"

"Oh my god. Oh my god!" Bouncing from foot to foot, I felt another wave of heebie-jeebies wash over me. "It's so bad, Hugh."

"What is?" he asked, joining me in the landing. "What happened?"

"Mark Allen!" I strangled out, eyes bulging. "He's back in Ballylaggin."

"That's not funny," my brother was quick to shoot down, eyes narrowed in disgust. "Don't say shit like that."

"I'm not trying to be funny." Stamping my foot in frustration, I pointed in the direction of the street and eyeballed my brother, willing him to believe me. "He's back, Hugh. I saw him with my own eyes."

Hugh's face turned a deathly shade of gray. "Tell me you're joking."

"I wish I could."

"He's back?"

I nodded vigorously.

"In Ballylaggin?"

Again, I nodded eagerly.

"Across the street?"

"Yes," I strangled out, gesturing wildly. "He's back."

"Motherfucker!"

"Whoa, where are you going?" I called out, watching as my brother barreled down the staircase like he was chasing a rare Pokémon. "Hugh, wait. Don't go over there!"

Too late.

Our front door was wide open, and my brother was stalking across the street like a man on a mission.

"Hugh!" I shouted, racing after him in my unicorn onesie. "You know what Mam said. We're not supposed to take sides, remember? Sadhbh's her best friend! We're supposed to stay out of it!"

Ignoring my protests, my brother walked right into Gerard's house without a hint of hesitation. Now, knocking or ringing doorbells wasn't something Gerard, Hugh, and I ever did before entering each other's homes, but this was different. Because usually we didn't intend on spilling blood, something I had an awful feeling my brother was hell-bent on doing tonight.

"Hugh!" I called out when I reached their front door and caught a glance of my brother's back as he bolted up the staircase. "Wait, will you?"

Moments later, the sound of a door slamming filled the air, followed by shouting.

Aw, crackers.

Clambering up the staircase, I didn't stop until I was standing in the doorway of Bethany's old room, eyes widening in horror. "Hugh, stop!"

"You have a lot of fucking nerve to show your face back here!" my brother roared while he pinned Gerard's stepbrother to the bedroom wall. "You fucking monster!"

"I'm…innocent," Mark strangled out, pulling and tearing at the hand Hugh had wrapped around his throat. "Ask…the…Gards…"

"I don't give a shit what the Gards say," my brother snarled, looking more furious than I'd ever seen him. "We all know what a piece of shit you are!" He slammed Mark against the wall. "How fucking *dare* you come back to this street!"

"Hugh, no!" Rushing to intercept my brother before he went too far, I squeezed between their bodies and pushed at his chest. "Let's just go home, okay?"

"Yeah, Hugh," Mark wheezed, using my intervention to break free from my brother's hold. "Listen to your sister."

"You fucking…"

"Let's go, Hugh!" I shouted, pushing at his chest in my bid to get him out of this room. "Walk away now or I'm telling Mam!"

"You stay the hell away from her!" Hugh warned, body trembling, as he jabbed a finger in Mark's direction while reluctantly allowing me to push him into the landing. "Do you hear me? You keep your goddamn eyes off her!"

"Or what?" the older man goaded.

My brother narrowed his eyes in challenge. "Fuck around and find out, asshole."

"Relax, kid. I'm married now," Mark spat out. "I have no intention of looking at your sister."

"I'm not talking about my sister," Hugh roared, chest heaving. "This is your one and only warning, asshole."

37

So, Who's the Big Spoon?

"GIBS, FOR THE LAST TIME, STOP BLEEDING SPOONING ME!" WAS THE FIRST THING I heard my best friend say on Wednesday morning, swiftly followed by the heel of his foot digging into my shin.

"Okay, *ow*," I huffed, blinking my eyes open when pain ricocheted up my leg. "That fucking hurt, Cap. You know I bruise like a peach."

"It was supposed to," Johnny grumbled, shaking my arm off before pulling himself up into a sitting position. "Since when have I *ever* given you the impression that I'm the little spoon in this relationship?"

"And I am?"

"Well, it isn't bleeding me!"

"I can't help it, okay," I huffed, flopping onto my back. "I'm used to cuddling Claire at night."

"And I'm used to cuddling Shannon." Reaching behind his back, he retrieved a pillow and smacked me upside the head with it. "Not my fucking flanker."

"Yeah, well, those Lynches are like breeding vessels, so if you think about it, this impromptu sleepover might have just saved your ass from joining Lynchy on his trip down early fatherhood lane."

"Hold up." Johnny narrowed his eyes at me. "Did you just call my girlfriend a *breeding vessel*?"

"Shh, don't be cranky," I coaxed, rolling onto my side to snuggle the pillow he tried to maim me with. "You said it yourself that you and Shan want a bunch of kids when you're older, so think of it as a compliment."

"I don't know what to think when it comes to the shit that comes out of your mouth, Gibs, I really don't."

"That's your problem, Johnny," I replied with a yawn. "You do too much thinking."

"And you don't think at all."

"Yep. Sounds about right."

"Care to explain the late-night visit?" he asked then. "Because I have to say, Gibs, you've done a lot of strange things since we first met, but creeping into my bed in the middle of the night is definitely a first."

"Yeah, sorry about that." I offered him a sheepish grin. "I probably should've given you the heads-up first, huh?"

"Would've been nice."

Grinning, I said, "Would it sound strange if I told you I get nightmares and you make me feel safe?"

"Only a lot," Johnny shot back, looking mildly entertained by my antics. "So, what happened?"

"Nothing much."

"Don't give me that shite," he argued with a shake of his head. "Did you have a fight with Claire or something? She's usually your first port of call."

"Nah, we're good," I replied, stretching out. "But I was over at her place when the Viper showed up, throwing her usual shade at me." Shrugging, I added, "Basically, I had to split before I snapped."

"Jesus Christ." Johnny narrowed his eyes. "That bleeding girl."

"Yep," I agreed with a tired yawn. "Oh, but it gets worse."

"I'm listening."

"So, I go back to my place after the fight."

"Yeah?"

"And I walk through the door."

"Keep going."

"And there he is."

"He?"

"Mark."

"Mark?"

"*Mark*," I repeated, giving my best friend a knowing look.

Confusion filled Johnny's eyes for the briefest moment before awareness quickly set in. "Oh *shite*…"

"Yep," I replied flatly, feeling my mood darken. "And apparently, he's planning on packing the family up and moving back to Ballylaggin. Fuck my life, huh?"

"Gibs, man, what's the story there?" he asked in a cautious tone. "I know shite went down when I first moved down here, but no one ever talks about it, and I've only heard bits and pieces from Feely, Hugh, and Shan."

"Trust me, Cap, bits and pieces are all you need to know," I muttered, feeling the four walls close around me at the thought. "It's in the past."

"Humor me, lad," he pushed, nudging my thigh with his knee. "Come on, Gibs, you know I'm always on your side when it comes to that girl, no matter what." Shrugging, he added, "But it would be a hell of a lot easier to defend you when I know the whole story."

"You don't need to defend me, Johnny." His words felt like a slap to the face and my entire frame stiffened. "Because I didn't *do* anything."

"I know, Gibs," he agreed calmly. "Never thought for one moment that you did, lad. But when it comes to you and Lizzie, I feel like I'm walking around with a blindfold on."

"I *really* don't want to talk about it," I mumbled sleepily, settling deeper into his epic mattress that I couldn't even pretend I wasn't jealous of. In fact, if I could find a way to smuggle it out of the manor and back to my house, I would do it in a heartbeat. *That's it, lad. Distraction. Good thoughts. Happy thoughts. Block it all out.* "It's so fucking pointless and we'll just end up going around in circles."

"Try me."

"Jesus Christ, fine." Sitting up, I wiped the sleep from my eyes and slumped against the headboard at my back. "Tell me what you already know, and I'll fill in the rest."

"Your ma left your da when you were eight and got with Keith."

"I was seven when she threw him out," I interjected with a heavy sigh. "But close enough."

"Meanwhile, Keith was a widower when he moved into your gaff with his kid…"

"Mark was no kid," I cut him off by saying. "That prick was fourteen when our parents got together."

"Okay, Keith moved into your gaff with his teenage son after your parents got divorced," Johnny deftly corrected. "Is that about right?"

"Nope, there was no divorce," I corrected. "You couldn't get divorced in Ireland back then. Mam moved them in while she was *still* married to my old man. They didn't get married until *after* my father and Beth drowned."

"Shite."

"Yep." Bristling, I gestured with my hand for him to continue. "As you were."

"So, Mark used to go out with Lizzie's sister…"

"Caoimhe," I filled in.

"Caoimhe," he repeated with a grateful nod.

"They went to Tommen together?"

I nodded stiffly.

"Where they in the same year?"

"For a while."

"So, Mark and Caoimhe must be close in age to Shan's brother, Darren," Johnny said, doing some pretty fast fucking math in his head. "I know Darren went to BCS, but they could've easily gone to the same primary school together?"

"I don't know, lad." I shrugged. "I barely knew of the Lynches back then. They didn't go to my primary school, remember?" Shrugging, I added, "I barely remember the lads I went to primary school with, let alone anyone else."

"But Keith and Mark are blow-ins, so he obviously didn't go to primary school in Ballylaggin, but Lizzie, Shan, Joe, Tadhg, and Ols all went to Sacred Heart, so I'm guessing Darren and Caoimhe did, too," Johnny muttered, more to himself than me as he mentally pieced the puzzle of my past together.

"You know, Cap, when I said tell me what you know, I didn't mean in this much detail," I joked. "Christ, you'd make one hell of a detective."

"I like to be thorough," he shot back, unaffected. "So, they went out together? Mark and Caoimhe?"

"Pretty much."

"And you guys already knew each other because of Lizzie and Claire being friends?" Frowning, he added, "And because Caoimhe used to babysit all of you guys when you were kids?"

"Pretty much."

"Come on, Gibs," he pushed. "Give me something here, will you?"

"What do you want me to say?" I snapped, feeling claustrophobic.

"More than the words 'pretty much.'"

"Fine!" I snapped, running a hand through my hair in frustration. "How about this: they went out together for a few years. He was a good-for-nothing prick, and she was a fucking eejit for going anywhere near him. If they weren't causing drama and scenes by breaking up every second weekend, they were fucking on the job like rabbits. Remind you of anyone?"

"Lizzie and Pierce."

"Ten points to Gryffindor," I cheered with a sarcastic clap. "Listen, everyone tried to tell her what a piece of shit he was, but she wouldn't hear a word of it. In Caoimhe's eyes, Mark could do no wrong, and fuck you if you told her otherwise. It went back and forth like that for years, fucking years, Kav, until she clearly came face-to-face with his true colors." Bristling with agitation, I rolled my shoulders in my attempt to stop the shudder racking through me. "After she died, a rumor went around town that she left a suicide note for her mother disclosing a rape. The Gardaí investigated and found nothing. Not a shred of evidence to support the Young family's allegations. Eventually, the investigation was dropped, and Mark graduated from Tommen and left Ballylaggin." Blowing out a breath, I gestured aimlessly before saying, "Leaving the rest of us to clean up his mess."

"Well, shite."

"Pretty much."

"So, even though there was no solid proof, Lizzie and her family are convinced that Caoimhe killed herself because of a sexual assault she endured at the hands of your mother's husband's son?"

"*Yes*," I confirmed with a nod, relieved that he didn't refer to him as *my* stepbrother.

"And Lizzie has it in for you because your mother is still married to his father?"

"Yep." I nodded. "That and the fact that Mam and Keith backed Mark one hundred percent, causing a whole heap of drama between our families."

"But you didn't?"

"Hell *no!*" I narrowed my eyes. "I tried to warn her years ago, but she wouldn't hear a word of it."

"But you and Lizzie used to be friends before this?"

"Yep," I replied with a nod. "We all were—although she tried her best to turn everyone against me after it happened."

"What do you mean?"

"Claire, Feely and Hugh," I bit out. "She wanted them to choose."

"Between you and her?"

"Yep."

"But they refused?"

"Yeah." Another nod. "And I'm fairly sure that's a lot of the reason why Hugh and Liz barely speak anymore."

"Shite." Johnny was quiet for a long time before asking, "Do you think he did it, Gibs?"

"Who?"

"Mark."

With my heart bucking wildly in my chest, I nodded stiffly.

"Jesus," my best friend whispered, rubbing his jaw. "And now he's back in town?"

"Yep."

"For two whole months."

"You got it in one."

"What a clusterfuck."

"Agreed."

"Well, you're always welcome to crash here," Johnny said before throwing off the covers and climbing out of bed.

"Cheers, Cap," I replied, settling back down in his supersized bed. "Legend."

"Anytime, lad." Grabbing his phone off the nightstand, he glanced briefly at the screen before stretching. "Right, come on. It's only half six. We can get a run in before school."

"Are you *mental*?"

"The only thing I plan on doing before school is sleeping—and maybe having a few of your mam's pancakes if they're on offer."

"Get up."

"Hard pass."

"Come on, Gibs, we have a match today."

"Exactly. I need all the rest I can get."

"Gibs!"

"Night, Cap. Love you."

Forty minutes later, I found myself a breathless, wheezing mess at the mercy of a masochistic Dub with a penchant for sadism when it came to his best friend's lungs.

"You're a monster," I strangled out, gasping for air, as I tried to keep up with his inhuman stride. Aside from the fact that it was pissing rain down on top of us, it was still dark outside. "Seriously, Cap. I'm just about ready to die here, lad."

"Come on, Gibs, you've got this," he called over his shoulder. "Keep the heart rate up, lad. You're on the last mile."

"That's what you said three miles ago," I wailed, while I contemplated throwing myself in over a ditch and letting the cows have me. "And I don't 'got this,' Johnny. I don't 'got this' at all."

"Yes, you do. Come on, lad, the house is just up ahead," he tried to motivate me by calling back. "At the top of the hill. One more big push and we're home."

"No, fuck it, I can't," I called back, feeling every muscle in my legs cramp up. "It's not worth it. Just go on without me."

"I'll ask my ma to make you pancakes."

Dammit.

"I want sugar and lemon juice, and I don't want to hear a word about wasted calories."

"Deal."

"Fine," I bit out, heaving my body up the steep country road that led to the manor. "The things I do for my stomach."

38

Rude Boys and Elephant Trunks

CLAIRE

Gerard Gibson was becoming a super ninja at evasion, somehow managing to avoid me all day at school, much to my disappointment.

I felt awful about the whole Lizzie drama last night and knew he had to be stressed about Mark's return. The fact that he hadn't shown up in my room last night, or appeared in the kitchen for breakfast this morning, only proved to me that things were a lot worse in Gerard's head than I originally anticipated.

Even though he didn't join us at lunch, I knew he was at school because I'd passed him in the hallway a couple of times while he was in full-blown erratic Gibsie mode.

Regardless of how unsettled I felt, I remained at Tommen after school to watch his game. Like a faithful friend, I stood in the torrential rain with Shannon and cheered our boys on just like I had at every other game.

After eight minutes of intense physical athletic performance, our school's rugby team ended up thrashing St. Andrews off the pitch with a final scorecard of 64–3, with Gerard receiving ten minutes in the sin bin for a tactical foul on the oppositions number 13.

Instead of waiting with Shan at the car for the boys to come out afterward, I found myself knocking on the changing room door instead, both unwilling and unable to let another minute tick by without talking it out with him.

"Hi!" I beamed when the door finally swung open. "Is Gerard there?" I fully appreciated the fact that the boys were probably celebrating in there, but I couldn't wait another second. Hence, my current overstepping of boundaries—and school rules. "I really need to talk to him."

"Who wants to know?" a boy I wasn't familiar with replied, keeping a firm hold on the changing room door to prevent me from entering, no doubt.

"Uh, me?" I rolled my eyes. "*Clearly.*"

"And you are?"

"Who am *I*?" I gave him a slow appraisal, taking note of the towel hanging precariously low on his narrow hips. "Who are you, more like?"

"Damien Cleary."

"And where did you come from, *Damien*?"

"I'm new," he replied flatly. "Transferred in from St. Pat's for sixth year."

"Well, Damien Cleary." I smiled sweetly up at him. "I'm Claire Biggs. I'm sixteen, a Leo, and a fellow Tommen student, and I really need to speak to Gerard, so if you could be a doll and grab him for me, I would be super grateful."

He stared blankly at me for several beats before attempting to close the door in my face.

"Hey!" I snapped, sticking my foot in the door and pushing it back open. "Rude much?"

"I might be new, but I'm not thick," he deadpanned. "There's no Gerard on the team, princess, so run along."

"*Excuse* me?" I narrowed my eyes. "Yes, there is. He just ran over two tries for your team, *Damien*."

"No, there's not. I think I'd know my teammates' names. Now fuck off."

My mouth fell open in shock. "Wow, you really *are* rude."

"Hey, you can't come in here!" Damien argued, when I pushed at the door and tried to squeeze past. "Lads, there's a crazy blond out here. Cover your cocks!"

"He's number seven on the team, idiot," I huffed, shoving past Rude Boy in my bid to get to my destination. "And *ew*! Like I would I ever want to look at any of your baby elephant trunks."

"Biggs, your sister's on the warpath."

"Hey, baby, this elephant trunk expands."

"Sure, it does, Robbie," I replied, rolling my eyes. "And I'm sure when it does, it's as easy to find as Where's Wally."

"Oooh, burn, lad!"

"So, this is what the boys' changing room is like," I mused, hands on my hips as I observed thirty or so teenage boys scrambling to get dressed, while feeling both impressed and jealous of the rugby team's top-notch facilities. Holy crap, they even had their own physio room. *Fancy.* "Well, I think it's fair to say that you all should be ashamed of yourselves," I added, pegging my nose from the overwhelming stench of teenage boy. "Because this place is a pigsty!"

"Whoa, Claire, this is the boys' changing room," Patrick called out, rushing to cover his dignity with a rugby ball. "You know you can't come in here, right?"

"Hi, Patrick!" I made a beeline for him. "So sorry for the intrusion, but I really need to speak to Gerard."

"He was late coming up from the pitch. Try the showers," he replied, using his free hand to point me in the right direction.

"Thanks so much." Smiling, I waved him off. "You're the best… Oh, and *nice* ball."

"Jesus."

"Claire!" Hugh roared, storming through another doorway only partially dressed in a pair of gray sweats. Yikes, he looked just as angry today as he had been last night. Clearly, sleeping on it hadn't brightened his mood. "What the hell are you doing?"

"Looking for Gerard," I explained with a huff. "And that new boy over there was super rude to me," I added, jabbing a finger in the direction of Damien. "He told me to fuck off."

"You told my sister to fuck off?" Hugh's attention immediately flicked to Damien, and I felt an immense amount of pleasure when he turned beetroot red. "In what world did you assume it was okay to speak to her like that?"

"My bad, Biggs. I didn't know she was your sister."

"It wouldn't matter either way," Johnny answered, appearing from the tall archway that led to the showers in a pair of black boxer shorts. "You're new, Cleary, so I'm going to give you a hall pass this time. But for future reference, we don't talk to our girls like that. You got that?"

"Yeah, I've got it." Rude Boy's face turned an even deeper shade of red. "Won't happen again, Cap."

Oh boy, it was quite the power trip to be around Johnny Kavanagh. The boy oozed intensity. *Lucky Shan.*

"*Yeah*, Cleary," I tossed out, feeling brave with the backing of the alpha. "You see that it doesn't!" And then, because I was still three years old in the prefrontal cortex of my brain, I poked my tongue out at him for good measure.

"You have about two minutes before Coach comes in for postgame analysis," Johnny explained, flicking his attention back to me. "Make it snappy."

"You're the best captain boss ever!" Patting his ridiculously hard pectoral, I scampered through the archway. "And good job winning your game."

Following the sound of running water with pep in my step, I stopped short when I rounded the corner and came face to back with a naked flanker. The moment my eyes landed on his bare butt, a high-pitched "Omigod" escaped my lips and I quickly slapped a hand over my eyes and backed up against the opposite wall, heart racing violently. "I'm really sorry for what I'm about to tell you, but I think I just saw your ladder dangling between your legs."

"So?" A familiar chuckle came from the shower area. "You've seen my ladder before."

My heart raced harder at that. "Uh, not from that angle, I haven't."

"What's up, Claire-Bear?"

"I've been trying to get ahold of you all day," I explained, feeling a ridiculous amount of relief at being in his company again. "You are a hard man to track down, Gerard Gibson."

"I saw you at school."

"No," I corrected, hand still clamped over my eyes as the damp perspiration on the tiles at my back began to seep into my school uniform. "I waved to you in the hallway between classes, and you waved back. That's not the same thing." Blowing out a shaky breath, I forced myself to address the elephant in the room. "Where the hell were you last night? I came over and you were gone. And *Mark* was there!"

The sound of flowing water abruptly stopped.

"Gerard?" I called out when he didn't respond. "Did you hear me?"

"Yeah, I heard you." His voice was closer now. "And yeah, I know." I felt his hand brush past against my arm, and it caused my entire body to ignite in a hot flush. "Sorry." I felt his hand on my hip, gently steering me to one side. "My towel is on the hook behind you."

"Okey dokey," I squeaked out, feeling my face grow hot from the knowledge that his naked body was so close to me. It was more than just that, though, because I wanted to open my fingers and peek. Not just peek. I wanted to *touch*. Remembering how it felt in my room last night when his big body was pressed against mine and his fingers were deep inside me...

"All clear." I felt him gently peel my hand away from my eyes. "The ladder is safely tucked away."

When I blinked my eyes open, I found that to be regrettably true. The white towel wrapped around his narrow hips was proof to that pudding.

Aw, crackers.

Feeling weak, I slumped against the tiles at my back. "So, Mark's back, huh?"

"Apparently so."

"You didn't know?"

"Nope," Gerard replied, resting a hand against the wall at my back. "No clue."

Breath catching in my throat, I swallowed deeply and offered him a small smile, desperately trying to ignore the heat flooding every inch of my body. "Are you okay?"

"Of course." He smiled, but it didn't meet his eyes. "I'm always okay."

"You didn't come over last night." I shrugged, feeling helpless. "It was..." *I didn't like it.* "Weird."

"Yeah, sorry about that." Exhaling shakily, Gerard reached up with his free hand and pushed his damp curls off his brow. "You were dealing with Lizzie, and I, ah, I had to get away."

"So, where'd you go?"

"Cap's."

"Oh."

"Yep."

Feeling slightly bereft at his response, I forced another big smile.

He smiled back at me, but again, it didn't meet his eyes.

Aw, crackers.

I didn't like this. Not one bit. Because Gerard might be physically standing in front of me, with nothing but a towel covering him, but internally he had several layers wrapped around his heart. "Talk to me, Gerard."

"About what?"

I narrowed my eyes. "About what happened last night."

He stared blankly back at me. "What about what happened last night?"

"Uh, *hello*? Lizzie basically attacked you and then you find out your evil step-brother is back in Ballylaggin."

"It's all good, Claire-Bear."

"Gerard," I snapped. "I know you're upset."

"I'm not upset."

"Yes, you are," I urged. "You have to be."

"And why's that?"

"Because *Mark's* back."

"I honestly couldn't give a damn, Claire."

"No, stop." Shaking my head in frustration, I reached up and knotted my fingers in the silver chain around his neck. "Don't do that."

"Don't do what?"

"Act the fool," I growled, yanking on his chain so hard he had to lower his face to mine. "Don't shut me out, Gerard. We've come too far for that."

"I'm not trying to do that," he said gruffly, nose brushing against mine. "I'm just…"

"You're just?" I pushed, fisting his chain so tightly I thought it might crack in my hand. Inhaling a shaky breath, I pushed off the wall, melding my chest to his. "You're just what, Gerard?"

"You're going to get wet," he noted, hooking an arm around my waist to steady us both.

"Don't change the subject," I warned, unwilling to take a step back. "You're just what?"

"You know it's a really bad idea to be in here with me, don't you?" he asked in a gravelly tone, and I could feel *exactly* why he would say that growing against my belly.

"Especially since…" His voice trailed off and he shook his head. "This is just a really, *really* bad idea, Claire-Bear."

"I don't care," I replied, feeling a little breathless as my heart continued to try to power drill its way out of my chest to get to his. "We need to talk, so just *talk* to me, dammit."

"And say *what*?" he asked softly, his breath fanning my face.

"How about you start by telling me how you feel."

"I don't feel anything." He stepped closer, causing my back to hit the wall once more, but this time his body was flush against mine. "Not about Lizzie. Not about him. Not about any of them." The move seemed to cause a shiver to roll through both of our bodies simultaneously. "I don't feel a damn thing."

"You're lying."

"No, I'm really not."

"Gerard," I cried out in despair. "Please!"

"Please what?" he demanded. "Please what, Claire? What do you want from me?"

"You!" My chest was heaving against his, my entire body screaming out for him, and I honestly felt like I might die on the mortal spot if he didn't put his lips on me. "I want you, Gerard!"

"I'm right here."

"That's not what I mean, and you know it," I strangled out. "I want you to talk to me about how you're feeling! I want you to open up to me, dammit!"

"I *can't*."

Devastation washed over me like a tidal wave. "Why not?"

"Because I love you too much!" he surprised me by saying. Expelling a pained breath, he dropped his head to rest on my shoulder. "Because I fucking *love* you, Claire Biggs."

The three words hurt to hear because they weren't what I needed from him in this moment, and the pain in my chest assured me that my devastated body had come to the equally devastating conclusion that these three words were all this boy would ever give me.

"I don't understand why you act like this," I croaked out, feeling like a masochist for pushing the same broken narrative. "I'm your best friend and instead of letting me in, you keep pushing me out."

"Claire."

"No. No more excuses, Gerard!" Shaking my head, I pushed at his chest and willed him to wake the hell up. "I'm right here, okay? I'm right here for you."

"I know that."

"Then *do* something!"

He didn't.

Instead, he opened his mouth. "Claire, if you could just..."

"No. Stop!" I shook my head. "I don't need any more of your excuses, Gerard Gibson." Chest heaving, I stepped around him and moved for the exit. "I need your truth."

39

Seventeen Going Under

GIBSIE

"WHERE IN THE NAME OF GOD HAVE YOU BEEN?" MAM DEMANDED WHEN I WALKED into the kitchen after school. "You didn't leave a note to say where you were going. You didn't take your phone with you. I couldn't call you; I couldn't text you, nothing! I have been going out of my mind with worry!" Slamming the roast chicken she was taking out of the oven onto the kitchen island, she turned to glare at me. "Thank god for Edel Kavanagh letting me know that you were staying over at her house, because my next port of call was the Garda station."

"My sincerest apologies, Mother," I drawled, dropping both my schoolbag and gear bag in the corner before making a beeline for the fridge, dutifully ignoring evil cat sitting on top of the kitchen table. "It's dreadful when your family member doesn't tell you shit."

"Excuse me?"

"You heard me," I replied, grabbing the carton of orange juice and closing the fridge.

"Gerard Joseph Gibson," Mam snapped, hands on her hips. "Don't speak to me like that."

Rolling my eyes, I unscrewed the cap and drank straight from the cartoon, my own personal nonverbal *fuck you* when I would never speak the words aloud.

"I saw the condition of your room," she continued, using a tea towel to wipe a dribble of chicken grease from the counter. "Your behavior last night was completely out of order."

"And your behavior when you didn't give me a heads-up about that prick rocking back into town *wasn't*?" I snapped, slamming the carton down on the counter. "Come on, Mam, what's good for the goose is good for the gander."

"So, because I wanted to surprise you, you decide to punish me by leaving the house and not telling me where you are? You are seventeen years old, Gerard, and until you turn eighteen next February, you are on my time, and that means no overnight trips without a phone call!"

"Punish you?" I gaped at her. "Mam, I walked through the front door last night and was blindsided!"

"Mark is *family*, Gerard," Mam exclaimed, throwing her hands up. "You should be happy to see him. And Keith! He made reservations for the four of us at Spizzico's to celebrate." Mam glared. "Some fecking celebration it was when you refused to break bread with your brother and then stormed off for the night."

"I should be *happy*?" I gaped at the woman like she had just spurted a second head. "Are you fucking with me? Mam, you know how I feel about him!" I practically roared, body trembling. "And please don't label that piece of shit as *my* family. You might consider him to be yours but I sure as hell don't consider him to be mine!"

"Is this because of the Young family?" she demanded. "Because of Lizzie? Do you plan to spend the rest of your life holding a grudge against Mark for something he didn't do?"

"It's not that he didn't do it, Mam, it's that they couldn't *prove* it," I spat back. "And you know damn well she's not my friend anymore," I added, feeling my chest heave from the pressure it was taking to breathe through this conversation. "Your perfect stepson took care of that."

"Gerard, he didn't do it," Mam stressed, trying a different approach by closing the space between us and placing her hands on my chest. "I promise you, from the bottom of my heart, your stepbrother *never* harmed Caoimhe Young."

My blood ran cold, and my entire body trembled. "Oh, you promise, do you?"

"Yes," she urged, nodding her head eagerly. "It was a vicious, nasty rumor spread by people who took the word of a grieving woman who misunderstood her child's suicide note."

"You don't know that, Mam," I choked out, trembling. "You *can't* know that."

"I *do* know that, Gerard." She tried to soothe as she reached up and stroked my face. "I do, love. Mark was completely innocent. The Gardaí proved that. And before you say anything else, I *saw* a copy of the note Caoimhe left her mother. I read the words. Catherine Young was mistaken, love. There was no rape to her daughter." Tears filled her eyes when she cupped my cheeks in her hands and offered me a watery smile. "Not only is Mark innocent, but he's *family*, love, and we look after our own."

"So, that's it?" I deadpanned. "According to you, Mark's innocent, the Young family is mistaken, and that's all there is to it?"

"Yes, love." With a nod of affirmation, Mam stroked my cheek once more before returning to her roast chicken. "That's all there is to it."

Motionless, I stood in the kitchen, watching as my mother tended to her roast chicken, and I never felt *less* hungry.

"So, you've never doubted him?" I challenged. "You're not even willing to consider that you might be wrong?"

"No."

"No?" I shook my head in disgust. "No to which question?"

"No, I've never doubted Mark," she replied firmly. "And no, I'm not willing to consider I might be wrong because I'm not wrong."

Well then.

"I'm not doing it," I heard myself say, body rigid. "Playing happy families with him?" I shook my head. "I won't do it, Mam."

"Gerard..."

Shaking my head, I turned on my heels and walked out of the kitchen, both unwilling and unable to continue this conversation.

There was no point because we were never going to agree on this.

Because my mother was unwilling to entertain a different scenario.

She wasn't willing to believe the truth.

40

Call My Bluff

CLAIRE

It was late October, three whole weeks had passed since the incident with Lizzie, and Gerard was back to his usual playful self.

Sitting in the lunch hall during big break the day of Halloween break, he casually draped his arm around me while he laughed and joked with our friends.

He was just as lovable as always, full of warm affection and flirty banter, but it wasn't real. It wasn't *him*.

I knew it was a front, his way of coping with stress, but the rest of the world found it hilarious, and the more they laughed, the more he performed for them, despite what it cost him.

Meanwhile, I slapped on a smile for the outside world, while stewing on the inside. Too immersed in my internal reeling to participate in the conversation unfolding around me, I leaned back in my chair and studied the chipped pink nail polish I had on instead.

Most of my frustration could be pinpointed to two areas. First, I was frustrated by Gerard's uncanny ability to pretend like lines hadn't been crossed between us when they clearly had. And second, I seemed to be even more frustrated by the fact that I desperately wanted to cross those lines again, while he showed zero interest.

Not only had he given me the first and best orgasm of my life, but he was pretending like it never happened.

I couldn't understand it. Because, in all honesty, if the shoe was on the other foot and I had the ability to do what that boy had done with his fingers and thumb, I knew I would be bragging from the rooftops about how epic my magic fingers were. Because dear lord, his fingers were *masterful*.

While Gerard tossed banter back and forth with his teammates, he traced his fingers innocently against my arm. The memory of just how *worldly* those fingers could be caused my face to flood with heat.

"What's wrong?" Hugh demanded, spooking me out with that freakish telepathic brotherly bond thing he could do. Even though we were twenty-two months in age apart, I swear my brother had the ability to sense my moods. "Claire?"

"Nothing," I replied, offering him a big smile. "I'm grand."

My brother didn't look convinced. In fact, his tone took on an accusatory note when he turned his attention to the boy sitting next to me and snapped, "What did you do now?"

"Me?" With a half-eaten lollipop hanging out of his mouth, Gerard stared blankly back at my brother. "What did I do?"

"That's what I'm asking," Hugh bit out. "What did you do?"

Gerard's brows creased in confusion. "Today?"

"To my sister, asshole," he shot back, gesturing to where I was sitting. The moment he did that, everyone's attention flicked to me. *Lovely.* "She's upset and I know you have something to do with it, Gibs."

"You're upset?" Concerned gray eyes landed on mine. "What's wrong?"

"Nothing." I forced a laugh and tugged on the sleeve of my jumper. "I'm perfectly fine."

"See?" Katie coaxed, patting my brother's shoulder. "Calm down, big brother. You're overreacting."

The look Hugh gave her assured me that he didn't think he was overreacting, but he *did* drop it.

Thank god.

After a few moments, everyone returned to their conversations and lunch, but a pair of silvery-gray eyes continued to watch me. "What?" I forced another laugh and nudged him with my elbow. "I'm fine, Gerard. Stop looking at me like that."

He didn't stop looking. Instead, he twisted in his seat, giving everyone sitting around the table his back, while giving *me* his full attention. His tone was low and serious when he asked, "Did I do something?"

Yes. "No."

"Claire."

I smiled back at him. "Gerard."

Catching ahold of the underside of my chair, he pulled it toward him, causing my legs to slide between his thighs. "Did I do something?" he asked again, leaning in close as he spoke, eyes focused entirely on my face. "Talk to me."

I smiled sweetly. "About what?"

His nostrils flared and I knew that he was tasting a healthy dose of his own medicine. "That's not fair."

I could have argued with him. I could have thrown a tantrum and demanded he confess his undying love for me right here in the lunch hall, but I already knew how he felt. Gerard's love for me wasn't something I ever needed to question. It was his unwillingness to offer me *more* that plagued my every waking hour.

"I'm going to say yes to Jamie," I blurted out and then held my breath while I waited for his reaction. I wasn't serious. I had no intention of going out with Jamie, and I wasn't typically a goading girl—meaning that I didn't cause unnecessary drama to get my way with boys. But I was growing weary of Gerard's pretenses and felt like this might be the push that he needed.

He stared at me for a long beat before a smile spread across his face. "No, you're not."

The way he said it, so confident and self-assured, instantly had my back up. "Oh yeah?" I narrowed my eyes in challenge. "Who says I already haven't?"

His smile faltered. "Tell me this is a joke."

"Nope," I replied in as breezy tone as I could muster. "No joke. In fact, I was just about to tell Jamie the good news, but I figured I'd give you a heads-up beforehand." Shrugging nonchalantly, I added, "You know, just in case."

"Just in case," Gerard deadpanned. "Just in *case*?"

"Yep." Nodding, I offered him another forced smile, while my heart hammered violently in my chest. "Just in case."

"Well then." Leaning back in his chair like I had slapped him, Gerard folded his arms across his chest and called my bluff. "You better hurry up and catch him before he leaves." He inclined his head to where Jamie was standing in line for lunch. "You know." He shrugged just as nonchalantly as I had before adding, "Just in case."

"Fine." The wave of rejection that washed over me had my pride forcing me to stand up and say, "I will."

"You do that," he called after me.

"Oh, don't worry," I tossed over my shoulder. "I'm going to."

"Fine!"

"Fine!"

Marching toward the lunch line, I balled my hands into fists at my sides and tried to steady my nerves.

Oh my god, Claire, what are you doing?

Abort mission.

Abort mission, dammit!

"Hey, you," Jamie acknowledged with a warm smile when I reached him in line. "How's it going?"

"Uh, it's going good." Swallowing deeply, I turned back to find Gerard glaring at me. Steeling my resolve, I swung back around to face Jamie and smiled. "Yes."

"Yes?" His brows furrowed for a brief moment before awareness dawned on him, causing a huge smile to spread across his face. "You're saying yes to a date with me."

Was I?

Was I really?

"Yes," I confirmed with a forced smile. "I'm saying yes to a date with you."

41

Karma Is a Chess Player

GIBSIE

MOTHERFUCKER!

"She's going out with him, Johnny," I snapped, losing my patience with the shoelace I was attempting to tie. "She's going the fuck out with him!"

"Yeah, Gibs, I know," he replied calmly, stooping down in the corridor to tie it for me. Something I was clearly incapable of doing these days. "You already told me a half-dozen times, lad."

"What am I supposed to do?"

"Nothing," he replied, sounding distracted as he glanced at the screen of his phone before sliding it back into the pocket of his school trousers. "You had your chance, lad. You let her go."

"I didn't let her go," I argued, coming as close as I ever had to blowing a head gasket. "I've never let her go a day in my fucking life."

"I told you this would happen." He pushed his dark hair out of his eyes. "I've been telling you for months, Gibs, but you wouldn't listen."

I narrowed my eyes in disgust. "Spare me the I-told-you-so spiel."

"I did," he urged, holding the door for a group of second-year girls to pass. "I bleeding told you to pull the finger out and lay your cards down."

"I wasn't ready!" *I'm still not.*

"But you're more than willing to lay your cards down with Dee."

"I never laid a thing down with that woman."

"You've laid plenty on that woman," he corrected before rehashing his earlier statement. "I told you Claire wouldn't wait around forever."

"*That,*" I pointed toward the office, "*was a* situation that suited me, Johnny!" I gestured wildly around me before adding, "*This* isn't suiting me one bit!"

"Well, then, maybe you've finally gotten a taste of your own money," Lizzie interjected, joining us in the courtyard. "Serves you right."

"Did I *ask* for your opinion?"

"Oh my god, I love it," she replied with a smirk. "Seeing you squirm. It gives me the utmost pleasure. He's taking her out tonight, you know. They're going on a date, and I *pray* she makes it official with Jamie. It'll serve you right for being such a waster."

Deep breaths, I mentally instructed myself, not about to take the bait she was casting out to me.

Turning to Johnny, she asked, "Have you seen Shannon?"

"She's with Joey," he explained, jabbing a thumb over his shoulder in the direction of the car park. "Over in the car park."

"Cool."

"Why are you civil to her?" I demanded when the Viper had swanned off in the direction of the car park. "You know she's the devil in a Tommen crest."

"I'm stuck between a rock and a hard place here, Gibs," my best friend admitted with a sigh. "She's my girlfriend's best friend."

And you're mine.

"Look, Gibs, I'm just trying to keep everyone happy here."

"Uh, hello?" I held my hand up. "I'm not happy."

"What am I supposed to do about that?" Johnny shot back, sounding flustered. "I gave you the right advice and you *didn't* take it."

"Well, you obviously weren't very good at getting the point across, now, were you?"

"Excuse me?" Johnny gaped at me. "Are you honestly blaming me for Claire going out with another fella when I *told* you it would happen?"

"Yes," I replied, unblinking. "And now, for your penance, I'm going to need you to spy for me."

"Spy for you?"

"Yes." I nodded enthusiastically. "You heard the Viper. Claire's going out with that prick today, and we're in a fight, so she's not going to tell me shit about how it goes." Grimacing I added, "All the juicy, homicidal-inducing details will be doled out to her other bestie."

"Shannon." Johnny sighed, quick as a cat.

"*Shannon*," I agreed, eyes gleaming with mischief. "And it just so happens that Claire's girl bestie happens to tell my boy bestie everything."

"If you call me your 'boy bestie' again, I'll have you committed."

"You have to spy and report back to me."

"I'll do no such thing."

"Ah, yes you fucking will," I huffed, hands on my hips. "Do I need to remind you of all the ice packs I supplied to your broken bollocks back in the day? Or the million favors I've done for you."

"I can't be spying on my girlfriend, Gibs." Johnny groaned, looking pained. "We don't keep secrets."

"See that's the thing, you won't be spying on Shannon," I tried to coax. "You'll merely be relaying information to the other person in your life who you've never kept secrets from." I eyeballed him. "Do this for me."

"Gibs."

"I'll beg," I threw out there. "Do you want me to beg, Johnny?"

"No, Jesus Christ, don't beg, ya eejit."

"So, you'll do it?"

"If she brings it up," he begrudgingly conceded. "But only if she brings it up. I'm not digging, Gibs."

"You're the best."

Johnny shook his head in dismay. "So, this is the teenage bullshit I chose to partake in instead of the pros."

"I know." Grinning, I clapped his shoulder. "Good decision or what, huh?"

"Or what," Johnny muttered under his breath.

"Can I ask you a question?"

"No, Gibs, Shannon didn't tell me anything about their bleeding date," Johnny snapped in an exasperated tone from his perch at his desk, where we had been since school ended two hours ago. Instead of doing something fun to kick off our midterm break, Brains had decided we needed to get all of our homework out of the way. "Nothing's changed since the last time you asked," he added, glancing at the screen of his phone. "Ten *minutes* ago."

"Not that," I replied, trying and failing to make sense of his notes from accounting class. Giving up, I closed the book and sprawled out on his bed instead. "I was going to ask you how it felt."

"How did what feel, Gibs?"

"When you kissed Shannon for the first time."

"It was a disaster," he muttered, scribbling furiously into a copybook. "I couldn't have handled it worse."

"What about the first time you were *with* her?" I questioned. "How did it *feel*?"

"If this is another one of your weird conversations, then strike it out, Gibs, because Shan's name isn't up for discussion. And especially not that kind of discussion."

"Ah, calm down, will you?" I grumbled, pulling myself up on my elbows. "I'm not asking you to give me intimate details about her—"

"Gibs!"

"All I'm asking is if it felt different with Shannon than say Bella, or any of the rest of them," I huffed, flopping back down. "You know, because of the feelings."

"The feelings?"

"Yeah, Johnny, the feelings."

"Hold up." His head snapped up and set down his pen. "Are you fucking Claire…"

"No," I snapped, not liking him saying her name and sex in the same sentence. *Jesus, karma was a bitch.* "And don't say the words 'Claire' and 'fucking' in the same sentence."

Johnny grinned. "Oh dear."

"What?"

"It's worse than I thought." There was a knowing glint to his eyes when he rolled his chair toward the bed and folded his arms across his chest. "Alright, Gibs. Ask your questions, lad."

"When you and Shannon were together," I repeated, rubbing the back of my head. "Was it different?"

Johnny nodded. "It couldn't have been any more different."

"Really?"

"Yeah, lad, really," he replied. "Feelings change everything."

"Meaning?"

"Feelings make you a whole lot less concerned with how you feel in the moment than how *she* is feeling."

"Break it down for me."

"It's like… You know that mad, desperate feeling to get there?" he explained, continuing when I nodded. "Well, it kind of switches up into a mad urge to get *her* there." He scratched his jaw as he thought about it for a moment. "It's like everything you used to care about switches into something deeper. Like your needs go on the back burner because your focus has switched to her."

"Jesus, that sounds terrifying."

"It is," he wholeheartedly agreed. "And it's not just a mental thing, either, lad. It runs deeper. It expands beyond the mental and emotional to the physical, and then, because she's good, it's better than it's ever been before."

"So, for you, being with little Shannon is the best it's ever been because of the feelings?"

"Because of the feelings," he confirmed with a smirk. "Messed up, huh?"

Sighing heavily, I folded my hands across my chest and stared up at his bedroom ceiling. "Yeah, so I think I have a similar affliction."

Johnny chuckled knowingly. "You're only figuring that out now?"

"What can I say?" I sighed heavily. "I'm a slow learner."

"Nah, Gibs," he mused. "You're a lot smarter than you give yourself credit for."

"Clearly not," I argued. "Considering she's going out with someone else."

"Then do something about it," Johnny urged. "Change the narrative."

"Change the *what*?"

"Go get your girl, Gibs!"

42

Second Thoughts

CLAIRE

"Do we really think this is a good idea?" I asked Lizzie as we wandered aimlessly through the lingerie section of the department store after school on Friday, after inviting ourselves along on our other bestie's mother and daughter shopping trip.

"Yes, we really do."

"And Jamie really said all those nice things about me."

"Hand on my heart."

"I don't know, Liz." I shrugged helplessly. "Maybe I should cancel."

"Well, I do, Claire. I know, and I am so proud of you," Lizzie praised, linking arms with me. "Seriously, you're doing the right thing here and no way in hell are you canceling."

"But it's so soon," I groaned. "He's supposed to be picking me up at eight o'clock tonight."

"Good," Lizzie encouraged. "The sooner, the better."

"How'd you figure?"

"Because the longer you're left to your own devices, the more you'll try to talk yourself out of it."

"And you really think going to the cinema with Jamie is a good idea?"

"Yes, Claire, I really do."

"Okay," I replied, chewing on my bottom lip as I tried to battle with the wave of doubt cresting like a tidal wave inside of my belly. "Let's hope so."

"Hope has nothing to do with it in this instance," my friend assured me. "Thor's been wasting your time for years now. It's time to move on and stop waiting for him to throw you a bone."

"Ouch, Liz." I winced. "Tone down the bitchiness, will you?"

"Sorry," she conceded with a shrug. "It's not directed toward you, I promise."

"I know," I replied. *But it still hurts.* "He's a good person."

Silence.

"He is, Lizzie."

More silence.

Resigned, I exhaled a heavy sigh and snatched a random pair of fancy knickers off the rail in front of me. "Oh look, what every girl needs in her wardrobe," I grimaced. "Crotchless knickers."

"Maybe we should slip them into Shannon's basket," Lizzie joked, pointing to where Shannon was browsing the Halloween section with her foster mam. "And see what Mrs. Kavanagh says when they ring up their stuff at the till."

"Can you imagine?" I snickered. "She would blow a head gasket."

"I know. I would pay good money to see it."

"They look kind of nice, though."

"What?"

"These crotchless knickers."

"Oh my god, Claire," Lizzie laughed. "Put down the knickers and step away from the rail."

When I turned back, I spotted Shannon and Edel at the counter paying. Edel had her arm wrapped around my friend's shoulder as Shannon showed her something on her phone.

"Can you imagine having to live with your boyfriend's mam?"

"I think it's perfect for Shan," Lizzie replied.

"Me too," I agreed, still smiling. "She needs the stability."

"And Captain Fantastic is nothing if not stable."

"True," I agreed, watching my bestie embrace her foster mam with a side hug. Laden down with shopping bags, Edel Kavanagh pressed a kiss to Shannon's head and smiled dotingly at her.

She would be okay.

I didn't need any other validation.

Shannon had been born to be a Kavanagh.

"Are you serious?" I asked later during dinner, completely engrossed in the story Edel Kavanagh was telling us. "You really lived with Daddy K when you were a teenager?"

"I sure did, love."

"So, it's like history repeating itself," I mused, popping another spoonful of ice cream into my mouth. "You and John Sr. Shannon and Johnny." I sighed dreamily. "It's like fate."

"Or bad parenting," Lizzie muttered under her breath.

"Liz!" I elbowed her. "Filter."

Surprisingly, Edel laughed at our fiery friend's cutting one-liner. "You're a hard one to know, Elizabeth Young, are you?" She smiled indulgently at her. "With all those hard outer layers."

Lizzie blushed and offered our host a small smile. "Sorry."

"Don't be sorry, love," Edel replied. "A woman should always have a bit of edge about her."

"Not this woman," I chimed in, gesturing to myself. "I'm a glorified circle."

"Oh, Claire."

"You're so weird." Lizzie chuckled, shaking her head. "I swear, she's been like this since junior infants."

"It's true," Shannon added, returning from the bathroom to take her seat next to Edel. "Claire's our personal pocket of sunshine."

Edel spent the rest of our meal fussing over the three of us before going to the counter to pay the bill.

"Can I have her?" Lizzie asked, when she was out of earshot.

"Nope," Shannon shot back with a chuckle.

"Then can we share?"

"Nope." Shannon smiled proudly. "She's all mine."

"So, ladies, what's the plan for the midterm?" Edel asked, returning to the table to fetch her handbag and coat. "Any exciting plans lined up for your week off school?"

"My mam's throwing a party for Hugh next weekend for his eighteenth," I heard myself say, falling into step beside the three of them as they left the restaurant.

"Oh? That's sounds sashing, love."

"His birthday is on Halloween."

"Oh, same as Seany," Edel mused. "Can you believe he's turning four?"

"No," Shannon answered with a small shake of her head, as she linked arms with Edel. "I can still remember when he came home from the hospital." Smiling sadly, she added, "I swear Joe didn't sleep for the first three months."

"Are you having a party for him?" I asked, desperate to keep the tone light. "Seany, I mean?"

"Do bears shit in the woods?" Edel replied with a laugh. "Of course we are. John has the bouncy castle ordered."

"He's getting a clown, too," Shannon interjected.

"A clown?" My eyes widened. "Can I come?"

"Claire!" Lizzie laughed, slapping my arm. "You can't just invite yourself like that."

"Oh, please." I rolled my eyes. "Like we didn't already invite ourselves to a free dinner."

"Still, though."

"Of course you can come, love," Edel replied. "You're all more than welcome. It's on at three o'clock next Saturday so it won't interfere with Hugh's party later that night."

"Yay!" I clapped with excitement. "Gerard had a clown once. I think it was his sixth birthday." I smiled at the memory. "I've always wanted to see one again."

"You see one every day," Lizzie tossed out with a smirk. "You live across the street from one."

I narrowed my eyes. "Ha-ha."

43
Cuckoos in the Nest

GIBSIE

WHEN I STROLLED INTO THE BIGGSES' KITCHEN LATER THAT NIGHT, I WAS AGHAST I tell you, a-fucking-ghast, to see Jamie Kelleher sitting on *my* chair at the table.

Christ, karma moved quickly.

"Gibs," Sinead acknowledged, intercepting me before I had a chance to toss the intrusive bastard of a cuckoo out of *my* nest. "I *know*," she said quietly, brown eyes locked on mine as she patted my cheek affectionately. "Best behavior now, you hear?" She grabbed a plate off the counter and handed it to me. "That's a good boy."

Nodding stiffly, I took my plate and walked over to the table, not stopping until I was standing in front of Fuck-Face himself. "You're in my seat."

"I didn't see your name on it, lad," Jamie joked, looking slick in his fancy black coat and gelled hair.

"It's right there," Hugh offered, using his fork to point out the word *Gibsie* engraved on the chair. "Move."

"Don't families usually eat dinner together?" he muttered under his breath as he begrudgingly took the seat at the end of the table.

"They do," Hugh replied with a sharp edge to his tone. "He *is* family."

"Is he here yet?" Claire asked, hurrying into the kitchen, looking better than anything Sinead could serve up. Seriously, this girl was the best thing that woman had ever cooked. "Because I'm running seriously late," she added, holding one high-heeled boot in her hand. "You're here?" Her eyes widened when they landed on Jamie. "Hugh, why didn't you tell me?"

"Because I'm not your messenger," he tossed back sarcastically, while he tucked into his plate of food, not bothering to look up at his little sister.

"Hi, Claire," Jamie said, immediately standing up and moving to her side. "You look lovely."

"Thanks," she replied, cheeks flushed. The smile she was sporting quicky faded when her gaze landed on me. "Gerard," she gasped, breath hitching in her throat.

I twiddled my fingers at her. "Claire-Bear."

Her face flushed bright red.

Good.

"Okay, boys, I'm off to work," Sinead cut the tension by announcing. "Hugh, load the dishwasher and switch it on before you go to Katie's… Oh, and Gerard, run the hoover around under the table after you eat, please, pet."

"Will do."

"Best behavior, boys."

"Always."

"And back home before eleven o'clock, Claire."

"Okay, Mam."

"Jamie, it was nice to meet you, love."

"You too, Mrs. Biggs."

"Oh, oh, oh, I almost forgot to ask." Quickly backpedaling into the kitchen in her green scrubs, Sinead asked, "A little birdie told me that you agreed to swimming lessons. Is that true, lad?"

Fuck no! I agreed to take a bath. I made no such commitments to stepping foot inside a swimming pool, but I refused to lose face in front of an asshole like Jamie Kelleher, so I nodded instead.

"You went back in the water, lad?" Hugh's interest was instantly piqued.

I nodded stiffly.

"I'm so proud of you, pet," Sinead stated, and then she blew all three of us kisses before dashing off for her shift at the hospital.

"Well, shit." Hugh set his fork down and gave me his full attention. "You really went back in the water?" He gave me a meaningful look. "How was it?"

"Bearable," I replied with a shrug. And then, because I was feeling bitter, I added, "Claire's an amazing teacher." I narrowed my eyes at the cuckoo with his arm around *my* lovebird. "Very hands on."

Jamie's nostrils flared, letting me know that he clearly got my drift.

Yeah, I'm watching you, fucker. I glared back at him. *Keep your goddamn hands off.*

"We better get going," he said, reaching for Claire's hand. "The film starts in half an hour."

"Oh, okay." Yanking her hand out of his reach, she flicked her eyes to me before shaking her head and making a bolt for the kitchen door. "See you later, guys."

"Toodles," I called after them, tone laced with an unhealthy dollop of sarcasm. The moment the sound of the front door slamming filled the air, I face-planted the table and groaned. "Fuck my life."

"You good, Gibs?"

"She's going out with him."

"Who?"

"Who?" I raised my head to gape at him "Mary McAleese. Claire, you spanner. *Claire!* Who else?"

"Yeah, and you should support it," Hugh replied, tone suddenly serious. "I mean it, Gibs. You need to let her go."

"Why?"

"Why?" Now, he was the one to eyeball me. "Because you've been leading her on for years."

"I haven't."

"You have, lad."

"I love your sister," I enunciated every word, knowing that it might lead me to an ass-kicking, but not caring either way. It was the truth. "I *love* your sister, Hugh."

"Not the right way," he replied, reaching for his fork once more. "Not the way she needs you to."

"Which is?"

"If you think I'm giving you tips on wooing my sister, you're off your rocket."

"I'm a wonderful woo-er."

"Sure you are, lad."

"I am," I huffed, folding my arms across my chest. "I can woo."

"You're a messer is what you are," he replied between mouthfuls of roast beef. "And that's grand. We all love your messy antics."

"But?"

"You're not exactly boyfriend material now, are you, lad?"

"Ex-fucking-scuse me," I gasped, practically falling out of my Seat in my outrage. "You're one to talk, Mister Seeing One Girl While Pining After Another One Entirely."

"Hey!"

"Hey right back," I snapped. "Don't deny it, fucker. You think you know everything about me? Well, I know just as much about you." Eyeballing him, I added, "Mm-hmm, that's right, I *see* you."

"You're talking out of your ass, Gibs," he bit out.

"I'm spitting facts."

"You'll be spitting your teeth out if you don't give it a rest."

"Fine." I held my hands up. "Keep on living in your bubble, lad."

"There's nothing wrong with my bubble."

"Except that it's a lie."

"Stop trying to turn this around on me, Gibs!" Inhaling a calming breath, Hugh forced calm into his voice when he said, "Listen, you're out for a good time and that's grand, lad. But Claire's over it. She's looking for a nice lad to take her out and hold her hand."

"*I* take her out," I argued, jabbing my chest with my finger. "*I* hold her hand."

"Yeah, her and how many other girls?"

"Are you implying that I'm some kind of fuckboy?"

"Are you insinuating that you aren't?"

"I'm not insinuating anything," I shot back. "I'm telling you straight out that I'm not."

"Says the fella riding the school receptionist."

"For the last time, I didn't ride the woman!"

"Sure thing, Gibs. Whatever you say, lad."

"It's the truth," I defended, rising to my feet. "I am *not* a fuckboy."

"Then prove it."

"Oh, don't you fucking worry, Hugo, I plan to."

"Well, look what the cat dragged in," Mam said when I walked into the sitting room. "How's the emancipation treating you, son? Have you had your fill of sulking yet, or are you planning on turning poor Edel Kavanagh's house into your own personal hotel?"

"Don't start," I grumbled, leaning in the doorway. "Are you alone?"

"Yes," she replied, pausing *Fair City*. "Keith's at the bingo."

"And *him*?"

"Up the country visiting a few college friends."

"Good," I snapped. "Let's hope he forgets the way home."

Mam sighed wearily. "Gerard."

Feeling my shoulders relax a little, I gestured to where my mother was sitting. "And you didn't go to the bingo?"

"No, Gerard, I didn't," she replied, giving me a pointed look. "Because contrary to your beliefs, I *am* here for you." Narrowing her eyes, she added, "When you decide to grace me with your presence, that is."

"You want to be here for me?"

"I *am* here for you."

"Fine." Stalking over to the couch, I threw myself down and draped an arm over my face. "Then be here for me."

"What's wrong?"

"Oh, I don't know, Mam, how about *everything*!" I wailed. "Do we have the good ice cream in the freezer?"

"Always for you, my little cherub."

"Good, because I'm going to need the whole tub," I groaned. "And a razor."

"Oh, Gerard, nothing is that bad, is it?"

"That depends on how you view heartbreak, Mam," I replied, pressing a hand to my chest. "Because if you took an X-ray of mine right now, you'd see it cracked in half."

"Ah, come on now." Mam laughed, turning to look at me. "What's all this moping about?"

"Claire," I strangled out, rubbing the sore spot of my chest. "She's at the cinema with another fella."

Mam gasped. "She isn't."

"She is." I twisted in discomfort. "Fuck, I think I might cry."

"When did this happen?"

"Tonight, right now, in front of my fucking face."

"Language, Gerard!"

"Mam!" I pulled myself up on my elbows to glare at her. "I'm dying from a broken heart here and you're worried about my language?" I shook my head and gaped. "This *hurts*, okay? I am in serious pain here."

"Love hurts, pet," Mam replied, smothering her smile with her hand. "And I'm sure this is all one big misunderstanding."

"I literally just watched her drive off in his car, Mam."

"I don't care what you saw," Mam argued, batting the air with her hand. "I know that girl adores the ground you walk on and has done so since you were both in nappies."

"Then you should know that the feeling is very much reciprocated," I shot back, not one bit embarrassed by my admission. "Which is why I am *dying* here!"

"I could have a word with Sinead."

"And say what?" I gaped at her like she had three heads. "Tell her that her daughter broke your son's heart? No fucking thanks, Mam. I'd rather die on my hill of pride right now."

"You could always tell Claire how you feel, Gerard."

"I have. I do. Daily!"

"You could mean it."

"I have never *not* meant it, Mam!" Disgusted, I flopped back down on the couch, only to howl out a groan when another thought poked through my depression. "Oh my god. Reginald! I'm going to lose custody."

"Ah, here now, Gerard Gibson." Mam laughed, throwing the remote at me. "Cop onto yourself a small bit, will you?"

"It's always the mother who gets to keep the children, Mam!"

"Son, Reggie's a hedgehog."

"She already has all the kittens," I groaned, biting my fist. "All I'm going to end up with is an ice-cream belly, and a tomcat that hates me."

"Brian doesn't hate you."

"No," I argued. "Brian is a deceiving bastard who only shows you his best side."

"Speaking of best sides," Mam said. "Are you planning on showing me yours any-time soon?"

"What do you mean?"

"Are you going to stay at home tonight?"

"Are they going to be coming back?"

"No, I already told you they're gone up the country for a few days."

"Then I'll stay."

She sagged in visible relief. "Good boy."

"But the minute he's back, I'm gone, Mam," I warned her.

She sighed sadly. "Oh, Gerard."

44

Kissing Boys in Cars

CLAIRE

I WAS QUIET THE ENTIRE DRIVE TO THE CINEMA, WHILE I LISTENED TO JAMIE HARP on about random hooligan attacks on parked cars at Tommen. Apparently, Jamie had been the victim of one such attack and, because of this, had resorted to driving his mother's Fiesta while the engine of his own car was being worked on at Tony's garage downtown.

I smiled politely and responded at all the right cues, but I would be a liar if I said I felt comfortable. In truth, I felt anything but. Seeing Gerard in my kitchen before we left for our date had thrown a spanner in midst of an already very bad idea. The look of betrayal in his gray eyes was undeniable, and I felt like such a damn fraud.

You are not a fraud.

You are doing the right thing.

Finally. After sixteen years of hanging on a limb, waiting for a boy who was never going to step forward for me, I was doing the right thing for myself and moving on.

If it's so right, then why does it feel so wrong?

When we took our seats at the back of the cinema, I felt more than a little uncertain. I wasn't used to sharing a couple's seat with anyone other than Gerard.

Usually, we brought a blanket and everything and made ourselves comfortable. I'd spent some of my favorite Saturday afternoons right here in Screen 2 with the boy across the street, watching matinee movies that ranged from cartoons when we were younger to romance, thrillers, and even gory horror.

In a weird way, I felt like I was cheating on him somehow by being here with another boy. A boy that wasn't him. It was a ridiculous way to feel, considering he'd been with lots of girls. But I couldn't help how I felt. I couldn't seem to trick my heart into believing this was a good idea, even though my brain was strongly encouraging me to be here with Jamie.

An anxious feeling tugged at my belly, but I pushed it down, needing to *not* let my heart talk me out of what my head knew was best.

Jamie had nice hair. It was dark and spiked and had the perfect amount of gel pushed through it. And he smelled really nice. I was a dinger for scents, and I could pick out his Hugo Boss cologne a mile off.

It was nice.

This was *nice*.

When he shifted in his seat during the movie and casually draped an arm over my shoulder, I felt a pang of panic gnaw at my gut, before swiftly shutting that down with a mental verbal warning. *This is fine. This is what you wanted. You're not doing anything wrong here, Claire. Just go with it.*

"Are you okay?"

"Yeah." Nodding, I smiled brightly up at him, trying to send the warmest, kindest vibes I could muster out into the atmosphere. *This is good. It's all good, and you're on the right path.* "You?"

"I'm really glad you decided to do this with me." His arm tightened around my shoulder.

My heart fluttered uncertainly, and it almost felt like it was trying to break its way out of my chest and fly back home to *him*. "Yeah." I smiled. "Me too."

"Good." Still smiling, he leaned in closer. "I think you're very beautiful."

Oh god.

Oh no.

Run, Claire, run!

"I'm hungry," I blurted out, turning my face away just in the nick of time. Jamie's lips grazed my cheek, and I quickly stuffed a handful of popcorn into my mouth. "Mmm! Tastes so…good."

Please don't say it.

Please don't say it.

Please, God, don't let him say it.

"So, we should do this again sometime," Jamie said when he pulled up outside my house after the cinema, and the cliché phrase made me internally gag. *How predictable.*

"It was a good night," I replied, polite while not giving him answer. "I had a nice time." Quickly unfastening my seat belt, I reached for the door handle and pushed the door open. "Thank you for inviting me," I added, turning back to offer him a polite smile. "I'll see you at school tom—"

My words were cut off when Jamie planted his mouth on mine.

Completely stunned by the abrupt move, I froze with my eyes wide open, and his lips clamped shut.

Oh my god.

Oh my god.

Ew, ew, ew!

When he dug a hand into my curls and tried to deepen the kiss by slobbering his tongue against my firmly closed lips, I arched backwards until my hands found purchase on the concrete footpath outside.

Scrambling backwards like a double-jointed ninja, I climbed out of the car and sprang to my feet. "Okay, *ew!*" I didn't even bother to try to hide the shudder that rolled through me. "Just…ew!"

"I'm sorry," Jamie replied, tone gruff and eyes full of darkened lust. "Was that too fast for you?"

"Uh, *yeah.*" Turning on my heels, I hurried up the driveway to my house, all the while ignoring the boy calling after me.

"Ew. Ew. Ew. Ew!" The minute I was safely inside my front door, I shook and shimmied around the front hall, feeling like spiders were crawling all over my skin. "Oh my god!"

"How was the date?" Hugh called out from the sitting room.

"Traumatizing," I called back, moving for the stairs. "He tried to lick my mouth, Hugh!"

I heard my brother snort in response. "I hope you kicked him in the nuts."

"I was too busy trying to evade his giant tongue."

"Nice."

"Believe me, Hugh, it was the opposite of nice."

"Then delete his number."

"Oh, don't worry, it's on the agenda." Gagging, I thundered up the staircase. "Right after I take a shower in Listerine!"

Cherub was on my bed when I walked into my bedroom after showering, looking like a sweet baby angel all nestled up in my dressing gown.

"Hi, my pretty girl," I cooed, clambering onto my bed to join her. "Did you miss me?"

I barely had time to get comfortable when my bedroom door swung inward.

"How was your *date?*"

"*Excellent*," I replied, narrowing my eyes when Gerard swaggered into my room without knocking. "Couldn't have gone better."

"Marvelous," he replied sarcastically. "I'm *delighted* for you."

"Thank you," I snapped back, furious with my heart for beating so damn fast at the mere sight of him. "So am I."

"Right, well, let's just get this over with, shall we?"

"Get what over with, exactly?"

"The matter of custody." Rolling up the sleeves of his school shirt, Gerard glanced around my room before finally settling his heated gaze on me. "You can't keep my kids from me. I have rights."

"Are you serious?" I shook my head and gaped at him. "Oh my god, Gerard, I'm not going to keep the babies from you."

"That's what you say now," he argued, moving for the basket in the corner of my room. "But I've been through this before, Claire." Reaching inside, he gently scooped Dick into his arms. "I know how it goes when the mam gets a new partner." Stroking him affectionately, he pressed a kiss to the top of his head. "I won't be pushed out of their lives."

"Gerard." My mouth fell open as my brain absorbed his words. "I would never do that to our family."

"That's what they all say, but I'm telling you now, if you even think about letting him meet our babies, I will lose my fucking mind, Claire," he added. "I mean it. It's bad enough that I had to watch him take you out tonight, but if I see him in this room with these cats, I will lose it."

"Oh, calm down, will you?" I snapped, clambering off the bed. "I went to the cinema with Jamie, I didn't accept a marriage proposal from him." Stalking over to him, I swiped Dick out of his arms and placed him back in the basket with his littermates. "I think one date is a little early for family introductions."

"That's what I thought, too," Gerard agreed, hands on hips. "But then I walked into the kitchen and found him with your mother and brother."

Aw, crackers.

He had me there.

"Listen, I didn't ask him to do that," I heard myself say, trying to reason with the part of my friend that had been damaged from his parents' behavior during his formative years. "I thought he would wait in the car." Shrugging helplessly, I added, "I mean, isn't that what boys are supposed to do when they take girls out on dates?"

"I have no idea, Clare," Gerard replied hotly. "Because the only girl I've ever taken out is standing in front of me."

"Gerard."

"I can take you," he blurted out. "If there's a film you want to see, I'll take you, Claire."

"That's not what tonight was about."

"Then what was it about?"

"Gerard." My heart jackknifed in my chest. "You know why I went out with him tonight."

"Nope," he stubbornly replied. "No clue."

"Yes, you do," I accused, mirroring his actions by planting my hands on my hips. "You know exactly why."

"Well, if you meant to hurt me, then congratu-fucking-lations, Claire, because it worked," he tossed back. "You succeeded."

"Well, now you know how I feel!" I shot back, feeling a million different emotions rush through me. "Oh my god!" I wasn't ashamed to admit that I stamped my foot in the heat of the moment. "You are so frustrating!"

"Me?" His eyes widened in outrage. "You're the one in the relationship when you're already in a relationship."

"I am *not* in a relationship, Gerard."

"Yes, you are," he roared back at me. "With me!"

"We are not together, Gerard."

"Yes, we are!"

"I'm not yours."

"Well, I'm yours," he came right back with. "I'm yours, Claire."

His words sucked the air out of the room, and I staggered back, feeling like he had physically struck me. The hypocrisy was suffocating.

"Then why didn't you think about me before you put your mouth on other girls!" I roared back at him.

His eyes bulged and he threw his hands up in frustration. "*What* girls?"

"How about Bernadette Brady for starters!" I threw back at him. "Hugh said you fingered her in second year, and you took a drink!"

"Bernadette Brady?" He gaped at me like I had lost my mind. "Jesus Christ, Claire, that was a million years ago. I don't even remember what she looks like!"

"Well, I remember how it felt when I heard about it and it hurt, Gerard." I pressed a hand to my chest and growled. "God, it's not fair. You are not being fair here! You're acting like there's one rule for you and a whole other set of rules for me!"

"Listen, I might have made a few mistakes in the past, and I'm far from fucking perfect, but contrary to popular belief, I'm not walking around town, ramming my tongue down other girls' throats, Claire!"

"Oh my god!" I screamed, throwing my hands up. "You just keep wrecking my plans, Gerard!"

"What plans?" he shouted back. "The plans you have with Jamie fucking Kelleher."

"With *any* other boys."

"Good!"

"Good?" I eyeballed him with intent to cause bodily harm. "Good? That's all you have to say for yourself?"

"Yeah, good." He doubled down by adding, "I'm not sorry, and I'm not stepping aside again!"

"Stepping aside?" I gaped at him. "Gerard, you chose to step aside!"

"Yeah, well now I'm choosing not to," he shouted at the top of his lungs. "I'll give you my weekends, Claire. I'll give you my weekdays, too. Whatever you want. Cinemas. Restaurants. Date nights. It's yours. Just promise me you won't go out with him again."

"You're only saying this because you're jealous," I shot back, trembling. "Because Jamie dared to kiss me when you weren't…"

"Hold up." His face paled and he pushed a shaky hand through his hair. "You kissed him?"

"No," I choked out, feeling my face flame. "I didn't kiss him."

"But he kissed you?"

"Yes."

Frozen to the spot, I watched as a million different emotions flickered in his eyes. "Jamie kissed you tonight?" he asked again. "At the cinema?"

"In his car," I croaked out.

"He kissed you in his car?"

"Yes."

Reaching up, he rubbed his chest before asking, "Was it good?"

I thought about it for a moment before saying, "No."

He swallowed deeply. "No?"

"No," I whispered, feeling my entire body tremble as I watched him watch me.

"Why wasn't it good, Claire?"

"Because it wasn't…" *you.* "Expected."

"Expected." He nodded to himself. "Okay."

"No." Heart aching, I stood in front of Gerard and locked my legs in place. "No, it's not okay, Gerard." Everything inside of me was demanding I go to him, and it was taking an inhuman amount of mental strength to stand my ground. "It's not okay at all."

Gerard bowed his head in defeat but didn't say a word.

"It's not okay," I repeated, readjusting the towel I had wrapped around me. "Because this *hurts*."

"Don't say that." His voice was barely more than a whisper and laced with helpless urgency. "Please don't fucking say that, Claire."

"This hurts me, Gerard," I repeated, refusing to let him off the hook this time. "Your behavior is hurting me."

"I love you," he stated quietly. "I always have. Take that whatever way you want. It's still the truth."

"You can't love me and then do stuff with other girls."

"Well, that's exactly what happened," he replied, voice torn. "I did stupid shit. Maybe it was because I was afraid, or maybe because I've never felt worthy of you." Shaking his head, he gave me one final glance before walking to the door. "Either way, I can't change my past."

45

Midterm Sadness

GIBSIE

"Jesus, Mary, Joseph, and the donkey," Edel Kavanagh shouted when we walked into her kitchen late the following Friday.

Well, Johnny walked in. Calling my manic, half-hunched hobble a walk was a bit of stretch.

"You're like a pair of drowned rats," she said, setting a pot of her famous stew on the table. "There's been torrential rain hammering down all day and you two lunatics decide to go out in it!" Banging and rattling cupboard doors, she set the table for the two of us as she continued to rant. "And don't even get me started on the gale-force winds outside. You could've been killed by a falling tree out there!"

"Relax, Ma," Johnny coaxed, pressing a kiss to her cheek before making a beeline for the pot of spuds on the stove. "It's only a bit of rain, and no trees maimed us."

"I made no such decision," I grumbled, collapsing in a heap at the table. "I opted for tea and biscuits by the fire. Your son was the one who forced me into a 10k run." When I shook my head, an impressive amount of rainwater sprayed around me. "So, you can blame him for any cases of sudden-onset pneumonia."

"Ah, Johnny," Edel scolded, disappearing into the hallway only to return a few moments later with a couple of towels. "Would you look at the condition of poor Gerard," she said before proceeding to dry my hair like I was a small child. "You know he has asthma."

"Thanks, Mammy K." Forcing out a wheezy cough for extra effect, I grinned up at my best friend while his mother fussed over me. "It always gets worse in bad weather."

"Bullshit," Johnny shot back, tone incredulous. "You have no more asthma than I have, ya bleeding chancer."

"I could have."

"You don't."

"Pneumonia then."

"The only thing you're going to have wrong with you is my toe up your hole if you don't pack it in."

"Jonathan!" Edel gasped. "Apologize to Gerard right this instant."

"For what?" Johnny demanded, eyes widening in disbelief. "He's the one faking a chronic lung disease!"

"We don't threaten anyone's backsides with our toes in this house," his mother countered, hands on her hips. "You know better."

Turning a comical shade of purple, Johnny opened his mouth to respond only to bite down on his fist with a growl instead. Pulling out a chair, he sank down at the table and glared at me. "I *apologize*, Gerard."

"*Thank* you, Jonathan." I grinned. "All is forgiven."

"What a relief," he deadpanned, but the kick I received under the table assured me that he wanted no such forgiveness. "Where is everyone?"

"Shannon's next door trying on Halloween costumes with Aoife," Edel explained, pointing a thumb in the direction of Lynchy's annex. "Your father's at work, and the boys have gone to the cinema with Darren."

"Darren?" Johnny's brows snapped up in surprise. "He's back *again*?"

"He's their brother, love," Edel replied calmly. "It's Seany's birthday tomorrow so Darren traveled down for the weekend." Giving her son a knowing look, she added, "He's welcome to visit them as much as he wants."

"Hmm," Johnny muttered under his breath, but made no other comment. I didn't blame him.

Darren was a dick to my best friend, and sure, a whole heap of crap had gone down in the past year that caused them both to set aside their differences, but at the end of the day, shit stuck.

"Speaking of Halloween costumes…" Edel disappeared down the hallway once more, this time returning with a pair of familiar leather pants. "These should fit you just fine now, Gerard, love."

"You fixed my pants?"

"It was no trouble, love."

"Aw, shucks." I beamed at her. "You really are Wonder Woman."

"I don't think he'll be needing them, Ma," Johnny chimed in. "Himself and Claire are on the outs."

"Wow." I glared at the side of his head. "Thanks for that, friend."

"Oh, no! Are you in a fight, love?" Edel asked, taking a seat beside her son. "You haven't broken up with the girl, have you? Because she's a keeper, Gerard Gibson."

"No, I haven't broken up with her," I grumbled, feeling that familiar pain in my chest at the thought of Claire. We hadn't spoken since last weekend. Since her date with *Jamie*. I wasn't even sure if we were still supposed to be wearing matching costumes tomorrow night, or if she had replaced me with *Jamie*. Fuck, now I was mad again. "I would never break up with her."

"True," Johnny mused. "Because breaking up with Claire would mean that you actually asked her out in the first place." Smirking, he added, "And we all know you're too pussy for that, lad."

"Language, Jonathan," Edel scolded, clipping her son around the back of the head, before locking her attention on me once more. "You haven't asked the girl out yet?" When I shook my head in response, she looked at me like I was sporting flowers out of my ears. "Why in the name of God not?"

"Because…"

"Because?" Johnny pushed, still smirking.

"Because," I replied, dropping my head in my hands. "Just because."

"You know, I'm not sure if I'm entirely comfortable with this scenario," I declared a while later as I sat on the couch in the annex with a squawking blob of blond curls on my lap. "He seems very nice, but I'm not supposed to hold babies."

"Why not?" Shannon laughed from her perch next to me, where she was protecting her nephew's head from lagging. "He really likes you, Gibs."

"Because my mam said so," I admitted honestly. "One time, I dropped my cousin from Scotland on his head, and there was like this whole heap of drama." Shifting in discomfort, I glanced down at the chubby little hand trying to snatch up my finger and felt a surge of panic. "I mean, Thomas was fine afterwards. It was only a mild concussion. He didn't even have to stay in the hospital that long, and the doctors were able to correct the whole eye thing, but Mam was adamant that I wasn't to hold any more babies."

"Okay, maybe that's enough holding for you." Wisely intercepting her son before he came to harm, Aoife backed away slowly. "In future you can just wave at Uncle Gibsie from a distance."

"Good decision," I agreed with a solemn nod.

"Here," my best friend said, bounding over to Aoife before Shannon had a chance to stand up and snatch him up. "Give your uncle Johnny a cuddle."

"No fair," Shannon huffed as she slumped back down on the couch and folded her arms across her chest. "It's my turn."

"Don't worry, Shan," Johnny shot back with a wink as he swaddled her nephew to his chest with a terrifying amount of confidence. "I'll cuddle you later."

"Oh shit." I choked out a laugh. His girlfriend's cheeks turned as red as apples. "Little Shannon." I playfully nudged her shoulder with mine. "Sounds kinky."

"Evening," a familiar voice filled the air and Joey appeared in the doorway, clad in oil-stained overalls.

"Evening."

"Lynchy."

"Hi, Joe."

Ignoring the rest of us, Joey strode through the open plan kitchen/living area, not stopping until he reached his girlfriend, who was sitting cross-legged on the rug, neatly folding stacks of their son's tiny clothes.

"Hey, stud," Aoife said, craning her head up to smile at the lad towering above her.

"Queen." Crouching down, he tipped her chin up and kissed her once. "You good?"

"All good, Joe," she replied, catching ahold of his chin with her small hand. "You?" To anyone else, it might look like she was staring into his eyes with loving affection, and hell maybe she was, but I had a feeling that she was checking for something. *His sobriety.*

"All good, Molloy," he quietly assured her with a wink before reaching into the pocket of his overalls and retrieving a packet of Rolos. Tossing them onto her lap, he stood back up and moved for the kitchen sink. "So, where are the boys?" Joey called over his shoulder as he washed up. "They usually hang out here on a Friday night. It's Ollie's turn to pick the movie."

Ah shit.

"Actually, Darren's home for the weekend," Shannon took one for the team and answered her brother, while the rest of us held our breath. Because while Johnny might take issue with the eldest Lynch sibling, it paled in comparison to the animosity that oozed from Joey. "He took Tadhg, Ollie, and Sean to the cinema."

Silence.

You could hear a pin drop.

Double shit.

All four of us watched Joey turn off the tap and reach for the towel hanging on the cupboard door.

Finally, when I didn't think I could take another second of the silence, he asked, "Did he come over here?" Clearly the question was directed at his girlfriend because he was staring at her with a look of blazing protectiveness in his eyes. "Molloy?"

"Joe," she began to say with a sigh. "Don't get mad—"

"Did he come over here?" he repeated, enunciating his words slowly. "Did he see my son?"

"He asked to," Aoife explained with a sigh. "I told him that I would have to talk to you about it first."

"And you, Molloy?" He never blinked once. "What did he say to you?"

"Chill, Joe, it's all good," she replied. "He was perfectly polite."

Her response seemed to appease Joey because relief flashed in his eyes. "Okay." He nodded once, shoulders relaxing. "Good."

"Joe, he really wants to make amends," Shannon offered gently. "He asks about the three of you all the time." Climbing off the couch, she padded over to her big brother and placed her hand on his arm. "I know you guys have your differences, and I get that, okay? I do. More than anyone. But Darren is AJ's uncle, too. The same as Tadhg, Ols, and Sean. The same way I'm his aunt. Won't you even consider letting him meet his nephew?"

"You mean the same uncle who tried to pay my son's mother to abort him?" Joey replied flatly, making a beeline for his son. "No, Shannon, I won't reconsider."

"Shite," Johnny muttered, handing AJ over to his father. "I don't blame you, lad."

"Not helping, Johnny," Aoife and Shannon groaned in unison.

"What? You don't step on another fella like that. Brother or not." Shrugging unapologetically, Johnny turned to his girlfriend. "I'm sorry, Shan. I know Darren's your family, baby, and you want to keep the peace. I get it. I do, and you know I've got your back no matter what, and I've always supported women's rights to choose for themselves. But if the shoe was on the other foot and he had tried to get you to abort *my* kid behind my back?" Johnny shook his head. "I don't know if I could handle it as calmly as your brother here."

"See," Joey bit out as he cradled his son in his arms. "He gets it."

Yeah, I got it, too, but I wasn't nearly smart enough to throw my two cents into this delicate conversation without making a mess of it. Therefore, I jumped up and rubbed my hands together before saying. "Do you know what I think might help ease the tension in here?"

"Oh god, what?" Shannon groaned, looking almost fearful of what I might say.

"Why don't you girls scamper off and try on your Halloween costumes for tomorrow night's party, while Lynchy and Cap handle the Code Brown in that kid's nappy that everyone is pretending to not be able to smell. Meanwhile, I'll throw a batch of cookies together."

"We don't have eggs." Aoife sighed. "Dammit."

"Never fear, blondie," I replied, rolling up my sleeves. "I'm a man of many talents—one of which happens to be the ability to improvise."

Joey arched a brow. "Since when did you start baking?"

"Oh, Lynchy, you're not the only one who leveled up last summer." I chuckled, moving for the kitchen. "Now, chop chop and change that kid before the smell sticks to my nostrils."

46
Birthday Cakes and Toe Flicks

CLAIRE

"I'm rich," I declared with a cheer when I bounced into the Allens' house on Saturday afternoon. Catching ahold of my work bag, I tossed it next to the cupboard under the stairs with a flourish before dancing into the kitchen. Rusted Root's "Send Me On My Way" drifted from the radio on top of the microwave, and the song filled my heart with warm childhood nostalgia.

"I had the best first day ever at work, I made forty euro, and I get to go to two birthday parties today!" Pirouetting across the tiles, I toe-danced to the fridge and then tossed in a little toe-flick-toe for good measure. "What a time to be alive!"

"Claire," Mam acknowledged with an indulging smile, as she rested a hip against the kitchen table, nursing a cup of coffee. "You're full of beans."

"*Two* birthday parties," I reiterated, snagging a bottle of Gerard's Sunny D from the fridge. "Today is a good day to be me, Mam." I turned my attention to the other woman, whose fridge I was looting. "Hi, Mammy Number 2."

"Hello, Claire, pet," Sadhbh Allen called over her shoulder as she concentrated on putting the final touches on what I knew was my brother's birthday cake. Packets of balloons, streamers, and birthday banners littered the kitchen table, a sure sign that the preparations for tonight's party were in full swing. "It's hard to believe it, isn't it, Sinead? That this day eighteen years ago, you were in the throes of labor with our little Hugo boss-man."

"Jesus, don't remind me, Sadhbh." Mam laughed. "Sixty-two hours of labor only to end up having an emergency cesarean section." Smiling, Mam shook her head before adding, "Pete passed out in theater and chipped his collarbone on the metal tray going down."

"And Joe ended up sitting at his bedside in the A&E for the night. I remember it well." With a piping bag of icing in her hands, Sadhbh piped a thin border of blue icing on the cake. "I was only a few months along with Gerard and absolutely petrified of what was to come."

"Ah, we figured it out along the way, didn't we?"

"We sure did."

"Did you use the red velvet base I made?" I asked, watching over her shoulder as she worked on the edible masterpiece.

"I sure did."

"Yay!"

"The texture was so rich," she added. "The perfect consistency."

"You know, it was Gerard who told me to add the vinegar to the batter," I explained between sips of my juice. "I thought he was crazy, but it was *genius*."

"Oh, you should see him at the bakery," Sadhbh agreed, using the corner of a napkin to clean up the corner of the silver cake board. "He spent the entire summer coming up with new recipes, and I have to tell you girls, each one was better than the last, which is amazing considering he couldn't turn on a microwave before the summer."

"It's in his blood." Mam smiled. "He's just like his father."

"Yeah." Forcing a smile, I pushed down the pang of grief that hit me when Joe Gibson's face flashed through my mind. "He is."

"Where are the boys?" Mam asked, thankfully giving me an out from my depressing memories. "At home getting ready for tonight?"

"Nah, Hugh's still at work," I explained, hoisting myself onto the island. "Some girl got sick, and he had to wait until her cover shows up. Patrick gave me a lift home from the hotel."

"Oh?" Sadhbh arched a brow. "Meaning my rogue is on the missing list again?"

Yep. I hadn't seen her *rogue* since he stormed out of my bedroom last weekend. We were in a fight, and a bad one, apparently, but I would never lose face in front of our mothers. Fighting or not, I have a level of loyalty to Gerard that went above and beyond frivolous teenage arguments. Even when Gerard clamped the shutters finely shut on his emotions, simultaneously blocking any exclusive access I may have had to the real *him*.

He'd been staying at Johnny's house most nights since Mark's return, meaning I had no late-night visitors to my room. Something I felt surprisingly bereft about.

"Gerard's not on the missing list," I heard myself defend, falling into the pattern of a lifetime. "He's just…"

"Being Gerard?"

"He's with Johnny."

"At the gym?"

"No, I think they're prepping for Sean's party." Frowning I added, "Although I doubt the bouncy castle will go ahead now that it's raining again."

"Oh, I almost forgot!" Mam walked over to her handbag and swiped a

Tommen-crested envelope out of it. "The school's newsletter arrived yesterday. They've decided to scrap this year's fifth- and sixth-year skiing trip to Andorra."

"What?" I wailed. "No! But it's my turn! I'm finally old enough to go and it gets *canceled*?"

"Oh, that's right, Sinead. I read that, too," Sadhbh agreed. "Apparently there was some issue with the school's insurance."

"Typical," I huffed, folding my arms across my chest. "Just *typical*."

"Tommen is holding a winter ball for the senior cycle to make up for it."

"A winter *ball*?" My body thrummed with excitement. "Like a ball-ball? Like the ones they have in the States? With gowns and tuxes and fancy-pants corsages?"

"Apparently so."

"Shut the front door!" Squealing with delight, I clapped my hands together with vigor. "Are you serious? *When*?"

"The week of Christmas break."

"Oh my god, oh my god." I jumped down from the counter. "I need to prepare." I paced the kitchen floor. "I need a dress and shoes, and jewelry, and… Oh crap, I need to color coordinate with the girls so we don't clash. And then I need to book the hairdresser, and organize photographs, and transport, and get my nails done, and…"

"Claire, love, Halloween is tomorrow," Mam interrupted with a chuckle. "Calm down. You have plenty of time."

"Plenty of time?" I gaped at her. "Mam, this is a *ball*. A real winter ball! These things take time to plan."

"How would you know? You've never been to one." Mam laughed. "And before you lose the run of yourself organizing photographers and limousines for your entire friendship group, you might want to think about who you're going to go with first." She winked at Sadhbh before adding, "Or is it just a given that you're going to go with Gerard?"

"Uh…*duh*?" I stared blankly at her. "Who else would I go with?"

"Another boy, perhaps?"

The memory of Jamie's giant tongue filled my mind, and I scrunched my nose up. "Ew."

They both grinned in unison.

"Oh, please." I rolled my eyes. "Like it's such a big surprise that I would want to go with Gerard."

"They *are* good friends, Sinead," Sadhbh noted, winking at my mam.

"*Very* good friends," Mam agreed with a smirk. "Very good indeed."

"So, is there anything you'd like to share with us?"

I blinked in confusion. "Like what?"

"You two have been spending a lot of extra time together."

"And if he takes her to the ball, then I presume that means he'll take her to his prom next summer."

"Is it called the prom now? It was called the debs back in our day."

"True."

"It's called the *grads* now," I explained, and then beamed when I registered what had been said. "Oh my god, I'm going to the *grads*!" Excitement bubbled over inside of me. "Yay! Two dresses!"

"Then you better start saving all your money from that job you started today," Mam teased.

"Nah, I think I'll keep my money and spend Dad's instead." I laughed. "Where is he? I better get a start on my swindling."

"At home in the office," Mam replied with a cheerful smile. "Deadline, remember?"

Another pang of sadness struck me square in the solar plexus, but I quickly shook it off, reminding myself that if I had been the one to lose my best friend that day then I, too, would have locked myself away from the world.

Okay, so maybe not for an entire decade like my father had, but I understood the sentiment behind his actions, even if I didn't understand the depression he battled on the daily.

Walking over to where my mother was standing, I wrapped my arms around her from behind. "Love you," I whispered, pressing a kiss to her cheek. "Queen."

Because my mother *was* a queen. How she continued to love my father through his dark times was beyond admirable. I was sure they had their moments, but never once in the ten years since Joe's passing had I heard Mam raise her voice to my father. Mam was a nurse, and because of that, I knew she had a certain level of understanding into what was happening in Dad's mind, but the way she unconditionally loved him through it all not only proved to me that people could be kind, but also that true love could prevail.

My parents had loved each other since childhood, and Mam continued to love Dad even when he didn't have the strength to love himself.

The sound of the front door slamming filled my ears moments before the man of the moment himself strolled into his kitchen, swinging his car keys. "Mothers."

The minute my eyes landed on him, standing in there in faded blue jeans and a white T-shirt, a fierce blast of white-hot heat ricocheted through my belly.

Aw, crackers.

"Claire-Bear," he acknowledged with a polite nod.

"Gerard."

"Where in the name of Jesus is your jumper?" Sadhbh demanded. "It's raining cats and dogs out there."

"I lost it at the disco last night, Mam," he joked, referencing a Sultans of Ping song. "When I was dancing…"

"Gerard." His mam narrowed her eyes. "You're not funny."

Proving Sadhbh wrong, my mam choked out a laugh. "Dancing in the disco." She chuckled. "Very good, Gibs. I just got the reference."

Gerard grinned in victory before training his attention. "I've been given orders by your bestie to chaperone you to the manor—and bring your costume."

My heart leapt. "You have?"

He nodded. "Apparently, all the girls are getting ready over at the manor after Sean's party."

47
Shut Up and Let Me Go

CLAIRE

TENSION.

That was the only word I could think up to describe the weird, clammy air that enveloped us on the car ride over to the manor.

Gerard hadn't spoken a word to me since he loaded my bags and Sean's birthday presents into the boot of his car. Suffocating under the weight of unspoken friction, I tried my best to ignore it by flicking through radio stations.

Problem was, it felt like every channel had decided to play songs that felt like they were personally targeting me.

Already, I had switched over Berlin's "Take My Breath Away," "Kiss Me" from Sixpence None the Richer, and Whitney's "Saving All My Love for You."

To be honest, I was beginning to think there was a conspiracy going on behind the scenes of our local radio stations and that they had all decided to gang up on my feelings.

When I flicked stations for the last time and landed on Norah Jones's soulful voice crooning out the lyrics of "Turn Me On," I gave up the good fight and threw my hands up in defeat.

Daring to cast a glance in his direction, I watched as Gerard drummed his fingers against the steering wheel, looking as cool as a cucumber. His external blasé bullshit appearance irked me in ways I never knew I could be irked. That's right: irked. Gerard Gibson was beyond *irking*.

Ugh.

Scowling, I folded my arms across my chest, and glared straight ahead. The wipers on his car were working double time trying to clear the heavy rain from his windscreen, and the fan was blowing a steady stream of hot air into the car, but the windows were still fogging up at a rapid pace.

Finally, after what felt like a lifetime when in truth it couldn't have been more than seven or eight minutes, Gerard broke the silence. "So, any more playdates planned with your precious Jamie?"

The catty way he said it had my back up. "Depends."

"On?"

"On whether or not he asks me out again."

His grip tightened on the wheel.

Ha! Take that.

"What's wrong?" I bit out. "Jealous much?"

"On the contrary," he tossed back, jaw ticking. "I've developed a hernia from the weight it's taking me to give a fuck!"

My mouth fell open and I glared at him. "You did *not* just say that to me."

"You know what, Claire, I think I just did."

I narrowed my eyes. "You are *such* an asshole."

"Maybe," he agreed in a hard tone. "But at least I'm not an asshole that goes around school talking about all the ways I plan to fuck you."

"Excuse me?"

Gerard shrugged unapologetically. "You heard me."

"Jamie said that about me?"

Silence.

"Gerard!" I snapped, twisting sideways in my seat to look at him. "What did you hear."

"Enough to know that he wants in your knickers."

"Well, at least someone does!"

"Nice," he sneered, shaking his head in disgust. "That's real fucking nice talk, Claire-Bear."

"Stop the car."

"Yeah," he snorted. "That's what I'm going to do."

"I said stop the car, Gerard Gibson!"

"You really want me to stop the car?" he demanded in a sarcastic tone. "On the side of the main road in the pissing rain?"

No. "That's what I said, isn't it?"

Releasing a frustrated growl, he threw on the indicator and pulled off to the side of the road. "Fine." He jacked the hand break and turned to glare at me. "As you wish."

48

Weather for the Ducks

GIBSIE

"Claire, come on, will you?" At a snail's pace, I continued to drive along beside her with my hazard lights on and the car window rolled down. "Just get in the car, please." Ignoring the honking horns from the countless pissed-off road users tailing me, I concentrated on the furious blond stomping down the side of the road instead. "You're going to get washed away." That was a very real concern of mine. It was raining so hard that even with my windscreen wipers switched to full speed, I was having a hard time seeing the road ahead of me. "You're not even wearing a coat, you wally!"

"Don't call me a wally, you big tool," she called back, upping her pace only to step in a huge puddle and splash herself in brown mud. "Ugh. Perfect! Just perfect!"

Jesus, what a mess, and I wasn't talking about her clothes.

"Claire," I coaxed, trying another approach as I leaned an arm out the window and tried to reason with her. "I'm sorry, okay? Just get in the car and you can kill me while you dry off in the warm!"

"Why?" she demanded, stopping dead in her tracks. She folded her arms across her chest and glared. "*Why* are you sorry, Gerard?"

"Why?" I shook my head in confusion. "Because I pissed you off enough that you climbed out of the car on the main road?"

"Ugh!" She stamped her foot in frustration and continued walking. "Tool!"

"Well, didn't I?" I called out, rolling along beside her once more. "I mean, you're obviously mad at me if you're willing to walk the full three miles to Cap's house."

"I'm not mad, Gerard," she called over her shoulder. "I'm *furious!*"

Spying the entrance to Ballylaggin Woods up ahead, I switched on my indicator and drove fifty yards or so up ahead and pulled into the gap.

Killing the engine, I threw the door open and climbed out. "Are you happy?" I snapped, throwing my hands up as I walked back to her. "Because we're both getting soaked now."

"Oh my god, just go away!" Claire shouted. "I don't want to see you right now."

"Well, that's too fucking bad because I'm not leaving you on the side of the road, *sweetheart!*" I snapped back, pushing my already drenched hair out of my eyes. "Anyone could take you!"

"Take me?" She threw her head back and laughed humorlessly. "Like who? Old Dinny Byrne from *Glenroe* on his tractor?" She rolled her eyes. "Get real, Gerard."

"I *am* being real," I shouted back. "You're the one acting like a lunatic here. And don't take the piss out of *Glenroe* when we *both* loved that show," I accused. "So, why don't you do us both a favor and climb in the car before we both get double goddamn pneumonia!"

"No."

"No?" I gaped at her. "Why the hell not?"

"Because you suck, Gerard Gibson!"

"I suck because I want to keep you safe?" I flailed my arms around in exasperation. "Oh yeah, I'm a right horrible bastard."

"You know what?" Narrowing her eyes, Claire stalked over to the gate I was parked in front of and climbed over it. "Go screw yourself, Gerard."

"Oh, so you're just going to take a gander through the woods now, are you?" I demanded, stalking after her. "Is that your genius plan, Claire-Bear?" I demanded, jumping the gate with ease. "Because it's a really shitty one."

"I don't care!" she screamed back, doubling her efforts to outwalk me. "Now stop following me!"

"I told you that I'm not leaving you alone to be kidnapped," I growled, absolutely following her. "You little demon!"

"Being kidnapped is sounding awfully tempting right now," she spat out. "At least it would save me from being anywhere near you, you big bull."

"Oh, so I'm a bull now?"

"Yep!"

"How'd you figure that one?"

"Uh, maybe because you look like one. Except that you have piercings in your nipples instead of your nose!"

"Are you saying that my tits resemble those of a bull?"

"If the *moo* fits, Gerard!"

"Take it back."

"No!"

"That was a very fucking hurtful statement to make."

"Good."

"Take it back."

"I said no!"

"Take it back, Claire, or I'll be forced to say something myself."

"Like what?"

"Like how the webbed baby toe on your left foot isn't cute," I called out. "I lied. It's weird as fuck!"

"Oh, you are such an asshole," she screamed, throwing her hands up. "Now I'm glad I said it. And you know what else, Gerard Gibson? Your jokes aren't even funny half the time. That's right. You have shit craic."

"How dare you!" I staggered back, feeling like she had physically struck me. "My craic is *ninety*."

"Your craic is mediocre," Claire called over her shoulder, storming through the tree line. "Now go away!"

"Jesus Christ," I growled, pressing my fingers to my temples. I shook my head, at a complete fucking loss with this girl. "Can you stop walking away from me for two goddamn minutes and just talk to me calmly so we can figure this out!"

"No, because it's always words with you!" she screamed, pushing her rain-drenched hair back from her face. "It's always words and smiles and conversations and I'm over it, Gerard!" She threw her hands up in the air—dramatic as always—as the heavens continued to pelt down on us. "Oh my god. What's the point in even arguing with you?" She shook her head and screamed, "You're never going to get it!"

"Get it?"

"Us, Gerard!" she screamed. "You don't get us!"

"Us?" Now I was the furious one. "You think I don't get us?" I demanded, upping my pace and closing the space between us. "Oh, I get us, Claire," I snapped, bristling with temper. "I've been getting us for a lot fucking longer than you!" Catching up with her, I grabbed her hand and pulled her back to face me. "Stop running away from me, dammit."

"Then why don't you do something about it?" she challenged, tears mixing with raindrops. "Huh?" She ripped her hand free and stormed off, only to turn back around and stalk back to me. "Dammit, Gerard, why won't you just show me how you feel?"

"I do!"

"No, you don't," she choked out, shoving me again. "You tell me." Tears dripped onto her cheeks as she cried. "You're always telling me, Gerard, when I'm standing here begging you to *show* me."

"I can't!"

"Why not?"

"Because it's not that easy for me."

"Why?"

"Because I'm afraid!"

"Of what?" she demanded, pushing at my chest. "Huh?" She pushed me again. "What are you afraid of?"

"You, Claire," I roared back at her, chest heaving. "I'm afraid of *you*!"

49
All Aboard the Feels Train!

CLAIRE

"ME?"

"Yes!"

"You're afraid of *me*?"

"*Yes!*"

"Why?"

"Because I fucking love you, Claire!"

"I love you, too."

"I know," he agreed. "That's what makes it even worse!"

"But that doesn't make any sense," I cried out hoarsely. Reeling from his admission, I stood in the rain, staring up at the only boy I ever loved and screamed. "None of what you're saying makes any sense to me, Gerard!"

I didn't want to be in love with him, and I was. It sucked. Big time. I wanted requited love. The proper kind. Like Shannon had with Johnny. And Aoife with Joey. Well, minus the drugs and the teen pregnancy. I just wanted a real relationship.

With *him*.

He marked me in childhood, and that mark had only scored deeper on my heart as the years went by. I knew him, though. He lingered on my heart. I couldn't seem to get past him.

Apparently, that was too much to ask because the boy I wanted was broken in the head. He didn't have the same feelings I had. He didn't work the same way I did.

"When has anything about my thought process ever made sense, Claire?" Gerard shouted back. "I know I'm fucking all of this up." He pushed a hand through his drenched hair and shrugged helplessly. "I'm not trying to purposefully upset you. I swear to Christ, I'm not, but that's what happens." He threw his hands up in defeat. "That's what I seem to do, Claire."

"Then you need to stop."

"I'm *trying*," he bit out through gritted teeth. "That's what I'm trying to do, Claire. I'm trying to talk this out with you!"

"I don't need any more words, Gerard," I clapped back. "I don't need you putting anymore words into the atmosphere that you don't mean."

"That I don't mean?" he demanded. "What have I *ever* not meant?"

"How about all of those lies you've fed me for the past sixteen years about loving me and wanting us to be together," I strangled out. "Only to turn right around and do the opposite every chance you get!"

"I *do* love you, Claire. I *do* want to be with you. I've *always* wanted to be with you. I just—" He stopped short and blew out a frustrated breath, hands moving to his hips. "If you just let me explain…"

"I *am*, Gerard," I urged, voice high-pitched and torn. "I *am* letting you explain. I have given you all the time in the world to explain. To figure it the hell out. Sixteen years, to be precise. But you can't come up with a good enough excuse off the top of your head quick enough, now, can you?" I shook my head. "Instead, you say all the right words and then you turn around and do the complete opposite." Teeth chattering from the cold, I stamped my foot in frustration. Big mistake. My shoe landed in a pothole, causing brown, muddy water to splash all over my tights. Again. Furious, I balled my hands into fists and screamed. "And now I'm muddy again!" I glared at him, heart racing at a thousand miles an hour. "And these shoes are *new!*"

"It's not about me finding excuses to not be with you, Claire," he roared. "It's about me knowing that you're the perfect person for me." Clearly furious, he slapped the heel of his hand against his forehand and hissed, "All the while knowing that I'm not!"

"What?" I shook my head. "That makes no sense, Gerard."

"Yeah, it does." Nodding eagerly, he ignored the raindrops that were trickling down his face. "I know you're better off without me, Claire. Okay? I *know* that." Releasing a shaky breath, he held his hands up and shrugged helplessly. "But I also know I'm not better off without you." He raised his hands in a helpless motion. "Not better off one bit."

"Oh my god," I cried out, beyond confused. "I never know where I stand with you."

"In front," came his quick response. "On top. Number one. Fucking always, Claire."

"I have been waiting all my life for you to make a move. For you to grow a pair and just tell me how you feel."

"You know how I feel."

"Stop it, Gerard!" I snapped. "Stop playing with my heart. I can't take it. Don't say it if you don't mean it, because breaking my heart by accident is one thing but doing it on purpose is another thing entirely, and I don't think I could come back from it."

"Who's playing?" he demanded. "I fucking love you, Claire Biggs."

"How can you say that?"

"Because it's the truth!" Gerard roared, turning a dark shade of purple as his outrage clearly grew. "I didn't choose any of this, okay? I was born and there you were, and I had these feelings. And they grew, Claire," he roared, stalked toward me. "Holy shit did they grow!" Looking more furious than I'd seen him in years, he hooked an arm around my waist and pulled me roughly against him. "Like neon fucking lit-up boomerang feelings that keep coming back no matter how far I push them away!"

"Oh yeah?" My heart decided to accelerate to the point where I felt like I was having physical chest pains. "Well, you can't just…" My breath was puffy, and my voice was torn. "You can't just…" Pained, I pressed the heel of my hand to my chest bone, while using my other hand to clutch my temple. "Oh god…"

"What?" He demanded. "What's happening to you?"

"I'm having a moment."

"You are?" Panic, anger, and confusion all filled his tone. "Holy shit, from what?"

"From *you*, Gerard," I groaned, fisting his drenched school shirt in my hand. "From you, because you just hit me with the feels train, okay?"

"The feels train?"

"Yes, the feels train, you big dick!"

"Well, *choo-choo*," he snapped back, tone laced with sarcasm as he pretended to yank on a horn. "Hop a-fucking-board, sweetheart. It's about time you decided to join me. Considering I've been on the same damn feels train for years—"

"Shut up."

"You shut up!"

"Shut up, Gerard!"

"No, I won't shut up because you're not the only—"

"I said 'shut up'!" I screamed, clamping a hand over his mouth, eyes locked on his and the rain hammered down on us. "Shut up, Gerard Gibson. Just shut the hell up already!"

One moment we were glaring, and screaming, and shoving at each other and the next we were *kissing*.

Somehow, and only God himself knew how it happened, my hand on Gerard's mouth had been replaced with my lips.

Desperately. Voraciously. Adoringly. Our lips collided in a frenzied hunger that had been building up for sixteen years and had finally bubbled over.

Kissing him felt like I had suddenly remembered the answer to a question that had been tormenting me for hours. You know the feeling of frustration when something is on the tip of your tongue forever, and you finally figure it out and relief floors you? Well, that's how I was feeling in this moment.

And if wasn't just me doing the kissing, either. Gerard didn't hesitate to reciprocate my kiss. Not for one millisecond. No, he was kissing me back, and I mean *really* kissing me back. With just as much flair and need and desperation.

Fisting my hair with one hand, he reciprocated every reckless thrust of my tongue with an experienced thrust of his own, while he pulled me roughly against him with his other hand, fingertips digging into the fleshy part of my hip.

Trembling violently, I clung to his shoulders, feeling my body grow weak. Seriously, my legs were shaking so violently, I could hardly keep upright.

Oh god.

Oh *god.*

It was the strangest, most perfect, most real and *right* feeling ever. I never wanted anything more in my life than this boy and all he could give me. He was too much and not enough all at once.

This kiss?

His lips on my lips?

His hands on my body?

His tongue in my mouth?

It meant *everything* to me.

I wanted to laugh.

I wanted to cry.

I wanted to... Oh, God, I felt so much in this moment, so much for this boy, that I wasn't sure what I wanted. I was floored by relief and flooded by feelings all in one breath. I only knew that I didn't ever want him to stop.

But then he did.

Tearing his lips away from mine, Gerard pushed his hair off his forehead, breathless and panting. "Fuck."

"No." Feeling panicked that he was going to slam the brakes again, I fisted his shirt and pulled him back to me. "Don't stop."

"I don't want to," he replied in a gruff tone, hands moving to rest on my hip. "Trust me. But you're going to get sick out here."

"I don't care," I croaked out, feeling like I would die right here on the mortal spot if he didn't kiss me again.

His gray eyes blazed with heat when he said, "Yeah, well I do."

50
Your Place or Mine?

CLAIRE

"So," Gerard said twenty minutes later, when he parked up outside his house, and finally broke the strained silence that had hung heavily in the air the entire journey home. For some reason, he'd driven us home instead of to Johnny's house, but I wasn't complaining. Not when home offered me a bigger chance of getting him alone.

"So," I replied nervously, feeling like my entire future rested on what came out of his mouth next.

"So…" He killed the engine and turned to look at me. "That was new."

"Yep." Nodding, I tucked my damp curls behind my ear. "Super new."

My response drew a smile from his lips. "This is a bit weird, isn't it?"

"So weird," I agreed with another eager nod of my head.

"What do you want to do now?"

"Uh." I shrugged sheepishly and replied with, "I don't mind," when I knew damn well what *I* wanted to do now. *A repeat performance.*

"Hmm."

"Yep."

Another weird silence enveloped us as we stared awkwardly at each other from either side of the car.

"Is your mam home?"

"No, she's at your house getting the food ready for the party with your mam."

"Oh yeah."

"Yep."

"Do you want to come over?" we both ended up asking the other at the same time before chuckling nervously and saying, "yes." Again, at the same time.

Clearing my throat, I unfastened my seat belt and pushed the car door open. "Well, I'm going to go home now," I declared in a far calmer tone than I felt. "Would you like to join me?"

"Yes," Gerard thrilled me by replying as he unfastened his own seat belt and quickly followed after me. "I would definitely like to join you."

"Excellent decision."

"Yes, I think so."

"I think so, too."

Gerard quickly fell into step beside me, and we walked up the driveway to my front door, shoulders touching. "Weather for the ducks."

"Perfect weather for the ducks," I agreed, pushing the front door open and stepping inside. "Hugh?" I called out, stepping aside for Gerard to follow me inside. "Are you home yet?"

"His car isn't parked in the driveway."

"True. He's probably at Katie's house."

"True," Gerard agreed, looking like a drenched god as he stood in my front hall, dripping rainwater all over the tiles. "That would make sense."

"And Dad's probably in the office," I offered, my tone a little breathless.

"Probably," Gerard agreed with a nod.

"So…" An illicit shiver of delight racked through me as I watched him watch me. "I'm going to go upstairs now." I moved for the staircase. "Would you like to come up to my room?"

My entire frame trembled with lustful anticipation when I felt his chest brush against my back. "It would be rude not to walk you to your room."

Yay.

Hurrying up the stairs, we both made a beeline for my bedroom. Closing the door behind us, I leaned against the frame and watched as he walked into the middle of the room. "So…"

I exhaled a shaky breath and sagged against the door at my back. "So…"

"About what happened in the woods." He pushed his damp hair off his brow again and glanced around in every direction but mine. "That was some kiss."

"I'll say," I agreed, heart bucking wildly against my rib cage. "Best first second-kiss ever."

"Agreed." Wandering over to a random shelf, he readjusted a lopsided teddy bear that was perched on top of it. "And what happened in my room that night." He roughly cleared his throat before adding, "That was…"

"Epic," I told him, tracking his every move with my eyes. "For me, at least."

"Oh, for me as well." With his hands behind his back, Gerard snooped around my room, investigating knickknacks on top of shelves and dressers that he'd seen a million times before. "I was thinking…"

"You were?" I blurted out, and then mentally scolded myself for interrupting him. "Go ahead," I said in a coaxing tone. "You were thinking…"

"I was thinking that I could do that again for you sometime." Shrugging, he added, "If you wanted me to, of course."

"Yes!" Raw, unadulterated heat blasted through me. "I would definitely want you to."

"Good." He finally settled his heated gaze on me. "Glad that's settled then."

"Yep." I nodded eagerly. "What a relief."

"Oh absolutely," he agreed, walking toward me. "So, uh, when would you like that to happen exactly?"

"Um…" Sagging weakly against the doorframe, I looked up at his face and exhaled shakily. "I was thinking maybe now?"

"I was thinking now, too," he agreed in a gruff tone, closing the space between us. "But we might miss the clown."

"I think I can survive without seeing the clown," I breathed, heart racing violently. "If you can?"

"Oh, I can definitely survive without seeing the clown," Gerard agreed, hands grazing my hips as he looked down at me, gray eyes full of heat. "Don't think I can survive without you, though."

He didn't have to say another word. I literally threw myself at him like a deranged lunatic. Catching me in midair, Gerard hoisted me up effortlessly as our lips collided with just as much urgency as earlier.

Holy crap, his lips were so soft and warm and perfect. He tasted like home and smelled like it, too. Trying to remain calm in this moment wasn't easy for me, but I tried my best. Gripping his big shoulders, I fell into our kiss as he walked us backwards, not stopping until we tangled up in a heap on my bed.

"Oh my god," I croaked out, collapsing on the couch beneath him in a flurry of entwined limbs and tangled hearts. "You're ridiculously good at that."

"What?" he asked, tone breathless, as he craned his head back to look at me.

"Kissing, Gerard," I breathed, chest heaving beneath him. "You're good at kissing."

"Well." With a boyish twinkle in his eye, he tilted his head to one side and grinned down at me. "I've been practicing for you."

"Don't push it," I warned, slapping at his chest.

"Duly noted," he replied with a solemn nod.

"In fact, don't say anything at all right now," I added, tilting my chin up to meet his.

"Shutting up, Claire-Bear," he promised moments before his lips returned to mine.

"Mmm, I know I said it already, but I think it bears repeating that you really are an amazing kisser," I said several minutes later when I broke free of his lips to gather some much-needed air. "Like *seriously*…" My eyelids fluttered when his tongue lapped at the piece of skin above my collarbone. "Amazing."

"You know I love you." He pressed me deep into the mattress with his big body, lips moving against mine when he bit out the words, "There's only ever been you for me."

His words thrilled me but not nearly as much as his actions, because I'd had his words my entire life, while his current actions were brand-new.

"You're so wet."

"I know," I squeezed out, breath hitching. "Keep going."

"No, I mean you're really wet," he replied, pulling back to gesture to my drenched clothes. "You're going to get sick, Claire-Bear." Hesitation flickered in his eyes then, and I wanted to scream *no* when he started to retreat. "What the hell am I doing? I better—"

"Don't you dare," I warned, wrestling him onto his back and grinning in victory when I came out on top. "You're not leaving."

"I was going to say I better get off so you can take a shower." He chuckled beneath me, palms up as I pinned his wrists to the bed. "Jesus, choke slam me, why don't you?"

Now, I had little to zero experience with kissing boys in bedrooms, so I could only put my bravado down to years' worth of binge-watching rom-coms. Well, that and the fact that I felt ridiculously comfortable around this boy.

Super proud of myself for the moves I had somehow managed to manifest in this moment, I straddled Gerard's lap without a hint of shame or reservation.

God, who even *was* I?

"I don't want to take a shower," I replied, tightening my grip on his wrists. "I want to keep kissing you." Leaning in close, I pressed a hard kiss to his swollen lips. "And the only way these clothes are coming off my body is if you peel them off with your hands."

When his big hands settled on the part of my legs where my skirt grazed my thighs, everything inside of me coiled tight with anticipation.

Gerard's eyes blazed with heat. "Is that so?"

A delicious throbbing ache settled low in my belly, encouraged every time his fingertips danced under the hem of my skirt.

Do it, I mentally begged. *Touch me everywhere.*

"I am so fucking scared of breaking this," he surprised me by saying. "Of wrecking what we have." He shook his head and exhaled a pained breath before saying, "I could sit on the fence for the rest of my life and still be nervous."

His admission curled around my heart like a blanket of warmth, and I shivered. Because this was his truth. He was lifting the veil inch by tiny inch and giving me an insight into his thought process. "You shouldn't be afraid to strike out, Gerard." Reaching down, I stroked his cheek to reassure him. "I would much rather live my life with mistakes under my belt than regrets chipping away at my heart."

"See, that's the thing, Claire," he urged in a pained tone. "I don't want to be your mistake *or* your regret." He pulled up on his elbows, gray eyes burning with sincerity and heat. "I can't fucking bear the thought of it."

"You're not, Gerard," I replied, holding his beautiful face in my hands. He looked so vulnerable in this moment that it made me physically ache. I wanted to soothe the fear in him. I wanted to chase his demons away. The ones that had been put there from witnessing the breakdown of his parents' marriage. "You could never be either one of those to me."

"This past week was fucking horrible," he admitted in a gruff tone. "Fighting with you puts me in a bad place in my head." He reached up and tapped his temple for emphasis. "When I'm not with you, it feels like I've misplaced a limb. It feels *bad*, Claire."

"I know, Gerard," I replied, desperately trying to ignore the tremor of doom that was building up inside of me. "It's the same for me."

"Please don't let me break this," he begged, gray eyes locked on mine. "I can't lose you, Claire."

"You won't." Leaning in close, I touched my forehead to his and whispered, "You couldn't lose me if you tried, Gerard Gibson."

A tremor racked through his big body. "That's really good to hear, Claire Biggs."

"I'm so with you." I pressed a kiss to the corner of his mouth and then pulled back to take his measure. "Are you with me?"

"Yeah," he replied gruffly, gray eyes locked on mine. "I'm with you."

"Don't go again, okay?" I kissed his cheek and reveled in the feel of his arm tightening around me. "Don't leave me."

"I won't," came his quiet reply.

"I'm serious." I knotted my fingers in the front of his T-shirt and released a shaky breath. "I need you to stay."

"And I need to stay," he agreed, pushing me deeper into the mattress. "So, don't stop needing me."

"Never," I vowed. "You're my best friend."

"I know."

I rolled my eyes. "You're supposed to say it back."

He smirked. "But what about Cap?"

Snatching up his hand, I placed it on my chest and said, "Does Cap let you touch his boobs?"

"Okay." Nodding vigorously, he pressed a kiss to my neck. "You're my number one best friend."

I closed my eyes and smiled. "That's better."

51

You Missed the Clown

CLAIRE

"What the hell, guys?" Shannon exclaimed when we barreled into the kitchen of the manor, laden down with presents, plastered into PVC leather, and about three hours late. "You missed the entire party. We cut the cake hours ago."

Yeah, we had missed the party, and I felt terrible about it, but the memory of Gerard's epic neck-kisses took the sting out of it. I had no clue where we stood with each other. Clearly, I'd never racked up a three-hour make-out session with a boy before, but he was acting friendly enough and hadn't slammed the brakes on his offerings of affection, so I could only hope that we were on the right path.

The boyfriend and girlfriend kind of path?

Maybe?

Hopefully?

Aw, crackers.

"I am so sorry, chickie!" Dumping an armful of presents on the table, I made a beeline for the miniature version of Joey. "Hi, Sean." Crouching down in front of the boy dressed in an expensive-looking rabbit costume, I readjusted the adorable floppy ears and smiled. "Happy fourth birthday, handsome."

He smiled up at me and I swear I had never seen a cuter bunny in my life. "You know what, pretty boy," I cooed, poking the tip of his cute button nose. "I think you might be even cuter than my kittens."

"You missed the clown."

"No, she didn't," Tadhg chimed in from his perch on the island. "She brought him with her."

"*She brought him with her,*" Gerard mimicked with a glare. "Less of the lip."

"Oh my god, Shan!" Springing to my feet, I took in the sight of my bestie's costume and whistled out an impressed breath. Dressed in a long, floating white dress with angel wings attached, she looked every inch Claire Danes's Juliet. "You look so beautiful."

"And you look so stupid," Gerard laughed, eyeing Johnny who had strolled into the kitchen, looking less than impressed in the silver armor costume that Leo's movie version of Romeo had donned.

"Says the fella sweating his bollocks off in cheap-ass leather."

"Whatever, lad." Unaffected, Gerard continued to grin at his bestie. "At the end of my movie, I drive off in a flying car. You drink poison and die." Shrugging, he added, "There's a clear winner here."

"Yeah," Tadhg interrupted. "And that's me." He gestured to his T-shirt and sweatpants before returning his disgusted gaze on Johnny and Gerard. "You both look like tools."

Johnny smirked. "I'll be sure to remind you of that in a couple of years."

"Yeah," Gerard huffed. "When your girl comes to you with matching Halloween costumes and puppy eyes."

Tadhg didn't respond to their retorts because he was too busy gaping at the boy who had just appeared in the kitchen doorway. "What did they *do* to you?"

"Don't fucking start, kid," the Joker—I mean Joey—warned when he marched into the kitchen, looking like the sexiest baddie I'd ever seen. "Just get your bags and let's get this over with." He pushed his temporarily dyed neon-green hair out of his eyes before lifting Sean into his arms. "I dropped Aoife and AJ over to her parents' place, and I told her I'd be back in an hour to take her to this stupid fucking party, so let's get this trick-or-treating bullshit done nice and snappy."

"You think I'm going trick-or-treating with you looking like *that*?" Tadhg gaped at him in horror. "Fuck no, I would rather shit in my hands and clap."

"Tadhg!" Shannon scolded. "Language."

"Besides, I'm not going this year," Mr. Attitude explained, ignoring his sister. "I'm too old for that shit."

"You heard Shan. Mind your language, kid," Joey barked in a far more authoritarian tone than their sister had used, and like a good little pup, Tadhg bowed down to the alpha of their family pack.

Oh wow.

Maybe, Shannon wasn't the lucky one.

Maybe Aoife was.

"Ah, would you look at all of them," Edel gushed, appearing from another doorway with Shannon's oldest brother in tow. "Aren't they only gorgeous, Darren?"

"You all look brilliant," Darren offered with a smile. Turning to his brother, he added, "Looking slick, Joe."

His compliment was met with stony silence from Joey, who completely ignored him.

Awkward.

Sighing heavily, Darren turned to his sister. "You look beautiful, Shan."

"Thanks, Dar," she replied, offering him a small smile. "Are you doing anything for the night?"

"Nah, I'll hang here with the boys," he replied.

Don't do it, Gerard mouthed from behind them, clearly knowing what I was about to say before I said.

"You can come to the party," I blurted out and then laughed nervously when I was greeted with horrified looks from Johnny and Joey. Meanwhile, Gerard face-planted his hand. *Oops.* "I mean, it's totally cool if you want to swing by for a boogie." *A boogie? What was I, forty? Jesus.*

Thankfully, Ollie decided to save me by trotting into the kitchen with his sexy saint of a foster father in tow.

"Wow, Ols," I grinned. "Fancy."

"I'm a barrister," he explained, dressed in a designer suit, with sunglasses perched on his nose. He even had his hair slicked back like one of those corporate lawyers in the movies. "Like my dad."

The entire room went silent, and I held my breath, not having one single iota of a clue what to say in response to his innocent comment.

Was it good?

Was it bad?

I had no clue.

All I could do in this moment was eyeball Gerard, who was eyeballing me right back.

"Okay," Edel broke the silence by saying. "Everybody, stand in together for a photo." Her voice was thick with emotion, but she masked it well with an enthusiastic tone of voice and an even bigger smile. "And give me your best smiles. You too, Darren, love. I want this one for the wall."

52

Double Bubble, Toil and Trouble

GIBSIE

THE HALLOWEEN/EIGHTEENTH BIRTHDAY PARTY SINEAD BIGGS THREW FOR HER SON turned out to be a roaring success. More people than I knew the names of were crammed into their three-story house, while the DJ she hired played a mixture of modern jams and Halloween classics. The drink was flying, the craic was ninety, and I was freaking the hell out.

Clammed up tighter than a duck's ass with tension, I followed Claire around the party like she had an invisible collar and lead attached to my neck.

I didn't know what else to do.

My mind was in a heap after our kiss, and while Claire found it effortless to socialize, mingle, and entertain the masses, I had been given no such instruction manual.

Did I hold her hand? Did I not?

Did I run for my life before I could fuck up our friendship? Or was it too late for running, and if so, should I apologize?

I honestly had no idea.

All I knew in this moment was that if the Viper didn't stop throwing shade at me, I was going to lose my mind. Already, Lizzie had tossed half a dozen snippy comments, both directed at me *and* at my expense, and I was running low on patience.

"Ignore her," Johnny instructed a little while later when he joined me outside. "She's looking for a reaction, lad. Keep on *not* giving her one."

"I'm trying," I bit out, taking a deep drag of the cigarette I'd bummed from Joey. Unlike him, I was more of a social smoker and only smoked OPs—a.k.a. other people's. "But she's everywhere I turn."

The words were no sooner out of my mouth than Lizzie stepped into the back garden. The minute her eyes landed on me, she released a furious growl. "Why do you always have to be everywhere I go?"

"I could say the same about you," I snapped back, bristling.

Johnny placed a steadying hand on my shoulder. "You're good, Gibs."

No, I wasn't. I wasn't *good* at all, and this girl only made my life a million times more miserable. Still, I offered my best friend a clipped nod and forced myself to comply and ignore her.

"He *sure* is good," Lizzie sniped. "A good-for-nothing traitor bastard!"

"Back off," Johnny warned, quickly cutting her off. "I get that you're one of Shannon's best friends, and I'm trying to respect that relationship, really I am, but don't walk over a line here, because he's my best friend and I won't hesitate to take his side."

Lizzie continued to glare at us for a long beat before turning around and stalking back into the house.

"You'd really take my side?" I asked, ignoring the sound of the door slamming.

"I'm already on your side, Gibs."

Well, shit.

"You know, you're like the brother I never had."

"Don't get messy on me, Gibs." He chuckled. "You haven't had that much to drink, lad."

"Yet," I corrected with a smile. "I'm so fucking glad your grandmother died when she did."

"Wow, thanks, Gibs."

"Because you're here," I tried to explain. "Fuck knows where I'd be if you hadn't moved to Ballylaggin."

Several hours later, as I threw shapes around the Biggses' jam-packed kitchen to the *Ghostbusters* anthem, I concluded that Johnny might be on to something when he labeled me a messy drunk. I certainly felt like a mess right about now.

"Nah," I slurred, toasting myself before necking my seventh ghost-shaped, vodka-jelly shot. "Fuck 'em all."

"Steady up on the shots, pet," Mammy Number 2 instructed, and then she did the unthinkable and took the tray out of my hand. "That's a good boy."

"Sinead!" I wailed, eyeing the tray longingly. "I helped make those."

"Yes, you did, Gibs," she agreed, squeezing my cheek with affection. "And now you can let the others help you drink them."

"Fine." Huffing out a breath, I slumped against the island and sulked. "Ruin my life, why don't ya?"

"Why don't you go and see what Claire is doing instead of standing around on your own all night, hmm?" Leaning a hip against the island, she smiled up at me. "I'm sure she'd love to have a dance with you."

"While I would love to dance with your daughter, it wouldn't be a wise move."

"Oh?" She smirked. "And why not?"

"Because I might be tempted to do more than just dance with her," I replied in a solemn tone. "I might be lured into performing the physical act of love."

"You do realize it's me you're talking to, don't you, Gibs?" Frowning, Claire's mam reached up and felt my brow. "As in Claire's mother."

"Oh yes." I nodded solemnly. "I'd know your tits anywhere. Thank you, by the way. For making Claire. You did a top-notch job on that one." Frowning I added, "The older one could do with a bit of work, but the younger one is perfect."

"Oh dear." Sinead sighed wearily. "I think it's time someone's mother comes to collect him."

"I think you might be right." Sighing dramatically, I swiped another shot from the confiscated tray and tossed it back. "Meanwhile, until she arrives, I must resume my dancing a safe distance from your daughter's perfect tits. Thanks for those, too, by the way."

53

Pumpkins and Punch-Ups

CLAIRE

Hugh and Patrick were drinking, Pierce and Lizzie were fighting, Katie and Aoife were dancing, Johnny and Shannon were sucking face, and Joey was out front trying to sober Gerard up, which left me in prime position for the title hostess with the mostest.

Honestly, I was the only one of my friends helping by handing out drinks and cleaning up rubbish. I knew I didn't have to, but I felt bad for Mam, who had put on such an impressive spread.

Dad had made a rare appearance at the party tonight and had miraculously decided to stay. I wasn't sure who was more surprised by this—Mam, me, or Hugh—because it certainly wasn't a common occurrence. I suppose it wasn't every day your firstborn came of age. I was glad for Mam that Dad had decided to make an effort. He even shaved, something he was known to go months without doing. They were sitting out back, sharing a bottle of wine, hence my stepping up to host in her stead.

The DJ was doing such a good job entertaining the guests by blasting Kaiser Chiefs' "I Predict A Riot" that I honestly didn't hear the ruckus coming from the front hall. It was the guests at the party, who started dropping like flies from my line of sight, that alerted me to trouble. The sound of something crashing against the wall, loud enough to be heard over the music, had me dropping my bin bag and bolting into the front hall.

Pushing through the huge crowd that had formed in the hallway, I battled my way to the front door, only to bite back a groan in dismay when my eyes took in the carnage unfolding in my driveway.

Harley Quinn had the Joker pinned to the side of my brother's parked car to stop him from fighting, while Juliet wept into her hands and Romeo tried to console her. On the other side of my brother's car, Gomez Addams was dipping Vivian Ward, having valiantly shielded her from a rogue beer bottle, while Edward Lewis straddled a dark-cloaked stranger on the front lawn. To top it all off, Morticia Addams had decided this was her ample opportunity to throttle Danny Zuko, while Uncle Fester was looking on gormlessly.

"Omigod, guys!" I shouted, running headfirst into the madness, because, of course, every alcohol-induced uprising needed a referee in the form of Sandra Dee.

It would have been hilarious if these people weren't *my* people.

"Who the fuck do you think you are coming on my property?" my brother was roaring, and the homicidal tone in his voice had me veering toward him. *Biggest problem first.*

"The Gardaí are on the way," Mr. Murphy from two doors down shouted. "They'll bring the paddy wagon and sort ye little toe rags out."

"Good," Hugh roared, fists still flying as he wrestled with the stranger on our lawn. "Tell them to bring more transport. Because if they put me in the same paddy wagon as a rapist, I'll kill him!"

Rapist?

Oh no.

Oh no, no, no, no...

"Hugh!" Sadhbh Allen came barreling across the street with Keith in tow. "Get off him this instant!"

"Hugh, no!" Katie cried out, covering her face.

"Don't touch him." Lizzie was quick to jump to my brother's defense when Keith caught ahold of Hugh and dragged him off his son. *Too quick.* "Get your fucking hands off him!" Not hesitating for one moment, she threw herself at Gerard's stepfather, clawing and scratching and slapping at every exposed piece of flesh she could reach. "Let him go!"

Now that he was free and back on his feet, Mark charged my brother, knocking all three of them onto the driveway, Lizzie included.

The minute Mark landed on Lizzie, she started to scream, and it was the worst, scariest, most feral noise I'd ever heard.

"Get the fuck off her," Gerard roared, momentarily calling a truce with his longtime nemesis as he rushed to her aid.

Refusing the hand Gerard had extended to her, Lizzie scrambled out from beneath the men on her hands and knees, shaking and crying uncontrollably.

"Shh, Liz," Shannon tried to console as she dropped to her knees and threw her arms around our friend. "Shh, Liz, just breathe, okay? It's okay. You're right here with me."

"Jesus Christ." Quickly unbuttoning his jacket, Patrick moved for the girls, not stopping until he was crouched down in front of them with his jacket draped over Lizzie's trembling shoulders.

"See what you did?" Hugh roared, drawing my attention back to where Johnny was standing firmly between both parties, with Mark and Keith on one side, and my brother on the other. Standing off to the side, with her hand covering her mouth, was Sadhbh, while Gerard was nowhere to be found.

"What the hell is going on out here?" Mam and Dad both demanded, arriving on the scene just as I was about to go look for him.

"Oh, thank god." Sadhbh sounded like she was close to tears when she saw my mother. "Do something, Sinead, will you?"

Mam, the levelheaded woman that she was, took in the scene around her before honing in on her co-culprit son. "Get into the house, Hugh," she ordered in a tone that left no room for arguing. "Right now."

"But..."

"You heard your mother!" That was Dad, and holy crap did he sound mad.

Hugh ran a hand through his hair in clear frustration and opened his mouth to say something, before wisely snapping it shut. Chest heaving, he stormed past our parents and into the house without giving the Allen family a backwards glance.

Hugh was followed inside a few moments later by a skittish-looking Katie, and then Shannon and Johnny, who Mam had instructed to take Lizzie up to my room.

By the time Mam restored order, our guests had wisely returned inside before any police showed up, leaving only myself and Patrick outside with the grown-ups.

"What in the name of God happened?" Mam asked in a calm tone of voice. "One minute they were all joking and laughing, and the next they were tearing strips out of each other." Frowning, she added, "I know Hugh is no angel, but he's not one to fist fight."

"It's my fault," Sadhbh was quick to blurt out, pressing a hand to her chest, as tears trickled down her cheeks. "When you called to say Gerard was after drinking too much, I should have come and got him myself." Sniffling, she added, "I sent Keith instead."

"And he sent me," Mark growled, spitting out a mouthful of blood and then dabbing at his busted lip. "You're lucky I like you, Sinead," he continued. "Because I have a good mind to press charges."

My father opened his mouth to respond, but Mam placed a steadying hand on his arm, letting him know with that simple touch that she was well able to deal with this man. "I appreciate that, Mark," Mam said, using that superhuman willpower and professional politeness that all nurses seemed to possess. "And I can assure you that he won't be getting off lightly with this."

I was quite sure that my mother had treated some morally questionable patients in her time, and it had prepared her for handling scenarios like this one. *Like the scumbag standing in front of her.*

My parents didn't like Keith Allen, and I knew for a fact that Dad in particular loathed Mark, but they loved Sadhbh and adored Gerard.

When everything went to hell six years ago, Mam and Dad had made the joint decision to both stand by and support what was left of Joe Gibson's family. Especially Gerard, who was my father's godchild. They had taken a lot of stick for their decision, namely by the Young family, but they had held firm and remained a constant in Gerard's life.

Speaking of … "Where's Gerard?"

When none of the grown-ups answered me, clearly too busy kissing ass and calling truces, I looked to Patrick.

"He took off down the street earlier."

"He did?"

Aw, crackers.

"Come on." Sighing wearily, Patrick reached into his pocket and grabbed his keys. "I'm sober. I'll drive."

54

Drowning Sorrows and Memories

GIBSIE

Nᴜᴍʙ, I ꜱᴀᴛ ɪɴ ᴛʜᴇ ᴄᴏʀɴᴇʀ ᴏꜰ ᴛʜᴇ ʟᴏᴜɴɢᴇ ɪɴ Bɪᴅᴅɪᴇꜱ ʙᴀʀ, ᴡɪᴛʜ ᴀɴ ᴜɴᴛᴏᴜᴄʜᴇᴅ pint and a storm raging inside of me.

Ignoring the Halloween festivities happening around me, I drummed my fingers against the table and pondered my next move. Running the entire way into town wasn't exactly the most sensible thing I had ever done, but I'd needed to get out of there before I lost it. Before I said something I would undoubtedly regret. The words that threatened to come out of my mouth held heavier restitution than I could bear to pay back.

But I would be a liar if I said I wasn't exhausted from carrying the weight of my secrets. The weight of the blame. The truth was I wanted to tell someone. No, the truth was I wanted to tell *Claire*. But I couldn't seem to find a way to open the can of worms I'd spent so many years sealing.

Where the hell was I supposed to go now?

Not home, that's for sure, and I couldn't go to the Biggses' house. Not when I knew *she* would be there.

It was so fucking hard to hate her when Lizzie cried like that.

When she made those sounds.

Because I knew those sounds.

Those sounds haunted my nightmares.

Even in my drunken stupor, I knew that I would never make the walk to Johnny's place in one piece. If I hadn't left my keys at the house, I could've bunked down in the bakery for the night.

"What's up, buttercup?" a vaguely familiar voice asked. Moments later, a curvaceous woman dressed as Catwoman, leather mask and all, plopped down on the bench next to me. "You look like you're contemplating taking a bubble bath with vodka and a razor."

"Maybe I am."

"Aw, Gibs," she coaxed, nudging my arm with her elbow. "Surely things aren't that bad?"

Gibs?

So she knew me.

Trying my best to blink away my drunken stupor, I stared at the woman.

"I have to say, you make a sexy Zuko, but you'd make an even sexier Batman."

Okay, now I *was* sure I knew her. Her lips were big and pouty, and I had seen them form the perfect O on more than one occasion. "Dee?"

Her smile deepened. "You really didn't recognize me?"

"No," I slurred, shaking my head. "I really didn't."

"I guess that's a good thing for us, hmm?" She shifted closer and sat on my lap. "No one will know it's us."

"Us?" I blinked away the bleariness. "There is no us."

"We'll see," she purred. "So, why aren't you at the party?"

"Party?"

"Yeah, Hugh's party." She rested her hand on my thigh. "It's happening tonight, right?"

The fact that she knew so much about my social life should have troubled me. Instead, it went clean over my head because I was too fucking wasted to give it a second thought.

When her hand moved too far north for my liking, I shook my head in protest. "Would you mind taking your hand off her dick, please?"

"Her dick?" Dee blinked in confusion. "Don't you mean your dick?" She full on palmed me before leaning in close and purring, "It doesn't feel like you want me to take my hand off."

"No, I meant *her* dick," I clarified, brushing her hand off my crotch and shifting sideways so that her ass was back on the bench and *not* on my lap.

"Her?"

"Claire," I slurred before pointing to my dick. "And don't get flattered by that reckless bastard because he's as blind as a bat and can't see whose hand is touching him." I slapped a hand against my chest before saying, "But he can."

"So, that's it?" Her tone switched from flirtatious to accusatory in an instant. "You're just saying no?"

"Yes, Dee, that's exactly what I'm saying." Reaching for my pint, I slid it toward her. "But here's a pint for your troubles."

"Gerard!" Claire whisper-hissed in the early hours of the morning when I collapsed in a heap on her bed, after tripping over several sleeping kittens littered around her bedroom floor. "You're back."

"I'm back," I confirmed, whipping off my T-shirt and tossing it over the side of the bed.

"Where'd you go?"

"For a walk."

"Where?" she demanded, sitting up. "Patrick and I looked everywhere for you."

"I'm back now."

"But where did you go?"

"Biddies."

"Are you okay?"

"Never better," I muttered as I wrestled myself out of my pants. "Fuck, these are like another layer of skin."

"Gerard." Her tone was laced with pain. "I was really worried."

Aw, shit.

Kicking my leather pants off, I turned to face her. "I'm sorry, Claire-Bear." Reaching up, I pushed a clump of wild curls off her face. "I didn't mean to do that."

"It's okay." She snatched my hand up in both of hers and held it to her chest. "Just don't ever do that again?"

I nodded slowly. "I won't."

"Good." Perched on her knees, she exhaled a shaky breath and sagged against me. "Because I really don't think my heart can take it."

"Yeah." The moment her forehead touched mine, my heart gunned in my chest, hammering so hard and violently that I honestly thought it might explode. "I know the feeling."

"Claire."

"Hmm?"

"Look at me."

When she did, I felt blindsided by the feelings that her brown eyes evoked from me. "Hi."

"Hi." Reaching up, I trailed my thumb over her bottom lip before swapping it for my mouth.

Her lips were soft, warm, and welcome and soothed something deep inside of me. Something that no amount of time or therapy could fix or reach.

Rolling onto her back, she took me with her, fingernails digging into the skin covering my biceps as I kissed her back with everything I had inside of me to give.

"I want you," she breathed against my lips as she let her legs fall open for me to settle between them. "All of you."

"What do you mean?"

"I want *your* body inside *my* body."

Oh Christ.

For the first time in my life, I wanted that too, and the knowledge *terrified* me. "Not tonight," I forced myself to say, lips moving to the curve of her jaw.

"Please," she urged, rocking her body against mine. "Please, Gerard."

"Not tonight," I repeated in a torn voice. "Not that, at least."

"No?"

I shook my head. "No."

"Oh."

She sounded so sad that I found myself seriously considering my sanity. "I can still make you feel good." I kissed a slow pattern down her body, not stopping until my head was between her legs. "If that's what you want?"

"Definitely." She nodded eagerly before flopping back on the pillows. "That's definitely what I want, Gerard Gibson."

55

Back to Tommen

CLAIRE

By the time school rolled around on Monday, I was so deep in my feels that I didn't think there was any saving me. Happy, wondrous, epic, first love feels that had consumed me to the point where I honestly felt like I was floating on air.

Sure, Hugh's party had imploded on Saturday night, and everyone had gotten in a huge fight, but I'd woken up in Gerard's arms yesterday morning and we had spent the entire day together. I didn't care that a large portion of that time had been spent cleaning up after the party and receiving lectures from our mothers. He'd been by my side the entire time and that was all I ever wanted.

Across the table, though, something was very off with my brother. Katie had her hand entwined with his on top of the lunch table, but while she was giggling at something Patrick and Gerard had said, my brother looked like he wanted to face-plant on the table.

Seriously, with his elbow resting on the table, Hugh slumped forward and stared down at his untouched lunch. I knew it couldn't have anything to do with being told off for fighting with Mark because he was fine yesterday. This sudden dip in mood was both new and concerning.

"Did you get bad news?" I asked, reaching across the table to tug on his sleeve.

"Huh?" Blinking, he looked up at me, wide-eyed and startled. "What?"

His eyes were bloodshot, with dark circles underneath his otherwise paler-than-usual face.

Aw, crackers.

Something was really wrong.

"Is it Aunty Sarah? Did Mam text you?" Panic gnawed at my gut. Our maternal aunt had a hospital appointment today. She was in remission from breast cancer. Our mother was taking her for her three-month checkup. I suddenly had the worst feeling niggling at me. "Did she get bad news at the hospital?"

"Sarah's grand," he muttered, resuming his post of slumping over the lunch table with his head in his hand. "Mam texted this morning. She's still in the clear."

Relief flooded me. "Then what's wrong?"

"He's been like this all day," Katie explained in a concerned tone, flicking her attention back to my brother.

"I'm grand," Hugh said quietly. "Just tired."

"Are you sure?" Reaching over with her free hand, she pressed the back of her hand to his forehead. "God, Hugh, you're spiking a temperature."

"Are ya sick, lad?" That was Johnny, who had turned his attention to his friend.

"Jesus, he is, Cap," Gerard added, straining out of his seat to catch ahold of my brother's shirt collar and yank him across the table. "He's burning the fuck up."

"You should go to the office," Patrick added, all eyes on Hugh now. "There's a bad dose going around the place."

"He said he's fine," Lizzie muttered from her perch beside me. "So drop it."

"I can drive you home." Pushing his chair back, Johnny stood up and reached for his keys. "Do you want to come for the spin, Shan?"

"I'm *grand*, lads," my brother bit out, breathing hard and fast now as he pulled at the tie around his neck and settled back down on his seat. "I'm just *tired*."

"You're clearly not," Katie pushed, fawning at him like he was a little child.

"You're right." Clearly unhappy with the attention he was receiving, Hugh reached up and gently removed her hand from his face before rising from the table. "I need to go home." Turning to Johnny, he added, "I have the car, Cap. I'll drive myself, but thanks."

"You sure, lad?"

"Yeah, I just need to lie down."

"Do you want me to come with you?" Katie asked, moving to follow after him.

"No, you should probably stay away from me," Hugh strangled out, offering her a half-hearted smile that didn't meet his eyes. "I could be contagious." When Hugh hurried out of the lunch hall, Katie still chose to rush after him.

"What a big baby," Gerard offered up. "Jesus, talk about milking the situation. Having everyone worrying about him."

"Why don't you do the world a favor and lose your voice, Thor," Lizzie spat out, turning to glare at him. "I swear if the world ended tomorrow, you would be the cockroach still slithering around the place."

"Don't you start with me, witch," Gerard warned, holding a hand up to warn her off. "We both agreed to a treaty, remember?" That was true. Johnny had laid down the law in the common room this morning. The rules were made very clear to both of them. "If we can't be civil, we stay silent. So, stay the fuck silent."

"Come on, guys." Shannon sighed. "Let's not do this today, huh?"

"Do what?" Lizzie clapped back. "Be irritated by his presence because I'm sorry,

Shan, but no can do. The fact that he's above ground breathing is enough to put me in a bad mood."

"Fuck you," Gerard growled, shoving his chair back and standing up.

"What's wrong, Thor?" Lizzie taunted. "You're always full of comebacks."

"Trust me, Liz, you don't want my comeback," he bit out, before stalking out of the lunch hall.

"Did you have to?" I demanded, dropping my head in my hands. "You were having a good morning." That was true. Lizzie had surprising pep in her step when she showed up at school this morning.

"Yeah," she wholeheartedly agreed. "Until he showed up."

"Lizzie," I growled in warning. "You have to drop this."

"I will," she assured me, leaning back to fold her arms across her chest. "When I'm dead."

"Yeah, I'm not listening to this shite," Johnny declared, rising to his feet. "I'll see ya later, Shan," he added, dropping another epic hair kiss to the top of her head before heading off in the direction of his friend.

"You know why he left, don't you?" I snapped. "Because if he didn't, he would have lost it with you."

"You think I care what Captain Fantastic thinks?"

"*I* care what Johnny thinks," Shannon offered calmly. "And you care what I think, so just sit with that for a moment before you snap back, Liz."

To my surprise, she did just that.

"So, that was one hell of a party, huh?" I tossed out, trying to calm the waters once more. "We're really lucky the neighbors didn't actually call the Gardaí."

"Pity they…" Stopping short, Lizzie calmly set her apple onto the table. "You know what?" She pushed back her chair and rose. "I think I'm going to get some fresh air."

"Good," Shannon praised, hurrying after her. "Fresh air works, too."

"What's happening to this gang?" I exclaimed when I was left alone at the lunch table with only Patrick for company. "I swear everybody is getting weirder by the day."

"Honestly, who even knows anymore." Shrugging his shoulders, Patrick unwrapped the tinfoil containing his sandwich and then proceeded to dump the entire filling out before taking a tiny bite of the crust.

"You don't like your sandwich?" I asked, interest piqued.

"I don't eat meat," came his quiet reply.

"You don't?" My eyes widened. "Since when?"

"Since I was five and had to help my father make black pudding," he replied with a grimace. "Trust me, it's a process you don't want to know the inner details of."

"Ew."

"Hmm," he agreed, using a plastic fork to slide everything off his bread, including the butter. "Not the normal reaction of a farmer's son, I can assure you." He grimaced again before gesturing to the leftover filling on the tinfoil. "Hence my mother's persistent efforts to get me to align with normal regulations."

"Oh well, who wants to be normal anyway?" I offered, giving him my warmest smile. "Besides, I have it on good authority that weird is a side effect of epic."

He arched a dark brow. "I thought the phrase was awesome."

"Meh," I dismissed, cracking open my can of Fanta and pushing it toward him. "Sip?"

"Nah, I'm good, Baby Biggs." He chuckled, shaking his head. "So, how's the great romance coming along?"

My face flamed with heat. "Gerard told you?"

"Didn't have to," Patrick replied. "Contrary to his actions and lack of impulse control, there's only ever been you for him."

My heart warmed at his words. "Really?"

"Really."

"Hey, thanks, Patrick."

"For what?"

"The clarity."

"Anytime."

"Speaking about great romances." Waggling my brows, I leaned in close. "I heard a juicy rumor around school about you."

His brows shot up. "You did, huh?"

"Uh-huh." I grinned. "Apparently you've been getting down and dirty with one of Aoife's friends."

"Is that so?"

"Yup."

"Hmm." Neither confirming or denying, he tore another piece of bread from his sandwich and popped it into his mouth.

Whoa, he would make a fabulous card player.

"Of course, that's if you don't have another girl from your long list of admirers lined up."

Now he did raise a brow.

"Patrick, come on." I laughed. "Don't look surprised. You're a total babe."

Another cynical brow raise.

"Most of the girls in sixth year have the hots for you."

"Uh-huh."

"Don't you care that girls are practically brawling in bathrooms over you?"

"I'm entirely uninterested in participating in drama, Claire. If that means I'm a loner or frigid, then I'll happily shoulder the label. They can think what they want about me. I'm not pushed."

"Wow," I mused. "How does it feel to be so secure in yourself?"

"Why don't you look in the mirror and ask the girl staring back at you," he shot back with a smirk. "Because from where I'm sitting, she's got a tight fist hold of her worth."

"Hmm." I smiled back at him, thoroughly enjoying this conversation and listening to his input on the world. "You're good with words," I offered. "When you use them."

"I use them," he replied. "Not everyone listens."

"Ooh, deep… Okay, pee break!" Pushing my chair back, I sprang up and moved for the door. "I'll be right back."

"Take your time." He laughed after me. "And too much information."

Smiling to myself, I skipped down the corridor in the direction of the girls' bathroom, stopping to call out, "Get a room," to the ridiculously attractive couple eating the faces off each other in the stairwell on my way.

"Mind your business," Aoife called back, not bothering to release her hold on Joey. "As you were, Stud."

Aw…I hope they had condoms in the annex.

Pushing the bathroom door inward, I stepped inside and then, because I was a sucker for a good echo, I tap-danced across the floor, enjoying the clickety noise the heels of my shoes made against the tiles.

"Hey, girls," I acknowledged, offering Helen and Shelly a wave before disappearing inside one of the cubicles to take care of business.

When I reappeared a few minutes later, they were both still there, leaning against the sinks with one of their camera phones in hand.

"What's up?" I asked, joining them at the sinks to wash my hands.

"Do you want to ask her?"

"Oh my god, hells, no! I'm not asking her."

"Well, one of us has to."

"What's up, girls?" I smiled. "Ask me what?"

Stepping behind Helen, Shelley pushed her forward and said, "Helen wants to know if it's true about you and Gibsie."

"What about us?"

"Are you with him?"

Excitement bubbled inside of me because I had waited sixteen long years to finally answer this question. "Yes." Beaming, I clutched my chest and feign swooned. "I am absolutely with him."

Instead of being thrilled like I had expected my classmates since first year to be for their fellow peer, they looked at each other with wide eyes.

"Why?" Instantly suspicious, I folded my arms across my chest. "What did you guys hear?"

"It's not what we heard," Shelley replied nervously. "It's what we saw."

"Saw?" I stared blankly. "I'm not following you."

"Show her, Helen."

"Show me what?" I demanded just as a camera phone was thrust in my face. "What is this?" I snapped, attention flicking between them. "What am I looking..." My words broke off and my breath hitched in my throat when I glanced at the screen of the phone.

The image was a grainy one, but it was clear enough to show Gerard sitting in the corner of Biddies bar in a compromising position with a girl dressed as Catwoman.

My heart stopped dead in my chest for a solid three seconds before slamming back to life with a vengeance. "Where did you get this?"

"We took it," Shelly admitted.

"When?"

"Halloween night."

Oh god.

Oh god.

Pain.

It was taking me over.

"It could be totally innocent," Helen hurried to say. "I mean, it was almost closing time, and we only stopped into Biddies for a couple of drinks, but he came in and sat in the corner by himself."

"That's when she showed up."

"She was clearly more into him than he was her."

"But they were still together when we left."

56

Graveside Visits

GIBSIE

WITH MY ARMS CLASPED LOOSELY AROUND MY KNEES, I SAT FACING THE HEADSTONE that read **Gibson** in a large, bold font.

The damp grass was seeping into my school trousers, and a light drizzle of rain had set in, but I didn't move a muscle. Instead, I continued to stare at their headstone, with her letter fisted in my hand and my heart on my sleeve.

"Dad, if you're listening, I could really use your help," I said, hoping that the wind could somehow get my message to the one person I needed to reach most in the universe. If that's even where he existed now. Who the fuck knew for sure?

"Beth, this is guy talk, so close your ears," I warned as I plucked at a blade of grass. "So, I finally kissed Claire. And she kissed me back, so I guess that means the joke's on you and Pete for always teasing Mam and Sinead about us ending up together." I smiled sadly at the memory. "Because I want to end up with her, Dad." I sighed heavily. "I really love her, Dad, and I want to tell her, but I'm so fucking scared of her walking away from me." I hung my head in shame. "I feel like I'm wrong on the inside." A shudder racked through me. "Like I'm *infected*."

Wishing like hell I had a cartoon baboon that could take me to the river to speak to my father one more time, I sniffed my emotions back and wiped a tear from my cheek. "I don't want to live like this anymore, Dad."

Because I was a wreck.

I couldn't get my body, heart, or mind to comply and work together. The three most dominant parts of me were in raging wars against each other, all pulling me in three different directions.

Still, no matter the path I took, whether it was my body, heart, or mind in the driving seat, I always ended up at her door.

That *had* to mean something.

It had to be a sign.

"Am I going to be okay, Dad?" I asked, placing my palm on the stones covering his grave. "Am I ever going to get over it?"

"Sorry, I didn't mean to interrupt," a male voice came from behind me, and I craned my neck back to see Darren Lynch, armed with a bouquet of flowers.

"Aww." I shoved my letter back into my pocket and feigned a swoon. "How did you know daisies are my favorite?"

"Always with the wisecracks."

"We'll be dead for long enough," I replied, gesturing around us. "Might as well crack the jokes while we're still aboveground."

"That's one way to look at it," Darren agreed with a reluctant smile.

"So, what are you doing on my turf, Darren Lynch," I mused, climbing to my feet. "Your mam's buried on the other side of the graveyard."

"Actually, I was bringing these to Caoimhe Young," he explained, waving the bouquet around. "I always bring her a bunch when I'm visiting my mam." He studied me for a brief moment before adding, "She was your babysitter, wasn't she?"

"So?" I shrugged. "She was everyone's babysitter."

"Do you want to come with me to visit her?"

I narrowed my eyes. "Why?"

"Because it's only half past two in the afternoon and you're sitting in a graveyard. Which means one of two things. Either you bunked off school on a whim and didn't think through where you would go, or you have a strange and morbid fascination with graveyards." He shrugged. "Either way, you clearly have some time on your hands, so why not?"

Well, he had me there.

"It would sound a lot better if it was the second thing," I decided to say as I fell into step beside him. "But I forgot my mam was at home."

"Rookie mistake." He chuckled.

"Says the fella who never skipped a day of school in his life," I shot back with a laugh. "I have it on good authority that you were a fair bit of a swat in your younger days, Darren Lynch."

"Hmm," he mused, and then stopped a few headstones up. "This is hers."

I didn't want to look at it, but I forced myself to read the name **Young** in a similar bold font to one on my family's plot.

Anxiety thrummed inside of me, making me feel faint because I shouldn't have come over here. I wanted to run, to hide, to shed my skin like a reptile and escape the evidence of the worst day of my life.

Because my worst day was her last day.

"She was a good friend," Darren said, placing the flowers on Caoimhe's grave. "She was an all-round good person, period."

"Yeah."

"You don't agree?"

I momentarily panicked when Darren picked up on my reservation. "I didn't say that."

"It's not about what you said," he replied. "It's about what you didn't say."

For a moment, I held my breath and wondered if he knew. But when he said, "The way she died hurt the people she loved but, in the moment, she couldn't see a way past her pain."

"So, you believe her?" I trailed my tongue over my bottom lip, feeling nervous. "You believe he did that to her?"

"I believe something happened," he replied carefully. "And I believe he's responsible for that something."

"You got over it when it happened to you," I blurted out, balling my hands into fists at my sides to hide my tremors. "If you could go back in time and Caoimhe was standing here in front of you, what would you say? What advice would you give her?"

"If Caoimhe was here, I would tell her that what happened to her doesn't define her." Darren looked me dead in the eyes when he said, "It defines him. He's the monster in the story. The shame is on *his* doorstep." He reached up and stroked his jaw before saying, "And I would tell her that it's never too late to disclose." His eyes burned with sincerity. "Never."

"He wouldn't have gotten prison time even if she had stuck around to prosecute him," I heard myself whisper. "Everyone believed him."

"I didn't believe him."

"No?"

"No," Darren replied, shoving his hands into his coat pockets. "And from personal experience, I can honestly say that living with a secret like that eating away at your soul is a much worse fate than disclosing and having people not believe you." He sighed heavily before adding, "The right people will listen, and they'll believe."

"I'm his age now, Darren," I strangled out. "I'm almost the exact same age he was when he did that to *her* and I'm responsible for my actions. I know the difference between right and wrong, and I would never do that to anyone, so why the fuck would he?"

"Because he's evil, Gibs," he said gently. "Some people are just plain evil."

"What happened to you in that home," I choked out. "Do you think it has anything to do with you turning out—"

"You cannot be turned gay or decide to be gay, Gibsie. You are born gay," Darren cut me off and said, clearly having some psychic ability to read my mind. "Being raped by another man was not a deciding factor in my sexual preference, nor had it any dominion over my sexual orientation, because I was born this way."

"Oh."

"But it *can* cause to you to physically recoil and withdraw from intimate situations with a partner."

"Even women?"

"Trauma sees no genders," he explained calmly. "It's an instinctive thing."

"Like the back-of-your-mind kind of thing?"

"Exactly," he agreed. "It's your subconsciouses way of alerting your body to danger, even when you might not be in any."

"Okay." I nodded slowly, soaking in every word he was telling me. "Good to know."

"Can I give you my phone number?"

I stared blankly at him. "Lad, I'm flattered, but I like pussy."

Darren smirked. "Just take my number," he said, retrieving a business card from his coat pocket. "Call that number when you're ready."

"Wait!" I called after him, but he was already walking away. "When I'm ready for what?"

He didn't respond.

57

How Could You?

CLAIRE

"Stop it, Cherub." Crying hard into my pillow, I tried to ignore the paw that was prodding and swiping at my hair. "Please, I'm trying to wallow in peace here." Nope. She was relentless in her pursuit of my curls. "Your squeaky mouse is on the floor." I hiccupped out a sob. "Go play with that instead of my hair."

Cherub didn't go play with her squeaky mouse, but she did jump off my bed when my bedroom door flew inward. "I need to tell you something," Gerard declared in a nervous tone as he strode into my room with an envelope in his hand. "Actually, I need to show you something…"

"Don't bother," I choked out, planting my face back in my pillow. "I already heard *and* saw."

"What?"

I couldn't take it.

I honestly couldn't.

A sob tore from my throat.

"Claire?"

Followed by another and then another.

"Jesus, are you *crying*?"

My heart shattered into a million pieces all over again when he sat down on my bed and brushed my hair off my face.

"Baby, what's wrong?"

"How could you, Gerard!" I strangled out, crying so hard that my chest heaved violently. "How c-could y-you?"

"I would answer you if I knew what the question was," he replied, tone laced with panic. "What happened?"

"You happened, Gerard." Giving him my back, I rolled onto my side and clutched my pillow to my chest. "You ha-happened."

"Okay, you need to talk to me," he half demanded, half coaxed as he rubbed my arm affectionately. "Because I have no idea what's happening here, sweetheart."

Feeling bereft and lifeless, I somehow found the strength to reach under my pillows and retrieve my phone. "Check my message from Helen."

Taking my phone, he quickly unlocked it and set to work on the task I had given him. I knew the moment he saw the picture because I felt his body tense up beside me.

"Please d-don't say it's n-not what it l-looks like," I strangled out, through heaving sobs. "Because she's sitting on your l-lap and has her h-hand on your w-willy. You had the n-nerve to crawl into m-my bed afterwards."

"Claire, it's not what it looks like." His voice was laced with a pained kind of urgency. "I swear it's not."

"I told you n-not to s-ay it."

"I can't not say it, Claire, because it's the truth," he tried to argue. "I swear to Christ, okay?" Pulling myself into a sitting position, I watched as he paced my room. "You have to believe me."

"I don't believe you!" I cried out hoarsely.

Gerard reared back like my words had physically struck him. "You have to believe me," he choked out. "*You*, Claire. *You* have to believe me."

I choked out another pained sob and covered my face with my hands.

"No, no, no, don't do this." Closing the space between us, he knelt on the floor next to my bed and took my hands in his. "I didn't do it, Claire, okay?" Reaching up with one hand, he wiped at my tears, but they kept on coming. "I didn't touch her."

"I want to b-believe you."

"Then believe me," he begged, wiping more of my tears away. "Because I would never do that to you."

"You s-swear?" Desperately trying to get a handle on my breathing, I pressed a hand to my chest and tried to calm the hysteria rising inside of me. "You p-promise you've n-never been with h-her?"

Nodding eagerly, he opened his mouth to speak but then hesitated. "I can promise you that I wasn't with her that night," he finally said.

My heart shattered once more. "Who is s-she?"

He hung his head but didn't respond.

"Who is s-she, Gerard?" I sniffled. "Catwoman! Who is s-she?"

Silence.

"I didn't cheat on you."

"Who is s-she?"

"Claire, it meant nothing, I promise."

"Who is s-she, Gerard!"

"I can't tell you."

"Why not?"

"Because I just can't, okay?"

"She obviously m-means something to y-you if you're refusing to t-tell me her n-name."

"She means *nothing* to me. Okay, Claire? Not a damn thing. You're the only girl who's ever meant anything to me."

"Then why would you d-do it?" I begged. "Why would you b-be with other g-girls?"

"I haven't."

"You h-have in the p-past."

"I don't know." He released a pained groan and dropped his head. "I don't know what the fuck is wrong with me."

"This c-can't go on."

"What can't?"

"Us."

"Us?" His eyes were wild with panic. "What do you mean, we can't go on?"

"I can't d-do this anymore."

"Claire, stop. Please. I won't look at her again. I swear." He closed the space between us and tried to pull me in for a hug. I resisted because I knew if I didn't it would be the end of me. I was losing myself in this boy deeper by the day, and if I didn't push the brakes now that there were huge red flags blowing around, then I was screwed. Because love was dangerous. It was wild. It was reckless with the human heart, and I was determined to protect myself from it. "Please don't do this. You're my best friend. I need you."

"I'm not being your fallback anymore."

"You have *never* been my fallback anything."

"Yeah, I have, and I'm done with it!"

"Claire."

"Just go, Gerard!"

"I'm so sad."

"Don't be. You had a narrow escape."

"Liz!"

"What? It's true. She did."

"It'll be okay, Claire," Shannon coaxed, smoothing a hand over my curls when she and Lizzie came over later that evening to cheer me up. Well, Shannon came over to cheer me up. Lizzie came over to give me the I-told-you-so lecture. "You two will figure it out."

"They better not," Lizzie growled, leaning back on my desk chair. "He's a dog."

"Liz!"

"What?" She shrugged unapologetically. "It's true."

"Hey, how's Hugh doing?" Shannon asked then. "Is he feeling better?"

"He's been locked away in his room all day."

"Did he say what's wrong?" Lizzie asked.

"Nope," I replied. "He's really out of it, though, so it must be pretty serious. I think Mam's making an appointment for him at the doctor for later in the week, which is abnormal when you have a mother who's a nurse. If Mam can't fix him, it's scary."

"He'll be fine," Shannon hurried to soothe, setting her hand down on my forearm. "It might be mumps or something random like that."

"Oh crap, for his sake, I hope not," I sniffled.

"Why?"

"Because the mumps can make men infertile."

"*What*?" Lizzie pulled herself up on her elbows and gaped at me. "Where in the name of God did you hear that?"

"From my mam," I explained, blowing my nose. "So gross."

"He sat next to Johnny at lunch today," Shannon said, worrying her lip. "Do you think…"

"Aw," I half laughed, half wailed. "Aren't you cute worrying about your boyfriend's reproductive organs."

"Johnny's grand." Lizzie cut her off with a sigh. "Because Hugh doesn't have the mumps."

"He might."

"He doesn't."

"You can't know that."

"Hey, maybe my brother needs to sit next to your brother, Shan," I sniffled, blowing my nose again. "He needs neutering like Brian."

"That's the spirit," Lizzie praised. "Stiffen that upper lip, Baby Biggs."

58

3:00 a.m.

CLAIRE

TIME WAS SUPPOSED TO BE A HEALER, BUT SEVERAL HOURS HAD PASSED AND I STILL felt every blade of betrayal in my back, without a hint of letting up. My emotions were in turmoil, and I kept switching between thinking I made a terrible decision to doubling down on my decision to protect my poor battered heart.

Was there a chance I had it wrong and was overreacting? Of course, but my heart wasn't nearly wise or weathered enough to take another risk. How could I willingly put my heart back in the ring with Gerard's when every time in the past it had been KO'd?

When my bedroom door opened, and Gerard appeared in the door a little after 3:00 a.m., like the lyrics of my favorite Busted song, I wasn't even surprised. Just sad.

"Will you do something for me?" he asked in the darkness. Taking my silence as a nod to continue, he asked, "Will you take a walk with me?"

"A walk?" Wow. I didn't recognize my own voice. It was croaky and hoarse.

"Please."

I could hear the seriousness in his tone. It was the only reason I threw the covers off and whispered, "Okay."

"Thank you."

Weary, I slipped into my dressing gown and toed on my slippers before moving for the door. "Just around the cul-de-sac, okay?"

"Whatever you want," he replied, following after me.

"So," I said when we stepped into the night air and Gerard pulled the front door out behind us. "Is this a 'deep and meaningful talk' kind of walk, or an 'outrunning your nightmares' kind of walk?"

It was at least -2 degrees and the sky was crystal clear, which was a no-brainer indicator of frost and ice, but Gerard clearly didn't seem to notice. Walking beside me in a T-shirt and sweatpants, he emanated heat.

"It's more of an 'I fucked up and I can't sleep from the guilt that's eating me alive' kind of walk."

My feet momentarily faltered, but I quickly recovered, desperately trying to keep my composure. "So, you *were* with Catwoman?"

"Not last Saturday night, I wasn't," he vowed. "I was in the past, but haven't been in a very, very long time." He reached for my hand, only to pull back at the last moment and sigh heavily. "I promise you faithfully that I haven't looked at, let alone touched another girl since last Easter."

"Okay." I shoved my half-perished hands into the pockets of my dressing gown. "I believe you."

"Don't," he warned, voice thick with emotion, clearly noticing my physical retreat.

"I have to," I whispered brokenly. "I'll never get over us if I don't try."

"Don't," he repeated, gray eyes locked on mine. "Don't let it go." He swallowed deeply. "Don't get over us."

"Gerard…"

He reached a hand between us and trailed his thumb over my bottom lip, not stopping until his hand was in my hair, tilting my face up to his.

"Don't do it." Trembling from head to toe, I reached a hand between us and covered his mouth with my hand. "Not if you're going to backpedal again." Expelling a shaky breath, I trailed my tongue over my bottom lip, tasting my trepidation. "Because I honestly don't think my heart could take it."

His eyes were focused entirely on mine in this moment as he slowly raised his hand to mine and peeled it from his mouth. "I meant it the first time." His chest was heaving from the sheer force of his breathing. "I meant it the last time." Hooking one strong arm around my waist, he pulled my body flush against his. "And I mean it now."

"Ger—" My words were swallowed up by his lips when they landed on mine.

What had started as a featherlight kiss quickly progressed into something much deeper and far more serious. The feel of his tongue in my mouth as it dueled with mine, taking slow, drugging swipes of pleasure.

"I've been a poor man for you," he broke our kiss by saying. "I see that now. It took me awhile, and I fully admit that I've been a little caught up in my fucked-up brain, but I'm seeing it now, Claire." His tone was charged, his eyes full of urgency. "I'm seeing *you*, okay? Not that I ever didn't. But I'm hearing you, baby." Exhaling a shaky breath, he dropped his head to rest against mine. "From here on out, I will follow you anywhere."

My heart leapt in my chest. "What do you mean?"

"I mean it's yours," he ground out hoarsely. "Whatever you want from me. It's yours, Claire."

"You really mean that?"

"I really mean it," he vowed, looking just as petrified as I felt. "I want to be your boyfriend and I want you to be my girlfriend."

"You do?" I squeezed out, trembling.

He nodded. "Absolutely."

"I'm scared now," I admitted, heart racing wildly in my chest as I looked up at him. "I don't want to get hurt." *I don't want you to hurt me.*

"I don't blame you," he surprised me by saying. "I know I've given you the worst impression of me at times, and I can't take any of it back, but you need to know that I never intended to hurt you."

"I understand that, Gerard, I do."

"Thank you," he replied, exhaling a sigh of relief. "For being the most understanding person I've ever met."

"I want to be with you," I heard myself admit, voice torn from the countless tears I'd spent. "I want everything you just said, but I don't..." I paused and shook my head, unsure of how to voice my thoughts aloud.

"It's okay," he was quick to reassure. "You don't need to make any decisions right now."

"I don't?"

"No, you don't," he confirmed, tipping my chin up and offering me a small smile. "We can put the brakes on until you're ready."

"We can?"

"Yeah, Claire-Bear, we can."

This time, when he reached for my hand, it felt distinctively different than all the other times.

It felt more important.

It felt like I was being seen and my feelings were being validated.

It felt like *forever.*

"You waited for me," he said, squeezing my hand. "Now it's my turn to wait for you."

59

I Can't Carry This Anymore

GIBSIE

"WE NEED TO TALK," WERE THE FIRST WORDS THAT CAME OUT OF MY MOUTH WHEN I found Hugh slumped on his bed the following morning. Clad in my school uniform, I eyed his matching one strewn across his bedroom floor and frowned. "You're not going to school?"

A muffled "no" sounded from beneath the duvet.

"But we have a match today."

"The answer's still no."

"Shit, you're really sick." My brows shot up. "I thought you were faking it at lunch yesterday."

"Whatever this is, can it wait?" he croaked out, pulling the covers down enough to look at me. "Because I'm in a real bad way here, lad."

"No." Closing the door behind me, I walked into his room and sank down on the foot of his bed. "It can't."

Hugh drew the covers back over his head and groaned. "Fuck my life."

"I asked your sister to be my girlfriend," I announced, deciding to get it out of the way right away. "I think it's fairly obvious by now that I'm in love with her, Hugh." Clearing my throat, I scratched my jaw before adding, "I'm serious about this, okay? I'm serious about *her*."

I had been up all night going over my raging thoughts and what I might say to my oldest friend. Because as much as we liked to fight and banter, this was a delicate situation, and I didn't want to fuck up our friendship. Hugh Biggs meant an awful lot to me—not as much as his sister clearly meant, but still. I needed him to be okay about this. I needed his approval. I needed him to know that I wasn't fucking around anymore. That his sister wasn't a game to me, and I was deadly serious.

I had been expecting violence, predicting it even, but when Hugh didn't react, I started to feel real concern for whatever affliction he had come down with.

"Did you hear me, Hugh?"

"I heard you, Gibs."

Hmm. My brows furrowed in confusion. "And you don't want to kill me?"

"I'm too fucking broken to kill you, lad."

"Jesus." Reaching for the covers, I pulled them back and studied his face. "Do you need a doctor?"

"No, because it's my own fault." Shaking his head, he pressed a hand to his forehead before asking, "What did Claire say when you asked her?"

"Well, she didn't immediately reject me so I'm taking that as a solid win," I offered with a sigh. "She's taking some time to think it over."

"Smart girl."

"Very smart," I agreed with a nod.

"Don't break her heart, Gibs."

My own one hammered hard when I heard his quiet request. "I won't."

"I mean it." His brown eyes locked on mine. "If you're serious about this, and I really fucking hope you are, then don't let her down."

"I *am* serious," I vowed, swallowing deeply. "And I won't let her down, Hugh."

"Good," he groaned, rolling onto his side. "Because I'm in no condition to kill you at the moment."

"Duly noted." Chuckling, I stood up and moved for the door. "Feel better soon, lad."

"Omigod!" Claire yelped when I crashed into her in the landing, all blond curls and flushed cheeks. "What are you..."

On my best behavior, I smiled warmly before stepping aside for her towel-clad body to scamper back to her bedroom. "As you were, Claire-Bear."

"You're up early."

"I'm a man on a mission."

"Oh." Cheeks still flushed, she lingered in her bedroom doorway, eyeing me uncertainly. "Hey, are you driving to school this morning?" She licked her lips and flicked a wrist in the direction of her brother's closed bedroom door. "Because I don't know if Hugh's going..."

"I'll be across the road when you're ready," I cut in and told her. "I'll be waiting patiently, Claire-Bear."

"Okay." A small smile tipped her lips upward, letting me know that she had caught on to the hidden meaning behind my words. "I promise not to keep you waiting too long."

When I crossed the street and went into my house, I was already on full alert for potential run-ins with my mother's asshole stepson. However, finding him in my room was neither something I had anticipated nor dealt with in a very long time.

The minute my eyes landed on Mark Allen sitting on my bed, the tiny hairs on the back of my neck stood to attention.

Immediately, my skin broke out in a clammy, feverish sweat, and if it wasn't for the fact that I was in his presence, I might have thought that I was coming down with whatever Hugh had. *But I wasn't the sick one here.* "Get out of my room."

"Still as messy as ever, I see."

"I said get *out* of my room."

"That's not the way you're supposed to greet your brother, Gibs," he replied in a casual tone, completely unaffected by the tension I was emanating. "Didn't Sadhbh teach you how to treat people by now?"

"You're one to talk," I shot back, remaining in the doorway. "You have a lot of fucking nerve to come in here."

"And why's that, Gibs?"

I narrowed my eyes. "You know why."

"Nope." Shaking his head, he rose to his feet and stretched. "I have no idea what you're talking about."

"Yes, you do," I bit out, feeling my entire body rack with tremors when I watched him approach me. "You know what you did."

"And what did I do?"

"You know," was all I could get out, and I fucking hated how small my voice sounded. Like I was seven years old again. Or eight, or nine, or ten, or even eleven. My breath hitched in my throat, and I had to force myself to not cower. "You *know*," I strangled out, chest heaving. "And she did, too."

"You're mistaken," he tried to fuck with my mind by saying. "Confusing nightmares with reality, I reckon."

"No, I'm not." I shook my head, feeling all kinds of fucked up and panicky. "I'm not confusing anything because I *know* what you did." Swallowing deeply, I forced myself to choke out the words, "I *remember*."

"Oh yeah?" Stopping just short of me, he folded his arms across his chest and smirked. "Prove it."

Trembling from head to toe, I sidestepped his body and moved for my bed. "Actually, I can."

"What's that, Gibs? The ineligible scrawl of a dunce child?" he goaded when I withdrew the crumpled-up letter from under my mattress. "Don't tell me that an illiterate, dumb cunt like you actually kept a diary?" He laughed again before saying, "Jesus

Christ, you did. You actually kept a diary like a little girl!" Humor and cruelty filled his features, sending me on a spiral back to a time in my life I didn't dare revisit. "Looks like, despite my best efforts, I didn't make a man out of you."

"No, not me." With trembling hands, I unfolded the note and held it up between us. "Her."

A wave of recognition flickered in his eyes, and he took a step closer. "Is that Caoimhe's handwriting?"

"It sure fucking is," I spat out, shaking violently. "Think I don't have proof now?"

His eyes flashed with panic before he quickly slapped on a confident bravado. "If you haven't show anyone, and you clearly haven't, it's because you *know* nobody will believe it." He narrowed his eyes. "Nobody will ever believe *your* truth over *mine*."

"There's only one truth, Mark," I forced myself to stand my ground and say, while I gestured to the letter in my hand. "And it's written in here."

He watched me watch him for the longest moment before taking a step in my direction, attention flicking to the letter. "Don't even think about it," I warned, quickly tucking it away in my pocket. "I'm not seven years old anymore, asshole."

"Why are you bringing all of this shit up again?" he tried to change the narrative by demanding. "It's in the past, Gibs. It's dead and buried."

"Maybe for you," I strangled out. "But I'm still living it every day."

He rolled his eyes like I was being dramatic. Like my memories and my pain and his action didn't ruin me on the daily.

"I want you gone," I heard myself say.

"That's not going to happen," he dismissed me by saying. "I have a job lined up over here, and I just put a deposit down on a house for my family in town."

"I want you out of my house and out of my town," I doubled down and told him. "Today. This morning. Right fucking *now*."

"Or what?"

"Or I'm going to tell."

"*Tell*?" He tossed the word out like it was something laughable. "Christ, what age are you?"

"I'm seventeen now," I bit out. "But I was seven when you raped me."

"Don't…"

"I was seven years old when you first raped me!" I said louder, refusing to be silenced a second longer by my fear of this man. "I was eleven years old when you finally stopped!" Blowing out a ragged breath, I glared at the monster standing in front of me with tears pouring down my cheeks and strangled out, "You took four years of my childhood from me, and I've been living in a prison in my mind every damn day of my life since. So, if you don't want to risk spending the next seventeen years of your life behind bars, you'll get on a plane and never come back!"

60

That's My Man

CLAIRE

I'D THROWN DOWN THE GAUNTLET WITH GERARD LAST NIGHT, ONLY TO BARELY MAKE it to the end of school today without throwing in the towel.

Who was I trying to fool?

I wasn't going to make him wait.

Not when I had all the self-control of a rolling pin.

When Gerard drove me to school this morning, he was his supersweet, super-adorable self, and that sucked because it only made it harder for me to keep my guard up.

Most people erected walls around their hearts to protect themselves, and some of those people, like Joey and Lizzie, were mighty talented at building said walls. I, on the other hand, clearly slept in the day that particular life skill was being handed out, because my walls were only knee-high at best and had been constructed with *gummy bears*.

By the time Shannon joined me in the stands that surrounded Tommen's central rugby pitch, I was close to self-combusting.

"Oh my god." She laughed, eyeing me with humor dancing in her eyes. "You look like Tigger from Winnie the Pooh." Snickering, she asked, "How many sweets did you eat today, Claire? Because you're literally bouncing on the spot."

"I know!" I squeezed out, thrumming with barely contained energy. "I swear, Shan, if I had a tail, it would be wagging like crazy."

"Wow." My best friend laughed, taking her seat next to mine. "I know you enjoy watching the guys play, Claire, but I've never seen you this excited for one of their games before."

She was right. While it was true that I enjoyed watching them play, it wasn't the reason for my current state of agitation. In fact, they were already twenty minutes into the first half of the game, and I had no idea of the score.

I presumed our side was wining, but that was more of a "Johnny Kavanagh being on our team" thing than a "Claire Biggs concentrating" one.

"Is that the new boy the guys were talking about?" Shannon asked, pointing to the boy wearing my brother's number 10 jersey.

"Oh, yeah." I wrinkled my nose up in disapproval. "That's Damien."

"You've met him?"

"Unfortunately." Rolling my eyes, I added, "He's stepping in today as fly half." My attention flicked to Gerard just as he won a line-out, and I couldn't stop myself from leaping out of my seat and cheering like a banshee.

My bestie eyed me from her perch while I bounced around like the Duracell bunny jacked up on steroids and fizzy cola jellies. "I guess it's safe to assume that you and Gibs made up."

I beamed back at her. "Yep."

"Good." Relief flooded her big blue eyes, and she smiled up at me. "I knew that picture Helen and Shelley sent you was taken out of context."

"He swears nothing happened."

"I believe him," my best friend replied without a hint of hesitation. "If he says nothing happened with Catwoman, then that's the truth."

"You do?"

"Absolutely," she replied with a nod. "He wouldn't do that to you, Claire. Not Gibs. His entire world revolves around you."

"You really care about him, don't you?" I mused, sitting back down to link arms with her. "Aw, my bestie approves."

"He's one of the good ones, Claire," she urged in a sincere tone. "Sure, Gib's a joker and a prankster and can say all of the wrong things at times, but his heart is as big as the moon."

"It truly is," I agreed with a dreamy sigh.

"I've never felt safe around boys or men," Shannon admitted, brow furrowing as she spoke. "For obvious reasons."

I winced. "Yeah."

"But I feel safe around Gibs," she told me. "Aside from Johnny, he's the only other boy whose hands I would willingly put my life in."

"Aw." My heart squeezed tight. "Shan."

"So, don't listen to Lizzie, okay?" she urged. "Listen to your heart." She smiled. "It won't steer you in the wrong direction, I promise."

My heart, like it knew it was being spoken about, started to thud violently in my chest. "He asked me to be his girlfriend last night."

Her blue eyes widened like saucers. "He did?"

Biting down on my lip, I nodded excitedly. "Yep."

"And what did you say?"

"I told him I was scared."

Shannon's eyes warmed in understanding. "That's okay, Claire," she soothed, reaching over to squeeze my hand. "Taking the next step in a relationship can be really scary."

"It really can."

"But it can also be really exciting, and freeing, and so incredibly liberating."

"He told me that he would wait for me," I explained, feeling my face grow hot at the memory. "For as long as it takes until I'm ready."

"But you're ready now, aren't you?" she mused knowingly.

"Yes." I exhaled a shaky breath and nodded eagerly. "I really *am*."

"Well, he's right here, Claire." My best friend grinned and gestured to the pitch. "That's your man."

"You're right." I stood up and nodded in confirmation. "That's *my* man."

61

Who the Fuck Is Damien?

GIBSIE

I WAS DEEP IN CONCENTRATION HAVING JUST BEEN THRUST SEVERAL FEET INTO THE air for another line-out, when the sound of Coach ranting and raving like a lunatic from the sidelines snagged my attention.

However distracted, I still managed to retrieve the ball midair and protect it with my body against the opposition's challenge as my teammates lowered me to the ground.

"Bring him down safely, lads," Danny roared, falling back to steer the pack from the rear. "Are ya alright, Gibs?"

"Yeah!" Shaking my head, I tried to refocus on the maul I was slap-bang in the middle of and feed the ball out to our scrum half, while twenty-nine other players roared and barked orders at both me and each other.

"Move, move, move," Robbie Mac roared when I somehow managed to break free with the ball in arm. "Fucking leg it, Gibs."

Jesus, I was not built for 80-meter solo sprints, but with no one to hand the ball off to, I gave it my best shot, face-palming the opposition's cheeky winger in the process when he attempted to take me down. Because if I had to exert this much energy, I wasn't about to let a ten-stone, lanky fucker like him steal my glory.

"Back yourself, Gibs," Johnny encouraged, bombing it up the pitch to flank me on the outside. "That's your try, lad!"

Johnny was right, it *was* my try, but when I touched the ball down behind the white line, I didn't join him and the rest of our teammates celebrating. Because I was too distracted by the blond being wrestled off the pitch.

I shielded my eyes from the watery sun to get a better look at the girl in the Tommen uniform being carted away. "*Claire*?"

"Gerard!" she called out, arms flailing, as she wrestled to break free of the coach, who was attempting to restrain her. "Omigod, hi! Nice try!"

"Thanks," I called back, too exhausted from my Michael Johnson–like sprint to run over to her. Cramping out like a motherfucker and still trying to catch my breath, I clutched my side and studied the scene unfolding in front of me.

"You can't run onto the field, Biggs," Coach argued, catching ahold of her shoulders. "We're in the middle of the Schoolboys' Shield, dammit."

"Omigod, rude much, Coach? It won't take a minute." Breaking free of his hold, she dropped to the ground and crawled under his legs before breaking into a sprint across the pitch. "Hey, Gerard, I need to tell you something!"

"Right now?" Johnny called out, looking less than impressed with her on-field intrusion.

"Yeah," Feely agreed with a frown. "Can't it wait until after the game?"

"No." She shook her head, and it caused her curls to bounce around her face. "I have to tell him right now. Hey!" Her words broke off when she was stopped short by our substitute number 10. "*You* again!"

"Me," he confirmed in a grim tone. "Get off the pitch, princess."

"Get your hands off me, *Damien*. I want to talk to Gerard."

Who the fuck is Damien?

"Are you on some special medication or something?" our number 10 demanded. "For the last time, there is no Gerard on this team."

"Yes, there is!"

"No, there's not!"

"Wow, you are so damn rude!"

"And you are so damn crazy!"

The amusement I was feeling at her random behavior was quickly replaced with anger as I watched one of my own teammates continue to block her path. And just like that, my feet were moving.

"Hey, 10!" I snapped, quickly closing the space between us. "Back the fuck up from my girl."

"See? I told you he was real. *That's* Gerard," Claire declared smugly, pointing a finger in my direction. "My *boyfriend*."

"No, that's Gibsie," this Damien eejit argued slowly. "As in Gibson."

"Uh, *yeah*." Claire rolled her eyes. "As in *Gerard* 'Gibsie' Gibson."

Meanwhile, I was still stuck about ten seconds in the past, having tripped over the words *my boyfriend* when they came out of her mouth.

"Holy fuck," I strangled out, feeling my chest heave when my heart decided to piledrive into my rib cage. "You really mean that?"

"That's what I needed to tell you!" Nodding eagerly, Claire shoved passed number 10 and barreled toward me. "I'm super sorry for interrupting your game, but it couldn't wait."

"I don't give a fuck about the game," I called back, catching her midair when she threw herself at me. "You called me your boyfriend."

"Yep." Grinning with mischief, she wrapped her arms and legs around me and leaned in close. "I sure did."

"What about the whole waiting thing?"

"I've done the waiting," she replied, leaning in close to stroke her nose against mine. "Sixteen years' worth."

"But I'm telling you now, Gerard Gibson, that I'm not the girl for flings and whimsical fleeting feelings, so if you can't give me one hundred percent, then you need to say it," she warned, brown eyes locked on mine. "This is your last chance to get out."

"I'm in," I heard myself tell her, and never in my life had I spoken more truth than I had in those two words. "I'm in, Claire Biggs."

"Good." She smiled. "Me too."

And then she kissed me right there in the middle of the field, with the whole school watching.

Holy fuck did she kiss me.

62

After-School Pacts

CLAIRE

Okay, so the repercussions of my impulsive behavior resulted in the following:

One full week's worth of lunchtime detentions for me, due to my inability to follow school rules. Ooh, and I had been given my very first red card from the referee, which I thought was kind of strange considering I had only kissed Gerard and hadn't participated in any illegal tackling.

Either way, it was *so* worth it.

When I was finally released from the office, after enduring a twenty-minute lecture from both Coach and Mr. Twomey on the importance of *not* mounting rugby players, Gerard was waiting outside for me. The moment my eyes landed on him, freshly showered and looking divine in his gray sweatpants and a long-sleeved black T-shirt, all of our principal's words of warning went clean out the window.

My heart boomed like a drum the entire way home from school, because it knew it was in trouble with this boy. Van Morrison's "Brown Eyed Girl" drifted from the stereo, but I couldn't hear a word of it over the sound of my thundering pulse.

I had a boyfriend.

Yep, me.

Better again, that boyfriend was *Gerard*.

When he parked up at the footpath outside my driveway, I couldn't stop myself from springing into action. Unable to cope with the frenzied energy whizzing around inside of my body, I unfastened my seat belt and crawled over the console, not stopping until I was straddling his hips.

"Jesus, Claire-Bear." Gerard chuckled, reaching under his seat for the lever that allowed him to push his chair back and give us a little more room. "You're happy."

"I am happy," I agreed, resting my hands on his broad chest. "I am *deliriously* happy."

His hand slipped under the hem of my skirt, fingers grazing my bare thigh, and I felt like I might pass out.

Because I wanted him, I realized.

More than anything.

More than my next breath.

"Hey, is that Mark?" Distracted by the sight of Mark Allen packing the boot of his father's Land Rover with suitcases, I turned back to Gerard eyes wide with excitement. "Oh my god, is he *leaving*?"

"Let's hope so."

"Yeah, let's."

Gerard didn't bother to look in Mark's direction, keeping his entire focus locked on me instead. "I love you, Claire." Inhaling a deep breath, he studied my face for a long moment, thumb grazing my chin, before exhaling. "I really love you, girlfriend."

"Aw." Practically melting on his lap, I leaned in and pressed a kiss to his lips. "I really love you, too, boyfriend."

When he knotted his hand in my hair and deepened the kiss, I really did melt on his lap. It was such a good kiss: slow, and smooth, and deep, and spine-tinglingly *perfect*.

"Gerard?" I said in a breathless tone when I broke our kiss a little while later.

"Hmm?" he replied, peppering my bare skin with epic, toe-curling neck kisses.

"You were my first kiss."

"Mm-hmm."

"And the first boy who touched me there."

"Mmm."

"And the first boy to lick me there."

"Mm-hmm."

"Well, I want you…" My words broke off and I moaned when his tongue traced over a particularly sensitive part of my neck. "To be my first everything."

The moment the words were out, Gerard froze, lips still on my neck. "Everything?"

Releasing a shaky breath, I nodded. "Everything."

"Just so we're on the same page…" Gerard paused to pull back and look at me. "You are talking about sex, right?" He eyed me cautiously. "Because I've been known to get it wrong a time or ten, and my ability to read between the lines is about as shocking as my ability to read in class, Claire-Bear."

"I am, Gerard." My face flamed with heat. "I *am* talking about sex."

"Okay."

His brows furrowed together as he studied me. "What, uh, what exactly about…"

"Omigod, Gerard, I want us to have sex with each other!" I blurted out, spelling it out for him in the most unsexy way imaginable. "As in, I want you to put your ladder in my tree."

"In your tree?"

Rolling my eyes, I grabbed his hand and pushed it between my legs. "Oh, your *tree*," he replied, awareness dawning on him. "You should have called it a bush, Claire-Bear. I'm not familiar with the whole pussies being trees terminology."

"Ew, no." I scrunched my nose up in disgust. "'Bush' is such a gross word."

"True," he agreed. "And you definitely don't have one."

"Nope." I smiled proudly. "The benefits of pound-shop razors."

He seemed to think about that for a moment before shaking his head. "So, back to the sex."

"The sex," I agreed.

"When were you thinking about it, uh, happening?"

"Um, I was thinking sort of now."

"Now?" Gerard looked a little panicked. "Like 'right now in the car' right now?"

"No, obviously not 'right now in the car' right now," I replied with a nervous laugh.

"Okay, good." He laughed nervously in response. "Because I was thinking Mr. Murphy always takes his evening stroll and I wouldn't want to traumatize the poor man."

"True." Forcing a chuckle, I glanced around the car before saying, "But, um, maybe right now in my room?"

"In your room?" His attention flicked to my mother's parked car. "With your mam downstairs in the kitchen?"

Aw, crackers.

"Maybe your room?"

"We could, but then *my* mam would be downstairs in the kitchen."

"Dammit," I groaned.

"We could…" Gerard started to say something but quickly shook his head. "Nah, forget it."

"We could what?" I begged, catching onto the tiny flicker of hope and holding on for dear life. "What? What could we do, Gerard?"

"We could always go to the tree house," he offered, and then winced in what looked like fearful anticipation of my reaction. "But obviously that's a really shitty idea, and no girl wants to have her first time in a fucking tree house—"

"You're a genius!" I exclaimed with excitement. "It's perfect."

"It is?"

"Yes." I beamed at him. "And I would *love* to do it in the tree house with you, Gerard Gibson, if you would like to accept my offer?"

"You know what, Claire Biggs." He sat straight up. "I think I would like that."

"Okay then," I replied, holding my hand out. "We'll have sex in the tree house."

"Okay," Gerard agreed, shaking my hand. "Let's go do that."

63

CLAIRE

"What took you so long?" I demanded when Gerard finally graced me with his presence twenty minutes later than agreed.

When we parted ways at the car with a fist bump, we had arranged to meet back at the tree house in thirty minutes. Taking the fastest shower known to mankind, I scrubbed, shaved, and polished myself to perfection before climbing the rickety ladder at the bottom of our garden with two minutes to spare.

Hiding in the tree house for the past fifteen minutes, with no sign of Gerard, had set my teeth on edge because paranoia had started setting in. "I thought you were after having second thoughts and had scampered off."

"No second thoughts," he called back and then tossed a duffel bag through the opening before climbing in after it. "I had to get supplies."

"Supplies?"

"Condoms, Claire."

"Oh *sugar!*" My eyes widened and I slapped a hand over my mouth. "I totally forgot."

"Never fear, I've got us covered."

"You're the best."

"Question." Kneeling on the floor of our tree house, Gerard reached for his bag and deftly unzipped it. "Did you come through the back?"

"No." I shook my head, watching as he withdrew a thick, fluffy duvet from his duffel bag. "My mam's in the kitchen, and I didn't want to risk an interrogation, so I snuck around the side of the house instead."

"Dammit, why didn't I think of that?" he muttered, all business, as he opened the duvet and placed it on the wooden floor of the tree house that we spent most of our childhood playing in. Then out came another blanket. A thinner one that looked suspiciously similar to the one my mam used when she took us on picnics. "It was almost impossible to get away from them."

"Them?"

"My mam's there, too," he explained, reaching for the back of his T-shirt. "Like a pair of hungry lionesses, they were." He whipped the fabric over his head in one swift move. "Grilling me over hot coals for gossip."

"Gossip?" I croaked out, mouth running dry when I took in the sight of his bare chest. God, he was so beautiful.

"Yeah." Shifting into a sitting position, he reached for his runners and pulled them off one by one. "Did you hear anything about a winter ball?"

"The Tommen Winter Ball?" I asked, following his lead by cattishly removing my T-shirt.

"That's the one." Off went his socks. "Apparently, it's happening next month, and I need to make sure that I put an order for a fresh-flower corsage and 'not one of those fake ones,'" he mimicked with a roll of his eyes. "Like I didn't already know to do that."

"I'm wearing yellow," I told him with a dreamy sigh as I clutched my hands to my chest. "And not a mustard or a pineapple yellow. Ew, and definitely not an ochre yellow. Think Andie Anderson's dress in *How to Lose a Guy in 10 Days* kind of yellow."

"Good to know." Reaching into the waistband of his sweatpants, he pushed them down his narrow hips. "I'll be sure to tell the florist not to give me any fruit or condiments."

My breath hitched in my throat at the sight of him.

He was so…big and broad and muscular.

Sucking in a steadying breath, I pushed my pajama shorts down and knelt on the duvet in my underwear. "I'm nervous."

"Yeah, me too," he agreed, tucking a foil wrapper into the waistband of his gray boxers before reaching up to push his hair back. "Who knew there was so many different shades of yellow."

"No, not about the color of my corsage, Gerard." I gestured to where he was kneeling in his boxers and then to myself. "I'm nervous about *this*."

"*This* doesn't have to happen," Gerard replied in a gentle tone. "It's okay if you want to wait." Closing the space between us, he placed his hands on my shoulders and smiled. "We don't have to do anything until you're ready."

"But I *am* ready," I reaffirmed, eyes locked on his. "I'm just…scared."

"Me, too," he admitted quietly.

My brows rose. "Really?"

"Really," he replied with a small nod. "What are you scared of?"

"Of it hurting."

"Same."

"You are?" Frowning, I reached up and wrapped my arms around his neck, shivering when the heat emanating from his skin penetrated mine. "But it doesn't hurt boys, right?"

Something flashed in his gray eyes then, a rare glimpse of vulnerability that was quickly replaced with his usual warmth. "I love you," he said, hands moving to settle on my waist. "I'll do whatever you want, okay? Just set the pace here, Claire-Bear, and I will follow you anywhere, okay?" He rested his forehead against mine and expelled a shaky breath. "But I meant what I said about waiting. If you want to just cuddle, then that's what we'll do…"

"No." I shook my head and pulled his big body flush against me. "I want you to be inside me."

"Fuck." Another pained breath escaped him. "Are you sure?"

"I've never been surer of anything in my life," I hurried to say, needing him to *not* put the brakes on this because I was tired of stalling. I'd been sitting in the passenger seat of a stagnant car for sixteen years, and Gerard, who was in the driver's seat, had finally found the throttle. It was everything. He was everything. "I want this, Gerard." And then, with trembling hands, I reached behind my back and unhooked my bra before casting it aside. "I want you."

"I love you." He tipped my chin up, gray eyes searching every inch of my face before locking on my eyes. "I always have."

And then he kissed me.

A full-body shiver racked through my body as his lips destroyed me for every other boy to come.

Please don't let there be more to come.

I just want him, God.

Let me keep him.

Instinctively, I slowly lowered onto my back, taking his big body with me, while his lips never stopped loving mine. The only thing separating our bodies was the fabric of our underwear, as we both ground against each other, finding an itch that I never knew desperately needed scratching. Well, he was scratching that itch right now. In fact, I never wanted his weight to leave my body because I couldn't remember a point in time where I felt this complete.

And then we started to touch each other. It was deeper. More serious. Harder. Softer. More loving. More everything. The shape of him, the feel of his skin on mine, it was too much. It was exactly what I'd been waiting my entire life for.

"It's okay," I whispered a little while later, when the rest of our underwear had been cast aside on the tree-house floor. "I want this." My heart hammered in nervous anticipation when he moved into position between my thighs, with a condom sheathing his impressive ladder. I didn't move an inch for fear of scaring him off. I needed him to not run away, because I honestly felt like I would die if this boy didn't join his body with mine. "You're shaking all over."

"Well, yeah," he croaked out, leaning in close to brush his lips against mine. "That's what happens when you're nervous."

"You're nervous?"

"I feel like I'm holding glass in my hands here, Claire." He pulled back to look at me, body trembling worse than mine in this moment. "Of course, I'm nervous."

Something tugged at my heart then, something deeper than affection, stronger than friendship, more permanent than forever, and I pulled up on my elbows. "I love you." Lips grazing his stubbly jaw, I nuzzled his cheek with mine and pressed another kiss to the corner of his mouth. "I want it to be you."

"I've only ever wanted it to be you," he whispered, as a full-body tremor racked his big frame. "I'll be as gentle as I can."

"Do it." Shivering in fearful anticipation, I grabbed his shoulders and kissed him hard. "Just go slow."

Blowing out a shaky breath, Gerard leaned forward, rested his brow against mine, and pushed.

And then he was deep inside of me.

The initial jolt of pain that coursed through me was enough to sting my eyes with tears, but I held my nerve, too enraptured in the moment to care. Because this boy. If there was pain to experience, I wanted it to be at his hands.

"Are you okay?"

"Yes." I nodded through the pain, through the feel of him moving inside of me, of connecting with me in a way that no other human had before. It was overwhelming and terrifying and beautiful all at once. "Don't stop."

He kept his weight off me by resting his forearm on the floor beside me. His free hand moved from my face to my thigh, hitching me closer, aligning our bodies until we connected in the most basic and primal of human ways.

His eyes were clenched tight while mine were wide open, taking it all in, every inch of him. All of my senses were in overdrive. The smell of the washing powder on the duvet beneath us, the salty taste of his skin around his throat when my tongue snaked out to taste him. The delicious weight of his hips and how when they rocked deeper, the pressure grew.

Feelings were flooring me. I was drowning in him in this moment. It was incredibly overwhelming. It was like playing the lottery for sixteen years and finally winning. The feeling of euphoria and uncertainty colliding.

I couldn't tell which one of us was shaking most. I thought it might be an equal effort because Gerard seemed as deeply affected by this moment as I was.

"Are you okay?" I whispered, cupping his neck with my hand. He looked like he was in physical pain, as he clenched his eyes shut and moved inside me. "Gerard?"

"Yeah." Nodding, he kept his eyes closed. "Keep talking."

"Talking?"

"Your voice." He released a pained groan and buried his face in the curve of my neck, hips still thrusting. "I need to hear your voice."

"Why?"

"Because I need to know it's you touching me."

64

Losing Virginities and Consciousness

GIBSIE

"So." Body rigid, I clutched the blanket draped over us and stared up at the roof. Seriously, I was so stiff I was halfway toward rigor mortis. "That was different."

"Very different," Claire agreed from her perch beside me as she also clutched the blanket and stared at the roof.

"Uh, sorry about the whole blowing my load before you got to come," I added. "I, ah, was overexcited."

"Oh no, no, I did," she was quick to answer.

My brows shot up. "You did?"

"Yeah." She nodded, attention still trained on the roof. "Once before and once during."

"Oh."

"You couldn't tell?"

"Nope. I was just freaking the fuck out the entire time."

"Oh." She blew out a shaky breath. "Well, I did, so…uh, good job?"

"Uh, thanks?" I shifted slightly, causing our shoulders to brush. "You too."

"Thanks," she squeezed out. "So, uh, did the condom stay on your ladder the whole time?" Shrugging, she added, "You know, with the whole piercing thing?"

"I don't know." I tightened my hold on the blanket, feeling a wave of panic wash over me. "I'm afraid to check."

"Yeah," Claire agreed, sounding equally panicked. "Me too."

"I didn't hurt you, though, did I?" I forced myself to roll onto my side to face her. After all, looking in her eyes when we talked was the least I could go considering what she just let me do to her body. "It wasn't too bad, was it?"

"What? No, of course you didn't hurt me," Claire replied, mirroring my actions by rolling on her side to face me. Her cheeks were flushed and her brown eyes bright. Smiling sheepishly, she reached over and stroked my cheek. "You were *so* good."

"I was?"

"*So* good." A girlie squeal escaped her, and she bit down on her lip, still grinning from ear to ear. "I can't wait to do it again."

"You can't?"

"Why do you sound so surprised?" she teased. "I bet you've heard that a hundred times before."

"Nope."

"But you…" She frowned in confusion. "You've clearly done that before."

"Nope."

"Wait." Her eyes widened to the size of saucers. "You're a virgin, too?"

I hesitated before asking, "What's your definition of a virgin?"

"For you, it would mean that you've never put your ladder in another girl's tree," she replied innocently.

"Then yes." I shrugged, "Or at least I was until half an hour ago."

"Omigod!" She bolted onto her feet and the move caused her to take the blanket that was covering both of us with her. "I can't believe this!"

"Is that a bad thing?"

"Gerard, it's an *amazing* thing." Twisted up in the blanket, she quickly dropped to her knees and scooted back to where I was sprawled out.

"Contrary to the bullshit that spurts from my mouth, I'm more of a flirt than an action man," I offered.

"You think filthy thoughts," she teased. "You could write a book."

"If I could write." I snorted. "I'm the best at the sex texts. You just ask any of the lads. I'm gifted." I grinned up at her. "I'm so fucking detailed that I could be a screenwriter on a porn set. I just… I fuck up the spellings and then everyone knows it's me."

"Did you keep it for me?" she asked, happily skipping over my random comments. "Your virginity?" Her eyes were bright with excitement as she bounced on her knees. "Omigod, I already know the answer, but I need to hear you say it."

"I've told you before, there's only you for me, Claire-Bear."

"Aww!" She clutched her chest and cooed at me like I was one of our kittens. "I so knew you were going to say that, but it sounds amazing anyway."

"Yeah, so listen," I began to say, while I mentally prepped for what was about to come. "You know the way I have that really bad phobia?"

"Of blood?" She nodded solemnly. "It's so bad for you, isn't it?"

"Hmm," I replied, voice cracking like a girl's as the mental image popped into my head and made me feel faint. "I know this is a strange request, but I was kind of hoping you would do me a solid and check."

"Oh, you mean *check*." Her eyes widened when she registered what I meant. "Me or you?" she asked and then started to remove the blanket from her body.

"Both," I replied and then swiftly clenched my eyes shut.

"Okay, ew!"

"*Ew*?" My heart started to thunder wildly in my chest. "Is that a good ew or a bad ew?"

"Uh, kind of both."

"Both?"

"Don't freak out, but I sort of bled on the both of us."

"Oh Jesus Christ." My stomach rolled. "Is it bad? Is there a lot? Is it on me? It's fucking on me, isn't it?"

"No, of course it's not *bad*," she huffed, sounding insulted. "And calm down, you big baby. It's just your typical run of the torn-hymen blood loss."

"Torn hymen?" I think I screamed. "What the fuck is *that*?"

"You know what that is, Gerard," she snickered. "You've had the talk."

"Oh my god, baby, you have to take the condom off," I strangled out, feeling faint. "Please, I'm begging you because if I have to look at your torn hymen—and I'm really sorry about tearing it, by the way—then I'll pass out."

"Gerard!"

"I'm serious," I strangled out, chest heaving. "I know I'm being a pussy, and I swear I'll make it up to you, but I will die on the mortal spot if I see blood, Claire. Die, I tell you!"

"You are being ridiculous," she huffed, but when I felt her fingers on my dick, I sagged in relief. "You know, in the movies, it's the men that look after the woman after sex," she complained as she rolled the condom off. "Not the other way around."

"We're not in the movies, Claire-Bear," I choked out. "We're in a tree house in your mam's backyard in Ballylaggin."

"Okay, lift your hips," she instructed a few minutes later. When I obliged, she pulled my boxers into position. "Just keep your eyes closed when you take a shower later and you'll be golden."

"And you?"

"Yes, Gerard, I'm perfectly decent again. You big baby."

I risked a peek and sagged in relief when my eyes landed on Claire pulling on her pajama pants.

"Sorry about the drama." I offered her a sheepish grin. "Hope you still love me."

"You're such a dope." She slipped her T-shirt back on and smirked. "But yes, Gerard Gibson, I still love you."

"Thank god for that." Feeling braver, I stood up in a stooping position to avoid the roof and went to her. "My hero."

"Claire! Gerard!" Sinead's voice echoed from the other side of the garden, followed by own mam's voice when she called out, "Dinnertime."

"Coming, Mam," Claire called back before turning to face me. "Poor innocent fools," she snickered. "They don't have a clue what we just did in here."

"Yeah," I started to laugh, but quickly sobered when my eyes locked on the white duvet. The white duvet with a crimson-red bloodstain. "Oh no, no, no," I heaved, feeling faint as I staggered backwards. "You have to get me away from it," I begged, and then, because I was a fucking eejit, I made a run for the door, only to smack my head off the roof beam above me.

The sound of Claire calling my name was the last thing I heard before everything went black.

65

Murder Weapons and Crimes of Passion

CLAIRE

"Gerard!" I screamed, watching as he face-planted on the tree-house floor with an audible thud. Seriously, he went down like a sack of spuds. "Omigod, Gerard?"

Nothing.

Not a peep.

"Are you dead?"

Silence.

"Omigod, I killed you!" I wailed, throwing my hands up. "I killed you with my hymen!"

Wailing like a banshee, I quickly snatched the bloodstained duvet up and threw it out of the tree house. "I am so sorry, Gerard," I cried as I bolted down the ladder. "I'll get help!"

Tripping off the last step of the ten-foot ladder, I scooped up the evidence of my crime of passion and ran for my life, screaming the word *help* at the top of my lungs.

"Claire?" Both of our mothers came barreling out of the house. "What in the name of Jesus happened?"

"Mam, I killed him!" I wailed, running into her arms. "I killed Gerard!"

"What happened?" Sadhbh demanded, looking frantic with concern. "Where's my son, Claire?"

"He's dead." Still wailing like a banshee, I pointed behind me. "In the tree house."

"How?" Mam asked in much calmer voice than either Sadhbh or I were displaying. "What happened?"

"Gerard!" Breaking into a panicked run, Sadhbh dropped her coffee cup on the lawn and bolted up the ladder of the tree house. "Gerard, love, it's alright. Mammy's coming!"

"What's wrong?" Dad demanded, appearing on the patio. "Jesus, I could hear you screaming from the attic."

"I killed Gerard with my hymen, Daddy!" I wailed, throwing the bloodstained duvet at his feet. "Here's the murder weapon for the Gardaí when they come to arrest me!"

"He's alive!" I heard Sadhbh call out from the tree house, and I swear, I almost collapsed on the lawn in relief.

"Oh, thank god," I cried, dropping my head in my hands. "Thank you, baby Jesus and the Virgin Mary for watching over us."

"Peter?" Sadhbh called out from the tree house. "Give me a hand with your godson, would you?"

"Claire." Mam shook her head. "I don't know whether to cry or kill you right now."

"I know!" I winced. "I'm super sorry, Mam."

"Okay, everybody, stand back," my father instructed a few minutes later as he carried my boyfriend down from the tree house in the fireman's carry position. "He'll be alright. He's just after getting a fright, that's all."

66

Hero Dads and Fireman's Carry

GIBSIE

Feeling faint, I hung limply over Peter Biggs's shoulder, knowing there was a huge chance he was carrying me to my death, but not having the ability to run away either way. Not only was the man rescuing me my godfather, but he was my girlfriend's father. The same girlfriend whose virginity was smeared all over my dick.

Don't look, lad.

Don't look.

"Are you going to kill me, Pete?"

"I haven't decided yet, Gibs."

"Okay, well, if you decide you are, can you give me a ten-second head start to get away?"

"You'll be lucky if you get five."

"I can work with five."

"If your father was alive to see this, he would have a field day."

"Gerard!" Claire cried out when her father set me down on the back lawn. "You're alive!" Making a beeline for me, she dropped to her knees next to me and peppered my cheek with kisses. "It's a miracle… Oh, your poor head." Her kisses were swiftly refocused on the huge lump that had sprouted out of my forehead. "My poor baby."

The look our mothers were giving us as they stood side by side with their arms crossed assured me that I would need another miracle to make it out of here in one piece.

"Bet you wish I killed you first," Peter muttered under his breath before walking back inside.

"Inside, Claire Biggs," Sinead ordered before storming into the house.

"Right now, Gerard Gibson," Mam added before stalking after her.

Ah shit.

"First and foremost, how are you feeling Gerard?" Sinead asked as she peeled the ice pack off my forehead and winced. "Oh dear, that definitely needs more ice. Let's just keep that on for another while."

Yeah, I bet it did. I'd almost decapitated myself off the roof of the tree house and was sporting a horn-shaped bump for my troubles.

While the fact that I currently looked like one of my girlfriend's unicorn stuffed animals was disturbing, it wasn't nearly as terrifying as the two women in front of me.

"Drink up, Gerard," my partner in crime said. Readjusting the blanket our mothers had wrapped around my shoulders after my rescue, Claire pushed the glass of 7up I was holding to my lips. "Sugar is good for shock."

"So, which one of you brainboxes decided it was a good idea to take off your clothes and fiddle around in the tree house in the month of November?" Mam demanded, hands on her hips. "Well. Come on. Fess up."

I pointed at Claire as inconspicuously as I could at the same time that she not so secretly pointed at me.

My mouth fell open. "It was *your* idea."

"No." Claire eyeballed me. "The tree house was *your* idea."

"Fair enough," I conceded. "But the whole ladder in the bush idea was all *you*!"

"Ew, say 'tree,' Gerard."

"Tree."

"Ladder in the tree?" Sinead questioned.

"Sex," Claire and I groaned in unison. "It means sex!"

"Oh Jesus," Mam groaned, covering her face with her hand. "Well, I hope you used protection, because the last thing our families need is a repeat of the Cherub and Brian fiasco!"

"We did, Sadhbh," Claire croaked out. "And we're both very sorry." She elbowed my side before adding, "Aren't we, Gerard?"

"Oh, yes." I nodded solemnly. "We're both very sorry and we'll never do it again."

"Ever," Claire chimed in, joining me in nodding-dog mode. "We promise."

"Do you think we were born yesterday?" Sinead arched a disbelieving brow. "You'll be back at it the minute our backs are turned."

"Exactly," Mam agreed. "Do you know how to tell when a teenager's lying?"

"When their lips are moving," Sinead answered for her. "Which begs the question; what are we supposed to do with the pair of you now, hmm?"

"You clearly can't be trusted to be left alone together."

"Which means sleepovers are certainly out of the question."

"And you can both forget ever stepping foot in that tree house again."

"That's right, Sadhbh. Over my dead body."

"And mine, Sinead."

"Ah Jesus," I choked out, reaching for Claire's hand. "They sound like they want us to get a divorce."

"Well, that's never going to happen," Claire replied, giving my hand a reassuring squeeze. "Gerard and I are life partners. You can't break us up."

"Yeah," I agreed with a defensive huff, gesturing to Claire. "What she said."

"I'll give you life partners," Mam grumbled, clipping me over the back of the head. "You better hope your swimmers were contained, Gerard Gibson, because if you make us grandmothers before you both come of age, I'll take you to the same vet as Brian and have you chemically castrated."

———————————

Being demoted to Hugh's room was a bust but I couldn't argue with Sinead's reasoning. In all honesty, I was lucky to be let through the front door again, never mind being given a place to sleep at night.

Tossing and turning like a deranged lunatic, I couldn't close an eye.

Not because of nightmares tonight.

No, because I was wired.

I knew I could go home if I wanted to.

Mark was gone. My mother had told me as much tonight. An unforeseen emergency on his wife's side of the family was the lie he fed Mam and Keith before he slithered off like the snake he was.

A part of me was furious with myself for letting him walk away for the second time, but an even bigger part of me was so overwhelmed with relief that it took the sting off.

Because at the end of the day, I had been carrying this cross for ten long years, and I had coped fabulously. I would continue to go on coping just fine once that monster was on the other side of the world from me.

The way I saw it, I was making the best of a bad situation. The worst had already happened to me, and I'd survived.

I had built myself up from the bottom, and I would rather die than let that bastard get the better of me again. I would never let him beat me again. He won the battle against the child version of me, but he would never win the war against the grown-man version of me.

The only way I could see it worsen, or him truly defeat me, was if people knew about it. That was the hill I didn't think I could climb, and *he* knew that. My shame was his power hold over me and had been for a decade.

Regardless of his abrupt departure, I wasn't ready to go back in my room. Knowing that he had been there again, touching my stuff, tainting the air… That made it hard to function.

Besides, I felt comfortable in the Biggs house. I always had. This house was my home away from home and the girl sleeping in the room next to the one I was currently residing in made it impossible for me to leave.

Climbing out of my makeshift bed, I padded out of the room, only to make the rookie mistake of stepping on the creaky floorboard in the landing by the staircase. Within seconds, the matriarch of the house was out of bed and patrolling the landing. "Back to bed, young man."

Like a criminal caught in the act, I raised my hand and froze on the top step of the stairs. "I was just getting a drink, I swear."

Nodding in approval, Sinead gestured for me to continue. "No pit stops on your way back up. Straight to bed, you hear?"

"Okay."

"I mean it, Gibs. I'll know."

Oh, Jesus Christ.

Climbing off the last step, I scooped up a wandering Dick. "How's my boy?" I cooed, cuddling him to my chest. "Jesus, you even smell like her," I mused when I dropped a kiss to his head on my way to the kitchen. "I could eat you up."

When I flicked the kitchen on, and the room was bathed in a dull-yellow hue, I almost dropped my pussy with fright. "Jesus Christ!"

Hugh was slumped at the kitchen table with his elbows resting on the table and his head in his hands.

"Where the hell did you come from?" I whisper-hissed. "I thought you were gone out when your bed was empty." Frowning, I asked, "Where have you been, lad?"

"Around."

"Are you okay?"

"I'm grand."

"Hugh, you're sitting in the kitchen at three o'clock in the morning, looking like someone died." Concern grew inside of me. "You're clearly not okay, lad."

"I've just…" Cutting himself off, my friend blew out a breath and shook his head. "It's grand. I'll fix it."

"Fix what?"

Silence.

"Fix what?" I repeated, taking a seat at the table.

"I'm in trouble, Gibs," he whispered, head down.

"Trouble?" Setting Dick back down on the kitchen floor, I gave my oldest friend my full attention. "What kind of trouble, lad?"

"The bad kind."

"The Joey Lynch kind?" I asked, feeling bad that my thoughts immediately shifted to Lynchy. "Is it drugs?"

"No, it's not drugs, Gibs."

"Then what is it, lad?"

When he didn't respond, I stood up and repositioned myself on the chair next to his. "Hugh." I placed my hand on his shoulder. "Talk to me."

"I *can't*."

"Come on, lad, it's me." I gave his shoulder another squeeze. "You can tell me anything."

He opened his mouth to respond, only to pause and then drop his head in his hands again. "Fuck it, it doesn't matter, lad."

"It clearly does."

"I can't talk about it," he admitted, looking like a broken man. Having said that, he pushed his chair back and stood up. "I can't even think about it."

Without another word, he walked out of the kitchen, leaving me with nothing but unanswered questions and my pussy for company.

67

Viper with a Tongue in the Common Room

CLAIRE

Seven whole weeks had passed since Gerard's ladder had taken its maiden voyage into my tree, and we were still going strong. Better than strong. We were titanium.

Sure, our mothers had turned into a pair of tag-teaming ninjas hell-bent on foiling any and all plans of teenage debauchery, but as the saying goes, where there's will, there's a willy, and Gerard and I had found ways of being together.

The best part of it all? Mother Nature had visited me on time as per our arranged schedule for the past four years. Every twenty-eight days for five days, she liked to stop by to let me know my eggs were capable of hatching.

The first visit after we were intimate was the most welcome visit of all because it reassured me that Gerard's pierced ladder hadn't pierced any holes in our protection. The second time was a glorious reassurance that I could have my cake and eat it, too. Not that I didn't want to have babies with Gerard. I did. I just wanted those babies to arrive many years into the future.

Today was Wednesday, and the last day of our dress fittings before the winter ball on Friday night.

While today was technically a school day, the light dusting of snow outside meant that our school had sent out a message to parents to let them know that due to adverse road conditions, attendance was optional.

Of course, the moment we heard the good news, Gerard and I had opted to spend our snow day at the manor, building snowmen and throwing snowballs around with our besties.

I *loved* when it snowed, even more when it snowed in December. It filled me with all the warm, festive fuzzies, and knowing that Christmas break was almost upon us and I was about to spend it as Gerard's *girlfriend*, well, that just sent my good mood soaring to new heights.

"He never asks for anything when we're being intimate," I told my bestie as we tried on our dresses for the final time. "Is that normal?"

"I don't know," Shannon replied, turning around to catch a glance of the back of her dress in the full-length mirror. We were in Edel Kavanagh's coveted office/dressing room, surrounded by designer labels and waiting for her to return with a measuring tape. "I'm not the best person to ask. Lizzie would probably have way better advice than me, Claire."

"Lizzie would rather scalp herself bald and offer her hair as sacrifice to the devil before she helped me with my relationship."

Since Gerard and I had gone public with our relationship, my friendship with Lizzie had cooled to the stage where it felt like there was an iceberg between us. She barely spoke to me at school anymore, she didn't sit with me in class anymore, we rarely hung out, and if Shannon wasn't there, she didn't even acknowledge my presence.

I would be a liar if I said it didn't hurt, but I would be an even bigger one if I said Gerard wasn't worth it. Because he *was*. He so epically was.

"When you're with Johnny, does he have anything in particular that he enjoys you doing to him?"

"Claire!"

"What?" I huffed. "You're my best friend, and best friends are supposed to dole out wisdom to each other."

"What if Edel hears?"

"But she won't, because she's still not back with her tape, so spill your beans, Lynch."

"Well." Shannon seemed to think about it for a long time before saying, "He's big into neck kisses."

"Neck kisses?"

"Uh-huh."

"I think Claire was hoping for something that pertained to his package, Shan." Aoife laughed, appearing from behind the curtain of the changing area in her dress. "Woo, I am rocking this MILF look," she said, gazing at herself approvingly in the mirror, while adjusting her giant boobs. "I know ladies are supposed to be modest and all that jazz, but honestly, girls, if I was a cake, I'd eat myself." Cackling to herself, she added, "And, let's be honest, I am *no* lady."

"Ask Aoife," Shannon blurted out, pointing at her sister-in-law. "But just don't do it while I'm in the room, okay? Because I really don't need to know the ins and outs of my brother's sex life."

"Your brother puts the *sex* in life, period," Aoife tossed over her shoulder. "My man is gifted, girls. He puts the D in BD energy."

I stared blankly. "BD?"

"Big dick," Aoife explained, and then, waggling her brows, she used her hands to illustrate in detail what I presumed was the length of her boyfriend's willy, which sort of resembled that of a giant cucumber and mildly terrified me.

"Oh my god." My eyes widened in horror. "He could touch your appendix with that thing."

"I know!" Aoife nodded gleefully, looking like the cat that caught the cream. "I'm a *lucky* girl."

"And now I'm going to go cry," Shannon groaned, hurrying off with her hands over her ears.

"Come to Momma, pretty girl," Aoife coaxed, gesturing for me to come closer. "Let me tell you how to seduce a man."

Armed with a world of general knowledge of the male appendage, courtesy of Aoife Molloy, and the dress of my dreams, courtesy of Edel Kavanagh, I practically glided on air through the doors of Tommen the following morning.

It was still snowing outside, but it wasn't nearly heavy enough to garner another optional snow day. Not that I minded either way. I was happy at school or at home. Besides, we only had today and tomorrow left and then we were free for two whole weeks.

"Morning, family," I called out in a lyrical voice when I pirouetted into the sixth-year common room, stopping under a rogue piece of hanging mistletoe to smack a loud kiss to Patrick's cheek.

"Morning," everyone chorused back at me.

"What was that for, Baby Biggs?" He laughed, wiping my lip gloss from his cheek.

"Check where you're standing, pretty boy."

As soon as Patrick looked up and noticed the mistletoe, he took three safe steps to the left—and out of danger. "Thanks for the heads-up." Pulling on the sleeve of his jumper, he shifted around in discomfort. "Those two girls from your year have been following me around all week with the stuff."

"Helen and Shelley?" I laughed. "Aw, see, Pa, I tried to warn you about the trail of girls following after you."

"Hmm," was all he said in response.

"How's my second favorite mam and dad?" I cooed when I reached Joey and Aoife, who were eating toast in the kitchen area. "I would say my first, but clearly that title goes to my own mam and dad."

"Clearly," Joey drawled, looking like he didn't quite know what to make of my

Christmas cheer. "You know, you'd make a killing as one of Santa's elves," he surprised me by saying. "Or at kids' birthday parties."

"She really would, right?" Aoife laughed. "Slap a princess costume on her, give her some face paints for the kids, and she could easily make 200 euro an appearance."

"I could?" Excitement bubbled up inside of me at the thought, and I bounced from foot to foot. "Really?"

"Oh, yeah." Nodding, Joey turned his attention back to his girlfriend. "She would make a killing."

"Oh my god." My eyes widened. "I'm going to be rich!"

"You're already rich," they said in unison before Aoife turned her attention to the quiet redhead sitting alone on the couch. "Hey, pretty girl! Did you get your dress sorted for the ball tomorrow night?"

Katie's face flamed with heat from the compliment. "Uh, yeah, eventually."

"Yeah?" Interest piqued, Aoife strolled over to the couches and sank down beside Katie. "Is it the green one you showed me in the picture?"

The door flew open then and Gerard stalked in grumbling about show-offs and passports, followed by a delighted-looking Shannon, who had a pair of mouse ears perched on her head. "I'm going to France!" she practically screamed, and then she barreled toward me waving around a pair of tickets. "For three nights, Claire!"

"Omigod," I screamed, joining her in the bouncing as I studied the tickets in her hands. "Whoa, you're not just going to France, Shan," I squealed with excitement. "You're going to Paris!"

"That's still France," Lizzie said in a lifeless tone, shoving past me on her way to the kitchen area. "Read a fucking map sometime."

Choosing to ignore her, I smiled brighter for Shannon's sake and focused my attention on the mouse ears perched on her ears. "That must mean you're going to the happiest place on earth?"

Beaming with delight, Shannon nodded eagerly. "I've never been on an airplane before."

"Don't get the hump, Gibs," Johnny said when he strode into the room a moment later. "It's my girlfriend's Christmas present, lad. I couldn't exactly bring you along, could I?"

"Ah, I don't fucking see why not?" Gerard huffed, moving to my side. "Heads-up, Claire-Bear, these two inconsiderate bastards are jetting off to *oui*, Paris without us." Huffing out a breath, he swiped Shannon's mouse ears and perched them on top of his head before turning back to me. "See this? Take a good look, baby, because unfortunately, this is the closest you're going to get to Mickey this Christmas, because unlike

Mister Limitless Cash Flow over there"—he paused to jab a thumb in Johnny's direction before continuing—"your stud muffin can only afford to take you to see Santa."

"Aww!" Swooning, I wrapped my arms around his neck and pressed a kiss to his cheek. "You're taking me to see Santa?"

"Ho, ho, ho, Claire-Bear." Waggling his brows, Gerard hooked an arm around my waist and pulled me closer. "And if you're really good, then maybe we can…"

"Oh my god!" Releasing a furious scream, Lizzie threw the glass she was holding, causing it to smash to pieces the moment it connected with the wall. "Can you both shut the fuck up!"

You could have heard a pin drop it.

The entire room went deathly quiet.

"Gibs," Johnny said, offering Gerard a subtle nod when he opened his mouth to speak. "Not worth it, lad."

"I know that," Gerard ground out. "She's the one who won't make peace."

"Peace?" Lizzie choked out, voice thick with emotion. "You honestly expect me to make *peace* with the brother of my sister's rapist?" She sneered. "The same brother with blood on his hands?" Narrowing her eyes, she spat out, "You supported him. You backed him up when I was supposed to be your friend. I would rather slit my wrists than ever make *peace* with you!"

"I didn't back him up," Gerard roared, losing his cool. "Believe me when I tell you there is no one on this planet who despises that bastard more than me."

"Keep telling yourself that, Thor. See if it'll help with your guilty conscience."

"I'm not listening to this."

"Because you're guilty."

"And you're wrong!"

"I'm right and you know it."

"Fuck you, Liz."

"Fuck you right back. I don't care if there wasn't enough evidence for the DPP to make a case against him. I know the truth. I read it with my own eyes. So, don't you dare stand here and lie to my face. Unlike you, I have the ability to read a fucking letter, asshole."

Whoa.

"Hey!" Johnny snapped. "Don't fucking go there."

"Oh, that's right, Captain Fantastic," she choked out. "Protect your lapdog."

"Johnny, wait. Please don't. She's hurting so bad right now," Shannon said, trying to plead her case, but Johnny shook his head.

"Shan, I love you, baby, but I'm not the audience for her narrative."

And that was that.

Our leader had taken sides.

The line was drawn in the sand, and after months of trying to keep the peace and appease his girlfriend, Johnny Kavanagh had taken his rightful place beside his teammate.

"You need to stop talking," Johnny warned, taking a defensive stance in front of Gerard. "And back off."

"You started this, not him," I threw out there before Lizzie could change the narrative. "You shouted, you threw the cup, and *you* brought it up."

"Why are you always siding with him?" she screamed. "I'm supposed to be one of your best friends."

"And I'm supposed to be one of yours," I shouted back at her. "But you've spent the past two months dictating how I should live and then talking down to me like I'm a child for making decisions that don't fit your perfect narrative."

"You know what happened."

"I know it didn't have anything to do with Gerard."

"My sister is dead!"

"So is Gerard's sister!"

"Yeah but see here's the difference, Claire. I didn't drown his sister, but his brother sure as hell drowned mine!"

"Guys, can we not?" Shannon tried to interject but it was too late to be brought down. The pot had come to the boils and confessions were spilling over the rim.

"No," Lizzie cried hoarsely. "Because I'm never going to be okay with you going out with him."

"And I'm never going to start asking for your *permission!*"

Looking like a wild, cornered animal, Lizzie shook her head and bolted for the door. "You can all go to hell."

"What the…" Hugh muttered, looking around down at the crying girl pressed against him. "What happened?"

"Ask the rapist protector!"

"Gibs?" Hugh asked, turning around. "What happened?"

"You know what, Liz?" Gerard replied calmly. "One of these days, you're going to have to make peace with the fact that the only person responsible for your sister's death is your *sister*."

The minute he said it, Lizzie snapped. She lunged for him, and that's when it all went to hell. Moving like lightning, Hugh intercepted her before she could reach Gerard.

"Let me the fuck go," she screamed, banging and hitting at his chest with the fury of a thousand demons. "I don't need you to save me!"

Hugh didn't let go. Ignoring her slaps, he wrapped an arm around her waist and pulled her close, using his free hand to cradle her face to his chest. Eventually, she grew limp against him, hands reaching up to clutch the fabric of his school shirt, as he talked heatedly to the boys.

"Get her out of here, Hugh," Johnny warned, as he kept a protective stance in front of his friend, looking less in control of his emotions than I'd ever seen before. "Go now, lad."

Meanwhile, Katie stood quietly looking on, with an unreadable expression on her face.

Keeping Lizzie tucked up against his chest, Hugh continued to speak to his friends, while he doled out instructions and caught a set of flying car keys midair. He flicked his gaze to his girlfriend, who simply nodded before turning away from the drama and packing her lunch box into her schoolbag.

Shielding her face from the view of dozens of our peers when he opened the door to the main hallway, Hugh walked Lizzie in one direction, while Johnny steered Gerard in the other. Keeping a supportive hand on his shoulder, he walked his best friend away from the carnage.

"She needs a doctor," Pierce, who was standing in the hall, came into the fray and declared. "That girl is seriously unwell."

"Don't fucking say it like that," Patrick snapped back. "Jesus!"

"Hurt people *hurt* people," Shannon offered. "I'm not excusing it, but please don't vilify her for not using healthy ways to cope with her trauma."

"Shannon, we all have trauma," Katie replied. "Not everyone projects it on other people."

"I think it's because there were so many unsaid conversations," Patrick offered, shifting in his seat. "One day she was here and the next she—"

"Wasn't."

"Exactly."

"Nothing was cleared up," he added.

"Exactly," Shannon agreed, nodding eagerly. "So, for Lizzie, she's still living that day on repeat."

"Kind of like the film *Groundhog Day*."

"Yes," she beamed at Patrick. "Just like *Groundhog Day*." She turned to the rest of us. "The years are passing by for the rest of us, but she's stuck in that moment." Shrugging, she added, "Time can't heal when it doesn't pass by."

68

Opening Up and Shutting Down

GIBSIE

THE LAST SEVERAL WEEKS HAD BEEN THE BEST OF MY LIFE, BUT IN A MESSED-UP WAY, they had also been the hardest. Because every day, I woke up and *lied* to the one person I wasn't supposed to keep secrets from. It was bearable when our relationship was platonic, but the shift that had come over me since we became more was like night and day.

I felt so tired all the time, like I was carrying this massive weight around that was becoming more unbearable with every day that passed. It wasn't until the morning of the winter ball that I finally came to the conclusion that I couldn't do this anymore.

I couldn't carry this weight another day.

It was too much.

It was too crippling.

With my arm wrapped tightly around the naked girl in my bed and my attention fixated on my bedroom ceiling above us, I thought about my options.

Could I say it?

Could I truly get the words out again, knowing that the one and only time I had spoken them before, they had fallen on deaf ears. I wasn't believed then, so what was to say that Claire would believe me now? Yes, she loved me, I knew that was true, but love didn't have anything to do with someone's ability to believe in monsters.

Concentrating on my breathing, I tried to repress the feeling of uneasiness, and when that didn't work, I held my breath in the hope that I might pass out and get a few minutes of sleep before my alarm clock went off for school. But all that seemed to do was make the sound of my pulse even louder in my ears.

Finding no comfort within myself, I flicked my attention to the tux hanging on the back of my bedroom door before settling my gaze on the sleeping beauty in my arms. She'd been asleep for hours, while I hadn't closed an eye. I wasn't comfortable in my own bed, having spent ninety percent of my nights sleeping in hers, so it didn't exactly soothe the anxiety ebbing away at me.

But having her here in my space, with her body touching mine, gave me a semblance of peace in this room that I didn't have before. She made me want to stay in this bed with her. She made me want to relax. Because I loved her. Every part of me. With every bone in my body. Defective and all as I was. I couldn't help it. It was instinctive. It was ever consuming. It was forever.

As my eyes trailed over her, I felt my heart anchor itself to her, both attaching and wrapping itself up in intricate knots around every part of her. I knew that I would never get over this girl, which made lying to her almost as unthinkable as disclosing to her.

Fighting an internal war that had me losing either way, I waited in silence until she finally roused from her sleep, bringing with her a smile that shone brighter than any sun over Ballylaggin.

"Morning, Mr. Smiley Face," Claire mumbled sleepily as she rolled onto her side and draped both her arm and leg over my body. "Mmm, my human radiator."

"Morning, Mrs. Smiley Face," I replied, feeling my entire body ignite now that she was awake. "Are you okay?" Her soft little puffy breaths tickled my chest, but I didn't move an inch. I needed the warmth that emanated from her. The light. "Are you sore?"

"I feel great," she replied sleepily, shifting closer until our bodies were once again melded together. "Last night was super fun."

Super.

I smiled when she used the word.

It was so fucking adorable.

And last night was more than just super fun. It meant everything to me. She would never understand how many demons she chased out of my room with her body. Being with her in this bed, the same bed where I'd endured countless nights of torture throughout the course of my childhood, was so cathartic, it was almost surreal.

Tell her, my heart commanded, *just tell her.*

"Do we really have to go to school?"

"No," I croaked out, pushing down my memories once more to live in the moment with the person responsible for keeping my heart beating since I was seven years old.

"Yeah, we do," she said with a sigh. "Mam will get a call from Dee if I don't show up at school, and then we'll be caught because she'll call Edel and will find out that I'm not at Shannon's house."

I shifted in discomfort.

"Are you okay?" She lifted her head to look at me. "Your body just went all stiff."

"I'm grand," I assured her, while trying to figure out what to do or how to phrase what I knew I had to disclose. "I need to tell you something."

"Oh?"

"Yeah." I swallowed deeply and closed my eyes while I mentally prepared for the very real possibility that she was about to walk out on me. "It's about Dee."

No, my heart protested, *it's about Mark.*

One thing at a time, another part of my mind whispered.

Tell her everything.

"Dee?" Claire asked with a frown. "Tommen office Dee?"

"Yeah." Licking my lips, I tried really fucking hard to think about my next choice of words, knowing that I couldn't screw this up. "I, ah, I…"

"You what?" Claire teased, reaching up to pinch my nipple. "What's got you tongue-tied, Gerard Gibson?"

Just fucking say it.

Be a man and tell her, dammit.

She deserves the truth!

"I was with her a few times," I blurted out and then held my breath in trepidation.

But Claire didn't react. Instead, she continued to smile up at me, waiting for the confession. Because she was too pure to consider something so fucking wrong. Jesus, Johnny was right. Saying it out loud sounded all wrong. It was icky. It made me feel dirty.

"Dee," I repeated, when she didn't get my drift or was just too sweet to comprehend the crap I'd gotten myself twisted up in. "I've been with her, Claire."

"What do you mean?" she replied, confusion etched on her pretty face.

"I mean I've *been* with her," I repeated, enunciating the word *been* in the hope that she didn't make me go into detail. "In the past."

"The past?"

"Yeah." I nodded slowly, feeling my heart rate rack up a dangerous volume of beats per second. "But nothing has happened since fifth year, and *nothing* has happened since we've been together."

When she continued to stare at me, unblinking, I released a pained groan.

"Please say something, baby."

"I don't know what to say," she replied, slowly pulling herself into a sitting position. "Because I don't understand what you mean when you say you've been with the school's receptionist."

"Dee's Catwoman, Claire."

Now she got it.

Pain encompassed her features and I wanted to die.

"Did you sleep with her?"

"No." I shook my head. "No, I didn't, I swear. I've only been with you like that."

"Then what…" Her voice trailed off and she pressed her hand to her forehead. "You've been intimate with her in *other* ways?"

"Yes."

"In ways you've been intimate with me, or the ways I've been intimate with you?"

I knew what she was asking, and I fucking hated myself for the answer I had to give her. "It was all me. I was the one doing the touching…"

"Shh!" She clamped a hand over my hand and shuddered violently. "I can figure it out without the finer details."

"I don't know why I let it happen," I admitted when she dropped her hand from my mouth. "I'm so fucking sorry."

"Why?" She stared at me like she didn't know me. Like I was a stranger instead of the person she'd spent her whole life with. "Why would you be with her, Gerard?"

"I don't know," I offered, feeling helpless. "There's something fucking wrong with me in the head."

"Why?"

You know. "I don't know, Claire."

"You *have* to know."

Tell her. "I don't have an answer for you."

She didn't respond to that, but she didn't run away, either. Instead, she sat in the middle of my bed, with the sheets wrapped around her and stared at her hands.

"What are you thinking?" I asked when I couldn't take another minute of her silence.

"I'm thinking," she began to say, only to pause. "I'm thinking…" Shaking her head, she balled her small hands into fists and glared at me. "I'm thinking she's going to get into a hell of a lot of trouble for going anywhere near my boyfriend!"

"Whoa, Claire," I quickly tried to reason with her, but I could tell by the way she bolted off my bed and started to dress that it wouldn't be easy. "You can't tell anyone."

"Can't tell anyone?" She looked at me like I had two heads. "Gerard, she's a *grown-up*, in an *authoritative role*, who's been making moves on a *student*!" Sounding furious, she quickly threw on her school uniform before searching my bedroom floor for her shoes. "She's not getting away with this, Gerard."

"Claire, I told you because I didn't want secrets between us, not because I needed you to storm in and save me," I snapped, feeling myself go on the defensive. "I don't need you to do anything, okay?"

"Well, someone needs to."

"Don't do anything," I warned shakily. "This is my business, not anyone else's."

"Gerard, she shouldn't have laid a finger on you!"

"I know that," I snapped back and then dragged a hand through my hair in frustration. "But it's over and done with now, so let it go."

"No, it's not." She shook her head. "Because if your mother knew—"

"Jesus Christ, Claire, I'm trying to talk to you here and you're not listening to me! You're not hearing me, dammit!"

"I *am* hearing you, Gerard."

"Then keep your mouth shut," I strangled out. "I don't need action. I just needed you to know, okay? I thought I was doing the right thing by telling you, but clearly, I was wrong. Either way, I told you that in confidence, so don't screw me over by telling anyone, Claire."

"*She* screwed you over, Gerard," Claire urged, throwing her hands up in despair. "Dee did that to you, not me!"

69
Payback's a Biggs

CLAIRE

BEYOND FURIOUS, I STORMED INTO TOMMEN ON THE FRIDAY MORNING OF CHRISTMAS break, feeling none of my usual peppiness or good cheer. The school's winter ball was happening later tonight, and usually, I cared deeply about social events, but I was too blown away by the bombshell Gerard dropped on me earlier to give a shit about dances.

Gerard thought I was overreacting massively.

I thought he was *underreacting* colossally.

This was *sick*.

What he told me was *wrong*.

What our school receptionist did to him was *perverted*.

After arguing the entire way from his house to school, we had parted on bad terms in the school car-park.

Beyond revolted by his admission, I made my way straight to the office, determined to put that woman in her place whether he wanted me to or not.

"Can I help you?" Miss Pervert asked with a tight smile when I marched up to the desk.

"Yeah." Resting my elbows on the countertop, I glared down at her. "I wanted to know if Mr. Twomey realized that he has a pedophile on the payroll."

To give her credit, she kept her nerve when she replied with a polite, "Excuse me?"

"Well, what else would you call a grown adult taking advantage of a fifteen-year-old boy?" I demanded, having managed to squeeze that tidbit of information out of my boyfriend on our way to school. Yes, *school*. Where we were both *students* and his abuser was a member of *staff*.

Ugh!

"I'm not following you."

"Then, let me make it clearer for you," I seethed, leaning over the counter. Lucky for her, we were alone. "I know what you did. I know all about your dirty little secret, and I think you're sick." My voice rose with my outrage. "You are *sick* in the head, lady!"

"I think you need to leave."

"Oh, I'm not going anywhere until I speak to the principal."

Her face paled.

"Yeah, that's right," I sneered, beyond furious. "Your ass is going to prison, Dee."

"I was twenty-one," she tried to explain. "I was going through a rough patch at home, and I wasn't thinking clearly."

"Nothing excuses what you did, you pervert!"

"Stop calling me that," she cried, dropping her head in her hands.

"What? Stop stating facts?" I demanded, unwilling to back down an inch. "You are *disgusting*!" Furious, I reached over the desk and knocked a stack of her neatly piled papers everywhere. "He was a *child*, and *you* took advantage of him."

"No," she continued to protest. "It wasn't like that."

"I have friends at this school," I told her, my body simmering with anger. "Friends with younger brothers who won't be safe with a pedophile like you working here!"

"I haven't," she choked out, clutching her chest like she was mortally offended that I would even think such a thing. "I would never touch a child!"

"You have, would, and already did," I shouted back at her. "You make me sick. People like you make me sick!"

The office door flew inward then, and Gerard appeared in the doorway. "Claire!" His eyes were wild with panic. "Stop it, will you?"

"Stop it?" I swung around to glare at him. "Stop it? I'm not the one that you should be saying *stop* to, Gerard!"

"It was consensual." He tried to placate me, reaching for my hands when they flailed wildly. "Hey, hey, shh…just calm down for a second *please*." Tone coaxing, he pulled me close and smoothed my hair back. "She didn't force me to do anything I didn't want to do, okay?"

"None of that *matters*, Gerard," I screamed, clutching his arms and willing him to *hear* me. "Because she shouldn't have touched you in the first place."

"I never slept with him," she strangled out, like there was a reward for being a slightly lesser version of a full-blown creeper. "I never touched his private parts."

"No, you just manipulated him into touching yours on the off chance that if you were caught, he could take the blame," I spat out. "Well, I see through you, lady, and I know him better than you ever could."

"Claire," Gerard snapped, snaring my attention once more. "Please don't do this."

I couldn't hear him in this moment.

I couldn't be reasoned with.

Because there was no reasoning to explain away what she had done to him.

It angered me that he couldn't see just how badly he'd been taken advantage of. It infuriated me to the point that I felt like physically lashing out at them both, which was an abhorrent feeling for me.

I'd slapped a grand total of one person in my whole life, and I still felt guilty for doing it. Still, it didn't stop the urge I had to claw her pervy eyes out of their pervy sockets.

"You need to make this right," I warned her, holding a hand up. "You need to go to the Gards and make a statement."

"Absolutely not," Gerard cut in, shutting me down in a commanding tone. "If you love me, Claire." He grabbed my face between his hands and forced me to look at him. "If you love me like you say you do, then you won't tell anyone." His chest was heaving, his eyes wild with a mixture of betrayal and panic. "If you do that to me, if you break my trust like that, I don't think I'll be able to get past it."

"Don't say that!" I strangled out, feeling helpless as he backed me into a corner with his unspoken threat. "It's emotional blackmail."

"It's my truth," he replied, still holding my face. "You need to *hear* me."

"I am hearing you, Gerard."

"Then do what *I'm* telling you I need you to do," he urged hoarsely. "Please, Claire!"

"Okay, I won't tell!" I cried out, feeling like a complete failure. Because I was a failure. I was failing the boy standing in front of me. "On one condition."

"Name it," he said with a relieved nod. "It's yours."

Sniffling, I pointed to his abuser. "She quits her job at Tommen."

"I'm not going to quit my job."

"Either you resign from your post with immediate effect," I snarled, breaking free from Gerard's hold to swing my glare on her. "Or I'll make sure that you're behind bars by the end of the day."

70

What a Disaster

GIBSIE

"WHAT IN THE NAME OF GOD WAS I THINKING?" LYING ON TOP OF MY BED IN MY TUX, several hours later, I howled like a banshee into the phone, repeating the same question I'd been asking myself all day. "Why, god, why do bad things happen to good people?"

"Because she's not a good person, Gibs, and your girlfriend was right when she called her a pervert."

I narrowed my eyes and glared at my phone. "Not fucking helping, Cap."

"I told you that you never should've touched that woman. From day one, I told you, but you wouldn't listen to me."

"Now you're really not fucking helping," I huffed. "I've a good mind to hang up on you."

"That wouldn't be such a terrible thing, lad, considering I need to take a shower and get ready for this bleeding dance."

"Don't you dare hang up on me in my need," I warned, pointing a finger at the phone, even though he couldn't see me. "I'm warning ya, Cap. I'll cry."

"Jesus, fine," I heard my best friend groan. "You can stay on the line while I take a shower."

Nodding my approval, I resumed my tale of woe, rehashing the same argument over and over until I ran out of steam.

"Do you want to hear something positive?" I heard Johnny ask over the sound of a shower motor running.

"Yes," I begged. "Badly."

"I'm proud of you."

I balked. "*Proud* of me?"

"You came clean to her, Gibs," he called back. "You got it off your chest. That couldn't have been easy, lad, but you did it."

"Johnny, she almost took leave of her senses," I deadpanned. "She *threatened* to have Dee arrested, she *forced* her to resign on the spot, and I'm not sure if she still wants to *be* with me. I reckon it's safe to say there is nothing about today that I can be proud of." Shuddering, I added, "It was a terrible fucking mistake on my part and one I won't ever be making again."

"Then I guess it's a good thing you only have one skeleton in your closet, lad."

"Yeah." I clenched my eyes shut and nodded. "Lucky me."

"Listen to me," he said when the sound of the motor running abruptly cut out. "I want you to get your tux on, splash some water on your face, walk your ass across the street, and give that girl of yours the yellow bleeding flower you've spent the last two weeks trying to hunt down. Shannon and I will be over in the limo in an hour, lad, so you best be ready."

"It's a Midas Touch rose," I muttered. "And what if she doesn't want to go with me anymore, Johnny?" My heart seized with dread at the thought. "I've known Claire my entire life, and I swear I've never seen her so angry."

"If you don't shoot, you don't score, Gibs."

"Trust you to toss out a sport's analogy when I'm having an existential crisis."

"Just go get your girl, Gibs," he instructed before the line went dead.

"Easier said than done, Cap," I whispered, scrubbing my face with my hand. "*Fuck.*"

Tossing my phone on my nightstand, I reached a hand under my mattress to retrieve the familiar folded-up piece of paper, and then, like the masochist I was, I unfolded the page and reread Caoimhe Young's suicide note.

The real one.

The one she left just for me.

71

Andie Anderson Yellow

CLAIRE

By the time the clock struck half past eight on Friday night and there was still no sign of Gerard, I resigned myself to the very high probability that I would be going solo to the winter ball.

Hugh had left over an hour ago to pick up Katie. Meanwhile, I remained slumped on the couch in my yellow satin gown, waiting on a boy who might never show up. Not that I cared if I didn't make the dance. I'd missed my appointments with both the hairdresser and the beautician, and I was feeling a whole heap less festive than I was furious.

To be honest, if it wasn't for the fact that my mam seemed so excited about the whole thing, I would have thrown on my pajamas and crawled into bed.

The fact that Mam had spent two painstakingly long hours straightening my curls and had phoned up her friend Betty to come over to do my nails and makeup only proved to me just how important this was to her, and I really hated letting my mam down.

She's not the only person you're letting down, my conscience hissed, and I wanted to cry.

I always like to think that I had a fairly straightforward moral compass. Wrong was wrong and right was right. But Gerard had forced my hand today, and now I felt like my compass was pointing in some morally gray area that I had never looked at before.

Dee had resigned. I'd watched her leave the school with my own eyes. It was definitively something to be satisfied about. But it wasn't enough. Because I would forever know what she did to Gerard, and whether he wanted to acknowledge it for what it truly was or not, he would forever have to shoulder that abuse. Meanwhile, his abuser got to start over wherever she liked with zero consequences for her senseless actions.

It wasn't fair.

"Claire?" Mam peeked her head around the sitting room door with a smile on her face. "Your date is here."

My breath hitched and I felt weirdly emotional. "He is?"

She pushed the door wide open and there he was, standing in his tux, with a yellow corsage in hand. And not just any flower. "You got me a Midas Touch rose?"

His gray eyes locked on mine, and he offered me an uncertain shrug. "Andie Anderson yellow, right?"

Swallowing down the lump in my throat, I forced myself to stand. "Right."

"You look beautiful, Claire-Bear."

"Thanks."

"Fuck," he groaned, noticing the tear I had attempted to discreetly wipe off my cheek. "Come on, baby, don't cry." Closing the space between us, he cupped my cheek and pulled me flush against him. "I don't want to fight tonight."

Shivering, I leaned into his touch. "Neither do I."

"Then let's just put it on the back burner until tomorrow," he said hoarsely. *It* being Dee. "Let's have a good night, okay?" His thumb traced over my cheek as he spoke. "You and me, and we can deal with everything else in the morning, okay?"

"Okay." I bit back a sob and steadied my breathing before whispering, "I thought you weren't coming."

"And leave my baby hanging?" His tone was gentle and coaxing. "Not in this lifetime, sweetheart." Taking my hand in his, he placed the corsage on my wrist. "You really do look beautiful."

"So do you," I squeezed out, feeling incredibly emotional as I entwined my fingers with his and looked up at his beautiful face. "I love you."

His eyes burned with warmth in response. "I love you, too."

"Aww, would you look at them, Sinead. Aren't they only adorable," I heard Sadhbh gush from the doorway moments before a bright flash almost blinded me.

"Oh, don't mind us," Mam cooed as she clicked furiously on her camera. "Just pretend like we're not watching and act natural."

"Bubba, put the corsage on Claire's hand again for us, will you?" Sadhbh asked her son. "I want a photo of that for the wall."

"Oh, good thinking, Sadhbh," Mam chimed in, still clicking away like a demon. "It would look smashing on the mantelpiece."

Thirty minutes later, we were sprawled out in the back of a limousine with our friends, having been subjected to a million different poses at the hands of our amateur photographer mothers.

"You know what, Claire-Bear, I'm sure your mam had her finger over the lens the entire time." Gerard chuckled as he leaned across the seats to clink champagne glasses with Shannon before returning to my side. "She's going to be pissed as hell in the morning."

"Oh god, let's hope not!" I laughed, taking the glass of champagne Johnny poured for me. "Otherwise, she'll make us dress up and do it again tomorrow."

"You look so beautiful," Shannon gushed for the dozenth time as she admired my hair. "I can't believe it's this long when it's straightened."

"Claire, you look very beautiful," Johnny acknowledged with a friendly smile before sinking down on the seat next to his girlfriend. "Now, where's my queen?" he purred, draping his big arm around her slim shoulders. "Every time, Shannon like the river," he purred, kissing her neck. "Every time, baby." He pulled back to look at her and released a masculine growl of approval. "You take the breath clean out of me."

"Is everybody good to go?" the driver asked, lowering the divider.

"Yeah," Johnny replied before quickly backpedaling. "Wait, does everyone have their tickets?"

"I have ours," Shannon chimed in, fishing two tickets out of her purse.

"I didn't even know we needed tickets." I looked at my friends. "We *need* tickets?"

"I have tickets," Gerard confirmed, reaching into his tux and then frowning. "Let me rephrase that to I have tickets on my nightstand."

"You're a bleeding train wreck, Gibs," Johnny groaned. "I swear you'd lose your head if it wasn't screwed on."

"I'll get them," I announced, moving for the door. "I need to pee anyway."

"Make it snappy, please," the driver called out.

"I beg your fucking pardon, good sir," I heard Gerard tell the driver when I climbed out of the limo. "Please refrain from telling my girlfriend to be snappy about anything."

Biting back a snicker, I made a beeline for his front door, kicking off my heels as I went. Bolting upstairs to the bathroom, I managed to relieve myself and wash up in record time before going in search of our tickets—something I was *so* not impressed about.

Considering the amount of money parents paid for their kids to attend Tommen, you would think they could have sprung for an actual hotel, but to find out they were charging us to dance around the P.E. hall? Well, that took the fecking biscuit.

Hurrying into Gerard's room, I moved straight for his nightstand, deftly kicking a pair of my tights under his bed as I went. *What Sadhbh didn't see couldn't hurt her.*

The tickets weren't on the nightstand like Gerard said, but they *were* on his bed, along with his phone, a lighter, a packet of chewing gum, and his wallet that I knew contained our emergency condoms. Opening my handbag, I scooped the lot inside and then bent down to retrieve a folded-up note that had fallen from the pile. Shrugging, I tossed that into my handbag with everything else before racing back outside.

"Got them," I declared when I joined my friends in the limo once more.

"Woo!" Gerard cheered, pulling me onto his lap and smacking an affectionate kiss to my cheek. "Let's get this show on the road!"

72

Save the Best for Last

GIBSIE

Feeling like Claire and I were somewhat back on track, I was determined to make sure that she had a good night. Maybe, with a bit of luck, I might end up wooing her to the point where she gave me a hall pass on my in-Dee-scretions.

Catching ahold of her hand the moment we got inside, I took my girl for a spin around the dance floor to the live band's cover of the Beatles' "Twist and Shout," not giving two shits if I was missing out on sacred time with the lads.

Tonight's mission consisted of making my girlfriend happy. I'd seen the tears on Claire's cheeks when I finally hauled my ass across the street tonight.

She looked genuinely surprised to see me.

Like she was prepared for me to let her down.

Not on my watch.

Now, it didn't take a genius to know that I was, hands down, the best male dancer within a ten-mile radius of Ballylaggin, but I was only as good as my partner. The blond bombshell herself who taught me everything I knew.

I'd been dancing with Claire Biggs since I could put one foot in front of the other, and we moved together on the dance floor the same way we moved together under the sheets.

Effortlessly.

I didn't know how she managed to do it, but she healed the broken pieces inside of me. She patched me up in such a way that I was a functioning man again. For *her*.

Only for her.

Happy to hand her off to her female bestie when she came looking for her, I continued to bop around to the band, quite content to be my own dance partner, because, in all honesty, my moves were wasted on the rest of them.

However, when the band kicked off their own haunting rendition of Sinead O'Connor's "Nothing Compares 2 U," I decided it was time for shots.

Squeezing past Katie, who was clinging to Hugh for dear life as they half danced, half hugged along to the poignant lyrics, I made a beeline for the lads' changing room where I knew I would find my people.

The minute I stepped through the door, I was greeted with a chorus of cheers from my teammates and a bottle of tequila.

"Come to me, you beautiful devil, you," I mused, gulping down as much as I could in one go without puking, which was surprisingly a lot more than most. See? There was a reason my mam called me special.

"Well, if it isn't Mister Nine Lives himself." Johnny chuckled, clapping my shoulder when I joined him at our usual spot on the bench. "I don't know how you managed to put that smile on Claire's face, lad, but keep that shit up."

"It's a gift," I replied, necking back another swig from the bottle. "Fucking cheapskates really shafted us out of the ski trip for this poxy dance?" I gestured around us. "Bad form, lads."

"Agreed," my best friend said. "But the girls seem to be thrilled with it."

"Speaking of girls." Feely rose to his feet. "We better get back out there before they come looking."

"We?" My brows shot up in surprise. "Who'd you bring, lad?"

He shifted in discomfort before saying, "Lizzie asked me to go with her."

"And you said *yes*?" I gaped at him in horror. "Are you mental?"

"Yes, I agreed to go with her, and no, I'm not mental," he replied calmly. "And no, it's not up for discussion."

"Fair enough." Shrugging, I downed another decent dollop of tequila before muttering, "It's your funeral, lad."

73

Cheat Sheets and Confessions

CLAIRE

"You're peeing again?"

"I can't help it, Shan. I have a super-sensitive bladder," I called back. "I've been like this since forever. Ask Hugh. He'll tell you. I used to wet the bed constantly when I was little."

"Too much information, Claire." Shannon laughed from the other side of the cubicle door. "Some things are best left unsaid."

"No, God, no!" I wailed when I pulled down my underwear and was greeted by an unwelcome visitor. "Why do bad things happen to good people?" Balling my hand into a fist, I shook it at the ceiling above my head. "You are two days early, you wicked, wicked torturer!"

"Oh my god, who?" Shannon called back. "What's wrong?"

"Mother Nature!"

"What about her?"

"She's here, dammit!"

"Do you want a tampon?"

"Ew, no, I don't put things in my tree."

"Tree?"

"Oops. Forgot I wasn't talking to Gerard. Hey, don't tell him I'm on my period, okay? He faints at the sight of blood, and I swear if he even thinks about it too much, he gets queasy."

"What a baby."

"I know." Reaching for my handbag, I quickly unzipped it and started to root inside. "I know I have a pad in here somewhere. I always take one with me, no matter what."

"Really?" Shannon asked. "You take one everywhere?"

"Mm-hmm. Everywhere," I called back. "I never leave the house without one after what happened to you at school last year."

"Oh god," Shannon groaned. "Don't remind me."

"Found it!" Grinning victoriously, I quickly handled my business before rejoining Shannon at the sink. "Quick, check the back of my dress."

"You're all clear," my bestie assured me, taking her time to inspect the back of my dress. "Close call."

"Tell me about it." Breathing a sigh of relief, I washed and dried my hands before inspecting my makeup. "Hey, Shan? You got any lipstick with you?"

"Sorry, I didn't bring any makeup with me."

"Hang on," I mumbled more to myself than her, as I placed my bag on the sink and rummaged inside. "I think I have a lip gloss in here."

"What do you have in there?" Shannon teased. "The kitchen sink?"

"A lady should always be prepared for any scenario," I joked, fingers landing on something light and papery. "Hmm."

"What's that?"

"I don't know," I mused, withdrawing the folded-up piece of paper. "It was with Gerard's stuff when I went to grab our tickets."

"I bet it's a cheat sheet for GTA," Shannon snickered, watching over my shoulder as I unfolded the a4 sheet of paper. "Both Gibs and Johnny keep cracking up because they can't clear the missions as fast as me."

I knew she was talking to me. I could hear her voice. But I couldn't make out a word she was saying because my attention was riveted to the words splashed across the page in my hand.

"Oh my god," Shannon gasped, leaning in closer to get a better look. "Is that from…"

"Caoimhe Young," I strangled out, hands trembling violently as my mind furiously fought to protect itself from the information my eyes were sending it.

"No," Shannon cried out, covering her mouth with her hand. "Don't read it, Claire." Too late.

Gibsie,

It is to my deepest shame that I write this letter.

Words can't express how sorry I am for the pain that my lack of belief has caused you.

I let you down. I understand that now, and if I could go back in time to that night, I promise I would take you at your word. I would protect you from him.

I have no way of making this better for you, or redeeming myself in essence because the bottom line comes down to the fact that I was supposed to protect you and didn't.

My biggest fear of all is that you won't believe me when I say I didn't know. I guess that's a hypocritical statement to make when I did the very same to you.

You told me and I didn't listen. You were a young child who trusted his favorite babysitter enough to disclose the horrendous abuse you had been enduring at the hands of your stepbrother, and that babysitter chose to let her teenage hormones blind her.

To say that I had rose-tinted glasses on when it comes to Mark is an excuse that I won't give you. Not you, sweet boy.

The fact of the matter is that I didn't want to hear it. I didn't want to see what was happening. I had this incredible blind spot that I couldn't see out of when it came to him.

But I saw tonight.

When I walked into your bedroom to check on you and found him pinning you to your mattress raping you, I think I died inside. Your eyes. You looked so broken. So defeated. You weren't making a sound. Your tears were as silent as my voice, and I am so sorry for that.

I don't know how I'm supposed to live with myself for allowing you to suffer like you have. I honestly don't think I can.

I've written you this letter, and I want you to take it to your mam. If not your mam, then take it to Sinead Biggs across the street. All you have to do is hand over this letter, sweet boy, and I promise you he'll get what he deserves.

(For all who read this letter, let it be known that I, Caoimhe Young, on the night of April 5th, 2000, witnessed my boyfriend, Mark Allen, raping his eleven-year-old stepbrother, Gerard Gibson, while I was supposed to be babysitting him. Let it also be known that eighteen months before witnessing this rape, Gerard Gibson disclosed to me that he didn't feel safe around Mark, and that he touched him inappropriately. And finally, to my deepest regret, let it be known that I, Caoimhe Young, believed my boyfriend's word over that of an innocent child.)

For my part in your pain, for my silence, I can never say sorry enough. I can only hope that my absence gives you some comfort, because while I know I wasn't your abuser, my lack of willingness to believe your truth hurt you in ways he never could.

Goodbye, sweet boy.

Caoimhe. x

74

Fade into You

CLAIRE

"CLAIRE, WAIT!" SHANNON CHASED AFTER ME AS I BOLTED OUT OF THE BATHROOM, down the hallway, and into the cold night air.

"Oh god."

I couldn't breathe.

"Oh god."

I couldn't *breathe*!

Collapsing in a heap on the ground, I lost all control of my upchuck reflex and vomited profusely.

"Looks like someone had too much to drink," Ronan McGarry snickered when he walked past me heaving my guts up at the side of the building.

"Looks like you need to mind your own business," Shannon hissed, sounding almost feral as she dropped to her knees beside me and shielded me from everyone's view.

"Well, if it isn't the little mouse who finally found her voice."

"Oh, fuck off, Ronan!" Shannon snapped.

"What did you…"

"I said 'fuck off!'" she screamed at the top of her lungs. "Now!"

"Jesus, relax," he muttered before stalking away in a huff. "You girls are crazier than your asshole boyfriends."

"Shan." Reaching for my best friend, I clung to her as my entire body racked with violent tremors and my stomach continued roll. "He raped…he raped…he raped…"

"I know, Claire. I read it, too," she replied, crying softly as she cradled my head to her chest. "Poor Gibsie."

The minute she said that, another wave of hysteria washed over me. "I need to f-find h-him!"

"No, no, no," she tried to coax through sniffles. "Not here, okay? Not like this."

"I have to!" I practically screamed as I tried and failed to get to my feet. "I have to ta-talk to h-him…tell someone what I just read!" On my hands and knees, I pushed myself up, and this time, my trembling legs managed to keep me upright. "Shan, did you read it?" I couldn't see through my tears, as I looked around wildly for her. "Did you r-read what that l-letter said?"

"I read it," she whispered, pushing my hair back off my face before gently prying the letter from my hands. "Listen to me, and this is very important, okay?" Sniffling, I nodded, watching as she carefully folded the letter and placed it inside her bra. "You need to *not* react right now."

"But I just…"

"I know," she urged, clutching my shoulders. "I know, and you know, but Gibsie doesn't know *we* know, and now is *not* the place for this conversation. Not in front of all these people."

"I can't pretend I didn't s-see it," I choked out, throwing my arms around her. "I can't, Shan. I'm not b-built like that." Not now. Never again. I'd let too many things slip on by throughout my life. The constant bullying from Lizzie. The mean jokes and jibes at his expense. His lifetime of discomfort living in that house with those people. Dee's predatory grooming of him.

No.

No more.

Not this time.

"I'm not asking you to pretend," she replied, comforting me. "I'm asking you to say nothing. At least for now. Not here, okay?"

"But I…"

"Don't do it," she begged with a sniffle. "Don't make him relive his worst memories in the middle of a school dance."

"I have to go to the authorities with this, Shannon!"

"I agree, Claire, I do, okay? But not here. Not this night."

"What am I supposed to do?" I sobbed. "I can't just *pretend*." I had to talk to him. I had to talk to Sadhbh. "Mam," I strangled. "I need to call my mam."

"Just follow my lead, okay?" she replied, hugging me tight. "We'll get through the dance, and then we'll figure out what to do next. I promise I'll look after you."

"But who w-will l-look after Gerard?" I strangled out. "Oh god, Shan, this is so wrong."

"He's with Johnny," she replied, pulling back to offer me a tearful smile. "There isn't anyone else in the world he's safer with right now than him."

"I don't need to figure it out, Shan," I choked out. "I know what I need to do." It was the same thing I should have done with Dee. "I have to report this." I swallowed deeply, feeling my chest heaving as my world imploded around me. "I have to tell."

Shannon didn't keep sanitary towels in her purse, but she did keep an emergency toothbrush and paste, something I found myself oddly grateful for.

It took a barricaded bathroom door and forty-five minutes of deep breathing exercises she'd learned from her trauma counselor to calm me down. In the end, she'd disappeared out of the bathroom, giving me strict instructions to stay put.

When she returned ten minutes later, it was with a tiny pill of diazepine she had somehow managed to weasel from Lizzie.

After another twenty minutes, I had managed to compose myself enough to return to the dance.

"Just keep smiling," Shannon whispered in my ear, and then gave my hand a reassuring squeeze. "Two more hours and it's all over, okay?"

Two more hours?

Wrong, wrong, wrong!

I couldn't cope with the weight of my conscience as it threatened to drag me under.

My breath hitched in my throat when my bleary gaze landed on Gerard. He was on the dance floor with Johnny and Patrick, and throwing shapes like it was going out of fashion.

Always the joker.

Hiding his pain behind a smile.

"Oh god," I choked out.

"No," Shannon commanded, giving my hand another squeeze as she led me onto the dance floor to join our boyfriends. "For *his* sake."

How could he do it? How could he live with his demons like this and mask his pain with a smile? I didn't understand it, but I knew in my heart that I could never in good conscience allow it to happen another minute. He deserved to be saved, and I was determined to do that. Never again would I sit back and watch his head go under the water. I would bring him to the surface even if it meant drowning our relationship in the process.

"There's my intended," Gerard declared with a wolfish grin, dancing toward me. "Where the fuck have you been, Claire-Bear?" His breath was fused with alcohol, but his tone was warm and loving. "You missed some serious belters. The band are on fire!"

"Mmm." I smiled as brightly as I could, but at best it was a watery one. I knew what Shannon said made sense. *Don't ruin his night.* But that seemed implausible to me, considering Mark Allen had ruined his world so many years ago. And Caoimhe? Jesus, I had so many conflicting emotions right now that I was afraid to delve too deeply into them. Anger and resentment were keeping company with my devastation, and I was starving for justice.

"You good, Claire-Bear?"

Another nodding smile.

It was all I could do.

Do more, Claire.

Just take him by the hand and walk outside.

Tell him you know.

Put your arms around him and offer him a safe place to land.

Then take him to the Garda Station and press charges on that monster!

When the band started to play their own rendition of Mazzy Starr's "Fade into You," Gerard took my hand and led me onto the middle of the floor. Pulling me close, he kept one big hand flattened against the curve of my spine, while using the other to hold my hand to his chest. Our bodies moved in perfect synchrony, like we'd been born to dance this dance together.

My heart was aching, a desperate feeling of loss and longing weighing heavily on my soul, but he was here. He was trying. He was mine. Unable to take the pressure in my chest another second, I reached up and grabbed his face with my hands.

"Are you o…"

Whatever he was saying, he never got a chance to finish as I pushed up on my high heels and kissed him.

Right there in the middle of the dance floor, I pressed my lips to his. It wasn't an erotic kiss or a seductive one.

I had to.

If I didn't kiss him, I was going to scream.

Instead, I kept my lips melded to his and clenched my eyes shut. Unable to get close enough or deep enough into this boy, I reached around and fisted his hair, keeping our lips fused together.

No.

It's not enough.

You need to do more.

You need to speak up!

Finally, when I felt like my lungs would explode from the effort it was taking to hold my breath, I released him and exhaled a ragged breath.

His gray eyes were locked on mine but neither of us spoke a word.

Instead, we just stared at each other, both clearly reeling in the moment, in our feelings, in each other.

"Claire." He shook his head ever so slightly, almost like he was disagreeing with something internal happening inside of his mind. "What's wrong?" he finally asked.

"Nothing."

"That's not true." He eyed me warily. "Tell me."

"I, ah…" I tried to smile, but I could barely get my lips to rise. "I…" *Just say it, dammit. Just take his hand and run. Save him, Claire!* "I'm just happy to be here with you, Gerard." The words tasted like betrayal on my tongue, because while there was no lie in what I told him, it wasn't enough.

"Claire." His lips parted and I watched as he licked his lips before dragging the bottom one into his mouth, teeth grinding furiously against the plump skin. It wasn't a method of seduction. It was a quirk of his. One he performed when he was anxious.

Because this was scaring him.

He was afraid of what was happening between us.

Me.

I was scaring him.

We were still dancing, moving in harmony to the music playing around us, but I wasn't here on the dance floor with him.

Instead, I was traveling back in time, mentally reeling as every quirky thing he'd ever said or done finally snapped into place like a heartbreaking jigsaw.

For most of his life, Gerard had been trapped in a room in his head, while I had been banging on the door, desperately trying to break him out.

Because his past was his prison, and our love was his getaway car.

I know, I mentally told him, *I know, and I believe you, and I will fight to the death to get justice for you.*

"Claire." His hands were on my shoulders, gliding up my neck before settling on either side of my face. "I love you."

My breath hitched in my throat because I knew what was coming.

This time when our lips collided, we weren't frozen still or stuck in an internal war because a decision had been made.

Cupping my cheeks in his big hands, and with his gray eyes locked on mine, he brushed his nose against mine affectionately. Once. Twice. And then his lips were on mine.

Feeling weak, I reached out to steady myself, finding purchase in the part of his shirt that was covering his chest. Fisting the fabric tightly in both hands, I fell into the moment, letting his lips guide mine like he had guided me a million other times in a million different ways.

I'm going to love you through all of this, I mentally told him, *even when I do something that's going to make you hate me.*

The lyrics of the song were dripping into my subconscious, and I was feeling every word in the deepest part of my soul. Every note seemed to hold a direct line to my feelings and desires.

Because I did want to fade into him.

I wanted to wrap myself around his broken body and chase his demons away with warmth and love. I wanted to cry because of the unfairness of it all. I wanted... I just *wanted*.

When his tongue touched mine in a slow drugging move, I felt my abdominal muscles tighten. Somewhere even deeper inside of me, I felt a delicious dull aching throb that seemed to have a pulse of its own.

The more he kissed me, the faster my heart beat, and the stronger the ache grew. It was a primal feeling I had no control over, one that seemed to take on a life force of its own. Being with him felt effortless because it felt so natural. Like this is what I was supposed to do. These lips were the ones my lips had been waiting for and no other lips would do.

These hands were the ones my body accepted without question or doubt.

This boy was the boy.

The boy my heart had been created to beat for.

The boy I was made to love.

It was effortless.

Clenching my eyes shut to hide my tears, I kissed him for all I was worth, telling him with my touch everything I couldn't say out loud.

I believe you, Gerard Gibson.

I believe you.

I believe you.

I believe you.

75

Let Me Do This for You

GIBSIE

THERE WAS SOMETHING VERY WRONG WITH MY GIRLFRIEND, AND I WASN'T SURE IF IT was because of the whole Dee thing, but Claire wasn't acting like her regular self.

First off, she had disappeared from the dance for well over an hour, and when she reappeared, she'd clearly been crying. After point-blank refusing to tell me what was wrong, she had clung to me on the dance floor.

When she started kissing me to the point where we were making a scene, I knew something was off, but I was too fucking drunk and horny to slam the brakes on her sudden neediness. Hence our current predicament.

With her dress pooled around her hips, and her tits on full display, she pushed me down on the couch in the empty sixth-year common room. We weren't supposed to be here clearly, but when she put her mouth on me, any and all rules went out the window.

Climbing on top of me, Claire straddled my hips and kissed me hungrily. I didn't understand any of this, but the harder she rocked against me, the harder I grew. "Fuck."

She was moving her body in ways I'd never felt her move before, like she was frightened of losing me or something. The only reason I noticed this behavior was because I felt it every time I was with her. When she unzipped me and slid her hand inside my boxers, I tensed.

"It's okay," she coaxed, palming me. Leaning in close, she kissed me gently before pulling back once more. With her brown eyes locked on mine, she released her hold on me and stood up. "Do you trust me, Gerard?"

"Yes." Instinctively, I moved to follow her, but she shook her head and pushed me back down on the couch.

"And you know I'd never hurt you, right?"

"Obviously." Confused, I leaned back and studied her face, unsure of what she wanted, but when she dropped to her knees in front of me, and reached for my waistband, I figured it out pretty quickly.

"Then let me do this for you."

"Claire, wait! I don't…" I began to say, but quickly stopped when I felt her mouth on me. "I've never..." Trembling violently, I balled my hands into fists and my sides, and kept my eyes locked on the top of her head as she worked me over with her mouth. "Fuck..."

"Thank you," she said a little while later when she readjusted her dress.

"Thank *me*?" My head clouded with lustful confusion when I tucked myself away. Mentally reeling from the sensations she drew from my body, I sat with my thoughts. With my trepidation. With my gratitude. Because Claire had just done something for me that I didn't think I would ever be able to cope with. But she did it, and I coped. More than coped, I *enjoyed* it. "I think it's safe to say that I'm the one who should be thanking you, sweetheart."

"Gerard, you know I love you so much." Her eyes were watery again and her tone of voice sent a spiral of panic through me.

"I love you, too, babe."

"No, I mean I really, really love you," she pushed, eyes locked on mine, tone as serious as her expression. "You're my first love." Her breath caught in her throat but she steadied herself before squeezing out, "You're my only love."

"And you're mine." Hooking an arm around her waist, I pulled her back down on my lap. "I know you keep saying there's nothing wrong, Claire, but I'm not stupid, okay? At least, not when it comes to you."

Her gaze dropped to her feet. "There's something I need to talk to you about."

"Okay," I drawled, keeping a firm hold of her waist. "Hmm?" Leaning in close, I stroked her nose with mine. "Tell me, baby."

She opened her mouth to respond then the door opened inward, and two bodies joined us in the darkness.

"Show me."

"No."

"Fucking show me."

"Why do you care!"

"You know why!"

"Fuck, I can't do this anymore."

"And I can? Jesus Christ, this is wrecking me. *You* are wrecking me."

Both voices sounded familiar, but it was the male voice that caused my girlfriend to call out her brother's name. "*Hugh*?"

"*Claire*?"

Busted.

Snickering I reached over the back of the couch for the light switch and flicked it on. "Looks like you and your sister both inherited the same filthy mind," I teased, but the shit-eating grin plastered on my face quickly morphed into a what-the-fuck expression when my eyes landed on my old friend in the dark with…

"*Lizzie?*" Claire demanded, twisting around on my lap to glower at her friend. "What are you doing sneaking around in the dark with *my* brother?"

Never one to miss an opportunity to throw shade at me, Lizzie tossed back, "What are you doing sneaking around in the dark with *my* enemy?"

"Don't you *dare* call him names," Claire warned, sounding more furious than I ever heard her. She sprang off my lap like a jacked-up backstreet fighter and paced the floor in front of the couch, hands balled into fists at her side.

"Whoa, Claire-Bear," I tried to coax, reaching for her hand. "It's all good."

"No, it's not," she replied tightly, not meeting my eyes. "Nothing is good in the world, and this school is full of fake people!"

"Fake?" I frowned. "Who's fake, baby?"

"Everyone," Claire repeated, voice rising.

"Jesus." Scrubbing his face with his hands, Hugh leaned against the wall at his back and exhaled a shaky breath. "If you're talking about me here, Claire, then yeah, I know how this looks," he told his sister. "But you need to trust me."

"Trust you?" Claire sneered. "Oh, please. There's nothing trustworthy about skulking around in dark rooms with your ex, Hugh." Turning her attention back to Lizzie, she narrowed her eyes in warning. "I don't care what you do with Pierce, or my brother, or Patrick, or any other boy in this town, but you keep *my* boy's name out of your mouth." She raised a trembling finger in warning. "I mean it, Liz. If you have *ever* valued me as a friend, you will stop with this tirade of abuse, because I'm not fucking around anymore. I've had enough of it!"

"Cut the bullshit, Claire," Lizzie snapped, unwilling to back down or even bend slightly. "You were never my friend."

"Yes, I *was*," Claire replied in a deathly cold tone. "Once upon a time."

"Once upon a time." Lizzie shrugged. "Past tense?"

"That's right," Claire surprised the hell out of me by saying. "Past tense, Liz."

"So, you're finally admitting that you're picking him over me?"

"Absolutely," Claire replied with a hint of hesitation.

Whoa.

"Did someone change the venue without telling the rest of us?" Feely asked when he strolled into the room moments later with the rest of the gang in tow. "Thanks a bunch for deserting us, lads," he added, oblivious to the drama unfolding around him. "Really appreciate it."

"Jesus, I'm starving," Joey stated, making a beeline for the kitchen area.

"Me, too, Stud," Aoife agreed, arms linked with Katie. "I'd do terrible things for a toasted sandwich right about now."

"Is everyone okay?" Shannon asked, casting a nervous glance in Claire's direction. "Claire?" She took a step toward her friend. "Are you *okay*?"

"No, Shannon," my girlfriend bit out, attention still riveted on Lizzie. "I'm not okay. I'm not okay at all, and if she doesn't stop talking shit about my boyfriend, I am going to lose my fucking mind!"

Double whoa.

Claire rarely used the serious bad words.

It just wasn't in her nature.

"Why are you trying to pick a fight with me, Claire?" Lizzie argued, voice cracking. "What have I ever done to you?"

"*To* me or *for* me, Liz?" Claire shot back. "Because from where I've been standing this past year, it's been a whole lot of the former and not much of the latter."

"You know I can't be around you when you're with him," she choked out, holding a hand up. "I told you that months ago, but you still decided to be with him."

"Because I'm in love with him!" Claire declared hotly. "Because he's been my best friend since forever!"

"And what have I been," Lizzie strangled out. "Dog shit?"

"You were a good friend for a long time," Claire admitted without a hint of hesitation. "But you haven't been a good friend since Caoimhe died."

"Since Caoimhe died?" Lizzie repeated, turning a deep shade of red. "You mean since his piece-of-shit brother drove her to suicide? Gee, Claire, I'm so sorry if you've been feeling neglected, but some of us have *actual* problems to deal with. Real ones that are a lot more serious than chasing butterflies or playing house with a litter of kittens!"

"None of what happened to your sister is Gerard's fault," Claire erupted. "And I am done sitting back and letting you throw shit at him. Do you hear me? I am done. So, if that means picking sides and losing friends, then I will gladly pick his side and I will gladly lose your friendship."

"It's all his fault," she screamed. "His brother killed my sister."

"Your sister killed herself!"

"Whoa!"

"Girls, just pull back a second and breathe, yeah?"

Lizzie reared back like I had struck her. "You did *not* just say that."

"Jesus Christ, Claire, don't talk to her like that."

"Stay out of this, Hugh! You don't know the full story."

"And you do?"

"Your sister killed herself," Claire doubled down and repeated. "Caoimhe did that to herself, and you can't spend the rest of your life laying blame on an innocent boy. Not when you don't know the facts. The real truth about what went down."

"I know exactly what happened," she strangled out. "Caoimhe was raped! That monster raped my sister and drove her to suicide!"

"You have it so wrong!"

"No, I don't. You're the one who's wrong. You're wrong, Claire. You're so fucking wrong!"

"Caoimhe wasn't the one who was raped!" Claire screamed at the top of her lungs, and I swear to god my heart stopped dead in my chest. "It wasn't her, Lizzie! Mark didn't rape your sister!" And then, she blew my world when she pointed a finger at me and screamed, "He raped my boyfriend!"

76

Murder on the Dance Floor

CLAIRE

As soon as the words were out of mouth, I knew I had made a fatal error in judgment. Good as my intentions were, my reckless urge to defend Gerard's honor had only resulted in exposing his throat to the enemy. Blind love led me into his arms, and blind loyalty led me to betray him.

Eyes widening in horror, my gaze flicked to his. "Gerard."

He just stared, frozen as a statue, unmoving, unblinking, unbreathing.

"Shit," Joey said quietly, sharp as a razor as he clicked onto the truth before the rest of the group. Blowing out a shaky breath, he held his head with both hands. "Fuck."

"I'm sorry," I strangled out, kicking into action, as I closed the space between us, attempting to touch and cradle his face in my hands. "I'm sorry, I'm sorry, I'm so, so, so sorry, baby." And I *was* sorry. For humiliating him. But I wasn't sorry for speaking out. I couldn't be. Not when my conscience was assuring me that for the first time in my life, I had done the right thing. Even when it was the scariest thing. "It shouldn't have come out like that," I hurried to soothe. "I know, okay? I know it shouldn't have, and I'm so sorry, baby, but I can't sit back on this."

Reaching up, he gently removed my hands from his face and placed them at my sides. And then he took a step away from me. And then another.

"No, no, no, no," I cried out hoarsely, running to barricade the door to stop him from leaving. In the background, I could hear everyone shouting, but I couldn't concentrate on a word anyone was saying.

I was too engulfed in the blazing fire of betrayal that burned in Gerard's eyes. "How."

One word.

It was only one.

But it held the weight of a lifetime of friendship with it.

"I found your letter," I admitted, feeling the tears from earlier return with a vengeance. "It was when I went up to your room to get the tickets." I shrugged helplessly as I tried to explain myself to the only person who mattered to me in this moment. "I took it by mistake. It was muddled up with your phone and wallet."

Betrayal.

It was written all over his face.

Everyone's attention had shifted to him, but he never took his eyes off mine, as he stared at me with a combination of surprise, horror, and betrayal storming in his gray irises.

A million different emotions waged a war inside of him, with betrayal coming out victorious. Some of our friends were shouting. Others were just staring. Someone was crying. I couldn't tell. I couldn't make sense of any of their voices. I was rooted to the floor in utter contempt for my recklessness.

"What are you talking about?" Johnny demanded, losing his cool as he looked around wildly, willing me to put the genie back in the bottle. "What did you say that for, Claire?"

"Johnny, don't," Shannon begged.

"You're such a fucking bitch!"

"Lizzie, stop it."

"What the hell does that mean?"

"What do you think she's saying, genius?"

"Are you saying it was *him*?"

"Obviously."

"Oh my god."

"No!"

"She's lying!"

"Everyone just back off." That was Hugh, who had come to stand beside me. Grateful for his presence in this moment, and the strong arm he had wrapped around my shoulders, I sagged against him, feeling weak and demoralized. "Fuck."

"Bullshit," Lizzie screamed, still spitting her pain like venom. "You're such a fucking liar, Claire!"

"Gerard," I repeated, voice cracking, as my hand shot to my mouth. *What did you do, Claire? Oh my god, what the hell did you do?* Ignoring Lizzie's verbal onslaught, I begged him with my eyes to not hate me. "Please."

He didn't respond.

Instead, he continued to stare at me like he was seeing a stranger instead of the person he'd spent his whole life adoring. Instead of seeing *me*.

"Gerard," I strangled out. "Please! It's okay. It's okay. You have nothing to be ashamed about here, baby. You didn't do anything wrong!"

"No!" Johnny barked, eyes wide and full of fear. "It's not him." He looked to me, willing me to take it back. "It wasn't him."

I hung my head in shame.

"Gibs," Johnny called out, bolting for the door in his bid to chase after his best friend. "Just hold up, will ya?"

But it was too late.

He was already moving for the exit.

"Gerard, wait!"

He didn't answer me.

He didn't look back, either.

Instead, he stormed out of the room faster than I'd ever seen him move.

Like we were attached by an invisible cord, I bolted after him. "Gerard, wait!"

Charging through the empty darkened hallways, I raced past a random couple kissing against the lockers, all while calling his name at the top of my lungs.

We weren't supposed to be inside the main building—it was off limits after 10:00 p.m.—and I knew there was a good chance that my screaming would alert a teacher to our breaking and entering, but I couldn't find it in me to care.

Everything I was, and all I would ever be, was focused solely on the boy up ahead. "Gerard!" I panted when I pushed through the exit door and caught a glimpse of him stalking through the courtyard. "Please wait!"

His jacket had been discarded in the courtyard right along with his bowtie. Stepping over both, I hurled my body forward, adrenaline pumping my legs in this moment. "Please," I begged, catching ahold of his shirtsleeve when I finally caught up with him. "Don't leave like this."

Taking his momentary hesitance as my chance, I threw myself at him. "I'm sorry, baby, I'm so sorry for it coming out like that," I cried, peppering every inch of his neck with desperate kisses as I clung to his big body. "I love you. I love you, I love you, I love you…"

"Don't." Breathing hard and ragged, Gerard placed his hands on his hips and bowed his head. "Please don't."

"I want to help you." Crying hard and ugly, I fisted his shirt, terrified that he might walk away again. "Please let me help you!"

"Claire, stop," he choked out, craning his face away when I tried to kiss him. "Please stop, will you?" A huge shudder racked through his big body. "I *can't* do this right now."

I wanted to push. I wanted to knock down his walls and storm his heart and secrets like he had done mine all those years ago, but the look in his eyes told me that he was seconds away from losing his temper with me. "Gerard, I want to help you if you just—"

"I don't want your help!" Reaching up, he pried my hands from his shirt and backed away from me. "I don't want anyone's fucking help, okay?"

"Gerard, please." My heart cracked clean open when I watched the first tear land on his cheek. "I'm here for you. Please talk to me."

"There's nothing to talk about!" His entire body trembled when he held a hand up to warn me off. "Because I'm fine, Claire! Do you hear me? I'm okay, dammit. I am *always* okay, Claire!"

His response only caused the both of us to cry harder. "You were raped."

"No." He shook his head, futilely denying what we both knew was the truth. "No!"

"Gerard, he's a predator," I tried to reason. "I can't sit back on this." Shaking my head, I felt my tears trickle down my cheeks. "I won't. Because what about the other children he comes in contact with?"

"That wasn't your secret to tell, Claire," he choked out, body shaking violently. "It was mine."

"It was your secret?"

"It was my fault!"

"That monster abused you, and that's not your fault!" I pushed, unwilling to back up or give up on him. "It's *not* your fault!"

"Don't look at me like that," he warned, using the back of his hand to roughly wipe at his eyes. "Don't fucking look at me like I'm not the same person you've been looking at for sixteen years!"

"I'm not, Gerard," I sobbed, desperate to console him. "I know who you are." My feet were moving straight for him again. "I do, baby. I know."

"Stop fucking looking at me like I'm broken, Claire," he snapped, backing up further when I tried to get close. "Stop looking at me, dammit!"

Oh god.

He was beyond broken and I couldn't break through the wall he had erected. Break through the lies he had invented to hide the truth. Like ivy on a house hiding the walls beneath, hiding the true colors and the cracks in the cement. He had cracks in him that I couldn't repair because he refused to acknowledge they were there in the first place.

"Gerard," I tried again, hearing my voice crack under the weight of my torrent emotions. "Please come back inside with me."

He shook his head slowly and continued to back up. "I don't want to hurt you."

"You're not hurting me by telling your truth, Gerard."

"I am," he strangled out, chest heaving. "It's hurting you now, Claire." Sniffling, he choked out a pained cry and ran his hand through his hair. "Fuck!" Losing his cool, he looked up the night sky and roared the word, "Fuck," at the top of his lungs. "You fucking push, Claire. You push and you push!" He threw his hands up helplessly. "And I don't have anything left to give."

"I have enough to give," I promised, reclaiming the space he put between our bodies. "I have enough for both of us."

"You hurt me," he strangled out, chest heaving. "You broke me, Claire."

Pain.

It devoured me whole.

"That was never my intention," I whisper-sobbed, clutching my chest, as his words ricocheted through me like buckshot. "I am so sorry for hurting you, and for it coming out like this," Sniffling, I sucked in a sharp breath, before adding, "But I'm not sorry for speaking up for you, Gerard."

My words were of no comfort to my boyfriend in this moment, because instead of taking the hand I had outstretched to him, he shook his head and stepped further away from me. And then he said the words that ripped my soul to ribbons. "I don't want to be your friend anymore."

"You don't mean that."

"Yeah, I do." Tears trickled down his cheeks as he cried. "I'm not your boyfriend, Claire Biggs, and I'm not your friend."

"Gerard!"

Familiar voices filled the air then, and I could hear Johnny calling out Gerard's name in a frantic tone of voice.

"No, Gerard," I started to say, but he had already taken off running. "Wait!" I cried, clutching my head in my hands. "Oh my god."

"Gibs!" When Johnny came thundering around the corner, he veered straight for me. "Claire? Where is he?" His breathing was hard and ragged as he looked around the empty courtyard. "Where's Gibs?"

"Claire," Shannon called out a moment later, as she came running toward me with the skirt of her beautiful white gown hitched up to her knees. "Oh my god, Claire!"

"I messed up, Shan," I cried out hoarsely. "I messed everything up."

"It's okay." With sympathetic eyes, she quickly moved for me, not stopping until I was wrapped up in her arms. "You didn't do anything wrong. Shh. Shh. It's okay."

"Talk to me," Johnny begged, watching on helplessly. "Please fucking talk to me, girls."

Keeping one arm wrapped around me, Shannon reached into her bra and retrieved the letter. Holding it up, she looked to me for permission. Slumping against her, I nodded weakly. "Claire found this in Gibsie's room tonight." Sniffling, she handed her boyfriend the note and then used her hand to wipe a tear from her cheek.

Wordlessly, Johnny unfolded the note and then, because it was too dark outside to read it, he reached into his pocket for his phone. Unlocking the screen of the phone, he held it over the letter as his eyes tracked every awful word.

His breath hitched and he dropped his phone, but instead of taking his eyes off the page, he slowly sank to the ground and felt around for it with a trembling hand. "Fuck…" His voice cracked and I watched as this huge boy, with limitless popularity and pull, broke down in front of us. "Fuck!" Head bowed, he clutched at his hair and continued to stare at the letter. "Fuck, Gibs." A pained cry escaped him. "Not you, lad." His big shoulders racked with shudders. "Not fucking you, Gibs!"

"Johnny," Shannon sobbed, shuffling us closer to him so that she could place a hand on his head.

"I know, baby." Almost instinctively, his hand shot out to clutch her leg. "I know."

77

I Don't Want to Be Your Friend Anymore

CLAIRE

"It's going to be okay." With one arm wrapped around my waist, Shannon led me back to the common room. "Johnny is going to find him."

"I should have gone with him," I replied, numb. "It's my fault."

"No, Claire, it's not. None of this is your fault, I promise." She stopped in front of the door and turned to look at me. "And you're in no condition to go running around town looking for him. Joey's not drinking. He'll drive us back to your house and we'll be there when Johnny brings him home. Because he *will* find him, Shan. He won't stop until he does."

"I can't deal with Lizzie right now, Shan," I admitted, gesturing to the closed door. "I can't." Sniffling, I batted a tear off my cheek. "Because if she says another word about Gerard, I think I might snap."

"Then wait out here, okay?" Shannon replied. "I'll go inside and get my brother."

"Okay," I agreed with a hiccup, not trusting myself to be anywhere near our other friend in this moment.

When Shannon opened the door a moment later and tried to slip inconspicuously inside, Lizzie's voice boomed through the air. "I don't care what she says. He's clearly after getting into her head and twisting everything around," she was screaming. "She's making all of this up to cover for him."

That was it.

That was all I could take.

Losing every ounce of self-control left inside of my body, I slammed my palm against the semi-closed door and pushed it back open.

"Making it up?" My voice was deathly cold as I stood in the doorway, eyes trained on the willowy blond. "Making it *up*?"

"Why would you do that?" Lizzie cried, turning to face me. "Why would you lie about my sister like that?"

"I didn't lie," I heard myself respond, knowing that the only thing I had left to lose had already bolted. "And I didn't make anything up." Narrowing my eyes, I gritted out the words, "Mark didn't rape your sister."

"Yes, he *did*! I read the words on her suicide note," she screamed, tears flowing freely down her cheeks. "I *know*, Claire!" Strangling out a heaving breath, she sobbed, "I *know* what he did to her!"

"You don't know anything!" I shouted back, losing my cool. "You don't have a fucking clue about what actually happened, Lizzie."

"And you do?"

"Yes," I screamed back at her. "Your sister is not the victim in this story. She was never Mark's victim. She was his fucking accomplice!"

You could have heard a pin drop.

Everyone's eyes landed on me.

"What are you saying, Claire?" Hugh demanded, making a beeline for me. "What the fuck does that mean?"

"It wasn't Caoimhe, Hugh," I cried when my brother's hands clamped down on my shoulders. "It was *Gerard*."

"What?" My brother staggered backwards, clutching his chest "What do you mean it was Gibs?"

"There's a note from Caoimhe," I tried to explain, feeling my entire frame rack with tremors. "Gerard kept it all along." Shuddering, I squeezed out, "It explains everything."

"How dare you!" Lizzie choked out, eyes full of horror and betrayal. "There's no other letter."

"How dare *you*," I challenged right back at her. "How fucking dare you treat him like you have all these years." I couldn't stop my tears from falling or my voice from rising. "And yes there is another letter, the real fucking letter, and I suggest that you read it, Liz. And then, once you have, you might want to start directing your anger at the right people." Narrowing my eyes, I spat out, "Because Gerard Gibson was never your target!"

"No, no, no, I know the truth." She desperately refuted my claims, tears streaming down her cheeks, looking more vulnerable than I'd seen her look since her sister's funeral.

She looked so broken, so utterly lost, that for a moment I had the strongest urge to fold her into my arms and make her feel better.

But I couldn't do it.

Not this time.

I couldn't bow to her anger.

Her pain belonged to her. Passing it around to the rest of us wasn't fair.

She wasn't the same little girl I'd grown up with, and while my heart truly broke for all the heartache she had endured, I couldn't live my life with this level of toxicity in it.

"I know what really happened," she continued to cry.

"You weren't there," I replied, striving for calmness when I felt anything but. "You don't know the whole story. You never did. None of us knew." Straightening my spine, I forced myself to add, "But we do now."

"He's trying to change the narrative."

"Of what?"

"Of my sister's death!"

"No, he's not," I shouted back. "Gerard has never done anything other than try to survive the horrendous hand of cards life dealt him."

"I don't believe you," she cried, roughly pushing Patrick away when he tried to hug her. "God, I fucking hate you so much right now, Claire!"

"Fine," I snapped back. "Don't believe me. Label me as a liar. If hating me fills a hole in your heart, then you go right ahead and hate me, but don't expect me to wait around and take your shit anymore. Because I'm done with it all. Including you."

"Claire." Shannon hurried to intervene. "You don't mean that."

"Oh, I've never meant anything *more*, Shannon," I ground out. "I can't do this with her anymore. I *won't*."

"I'm not doing this with you," Lizzie sobbed.

"Well, I am absolutely doing this with you," I spat back. "Because I am done holding my tongue, and I will never allow you to use him as your personal punching bag ever again."

"You are such a *bitch*."

"And you are such a bully," I roared back. "You know, Gerard took your bullshit for years." Furious, I shook my head. "He knew the truth and let you treat him like that. Let you try to meddle and twist and turn his friends against him." I narrowed my eyes in disgust. "That was you, Lizzie. *You* did that to him, but it stops now. Do you hear me? Go and get help. Sort your head out because I'm done walking this road with you. I'm stepping off!"

"Guys, please," Shannon offered up. "Please don't fight."

"I'm not fighting, Shannon," I stated. "I'm just done."

"We can fix this, guys," Shannon tried to plead. "Come on. After everything we've been through. We can get through this together."

"I can't." Lizzie hiccupped a sob. "Not after tonight."

Neither could I. "Don't ever speak to me again, Lizzie Young," I warned, and then, truly disappointed in myself, I walked away from one of my oldest friends in the world for the sake of another.

78
I Love the Bones of Ya!

GIBSIE

"Gerard, please," Mam tried to coax, but I couldn't be talked down or consoled in this moment. I was too far gone. Everything I had worked so hard to build back up after he destroyed me had been snuffed out in an instant.

I didn't know how I got home from the dance. I didn't know if I was in another nightmare, or if I was even breathing. I couldn't make sense of a fucking word of anything.

His hand was on the back of my neck, pinning my face into the mattress. "Daddy," I tried to scream, but he couldn't hear me all the way from heaven. "Come back and take me with you."

"Just stay down and take it, you little bastard!"

"It hurts," I strangled out, my body bowing in agony when I felt something impale me from behind, ripping my small body in half.

"That's it," he grunted as he continued to hurt me, pushing me, deeper, harder, rougher. "I'll make a fucking man out of you, ya little pussy."

"Stop." I was crying. I knew I was. My mouth was open, I could feel tears trickling down my cheeks, but my voice wasn't coming out. "Please stop."

Numb, I felt the life leave my body, fading quicker every time he rammed his privates into mine, as the pain grew worse, and my mind started to wander away…

Feeling cornered, I came out swinging, ripping and tearing at anything I could get my hands on in the moment, seeing nothing but his face everywhere I turned. "Keith, stop him, please! He's going to hurt himself!" I could hear my mother saying somewhere in the distance, but her face was gone from my sight. I couldn't see anything but *him.*

Curled up in a ball on my bed, I watched as he stood over me and zipped up his school trousers. He wore the ones the older boys wore. The boys who went to secondary school.

"You know the score, baby brother." Sitting down on the edge of my bed, he pushed my hair out of my face and reached between my legs. "Keep your mouth shut and I'll keep going easy on you."

Trembling, I didn't dare answer him or look in his direction. I knew better. I knew what happened when I didn't behave. When I didn't give him what he wanted.

"Good boy. You're always okay, aren't ya?" He stroked my cheek and then stood back up. "I'll see you tomorrow night."

I waited until my door was closed before checking myself over and pulling my Power Rangers pajamas bottoms into place, shuddering when my hand emerged with the familiar sight of blood…

I knew I had lost touch with reality. I could feel my sanity slipping back at the school. The tiny shred of dignity and pride I had managed to hold on to for the past ten years had finally upped and left me.

"I'm going to marry you when I'm a big girl," she told me, reaching across to press her Barbie's face to my action figure. "You'll be my shiny prince in the white garner, and I'll be the princess." When she grinned at me, I felt my lips smile back. Because she didn't have any front teeth and I thought she looked so silly.

"You're really going to marry me?"

"Uh-huh." Her brown eyes were big and happy, and she smelled like sunshine. "I'm going to take you to my castle in the North Pole, where we can build snowmen all day and Santa flies over our castle every night to give us presents."

"Does your castle have a chimney?"

"Hmm, don't think so."

"Then how is Santa going to leave us presents?"

"Santa's supersmart," she explained. "He'll get your daddy to fly down from heaven and use magic to open the door…"

"What happened to him, Keith?"

"I don't know, Sadhbh. Maybe he took something at the dance."

"Call one of his friends. If he did, then we need to call for an ambulance!"

"I'll go and get Sinead."

"Be fast about it!"

"Why would you say that?" Leaping off the couch, Caoimhe moved as far away from me as she could get. Like I was dirty. Like I was bad. "Are you telling lies, Gerard Gibson? Because that is the worst, most awful thing you could say about a person."

"I don't know," I heard myself reply.

"You don't know if you're telling lies or you don't know why you said it?" she demanded, hands on her hips. "I'll give you one more chance to tell the truth." Her eyes looked so mad. "Then I'm telling your family what you said."

"I…" I shook my head, feeling so sad because I knew what she wanted me to say, and I wanted to please her. She was my favorite babysitter. She told the best bedtime stories, *and nobody came in my room when she was here. I didn't want her to go.* "I…" *Frowning, I thought really hard about what to do, trying to find the words that would make her happy and like me again.* "I…was…making a joke?"

"Oh, thank god!" *She sighed out this big, loud breath and then she came back to me.* "You must never say things like that, Gibs." *She sat down on the couch beside me.* "I know I was your babysitter before I was Mark's girlfriend, but you can't make up stories about him because you're jealous…"

"Claire? It's Sadhbh, love. There's something wrong with Gerard. I think he might have taken something at the dance. I need you to come home right now. If you know anything about what he might have taken, you need to tell me now."

"What's she saying?"

"What, Claire? I can barely hear you, pet. Just calm down and stop screaming, love. Tell me what happened."

"Sadhbh?"

"Shut up, Keith. I'm trying to hear the girl. The line is bad and she's bawling her eyes out."

"See?" *the blond in the office encouraged, pressing the palm of my hand against her breast.* "That feels nice, doesn't it?"

I nodded slowly.

"Have you touched a woman before?"

I shook my head.

"Do you like how it feels?"

I nodded again.

"You're so cute." *Smiling, she reached for my other hand and pushed it into the waistband of her skirt.* "You can practice on me if you want…"

"Gibs."

"Oh, Johnny, thank god, you're here. He's after losing it. I don't know what to do for him. He's after putting his hand through a mirror and everything."

"Sadhbh, I need you to read this."

"What is it, Johnny?"

"Just read it *please*."

"Don't go near him, Kavanagh. He's too out of control."

"I'll be grand. Just give me a few minutes with him."

"Kavanagh, be careful, he doesn't seem to know who we are."

"He knows who I am, don't ya, Gibs? It's alright, my old buddy. Cap's here."

"Alright, class, eyes to the front of the room," *Mr. O'Donovan ordered when he walked into our classroom on Monday morning with a tall, dark-haired boy in tow.* "We have a new boy joining the class," he explained, clapping the tall boy on the shoulder. "This is Jonathan Kavanagh. He and his family moved down from Dublin this past summer, and I want you all to make your best effort to make him feel welcome." He squeezed the scowling boy's shoulder again. "From what I hear, we can expect great things from this one on the rugby pitch." Turning to the boy, he said, "Kavanagh, why don't you take a seat down the back of the class with young Gibson," before pointing at me.

Still scowling, the boy sauntered through the rows of desks with his head in the air. I knew the lads would say it made him look like a cocky fucker, but I thought it was great.

Dropping his schoolbag on the floor next to mine, he pulled his chair back and sank down, still scowling, still looking like he thought he was too good for the rest of us.

"How's it going?" Robbie Mac whispered, turning around from the desk in front of us to introduce himself. "Robbie."

"Johnny," the boy sitting next to me acknowledged with a polite nod.

"So, you're into the rugby, are ya, Johnny?"

His lips tipped up in a small smirk. "You could say that."

"Well, me and some of the other lads from class usually have a game after school on Mondays. You should come."

"What about you?"

It took me a moment to realize that he was addressing me. "Me?" I asked anyway, just to be sure, because aside from Hugh and Feely, no one else in class bothered a whole pile with me.

"Yeah." Johnny nodded. "Do you play?"

I opened my mouth to answer but Robbie got there first. "Who, Gibsie?" He snickered into his hand. "He can't play sports. He faints at the sight of blood." He snickered again. "He the class's personal Billy Elliot." More laughing. "He likes to dance with the girls."

I felt my face grow hot from embarrassment and quickly dropped my gaze to the copybook open in front of me, fully expecting the boy sitting next to me to be a perfect candidate for the dickhead club. The copybook littered with my own scrawling handwriting I could barely read.

"So?" Johnny surprised me by saying. "You think there's something wrong with dancing?"

"You don't?"

"No."

"Shit, maybe the sir put you at the right desk when he sat you with him," Robbie snickered, gesturing to me.

"Maybe he did," Johnny replied coolly.

"Whatever, girls," Robbie sneered before turning back to face the front of the class "Enjoy each other's company."

"I'm Johnny." He held his hand out to me. "Johnny Kavanagh."

"Gerard Gibson," I replied, accepting his handshake. "But everyone calls me Gibsie."

"So, Gibsie, is everyone in this class a bleeding eejit like that one?" he asked, pointing to Robbie.

"There's a couple of good ones," I replied, feeling my lips tip up in a smile. "But yeah, pretty much."

Johnny nodded solemnly. "And who's your best friend out of all of them?"

"Me?" My brows shot up. "Well, I'm, ah, I'm good friends with those two over there." I pointed across the room to where Hugh and Feely were sitting. "But I wouldn't say I have a best friend in here." Smiling, I added, "I have a girlfriend. She's at a different school, though."

"Is she your friend or you girlfriend?"

"Both?"

"Hmm." Johnny seemed to mull that over before asking, "Do you want to be my best friend?" He shrugged. "Looks like I'm not getting out of this town anytime soon, so I might as well put down some roots."

"Me?"

"Yeah, you."

"You want me to be your best friend?"

He nodded again, and I could tell from just one interaction with him that he was sharp. This lad was nobody's fool. He had clearly taken everyone's measure and, for some strange reason, had decided that I was the best of a bad bunch.

"So, what's it going to be, Gibs?"

"Yeah." I smiled. "I'm in."

"Nice one," he chuckled. "Now, the first thing we're going to work on is this phobia of blood." Smirking, he nudged my shoulder with his. "Because I've a feeling there's an unmerciful beast of a flanker inside you just waiting to come out…"

"Gibs."

"Come on, Gibs, lad, it's me."

"Come back, Gibs. Come on back to me."

My best friend's familiar voice filled my ears, and I whipped around to find him standing in the middle of my bedroom with his hands in the air. "Johnny?"

"The one and only." His tone was soft, coaxing, and laced with approval. "See? I knew you could hear me, fucker."

Feeling panicked, like I had just been chewed up by one of my night terrors and then spat back out into the real world, I said, "Johnny?"

"It's me, Gibs." He took a step closer, hands still raised. "I'm right here, lad."

I looked around my room, feeling the familiar swell of hysteria rise up as my eyes took in the carnage. I did that. I knew it had to be me. Everything was trashed. My bed. My furniture. My walls? The curtain? "Jesus Christ!"

And my mother? I cast a panicked glance in the direction of my mother. She was standing in my bedroom doorway with her head in her hands. Keith was standing behind her, looking as pale as a ghost.

"That's it," Johnny continued to coax but when his voice cracked, I noticed the tears trickling down his cheeks. "Just stay with me, Gibs."

Why was he saying that?

Why was he crying?

"Why the fuck was *I* crying?"

"Gerard!" Claire's voice cut through all of the bullshit and haze, and I turned just in time to find her being held up by her brother.

"What the fucking happening?" I demanded, feeling panicked as everyone stared at me. "What did I do?"

"Nothing, Gibs," Johnny was the one to answer me, taking another step toward me. "I just…" Pausing, he licked his lips and glanced at my hand before quickly retraining his attention on my face. "Can you hear me?"

"Of course I can hear you!" I snapped. "Why the fuck wouldn't I hear you?"

His attention shifted to my hand again and that's when I looked down. "Oh Jesus Christ."

Blood.

Thick crimson blood was flowing freely from my hand, dripping steadily onto the carpet. The massive shard of broken mirror I was clutching was no doubt the culprit of my bleeding. "Jesus," I strangled out, immediately tossing the shard away from my body and then heaving when I noticed just how badly drenched in blood my dress shirt was. "I didn't… I wasn't…" Shaking my head, I staggered backward, feeling weak from the sight of my head. "I would *never* hurt any of you."

"Everyone here knows that, lad," Johnny agreed, closing the space between us. "You're a good man. You wouldn't hurt a fly. So, don't you worry about that, alright? Because it's not any of us that we're worried you'll hurt, Gibs."

"I didn't mean to." I hurried to appease, roughly batting my tears away as blood poured from my right hand. "I don't know how I'm still standing," I mumbled, somehow managing to not pass out from the sight of it. "I think I might be in a bit of shock or something, Johnny." I reached up with a trembling hand and tapped my head. "I think I might be gone a bit wrong in here."

"Don't worry about it…" His voice cracked when he grabbed the back of my neck and pulled me roughly against his chest. "It happens to the best of us."

"I'm okay, Cap," I mumbled against his shoulder as he held me in his arms. "I'm always okay."

"*Oh god, Gerard, is it true?*" My mam was crying in the distance.

"*What do you mean, is it true?*" That was my old friend Hugh. "*Of course it's fucking true, Sadhbh! Look at him.*"

"Gibs!" *Was Feely crying?*

"Gerard!" *My walking heartbeat.*

"Can everyone just clear out for a few minutes," I heard my best friend command, chasing all the voices away. "Gibs and I are having a bit of a moment here, and we don't need ye bunch of bleeding babies crying around the place, now do we, Gibs?"

"No." Numb, I leaned my cheek on his shoulder and let him hold me. "No crying babies."

"He needs to have that arm seen to, Johnny, and the Gards are on the way."

"And that's fine, and he will get it seen to," Johnny replied in a coaxing tone as he lowered us both to the floor. "Just give him a minute."

"They know, don't they?" I whispered, slumped against him. "Everyone knows."

His arms tightened around me, and he pulled me closer. "You're going to be okay."

"All the things he did to my body." Feeling lifeless, I stared blankly ahead, feeling the tears trickling down my cheek. "I didn't want any of it, Johnny."

"I know you didn't, Gibs…" He choked out a pained cry and continued to rock me back and forth. "I believe you."

"I don't want her to know."

"Claire?"

I nodded, feeling empty. "She won't be able to love me now."

"She already loves you," he strangled out. "We all love ya." Sniffling, he pulled me closer and pressed a kiss to the top of my head. "You're the best friend I've ever had, and I love the fucking bones of you, ya mad eejit." He choked out a pained laugh. "And if you think this is going to chase me off, then you've another thing coming, fucker, because I'm never leaving you. Do ya hear me? Because you're my Gibs."

"And you're my Kav."

"That's right." He was crying hard now, and I think I was, too, but I felt so safe with him that I didn't fight the noises and words and sounds that poured out of me. Instead, for the first time since my father died, I let it all out.

79
The Aftermath

CLAIRE

THE FOLLOWING AFTERNOON, I SAT ON THE FOOTPATH ON MY SIDE OF THE ROAD AND watched as Sadhbh Allen ushered another Garda inside the house.

The Gards I had spoken to last night were in uniform, but this one wasn't in uniform, which led me to believe that he might be the detective on the case. I couldn't be sure because I wasn't allowed to cross the street, much less ask.

"That one is the detective inspector." Handing me over a mug of hot chocolate, Shannon joined me on the footpath with a mug of her own. "I met him once when he was working on my family's case." She blew into her mug before taking a sip. "He's one of the few I actually liked."

Numb, I kept my attention trained on the bedroom window that looked directly into mine. The curtains, which had been drawn closed since last night, finally started to move.

When the curtains were drawn back and his bedroom window opened outward, hope filled my heart at a rapid pace.

Was he up?

Was he talking?

Johnny appeared at the window then, clearly the culprit for opening it, and I felt my hope shrivel up and die in my chest. His attention locked on us, and he offered me a private wink before disappearing from sight.

"I should be with him," I declared hoarsely.

"I know it feels that way, but the kind of questions the detectives have to ask him wouldn't be good for you to hear." Fussing with the blanket draped over my shoulders, Shannon pulled my hair out of my face and tied it in a loose bun. "And it wouldn't be good for him to know you heard them."

"But Johnny gets to stay," I said brokenly. "I'm his best friend, too."

I remembered all too well what Gerard had said to me last night, and how he had ended both our relationship and friendship, but it wasn't over for me. It would never be over for me. Because we were a part of each other.

"Yes, and I know that's not easy for you when you want to be there so badly for him." Shannon wrapped her arm around my shoulders and sighed sadly. "But Johnny is the only one Gibsie wants to see right now, and we need to respect his wishes."

"I love him, Shan." Not bothering to blink the tears from my eyes, I turned to look at her. "I need him to be okay." *I needed him, period.*

She nodded in understanding.

"I'm sorry for how it came out but I'm not sorry that it came out," I confessed, chewing on my lip. "Does that make me a bad person?"

"No, it makes you a strong person, Claire."

"I just want him to open up to me."

"Patience," Shannon said softly. "You need to give him time. It takes a long time to get to that point, Claire. It's not so easy for everyone. There's trauma in his past, and right now he's living in it. But he'll find his way to you."

"Like you found your way to Johnny?"

"Yes," she replied with a nod. "But it didn't happen overnight, and I am so grateful that he had the ability to be patient with me. To show me that love can be kind and patient and everything I had never experienced before." Shivering she added, "Because I was so desperate to keep him out back then."

"Why?"

"Because I didn't want him to see the ugly in me and turn and run."

"You've never been ugly a day in your life," I told her. "Not on the inside or on the out."

"I appreciate you saying that, Claire, but that's how it felt. I truly couldn't get past my…well, my past. It took a lot of time and coaxing and gentle persuasion. Broken people don't display the same traits. Look at me and Joey. We couldn't be more different in our approach to life if we tried. Look at Ollie and Sean. Hell, look at Tadhg. We all lived in the same home and approach life with completely different perspectives."

"I don't want to be patient," I admitted. "All I want to do is charge in that door and fix it for him. To make everything better."

"You can't," she replied, tone laced with empathy and understanding. "You can't fix him or make it better. He has to do that for himself."

"But it hurts so bad to see him hurting."

"I know," she agreed, reaching over to squeeze my hand. "It's the helplessness that hurts the most, right?"

"Right."

"You can help him by staying," Aoife said, joining us on the footpath with her small son in her arms.

I shook my head in confusion. "Staying?"

"And by hanging in there," she confirmed wisely. "And by trusting that the boy beneath the broken can find his way out of the darkness. It's not easy. It hurts like hell, and you'll want to run for the hills at times. And he'll push away to the point where you doubt your own sanity. But your ability to love him through it is what will make the difference. Because, at the end of the day, that's all we can do, babe." She sighed heavily. "Love these boys with our whole hearts, and hope and pray that they'll pick themselves back up and show us that they're worth the pain. That they're *worth* fighting for."

80
It'll Be Lonely This Christmas

CLAIRE

"Claire?" Mam smiled across the table at me, but just like all the other smiles since that night, it was a forced one. "Come on, pet, at least try to eat something."

Numb, I continued to slump against my chair, while my plate remained untouched.

"Please, Claire," she tried again, voice wavering. "It's Christmas."

"No, it's not," Hugh surprised me by saying. "Because Christmas means family." He inclined his head to the empty chair at the table. The chair with the word *Gibsie* carved into it. "And we're one family member down."

My attention shifted to his empty chair, and the void that had been steadily growing inside of my heart morphed into a great abyss. Lonely didn't begin to touch the surface of how desolate my life had been this past week. I felt his absence everywhere. It was like someone had left the back door open overnight and all the cold had seeped inside. The Christmas presents under the tree with my name on them had been left unopened, because in my mind, if there wasn't a Gerard Gibson–shaped present left out for me, then I didn't want to hear about it.

Reeling from the discovery of Caoimhe's letter, I felt like everything had gone to hell in a handbasket. The guilt I felt for Gerard's public humiliation was stifling. It made it hard to breathe at night. Because I hadn't seen Gerard since the night of the winter ball and I was terrified that I never would. Not the way we were, at least. Not like before.

"Come on, you two," Dad encouraged, clearly doing his best to step up and support Mam through the storm that had settled over our home. "You can't go on a hunger strike."

"Yeah." Reaching up, Hugh snatched the paper hat he won in a Christmas cracker off his head and tossed it down on his equally untouched plate before pushing his chair back. "I'm going for a walk."

"No, Hugh." Dad set his fork and knife down. "This is not the right way to handle things, son."

"No, Dad, it's definitely not," my brother agreed with a sneer. "But if I handled things *your* way, then I would never come out of the fucking attic."

"Hugh!"

"Don't you feel responsible, Mam?" My brother asked the unspoken question that hung heavily over my family. "Because I sure as hell do."

"You are *not* responsible for what that monster did," Dad cut in. "So, get those notions out of your head, son."

"Oh, so *now* he's a monster," Hugh sneered, throwing his hands up. "He's always been a monster, Dad. Liz has been trying to tell everyone for years but not a damn person would listen."

"That's different," Mam interjected in a weary tone. "Lizzie and her family were mistaken."

"How do we know that?" Hugh demanded. "Huh? How can we ever be sure of anything ever again when for four years our best friend was being raped right across the street. Every fucking night by that monster!"

A sob escaped me, and I dropped my head in my hands.

"The way I see it is two innocent families were ruined by one monster," Hugh continued hoarsely. "And now those families are at loggerheads when they should be working together to take the bastard down."

"Hugh!"

"He wasn't even arrested!" Beyond livid, my brother continued to rant and rave at the top of his lungs while his big frame shook violently. "Just because he's out of the country. What utter bullshit! He continuously rapes a seven-year-old child, and he just jets off to play happy families with a woman who doesn't have the slightest inkling of how much danger her son is in around his father!"

"I am *not* the law," Mam replied, tears filling her eyes. "And I feel plenty of guilt for not seeing the signs, Hugh Andrew Biggs. Plenty."

"So, please spare us the guilt trip," Dad said thickly. "Because your mother and I are already drowning in regret."

"Yeah? Well, join the fucking club, Dad."

"Hugh, wait. Don't just walk out," Dad called out, but it was too late, because my brother had already stormed out of the house, slamming the front door behind him.

"Please just sit down," Mam began to plead when I followed suit and pushed my chair back. Because I couldn't do it, either. I couldn't sit, and smile, and be festive when our world had imploded around us less than a week ago.

"Sorry," I told my parents, abandoning Christmas dinner as I hurried to catch up with Hugh.

When I stepped outside, I found my brother in the driveway, leaning against his parked car. With his arms folded across his chest, he stared at the house across the street. They always had the best lights on the street, but today, it was in darkness.

Because Sadhbh and Gerard were gone. I knew. I'd watched them drive off in the back seat of John Sr.'s Mercedes three days ago. Soon after, Keith Allen had filled his Land Rover with his belongings before he too left the street. In the opposite direction.

"Have you heard from them?" I croaked out, leaning against the car beside my brother.

"Once." Hugh nodded stiffly. "Johnny called when they arrived at his parents' house in Blackrock."

According to Shannon, the Kavanaghs had offered their Dublin home as a sanctuary to Gerard and his mother while his stepfather moved his belongings from the house. A legal separation had already been put in motion, and Sadhbh had decided it best to remove her son from the home until all traces of Keith and his son had been wiped away.

"Did he say how Gerard was?" I managed to ask while my heart hung by a thread. "Do you know when they're coming home?"

While John Sr. had driven the Gibsons to Dublin, it was his son who had remained by their side at the property. Johnny hadn't left Gerard's side for more than a couple of hours since the revelation. He'd even missed Christmas at home to be there for his friend, and it warmed my heart to know that wherever Gerard was right now, he had Johnny.

Hugh shook his head. "I heard something about them coming back before the new year, but I'm not sure."

I was quiet for a long time, mulling over this new information while I continued to replay the night of the dance on a loop in my mind. "Do you think he'll hate me forever, Hugh?"

Sighing heavily, my big brother unfolded his arms and draped one over my shoulders. "I don't think he knows how to hate, Claire." He sighed again. "He's been given so many reasons to hate the world, but it's just not in his nature."

"Because he's such a good person," I squeezed out, feeling my emotions go haywire again. "He's always called me sunshine, Hugh, but knowing what we do now, knowing how badly he suffered in silence and continued to smile?" I shook my head and exhaled a shaky breath. "I don't think there's another person on this earth more deserving of the title."

"Yeah," my brother agreed quietly. "I know what you mean."

"What's going to happen?" I asked.

"What do you mean?"

"After Christmas, when we go back to school. Nothing's going to be the way it was before." A shiver rolled through me. "But I'm with him, Hugh," I whispered. "I'm all in with Gerard."

Nodding stiffly, my brother continued to stare right ahead, but I knew he knew what I meant. He understood the importance of what I said. There was no coming back from what had happened. "You loved her once."

"Yeah, Hugh, we both did, and look where it got us."

"Don't turn your back on her, Claire." He swallowed deeply. "She needs you."

"She might need me, Hugh," I replied hoarsely. "But I don't need her."

"Don't say that, Claire. You're not cruel."

"No, I'm not," I agreed. "But I'm not a liar, either."

His arm dropped from my shoulder. "Claire."

"I can't let it go, okay," I strangled out. "I can't get past the way she's treated him. Knowing that he's been shouldering this weight on his own for years and taking her abuse. I kept quiet because I believed what Lizzie believed. But knowing the truth changes everything. I can't go back. I won't."

81

I've Made My Mind Up

GIBSIE

"At this stage of the investigation, I'm afraid we have no further updates."
We'd been back from Dublin for less than an hour, and already the Gards were at
the door.

I knew it would be a regular occurrence for the next while—John Sr. had told me as
much—but it didn't make it any easier. Because when they sat me down and tried to coax
and coddle me, they seemed to forget that they *weren't* talking to the seven-year-old child
I had been when it started. I wasn't that same little boy who had buried his father and sister
the month before his stepbrother pinned him to the edge of his bed and defiled his body.
I wasn't the eight-, nine-, ten-, or eleven-year-old version of that kid anymore, either.

I was seventeen years old, with the body of a full-grown man, and I dared any
motherfucker to put his hand on me now. I had a girlfriend, and friends, and a life that
I *refused* to put on hold just because the adults around me had finally gotten the memo.

I'd made it this far and it wasn't from rocking in a corner. Sure, I took a short leave
of absence from reality when everything came out, but I had a firm handle on my sanity
again. Well, whatever little bit I had in the first place.

I wasn't sure if I would ever fully get over what happened, and to be honest, I wasn't
even sure if I was handling it in a healthy way, but I knew I couldn't erase it or escape
it, so I just kept *going*. And knowing that there was a small chance this might stop him
from fucking up another kid's life gave me a sliver of comfort. Either way, today was
New Year's Eve, and I had zero plans to carry that bastard's burden into 2006.

"No further updates?" Wiping her nose with a balled-up tissue, Mam stared at
the detective sitting opposite her at our kitchen table. "So, that's it? He's still walking
around a free man?"

"As of now the relevant authorities in Mumbai liaising with the Garda Siochana
have been unable to locate Mark Allen. According to airlines officials, he never arrived
at Shirdi International Airport on the dates you provided us with."

"So, he could be *anywhere*?" Mam demanded, and then cast an anxious glance in
my direction. "He could be still in Ireland?"

"Please try not to worry, Mrs. Allen," the detective continued to say. "The relevant authorities are working tirelessly to see that man located and prosecuted to the full force of the law."

Rolling my eyes, I retrained my attention on the game of Snake I was playing on my phone.

"And don't you worry either, Gerard," the detective added. "Every effort has been put in place to ensure your protection."

"Whatever you say," I replied, thumbs tapping furiously on the keypad of my phone. "Either way, I wasn't worrying."

"Gerard," Mam sobbed, reaching a hand over to place on my arm. "You're perfectly safe now, pet. The locks have been changed and we've been granted an order of protection from the courts."

"Good to know, Mam," I replied with a nod, my attention trained on the snake jetting around the screen. "Fuck, this round is a tricky one."

"I don't know what to say to him," Mam told the detective. "He keeps brushing it off."

No, I didn't keep brushing anything off. I was trying to live my life the same way I had lived it since she moved those assholes into my house.

All of this shit might be new and terrifying for my mam, but I'd been living in a constant state of fear for ten years, unlike the ten days she had under her belt. What she was feeling now was what I had felt every time the clock struck *bedtime*.

"You are remarkably composed."

"I'm remarkable, period," I replied, choosing not to tell him that the drugs the psychiatrist had prescribed me were *remarkably* effective. I felt sorry for Joey, the poor bastard, knowing that he would never be prescribed another ride on the roller coaster of narcotics like I had been.

"There is also the matter of Deirdre O'Malley," the detective said. "Without your statement, the DPP are unable to go any further with the prosecution."

"Well, that's fabulous news," I declared, setting my phone down. "The first bit of good news I've heard since this whole fucking mess kicked off."

"Mess?" Mam gaped at me. "Gerard, pet, this is your life we're talking about."

"I know it's my life we're talking about," I shot back. "I'm the one who's been *living* it."

She flinched and then a sob tore from her throat. "I didn't know."

I didn't know.

Three words that in my limited experience in life were about as useful as putting a condom on your dick *after* sex. If I had a euro for every time someone had said "I didn't know" to me this past week, then I would be a wealthy lad. I knew it was said with good intentions, but that didn't help. I didn't need Mam or anyone else that I loved to validate their ignorance or reaffirm how they didn't do me wrong. I knew they didn't know. That's how it had to be. That's how I stayed alive.

"Gerard," Mam snapped. "That woman *abused* you!"

Actually, that woman had kept my head from going under at a time in my life when I was drowning, but I didn't bother explaining that to either one of them. Because I knew what Dee had done was wrong. She'd stepped over lines that should never be crossed, but that didn't mean that I wanted any hand in being her judge, jury, or executioner.

"Son, you're going to have to talk to one of us," he pushed. "We have statements from several students at Tommen College to confirm your statement—if you would *just* give it to us in writing."

"I *am* talking to one of you," I replied calmly. "I have talked to *all* of you, but I'm not saying what you want to hear, so they keep sending more of you to talk." I shook my head. "I've made my mind up."

"Gerard," Mam sobbed. "Please reconsider."

"I have *made* my mind up, Mam."

———————————

"Happy now?" Johnny demanded when he sauntered into my room later that night with the DVD box of *Love Actually* in hand. "I had to pry the bleeding box from Tadhg's fingers."

"Kid's got good taste."

"On the contrary, lad, I think it's safe to assume that his attachment to the film has a lot more to do with the full-frontal nudity than Hugh bleeding Grant."

"Ah, I'd hardly call it full frontal," I snickered. "You can only see yer one's tits."

"Yeah? Well, tell that to my ma." Huffing out a breath, he tossed the DVD on my lap and sank down on the beanbag next to mine. "Because I've just had to endure a forty-minute lecture from the woman on the importance of not corrupting innocent minds with blue movies," he grumbled, snatching his controller.

"Imagine thinking *Love Actually* was a bluey."

"Gibs," he deadpanned. "You're talking about the woman who still covers my eyes when there's even the hint of kissing on the telly." Unpausing the game of FIFA we'd been playing earlier, Johnny tapped on the buttons of the PlayStation controller. "Happy fucking new year to me, huh?"

"Nah, you still have a couple of hours before midnight to turn it around."

"2005." My best friend shook his head. "What a crazy fucking year, huh?"

"Yep." I sighed heavily. "It's been a memorable one, alright."

"Do you remember New Year's Eve 1999?" he asked then, lips tipping up.

"Do I what." I groaned, shuddering at the memory. "I thought your mother was going to kill me."

"Lad," Johnny chuckled. "You threw an entire bucket of water on an open fire."

"Only because I thought the flames were getting out of control."

"Gib, the fire was in the *fireplace*."

"Exactly my point, Johnny," I replied. "I thought we were having a chimney fire. How was I supposed to know the smoke would backfire like that?" Shrugging, I added, "I was *trying* to save the manor from burning down."

"Yeah, well there certainly was plenty of steam coming out of my ma's ears when the soot destroyed her new wallpaper."

"She stills brings it up, you know," I muttered. "Every Christmas."

"Hmm." Chuckling softly to himself, Johnny miscalculated a dive against my player that resulted in my team scoring. "Shite."

"You're shit at PlayStation, Cap."

"Says the fella wearing a kangaroo onesie."

"Hey, don't knock the onesie, lad." I grinned. "Besides, onesie or not, I can still kick your ass at PlayStation."

"Yeah, well, maybe I'd be better at it if I actually had some free time."

"True that," I mused, scoring another goal on his team. "I hear live-in girlfriends can be quite the distraction."

"Speaking of girlfriends," he said in a careful tone. "Have you seen yours yet?"

And there it was.

The million-dollar question.

I hadn't seen Claire since the night of the dance, and the more days that passed without seeing her, the harder the thought of *facing* her became.

Because I could handle the Gard's questions, and the sympathetic side-eye glances from Johnny when he thought I wasn't looking. I could handle my weeping mother and the wrath of the Young family. I could handle the whispers, I could even handle the stares, but what I *couldn't* handle was Claire Biggs looking at me as less than a man.

It didn't matter if it was an irrational fear or not, the thought of my girlfriend looking at me in any other way that she had for the past sixteen years made me want to throw in the towel.

"We broke up," I reminded him, feeling a pang in my chest at the memory.

Johnny rolled his eyes. "Excuses, excuses."

"I said some bad stuff the last time I saw her, Cap."

"So?"

"So, I'm still pissed."

"Well, she's not holding on to any of that, Gibs," he replied. "Trust me, lad."

"Then I guess I'm still working up to it."

"Shannon's over there."

"Bet little Shannon loves me right now," I mused. "First, I stole her fella over Christmas, and now he's spending New Year's Eve in my room, getting his ass kicked on the PlayStation."

"We'll have plenty more Christmases together," he replied quietly.

"You can go over to her, you know," I said, giving him the permission he clearly thought he needed. "You don't have to sit around babysitting my ass for the night because I'm *okay*, lad."

He looked at me with that sad look and then quickly blinked it away. "You think this is a pity date?"

I arched a brow. "Well, isn't it?"

"I'll make a deal with you," he said, tossing the controller down. "I'll go across the road and ring in the new year with my girlfriend if you do the same with yours."

82

New Year's Eve

CLAIRE

"I'm going to die alone with only my cats for company!"

"No, you're not."

"Yes, I am, Shan," I declared from my perch under the Christmas tree. Okay, so maybe *perch* wasn't an accurate word for being strewn on the flat of my back, in my unicorn onesie, with a deflated party streamer hanging out of my mouth. "I'm already a crazy cat lady." Sighing dramatically, I reached up and petted Cherub, who was perched on my chest, purring in contentment. *At least one of us was happy.* "But it was cute when I had a partner in crime."

"Does that not hurt?" Shannon asked, sounded distracted.

"Oh, indeed it does hurt, Shan," I replied solemnly. "In fact, I don't think I remember what it feels like to not have a pain in my heart."

"Not your heart, Claire. Those kittens are latterly ripping and tearing at your hair," she laughed, pointing to where Tom, Dick, and Harry were using my curls as kitty toys. "You look like Medusa with your hair splayed everywhere."

"They're going through a challenging time," I explained sadly. "They miss their father." Another weary sigh escaped me. "You might think it would be me, but nope, Gerard's the disciplinarian when it comes to dealing with these bad kitties."

"You know, I have to admit that I never thought about it." She chuckled and then she snapped up her phone when it vibrated on the arm of the couch.

"Let me guess," I groaned. "It's a text from Johnny to wish his little river a happy new year with a ton of smoochy kisses."

"Actually, it is Johnny."

"F my life, Cherub," I whimpered. "Don't ever leave me."

"Claire?"

"Hmm?"

"It's like three minutes to midnight. Do you think we'll be able to see the fireworks in town from your road?"

"Probably."

"Oh good." Stuffing her phone into the front pocket of her dressing gown, Shannon sprang up with a little too much pep in her step, given my existential crisis that was in full swing. "Let's go outside and watch."

"Why bother?" I moaned. "We can just watch it on the telly."

"Get up," Shannon ordered with a laugh as she reached down to grab my hand. "You are not ringing in the new year under the Christmas tree with your cats," she added, pulling me to my feet. "We are going outside to ring it in properly."

"Fine," I huffed, pulling my unicorn hood up. "But I'm not even going to be cheery." Sulking, I allowed her to push me out of the house. "And I also reserve the right to…" My words trailed off when I stepped out of my house and locked eyes on the boy standing on the other side of the road in a kangaroo onesie. "Gerard?"

"Claire-Bear."

"Happy New Year, bestie." Shannon chuckled in my ear. "Love you." She pressed a kiss to my cheek before sprinting across the road to the other boy. "Hi, Johnny."

"Hi, Shannon," he replied, caught her effortlessly when she threw herself into his arms. "Happy New Year, baby."

The moment our eyes locked, the sound of fireworks erupting filled the air. Moments later, the night sky exploded with colorful sprinkles of twinkling lights.

"Gerard?" My breath caught in my throat, and I had to give my chest a little thump to reset my heart because when he raised his hand and waved at me, it flatlined.

And then he was crossing the road, walking toward me with strong, purposeful strides.

Unfortunately for me, the ability-to-remain-cool gene clearly skipped me over, and every tip, trick, and lesson on seduction Aoife had given me went right out the window.

Waving back at him like a demented cat lady, I almost broke my neck in my rush to get to him, trip-tumbling over my furry slippers and then sliding over a particularly icy patch of the driveway.

"Jesus." Gerard chuckled, hooking an arm around my back and pulling me to safety before I could fall on my ass. "Those slippers are an accident waiting to happen." Setting me back down on my feet, he inspected them with a mischievous glint in his eyes. "I love them."

"You're not supposed to tell my slippers you love them, Gerard," I complained, fisting the front of his onesie. "You're supposed to tell me."

"Really?" He slipped his hands into his kangaroo pouch and tilted his head to one side. "I thought that was already a given."

My heart began to race, and I shook my head. "I, ah, I'm not, I mean, I wasn't too sure if you still did."

"Love isn't a tap, Claire," he said, closing the space between us. A swell of emotion bombarded me, threatening to consume me to the point of passing out. "It doesn't turn off that easily."

"No," I agreed with a heavy sigh. "No, it doesn't."

"So." Taking a safe step back, he shoved his hands into his kangaroo pouch and shrugged. "Do you want to talk?"

Yes, I wanted to scream at the top of my lungs, but fear of chasing him off had me swallowing down my excitement and offering him a timid nod instead.

Slip-sliding across the driveway, I fell into step beside him as we embarked on the familiar route to the tree house. It was a trip we had taken thousands of times, but this time there was a heavy weight blanketing us. Like impending adulthood and sadness and hope all weaved into one complicated weighted blanket.

"Careful," I couldn't stop myself from tossing out when I climbed up first and then watched Gerard narrowly avoid that beam that had almost poleaxed him on our last venture. "Dad's not home to save you this time."

"Funny," he mused, gingerly maneuvering around the beam before taking a seat on the tree-house floor opposite me. "He's actually gone out this year?"

"Yep." I nodded, mirroring his actions by sitting cross-legged opposite him. "He took Mam out for dinner and drinks."

"Jesus." Scrubbing his jaw, he glanced around aimlessly. "That's a first."

"First New Year's Eve since the accident," I agreed.

"Hmm."

Unable to help myself, I let my eyes roam all over Gerard, soaking him in, all the while resisting the urge to fold myself into his arms. There were too many unspoken words between us for that. Conversations needed to happen first.

"So, ah…" Plucking on a loose thread, Gerard glanced around again before finally settling his attention on me. "Let's just get this out of the way, huh?"

"Okay." Nodding in agreement, I sucked in a sharp breath. "But before anything else, can I just say that I am so sorry for how it came out, Gerard."

"How it came out," he repeated slowly. "Don't you mean that you're sorry that it came out at all?"

"No, I mean I'm sorry for how it came out," I confirmed, steeling my resolve. "I can't be sorry for speaking up for you, Gerard. I won't be."

"That wasn't your letter to read, Claire."

"No, it wasn't," I agreed shakily. "But it also wasn't your burden to carry alone, Gerard."

He stared at me for a long beat before his shoulders sagged in defeat. "I was doing okay." His dropped his head when he spoke. "I was doing just fine, Claire."

"No." I shook my head. "No, you weren't."

"How can you say that?" he demanded, tone hard.

"Because I know you better than I know myself," I countered, unwilling to back down in such a colossal moment. "I'm only sorry that I didn't see the signs earlier."

"Signs," he muttered under his breath.

"Yes, Gerard, signs," I snapped, tone urgent. "We've all let you down here. Every last one of us, and for that, I am so damn sorry. I should've seen the signs. I should've been someone you could've come to, but I wasn't, and I will never forgive myself for it."

"Claire, please." He groaned like he was in physical pain. "Can we not?"

"We *have* to," I urged, hearing the heartbreak in my own voice. "Gerard, we have to talk about this. We have to go there."

"I've never hurt you," he choked out, eyes flashing with emotion when they locked on mine. "I've never hurt anyone. I was being a good person, doing good things, keeping up appearances, and I didn't need the whole fucking world knowing what a weakling I am!"

"You think you're weak?" My mouth fell open. "Gerard, you're the strongest person I've ever known."

"Bullshit," he snapped back. "I feel more powerless now than I did when I was seven, Claire."

"You do?" I sucked in a sharp breath, feeling horrified. "Why?"

"Because everyone knows." Breathing hard, he reached up and shoved a hand through his blond hair. "I am so fucking humiliated and there's nothing I can do about it. There's no rewind button for me, Claire. I'm going to be tarred as a victim for the rest of my life." A pained shudder escaped him. "I don't know how I'm supposed to face school next week, much less the team, and all of my friends."

"With your head held high," I bit out, desperate to comfort and encourage him. "Because you did nothing wrong here!" My heart broke for him, and I couldn't stop myself from reaching for his hand. "I never wanted to cause you any pain." Thankfully, he didn't push me away. Instead, he allowed me to entwine his fingers with mine. "But I couldn't keep this secret."

"I know you couldn't," came his broken whisper. "But now I don't know if I can."

I felt my heart splinter. "What does that mean?"

"I never wanted you to know about it, Claire. About that part of me. About that ugliness." He shrugged, his attention focused on our joined hands. "And now you do, I don't know how we move forward."

"Together, Gerard," I urged. "We move forward together. Because I'm still right here," I croaked out, needing him to know that I would never leave. That I would always be here by his side. "I'm still your Claire-Bear."

"It's different now."

"Different isn't bad, Gerard."

"I don't know if I can be your Gerard anymore."

An internal sensation that I could only assume felt similar to that of a straw breaking a camel's back occurred, and I erupted.

"How dare you." Furious, I snatched my hand back and pulled onto my knees. "How dare you say that to me?"

"Claire…"

"No, no, no." Shaking my head, I scrambled for the opening, not stopping until I was at the bottom of the ladder and moving for the back door of my house.

"Jesus Christ, Claire, wait a minute, will you?"

"For what?" I called over my shoulder, hearing his footsteps crunching through the icy lawn. Was I exploding in frustration, or in anger, or in love? I couldn't tell, but emotions were battering their way through my chest and out of my mouth. "For you to break up with me twice? I don't think so, Gerard."

"I'm trying to talk this out with you," he snapped, catching ahold of the patio door before I could slam it shut. "That's what you want, isn't it? This horrible fucking conversation? I mean, this has to be what you want. It's why you told the goddamn world about that letter."

"No, Gerard, I told the world about that letter because I wanted to protect you! Because I wanted justice for you. Because I wanted to stop a pedophile from abusing other children! You're having this conversation because you're trying to block me out," I argued back, reluctantly stepping aside for him to enter my kitchen. "You're freezing me out, Gerard, because that's what you do when it gets too deep. I jump and you falter." When we were both inside the house, I slid the patio door shut with a loud thump. "That's what you've always done, and I'm not putting up with it anymore."

"Are you *serious*?"

"I've never been more serious in my life." I turned to face him. "I won't apologize for what I did because I love you. Do you hear me? I love you, Gerard Gibson. I love the boy you were, and I love the man you've become." Releasing a frustrated growl, I stalked toward him and planted my hands on his chest. "And I will stand up for all of your forms, baby, boy, or man! I will fight for you even when you can't do it for yourself because that's what best friends do." Knotting my fingers in his onesie, I glared up at him before adding, "And I will *never* apologize for it."

Stormy gray eyes locked on mine. "You can't love me the same way."

"You're right," I agreed. "Because I love you more."

"Don't lie." His voice was heartbreakingly vulnerable in this moment. "Please don't say it if you don't mean it."

"I love you more," I repeated, tone unwavering. "I want you more. I am disgustingly attracted to you, Gerard Gibson, and nothing about your past can change that."

"Claire." When his hands rested on my waist, an illicit shiver racked through me. A mirroring shiver racked through his big body. "I just… I don't know where I'm supposed to go from here."

My heart broke just a little bit more from his admission, and the truth was I didn't know either, but I knew we were supposed to go on together. So, I told him just that. "We, Gerard." Reaching up, I pushed my hand through his hair and offered him what I hoped was a reassuring smile. "Where we go from here. We're a team, remember?"

A melancholy mixture of sadness and hope filled his eyes. "You really mean it, don't you?"

"Yep."

"So, where do we go from here, Claire-Bear?"

"Well." I shrugged. "I could start by wishing you a happy new year and you could follow it on by kissing me."

"Is that so?" A familiar smile ghosted his lips, and I soaked it in. "Then you better start."

Clearing my throat, I smiled up at him. "Happy New Year, Ger…"

My words were swallowed up by his lips when they crashed down on me.

Immersed in the feel of his big body pressed to mine, of his lips on my lips, and his skin on mine I kissed him back with a hunger that bordered on frenzied. Because every second of panic, pain, guilt, and fear of the unknown that had built its way up inside of me since the dance was exploding out of my head and into this kiss.

"I love you," he whispered, lips trailing from my cheek to the curve of my neck. "It's always been you, Claire-Bear."

I knew he was telling the truth because it was the same for me. It had always been him. No one else got a look in.

"I just need some time to figure out who I'm supposed to be now," he explained hoarsely when he broke our kiss. "I've been hiding for so long that I don't even know who I am." Expelling a shaky breath, he rested his hands on my shoulders and offered me a vulnerable shrug. "And I'm going to need some time to do that."

83

Snakes and Ladders

GERARD

EVERYTHING FELT LIKE IT WAS UPSIDE DOWN.

I knew that statement didn't make sense, but it was how my life felt since the winter ball. Keith was gone, my mother was in manic helicopter-mother mode, and I was slowly losing my shit one hug at a time.

I wanted my mother's attention and affection about as much as I needed it, which was not at all.

Because it made it worse.

Because it made it more real.

My secret was out, the whole world knew, and I couldn't change the narrative. I was a publicly proclaimed victim and I fucking loathed it.

The thought of school on Monday was almost too much to take, and I honest to God had no idea how I was going to face the team. In truth, I had a strong inclination to sell my soul for a rewind and erase button.

"Are you sure you're warm enough, pet?" Mam asked late Saturday night when she walked into the sitting room to check on me for the hundredth time.

"Yes, Mam."

"I can put another block on the fire."

"It's warm enough, Mam."

"Are you sure now, love? Because I don't want you to be cold."

"Mam, all I'm short of is a fucking apple in my mouth and you could roast me on a spit," I shot back, gesturing to the roaring fire in the fireplace, and then to the fact that I was clad in a pair of shorts. "Relax, will you? I'm grand."

The concern in her eyes assured me that she had no intention of ever relaxing again. "What about you, Claire, pet?" Mam's attention flicked to the blond leaning over the coffee table opposite me, trying to block my view of the dice she rolled in our current game of snakes and ladders.

"I'm grand, thanks, Sadhbh," Claire replied, tongue peeking out of the corner of her mouth as she craftily skipped over a snake on the board game. "I'm roasting, actually."

"Cheater," I accused, snatching her counter and pushing it down the snake. "You rolled a four."

"I rolled a five," she argued, but it was a half-hearted argument because she was the world's worst liar with two apples for cheeks that gave her away. "Don't make me go down the snake, Gerard."

"It's not me." I laughed, holding my hands up. "It's the rules of the game."

"Then break the rules," she encouraged, giving me a pleading look. "For me?"

Rolling my eyes, I gave in and set her counter down on her chosen spot.

"You're the best," she cheered, shimmying and dancing on the spot before snatching up the dice again.

"Hey, it's my turn."

"Yay! Two sixes." Ignoring me, Claire moved her counter up another ten spots before offering me a gleeful smile. "I love playing with you."

I'm sure she did. Since our truce on New Year's Eve, that's all we seemed to do. Play board games where she cheated and I indulged her. It was almost like nothing had changed between us.

Almost.

But it was still there, my secret still hanging heavily in the air between us, and it couldn't be fixed. She was Claire and I was still me, but we had somehow fallen back into the friendship version of us rather than the couple. I wasn't sure if that was my fault or because she wasn't comfortable with me anymore. It was a mindfuck that I didn't like to think too deeply about. Hence the board games. But one stark conclusion I had come to in the middle of the madness was this: I might not know who I was or where I fit in the world, but I knew without a shadow of a doubt that I didn't want any of it without Claire Biggs.

Or Cap.

"Right, well, I'll be out in the kitchen if either of you need me," Mam said before reluctantly retreating from the room.

I waited for her to close the sitting room door behind her before blowing out a breath. "I don't know how much more of this I can take, Claire-Bear."

"Sadhbh's just worried about you," she replied, rolling the dice for a third time in a row and then purposefully skipping another snake she landed on. "Don't be mad at her, Gerard."

"I'm not mad," I replied, leaning against the couch. "I'm just…" Shrugging my shoulders, I blew out a frustrated breath. "I'm aggravated."

"With your mam?"

"With the world."

437

Smiling sweetly, she batted her big brown eyes. "Even me?"

"Especially you." A reluctant smile spread across my face. "You're the worst, culprit."

Snickering, Claire stuck her tongue out, and I swear the mere sight of her caused a swelling sensation to my heart that could be mistaken for medical complications. Lucky for me, I knew these chest pains were a direct result of the repercussions of love.

Because I loved her.

Jesus, I loved her with every bit of me.

This past week, she hadn't left my side, even though I was shit craic right now. It didn't matter to Claire. There were plenty of unspoken conversations I knew we had yet to have, but I wasn't willing, and she wasn't pushing. I didn't know if I would ever be ready for the conversations I knew would need to happen in our future, but for now, we seemed to have settled on a vague—albeit throat-baring—common ground.

"You're staring," she informed me in a teasing tone.

"Am I not allowed to?" I tossed back, and the question seemed to stump Claire. Worse than stump her, it caused her to suck in a sharp breath. Because this was the first time either of us had crossed that particular threshold since that kiss in her kitchen.

Tilting her head to one side, she eyed me carefully. "Are you flirting with me, Gerard Gibson?"

Was I?

Of course I was.

But could I handle the repercussions?

Time would tell.

Feeling a little exposed and a whole lot vulnerable, I shrugged helplessly. "Am I not allowed to?"

"That depends."

"It does?" My brows shot up. "On what?"

"On how quickly we escape your mother and get across the street." Grinning devilishly, she leapt to her feet and held her hand out to me. "Because your mam is like a sniffer dog, and I am in dire need of some X-rated Gerard Gibson snuggles."

Well, shit.

She didn't need to tell me twice.

Springing off the couch like a boomerang returning to its owner, I took her hand in one hand and offered her a sailor's salute with the other. "Lead the way, Captain."

"Okay, but before we go ninja-stealth mode, I just want you to know that I am deliriously in love with you, find you ridiculously sexy—like seriously, super-duper sexy—and have no plans to push you for anything more than you've given me." Her words came out fast and furious, like an admission she'd been holding in for a long time.

Reaching up, she cupped my face with her hands and pushed up on her tiptoes. "Because I have everything I need standing right in front of me." She pressed a soft kiss to the corner of my mouth. "We've got all the time in the world for the sad parts." When she pulled back, she smiled devilishly. "Right now, I'm thinking we should concentrate on the happy parts."

"Oh yeah?" I grinned down at her. "What happy parts were you thinking we should focus on?"

"Well." She grinned mischievously up at me. "I was thinking I could concentrate on your ladder, if you focused on my tree."

"I'm in," I declared without a hint of wavering. "Fair warning, though, my ladder is already semi-erected."

"We'll see."

"Fuck me!"

Forty minutes later, I was back in her room, back in her bed, with my clothes discarded on her bedroom floor and her naked body draped on top of me.

"Is this okay?" Claire breathed against my lips. "Me touching you like this?"

"It's all okay," I groaned, reveling in the feel of her hands on my body. "More than okay."

"I'm right here with you." Rocking on top of me in the most primal of ways, she took my hands and placed them on her skin. "It's just you and me."

Unable to stand the pressure in my chest another second, I sat straight up, and readjusted her on my lap. The move caused us both to groan in pleasure. It was so much deeper like this.

In every way.

"You make me feel like it's possible," I heard myself tell her as our bodies continued to move in perfect rhythm.

"Hmm?" A bead of sweat trickled down her neck, and I followed it as it trailed between her breasts. "Like what's possible?"

"Like everything is going to be okay again." Tightening my hold on her hips, I moved faster, feeling that familiar surge of urgency taking over my body. "Like I'm going to be okay."

"Because it is," she urged, her words a breathless rasp as she gripped my shoulders and rocked her hips furiously against mine. "Because you are."

"Yeah." Breathing hard and ragged, I cupped the back of her head and pulled her forehead to mine. "But you make me believe it."

"Gerard, I–I..." Her words faded but her eyes never left mine when she started to tremble. Her body jerked and spasmed, and just like dominos crashing, I followed right along with her.

———————

When I blinked my eyes awake on Sunday morning, I was greeted by the sight of a pair of mischievous brown eyes looking at me.

"Whoa," I choked out, almost having a goddamn heart attack from how close said eyes were to my face.

"Morning," Claire chirped, as she sat cross-legged on her bed watching me, with a megawatt smile etched on her pretty face. "Guess what you did last night."

"Took you to heights of pleasure you never knew existed?"

"Okay, guess what else you did last night."

"What did I do?"

"You slept!" Shuffling around with barely constrained excitement, she clapped her hands together. "For three straight hours!" Her smile widened. "No nightmares. No sleepwalking. Just sleeping. I watched."

"You...watched?"

"Uh-huh." She nodded before adding. "You were right about the snoring, by the way. Unfortunately, I am the culprit."

"Told you so," I mused, pulling myself into a sitting position. "Now, can we rewind to the part where you admitted to creeper-watching me while I slept?"

"Oh, please." She rolled her eyes. "Like you haven't watched me sleep a million times."

"I don't watch you sleep, Claire. I listen to you sleep. The entire house does."

"Oh my god, stop. I am not that loud," she huffed, slapping my arm. "Besides..." She winked. "I have it on good authority that I have a cute snore."

"Whoever told you that was trying to get in your knickers."

"Well, he got in my knickers last night."

"And what a lovely pair they were."

Snickering, she reached for a pillow and then proceeded to hit me upside the head with it. "Come on, Gerard Gibson," she said, leaning in to press a kiss to my cheek. "Take a walk with me."

84

The Great War

CLAIRE

I<small>T WAS</small> J<small>ANUARY</small> 6, 2006, <small>THE FIRST DAY OF A NEW SCHOOL TERM, AND</small> I <small>WAS NERVOUS</small> to see what 2006 had in store. If it was anything like the year we had left behind, then we were in for a bumpy ride, but the boy whose car I was sitting in sure made for great company.

Everything had irrevocably changed in our lives. Not just for Gerard, but for me, too.

I felt different now.

Older.

Jaded.

Awake.

I knew we had a long way to go, and Gerard was only starting his healing journey, but as long as we stuck together, I knew we would make it.

2006 would be our year, I decided.

No more walls.

No more secrets.

Whatever came our way, we would face it together.

We would be alright.

"It's going to be bad in there," Gerard dragged me from my thoughts by saying. Parking up in his familiar spot, he killed the engine and jacked the hand brake before turning to face me. "With Lizzie."

Yeah, I already knew that.

The dynamics of our entire friendship circle had been fractured, and while some things had changed for the better, namely mine and Gerard's relationship, a whole heap more had changed for the worse.

Going backwards wasn't an option for any of us. Straight ahead was the only direction available.

Lines had been drawn in the sand, sides had been taken, and for the first time in my life, I felt like I was standing on the precipice of both greatness and pain. Nothing was going to be the same this year. But we had each other. And right now, that was all we needed.

"I know that you're in a really bad position," my boyfriend continued to say, his cheeks reddening as he spoke. "But I just need you to know that I'm not expecting you to take sides, okay?" Expelling a pained breath, he reached for my hand and pressed a kiss to my knuckles. "You can be both."

"Both?"

Nodding slowly, he pressed another kiss to my knuckles. "You can be her friend and still have me." Reaching across the console, he tucked a rogue curl that had escaped my ponytail behind my ear. "It doesn't have to be one or the other."

"Actually, it does," I heard myself tell him.

Gerard's brows furrowed. "I'm not following."

"I said it does matter, Gerard," I explained, curling a hand around his neck to pull his face to mine "Because I've learned a lot about myself this past year. About who I am, and who I love, and who I want to be. And I'm not afraid anymore to stand up for myself, or for what I believe in, and especially who I believe in," I admitted. "And it's you, Gerard. All paths lead to you." I shrugged helplessly. "So, if I have to step on a few toes along the way, then so be it. Because from here on out, we're a team. And if the whole world tries to take you on, then they have to take me on, too." Smiling, I pressed another kiss to his lips, before saying, "You come first, Gerard."

"I do?"

The uncertain vulnerability in his voice caused a surge of protectiveness to grow inside of my heart, and I pulled him closer, having made my choice. "You do."

"I won't mess this up, Claire," he vowed hoarsely, taking my hand in his. "But I'm not going to tell you. I'm going to show you."

"Wow." I beamed at him. "You actually listen to me, don't you?"

"Every word, Claire-Bear," Gerard replied with a wink. "Every word."

"Get a bleeding room," a familiar voice called out moments before the bonnet of Gerard's car was drummed on. "You're on my time now, Gibs."

Repressing a groan, Gerard dropped his head on my shoulder and sighed. "I told you that I've quit the team, Cap."

"And I told you that I don't accept resignations." The driver's door was yanked open. "Now, kiss your girlfriend goodbye, tell her you'll see her at lunch, same as always, and get your hole in that changing room." Reaching into the car, Johnny unfastened Gerard's seat belt and hauled him out of the car. "Because we have a Schoolboys' Shield to win, and I have no intentions of letting Royce take the win this year."

"Well, aren't you the biggest brand of hypocrite known to mankind," Gerard grumbled as he wrestled with his best friend outside the car. "Hey, don't fucking pinch me, Jonathan."

"Then don't bleeding scrawl me, Gerard."

"Are you ready?" Shannon's familiar voice drifted through the open passenger window of the car and I turned to smile at her.

"Yes, but I'm nervous."

"Welcome to my world," she replied with a soft laugh. "I seem to spend my life in a constant state of nervous trepidation."

"Still?"

"Oh, yes." She nodded, still smiling. "It's my calling."

"Have you seen her yet?" I asked when I climbed out of the car and retrieved both my bag and Gerard's from the back seat. "Lizzie?"

"I have," Shannon replied in a careful tone, falling into step beside me. "She's not in a good way."

"It's not my problem," was all I could say.

"Claire."

"It's not, Shan," I pushed. "I wish her the best, I hope she finds happiness, but I can't be in her corner anymore."

"Well, I'm still in both of your corners," Shannon replied sadly. "I love you both and I won't pick."

"I'm not asking you to."

"He, on the other hand, has picked," she offered, pointing up ahead to where Johnny and Gerard were still grappling with each other in the courtyard. "He's Team Gibsie until the end of time."

"Yeah," I replied, readjusting both bags on my back. "Me too."

"Are you ready for this, Shan?" Johnny asked when the boys returned to us, both breathless from their exertions. "Another six months of Tommen, baby."

"I'm as ready as I'll ever be," I heard my bestie reply before slipping her hand into his. "I've got this."

"You absolutely do," Johnny agreed in that calm, reassuring tone of his, giving her hand a squeeze, while simultaneously reaching over to clap Gerard on the back. "You both do."

"You really have got this," I whispered in Gerard's ear when he reached for his school-bag. The nervous tremor in his body caused my heart to ache. This was hard for him. Worse than hard. This was torture for him. But here he was, still standing, still smiling.

"Yeah." Reaching for my hand, he entwined our fingers and offered me a reassuring squeeze. "Let's get this over with, huh?"

Following a few paces behind Johnny and Shannon, we walked through the familiar doorway of Tommen College hand in hand. The minute we stepped inside, the gawking and staring began, though thankfully nobody was stupid enough to *actually* comment.

"So, this is what being in a fishbowl feels like," Gerard tried to lighten the mood by saying as we walked through the crowds in the direction of the sixth-year common room, ignoring the countless eyes boring holes through us.

"True," I mused, giving his hand another reassuring squeeze. "Or what being Johnny Kavanagh must feel like."

"Ignore them," Johnny, who had backpedaled through the crowd told us, before adding in a much louder voice, "People have short memories and big staring problems in this bleeding school."

That did the trick.

People couldn't look away quickly enough.

Grateful for Johnny's intervention, I let him take the lead, knowing that there was something about the Dub that calmed my boyfriend. Johnny made Gerard feel grounded, and right about now, Gerard needed all of the grounding he could get.

The shift in our friendship circle couldn't have been any clearer when we entered the sixth-year common room a few moments later and were met with what I could only describe as the great divide.

While Johnny, Gerard, and I stood in the doorway, Aoife and Katie sat on one of the plush leather couches, while Patrick sat on the other, strumming softly on his guitar. Meanwhile, Hugh was leaning against the window with his head in his hands, while Joey and Lizzie spoke in hushed whispers in the kitchenette area. Standing in the middle of the room, looking torn, was Shannon.

"The core eight fractured," Helen voiced my thoughts aloud, when she sidled up to me and said. "Wow, I never thought I would see the day."

"Don't you mean core ten, Hels," Shelley interjected, gesturing first to Joey and then to Aoife.

The moment Lizzie's attention landed on us standing in the doorway, I felt the air change around us. It grew cold and thick and clammy all at once. Her blue eyes flicked from me to Johnny, before settling on Gerard.

Unable to stop myself, I took a protective stance in front of him, letting her know that I wasn't here to play. I *would* defend this boy with everything I had in my armory. To the death.

"Well, this is awkward," one of the girls muttered. Shelley or Helen, I couldn't tell which one. I was too focused on the stare-down.

The feel of a hand tugging on mine dragged my attention from Lizzie, and I turned to look at Gerard. "Take a walk with me, Claire-Bear," he said softly, thumb gently tracing over my knuckles.

"Anywhere," I replied, squeezing his hand. "I will go anywhere with you, Gerard Gibson."

A mixture of relief, sadness, and love shone in his eyes. "Right back at you, Claire Biggs."

And then, without another glance, I turned on my heels and walked hand in hand from the room with the only boy who would ever lay claim to my heart.

Trouble was brewing between our friends.

I could feel it.

I could taste it.

But the lines had been drawn.

And I would forever stand with this boy.

After all, taming 7 had been the adventure of my lifetime.

Song Moments, Vibes, and Feels

ALL the feels from Claire's POV: Taylor Swift—"Willow"

Gibsie in his own head: Anson Seabra—"I Can't Carry This Anymore"

Gibsie's resilience: Sekou—"Better Man"

Kissing in the rain: Taylor Swift—"The Way I Loved You"

Gibsie and Johnny: George Ezra—"Coat of Armor"

Songs for Claire

Taylor Swift—"You Are in Love"
Aoi Teshima—"Young and Beautiful"
Taylor Swift—"Don't Blame Me"
Ella Henderson—"Hold On, We're Going Home"
The Sweeplings—"In Too Deep"
Grace Grundy—"Put Me Back Together"
Kelly Clarkson—"My Life Would Suck without You"
Maddie & Tae—"Friends Don't"
Taylor Swift—"Today Was a Fairy Tale"
Taylor Swift—"Paper Rings"
Pink—"True Love"
Avril Lavigne—"Mobile"
Abby Anderson—"Make Him Wait"
Sheryl Crow—"I Shall Believe"
Kelly Clarkson—"I Do Not Hook Up"
Ruth B—"Lost Boy"
Avril Lavigne—"Tomorrow"
Lady Gaga—"You and I"
Taylor Swift—"Love Story"
Picture This—"17"
Taylor Swift—"Fearless"
Taylor Swift—"Cardigan"
Avril Lavigne—"Things I'll Never Say"
Taylor Swift—"Wildest Dreams"
Uncle Kracker—"Smile"
Justin Timberlake—"Mirrors"
Black Eyed Peas—"Where Is the Love?"
Taylor Swift—"Maroon"
Alicia Keys—"No One"
Amy Winehouse—"Will You Still Love Me Tomorrow?"

Leona Lewis—"Colorblind"
Karizma Duo—"Save the Best for Last"
Taylor Swift—"Willow"
The Mayries—"Back to You"
Taylor Swift—"Long Live"
Ciara—"Love Sex Magic"
Tina Arena—"Show Me Heaven"
Taylor Swift—"Enchanted"
Miley Cyrus—"7 Things"
Cher—"The Shoop Shoop Song"
Salt-N-Pepa—"Whatta Man"
Leah Kate—"Fuck Up the Friendship"
Katy Perry—"Unconditionally"
Taylor Swift—"Our Song"
Colbie Caillat—"Bubbly"
En Vogue—"Don't Let Go"
Texas—"Inner Smile"
Alanis Morissette—"Head over Feet"
Sandi Thom—"What If I'm Right"
Bic Runga—"Sway"
Taylor Swift—"The Best Day"
Taylor Swift—"It's Nice to Have a Friend"
Camila Cabello—"In the Dark"

Songs for Gibsie

Sam Fender—"Seventeen Going Under"
Anson Seabra—"I Can't Carry This Anymore"
Anson Seabra—"Trying My Best"
LANY—"anything 4 u"
Stefan Lee Krantz—"Wherever You Go"
Nelly Furtado—"Try"
Picture This—"Take My Hand"
Sum 41—"Fat Lip"
Dermot Kennedy—"Lost"
Mitch James—"21"
R.E.M—"Shiny Happy People"
LANY—"cowboy in LA"
Five for Fighting—"Superman"
Wrabel—"Poetry"
Gary Jules—"Mad World"
Ed Sheeran—"Shivers"
Dermot Kennedy—"Kiss Me"
Blink-182—"Another Girl Another Planet"
The Fray—"You Found Me"
Busted—"Falling for You"
Smash Mouth—"All Star"
McFly—"Broccoli"
Kid Rock—"First Kiss"
Bell X1—"The Great Defector"
Noah Guthrie—"Sexy and I Know It"
Mr. Probz—"Waves"
Andy Grammer—"Honey, I'm Good"
Bowling For Soup—"High School Never Ends"
Third Eye Blind—"Semi-Charmed Life"
James Morrison—"Once When I Was Little"

Brooks Jefferson—"Two of a Kind"
Justin Bieber—"Anyone"
Keith Urban—"Somebody Like You"
McFly—"All about You"
The Kooks—"She Moves in Her Own Way"
Blink-182—"Josie"
Scissor Sisters—"I Don't Feel Like Dancin'"
David Gray—"This Year's Love"
Steve Acho—"Glycerine"
The Charlie Daniels Band—"The Devil Went Down to Georgia"
Picture This—"Jane"
Ed Sheeran—"Hearts Don't Break Around Here"
Munn—"The Reason I Hate Home"
Jonah Baker—"Don't Blame Me"
Wheatus—"Teenage Dirtbag"
Eminem—"The Monster"
Counting Crows—"Accidentally in Love"
Robbie Williams—"Angels"
Bloodhound Gang—"The Bad Touch"
The Offspring—"Pretty Fly"
Avicii—"Wake Me Up"
OMI—"Cheerleader"
Luther Vandross—"Dance with My Father"
Steve Miller Band—"The Joker"
Matt Nathanson—"Laid"
James—"Sit Down"
Jay-Z, Linkin Park—"Numb/Encore"
Sinead O'Connor—"Take Me to Church"
Ed Sheeran—"Shape of You"
Audioslave—"Be Yourself"
X-Ambassadors—"Unsteady"
Nickelback—"Far Away"
Declan J Donovan—"Fallen So Young"
Sean Paul—"Like Glue"

About the Author

Chloe Walsh is the bestselling author of the Boys of Tommen series, which exploded in popularity. She has been writing and publishing new adult and adult contemporary romance for a decade. Her books have been translated into multiple languages. Animal lover, music addict, and TV junkie, Chloe loves spending time with her family and is a passionate advocate for mental health awareness. Chloe lives in Cork, Ireland, with her family.

Join Chloe's mailing list for exclusive content and release updates.